THE BLUE NOON

Also by Robert Ryan

Underdogs
Nine Mil
Trans Am
Early One Morning

THE BLUE NOON

Robert Ryan

Chapter thirty-nine reproduced by kind permission of the *Daily Mail*

First published in 2003
by Review

An imprint of Headline Book Publishing

10 9 8 7 6 5 4 3 2 1

The Blue Noon is a work of fiction,
based on, and inspired by, true events.

Cataloguing in Publication Data is
available from the British Library

ISBN 0 7553 0176 5 (Hardback)
ISBN 0 7553 0177 3 (Trade Paperback)

Typeset in JansonText by
Letterpart Limited, Reigate, Surrey

Printed and bound in Great Britain by
Mackays of Chatham plc, Chatham, Kent

HEADLINE BOOK PUBLISHING
A division of Hodder Headline
338 Euston Road
LONDON NW1 3BH

www.reviewbooks.co.uk
www.hodderheadline.com

For Deborah and Lottie

Prologue

Paris Detention Centre, Porte des Lilas, 1945

By the time the three military policemen delivered him to the gaol it was after midnight and he had a closed eye, a split lip and a football-sized knee from a truncheon blow. They had to drag him up the worn stone steps to the guardroom on the third floor, the political section, where he was forced to strip out of his US Army uniform.

It might have been spring outside, but it had failed to penetrate the ancient walls of the fort that served as the Allies' detention centre and he was soon shivering. He had enough sense, though, not to try to hide his nakedness. He had been in this state before, and any attempt to cover his genitals or to assume a defensive posture was like blood in the water to sharks. The Redcaps were itching to use their truncheons again. He had to minimise the risk of that happening.

The guards took their time completing the transfer paperwork and as his teeth started to chatter he shuffled a few steps towards the ancient pot-bellied stove in the corner, but one of his captors slapped him back into place with an open hand. He could taste blood now.

His arrest detail finally departed with a farewell poke in the ribs, and he was left in the charge of the Paris Detention Centre guards, one Englishman and an American. They threw him a set of blue coveralls and thin, grey underwear and he dressed as quickly as his damaged knee would allow.

'What's with the American uniform?' asked the Yank as he picked up the discarded jacket and binned it. 'You ain't one of us.'

'Seconded,' he said through his clashing teeth. 'From the British army.'

The American looked down at the charge sheet and ran his finger along the list. 'So how come it says under item fifteen: impersonating an American officer?'

'Misunderstanding.'

'Yeah. Hey, you hear what the sentence for that Guy William Joyce was today? Your Lord Haw Haw?'

'Strictly speaking, I think he's yours,' the prisoner said. The famous traitor was American born, although since he had taken UK citizenship, the British had decided they should have the privilege of punishing him. 'But I can guess.'

The American sniggered. 'I think you'll be doing better than that, pal. I think you'll be following his footsteps up that scaffold.'

He didn't like the Yank, and was relieved when the Englishman indicated he should accompany him down the corridor to the cell. The guard unlocked a cupboard on the wall and took out a Colt sidearm along with an almost medieval key.

'Nasty eye,' he said as they left the guardroom.

'It's worse from the inside.'

'And the leg?'

'It's going to be an interesting colour tomorrow.'

'Fell downstairs, did you?'

'I suppose I did.'

'We get a lot of that.' The guard stopped before cell eight, turned the heavy key and pushed the battered steel door open.

'Can I see a doctor?'

'You'll live till morning,' the man replied. 'In you go, Mason.'

He limped inside and lowered himself gingerly onto the bed. It had been a long night, and one that had started so promisingly. Women, he thought bitterly, they really will be the death of me.

'I suppose you want a cuppa?'

'Yeah,' he said, modulating his cockney accent to mimic his gaoler's. 'I could murder a cup of tea.'

The guard laughed. 'I'd watch what you say, mate. You're in enough trouble as it is. That's the longest bloody charge sheet I have ever seen.'

As the Englishman turned to leave, the prisoner asked quickly: 'I don't suppose there is any chance of a typewriter, is there?'

'A typewriter? At this time of night? You'll wake up half the block.'

'No. For tomorrow.'

'I doubt it, mate. What's it for? An appeal?'

He hadn't even had a trial yet, but he knew everyone thought the verdict a mere formality. 'Something like that.'

'I'll see,' the man said grudgingly, then hesitated. 'Is it all true, Mason?'

'Is what all true?'

'What they said about you on the detention order and the charge sheet? What you did?'

The prisoner smiled grimly as he thought about the charges, a seven-year fairground ride around Europe reduced to nineteen stark indictments. Was it all true? Well, he couldn't deny the bare facts. His salvation would be in the details, if he could make anyone listen. 'Pretty much,' he finally said.

The Englishman nodded and said quietly: 'In which case, you can shove the typewriter up yer arse.'

Part One

One

Hong Kong, 1938

Harry Cole lit his first Capstan of the day and gazed over the waters of the bay to the dark shape of Stonecutter's Island, wondering how the gun crews out there had fared during the night. Two hundred dead and counting on the mainland, that's what they were saying. Mostly Chinese, of course, and nearly all refugees from the sprawling shanty towns that had colonised the foot of Lion Rock.

The *daih fung*, the big wind, had dashed itself around the hillsides, creating berserk vortices that tore at the tin, wood and canvas of the makeshift homes. The torrents of water it had sucked from the ocean had transformed the thin soil of the hillsides into a thick sludge that had swept through the compounds, pulling the weakest individuals into its glutinous embrace.

Out in the Straits, the sea was still boiling in the aftermath, its surface thick with the detritus of the storm. Harry turned to face the ugly sprawl of the Sham Shui Po barracks, where various sappers inspected walls and roofs for damage, and the red-eyed men of the First Battalion were bullying and cursing the gangs of coolies charged with clearing the debris.

A Number Nine storm, the old hands claimed, one short of a direct hit. If that was a nine, Harry would hate to see a ten: the barracks' church tower had gone, casually sheared off and carried into the hills. The Other Ranks' dining room was so much kindling, although the Officers' Mess and Club were still standing, because, as always, they were the best built bit of kit on the barracks. A *mafoo*, one of the Chinese stable coolies, walked by, pulling two jittery horses behind him, the beasts still snorting with residual terror from having the roof torn off above their heads.

Harry closed his eyes and the familiar show-reel played. In his mind he saw the crimson robe fall from her shoulders, held his breath as she stepped forward out of the shadows. It had been a week since he had stood behind the carved screen that formed the false wall of the spartan room where he watched the girl Suki perform for Colonel Parkhill, his CO. He had felt certain that his Colonel and the girl would hear the drumming of his heart from his hiding place, but the lovers had other things on their minds.

Harry had marvelled at the colour and texture of her young body in the soft orange glow of the lanterns and he almost groaned as she climbed on top of the prostrate Colonel. A tap on the shoulder from Mister Eric, the whorehouse's manager, and he had left, taking the vivid scene with him.

Harry and Mister Eric – not, of course, his real name, he was Lam Sang to the locals – had had business. There was always business to discuss. In the past few years, Harry had moved from London's Hoxton, Bethnal Green, and the West End, to Surrey – with a short diversion into Wormwood Scrubs – then out to Singapore and now Hong Kong. Just a change of venue, that's all.

The basics were always the same – all you had to do was get the language right, so there were no misunderstandings.

Hence he had Jimmy the barman from the Officers' Club teaching him a few basic Cantonese phrases. Most of the expats derided it as a total waste of time, especially as the Chinese all spoke pidgin anyway. Harry disagreed, it was still the locals' manor, no matter how many fancy hotels, gun emplacements and tram systems the British put in, or how much they excluded them from their clubs and the whites-only housing on The Peak, the highest spot on the island. Learning the Chinese ways, even if it was just how to say hello, was simply a mark of respect.

'Cole.'

Harry flung the cigarette over his shoulder and straightened as he spun round. Striding towards him, splashing across the sodden ground, was the beefy form of Regimental Sergeant Major Cross. He was one of the permanent Hong Kong garrison, as attested by the deep walnut colour of his knees, an NCO who had been moved up from Stanley to show the First Battalion the ropes.

'Sir,' Harry said quickly. At his full height of a shade under six foot, Harry was almost a head higher than the RSM, but Cross carried a couple more stone of muscle, upholstered with what looked deceivingly like baby fat.

'What you doing out here, Corporal? Half the barracks looks like shit and you're out here sucking on a Woodbine.'

A Capstan Extra-Strength, he almost corrected, but thought better of it. 'The MO sent me out for a break, sir.'

Harry flinched as a fat hand shot out and cupped his forehead, checking for fever. 'The MO? He give you any more quinine for the malaria?'

'Offered it. But you know what that stuff's like. You get Bow Bells goin' off in your head all night.'

'You take it, Cole, I don't care what's goin' on in your head.

I've had two bouts of the shivers, boy, and I tell you, it's worse than anything the quinine can do. You're driving the Colonel today?'

'I am.'

'Well, before you do, report to me at the Officers' Mess. You was an orderly once, wasn't you?'

Harry nodded. For all of three weeks in Singapore, till a little confusion over the brandy stocks.

'Wolsey is out of action,' offered Cross.

'Out of action?'

'Touch of the Cubans.'

Harry suppressed his smile. A piece of old Havana, a touch of the Cubans, something burning on the Spanish Main – nobody knew why, but the Hispanic Caribbean provided most of the euphemisms for a good old dose of the pox in Hong Kong.

'I need someone who knows his way around an optic, get the *drinkboys* working on Ladies' Night. You think you can handle that?'

'Yes, Sarge.'

'Good. Off you go. And take your bloody quinine.'

Harry walked back to the barracks, only grinning when he was sure Cross couldn't see his face. Running the bar at Ladies' Night, all pink gins and dull small talk? A piece of piss.

Of course Harry didn't have malaria. When the orders came to reorganise as a machine-gun battalion in anticipation of shipping out to Hong Kong, he had suddenly seen the future. It involved lugging either a Vickers or, worse, its metal boxes of ammunition through some godforsaken jungle or, in the case of the New Territories, a sodding wet, mosquito-infested paddy field. He'd been long enough in Singapore by then to know you could get anything you wanted on Amoy Street. Even a bitter potion that would mimic malaria by causing a fever and making your skin look jaundiced. The metallic after-taste that lasted three days was just about worth it.

A squad of soldiers double-marched towards the docks, rifles across their chests, causing a couple of *mui-tsai*, the indentured servant girls, to step out of their way. After a typhoon there was always the threat of looting, and Harry was certain these men were off to make sure the rice *godowns* were secure. Later in the day they would be on *congee* duty, distributing the mix of rice and salt to the poorest inhabitants of the city, a lesson learned in the 1920s after the riots when the typhoons kept the rice boats away for days on end.

Harry reached the barrack gates, nodded at the sentries and stepped over the growing pile of roofing tiles that were being swept together by coolies, overseen by the sweat-stained soldiers of First Battalion.

'Best get them out of the way, lads,' he said to his colleagues. 'Colonel's car comin' through in a couple of hours and we don't want a puncture, do we?'

'Fuck off, Cole,' came the reply in unison.

Harry laughed. He had been thinking, what with the order to be ready to defend the International Settlement in Shanghai from the Japanese army at twelve hours' notice, that he had better come up with a way of fucking off pretty soon.

Colonel Parkhill was new to the First Battalion, but not to Hong Kong, having completed a tour of duty three years previously. He'd been given the command of Harry's unit when the previous CO was shifted off to Palestine. Parkhill knew the value of a good driver and picked Harry because, although he was on light duties, he alone in the battalion boasted a First Class Motoring Certificate from the demanding Reading course. He wasn't to know it had cost Harry a fiver from a fly corporal at Aldershot. Fake or not, Harry made sure he impressed the Colonel with his ability to keep the ride smooth over Kowloon's tricky roads, to abuse roundly the local *ricksha'* coolies ('*diu lay lo mo hail'* – fuck your mother's hole – was one of the first phrases Jimmy taught him) and to keep the Colonel informed of the mood of the troops.

Harry drove the Colonel's Austin out of the barracks and south, past the shoe and incense factories towards the strip of watercress fields that separated Sham Shui Po from the tenements of Kowloon proper.

'How are the men, Cole?'

Harry looked in the mirror. The Colonel had put down his papers and was fiddling with his pipe, excavating the bowl with a knife, but Harry knew he wasn't simply making conversation. Drivers were meant to double up as weathervanes.

'Concerning what, sir? The typhoon?'

'The reorganisation.'

Harry shrugged and marshalled his thoughts. He recalled a conversation he had overheard between two warrant officers, and played it back as his own. 'Now they have got used to the guns, sir, not too bad. However, I do feel some men in the anti-tank company are wondering if their howitzers are the most appropriate weapon for the terrain. Assuming we'll be defending the bridges to the north, sir, over the—' *What was the bloody river called?* '—Shum Chin. The thinking is that the best strategy would be to blow the bridges to stop the enemy tanks, sir, then pin the Japs down with the Vickers.'

Harry saw Parkhill frown. 'Might not come to blowing bridges, Cole. The twelve-hour order is about to be rescinded. We are now on twenty-four to Shanghai. My guess is it'll be forty-eight before long.' This was no idle tidbit, but a reassuring rumour to be circulated through the ranks by Harry on his return. 'Where are you going, lad?' Parkhill snapped.

Harry had followed the waterfront to the harbour, the route the Colonel usually preferred, making a left onto Salisbury Road.

'Peninsula Hotel, sir.'

'King's Jetty, Cole. I'm off to see the Governor.'

'Sir. Sorry, sir. Thought it was a normal Wednesday.'

'Does it look like a normal Wednesday?' He waved his still unlit pipe at a drunken tower of bamboo scaffolding, leaning dangerously across the Hankow Road while a gang of shirtless erectors battled to make it secure with streams of rattan.

'Sir.'

Harry spun the car around, ignoring the muttered protests of the cyclists and *ricksha*' coolies, and swept down to a Victoria Harbour getting back to chaotic normality. Now the winds had dropped, the lighters, the scruffy coasters and the bobbing *walla-wallas* had recolonised its waters. A Short flying boat made its approach, klaxon blaring to clear the way for its landing. The Governor's launch was waiting at the jetty, rising and falling with the chop, the official plumage atop the wheelhouse looking a little threadbare. As Cole opened the car door for him, Parkhill said, 'I'll be three hours, Cole.' Harry nodded. He waited until the launch had cast off, heading for Blake Pier, before stepping back into the Austin and driving along the waterfront for some meetings of his own.

Harry parked the staff car in its usual bay on the eastern side of the great U-shape of the Peninsula adjacent to the railway station. He pulled his small kitbag from the boot, paid the usual fifty cents to the *carboy*, and walked back to the end of Hankow Road and stood for a few moments revelling in the sight and sounds of this Asian Babylon, from the illegal fan tan gaming den to his right, to the opium divan, selling its adulterated dope, opposite, and the low-rent brothel next door.

Harry walked the twenty yards to Kumar the tailor's place and stepped inside the cramped store, setting off the tinkle of bells.

Fifteen minutes later when Harry emerged, he was dressed in the cream linen and silk suit that Kumar had tailored for him and allowed him to store in the shop. It had been on only two outings so far. Harry slipped the matching lightweight panama on his head, the tortoiseshell glasses on his nose, lit a small cheroot and strode onto the main street, not as Lance Corporal Harry Cole, but as Rupert Wayne, industrial dye importer.

As he walked into the lobby of the Peninsula Hotel, past the flunkies in their black uniforms and pillbox hats, Harry felt the familiar flutter in his stomach. This was the big league, where the *taipans*, the bosses of the Hutchisons and Mathiesons and Jardines and Coxes and Butterfields and Swires and the other great trading houses held court, eating and drinking from the finest china and crystal under the lofty panelled ceilings of the vast lobby.

He nodded at the staff and checked his watch, an Omego, an almost perfect Chinese copy of the famous Swiss make, before heading for the bar. He would give himself an hour, no more.

Harry adjusted his tie as he stepped into the over-worked splendour of the Moorish-themed bar, and rapidly assessed the status and suitability of the drinkers. He settled on the solitary chap at the bar, the one with the slightly daft grin on his face.

He slid onto the adjacent stool and ordered a vodka and tonic. It would cost about two weeks' army pay, but with a modicum of luck it wouldn't be on his tab. He examined himself in the mirror, making sure he looked the part. Harry's face was handsome enough, although he was never sure whether the slightly bent nose and the chipped tooth from his brawling days in the East End of London detracted from his looks or gave him a slightly raffish, lived-in air. After all, they could easily be a proud memento of the rugger field. Satisfied, he turned and addressed his new companion.

'Don't think we've met.'

'No, don't think we have,' the man replied.

'Unless you know Henderson. Could have met you at his place.'

'Henderson? Is he the one in NT transport development?'

'That's the chap. Been to his house at . . . now where was it . . .'

'Fanling. Next to the golf course.'

'Of course.' Harry had spoken to a Henderson the previous week in the hotel, but he had no idea if they were talking about the same man. It didn't matter. He took a large gulp of his drink and pointed at the man's nearly-full glass of scotch and ginger. 'Ready for another?'

'Uh, no thanks. Thing is, had two already. I'm going home at the weekend. Nine months away from this place.'

That accounted for the grin. He was Boat Happy. Civil servants worked four years on, seven months off, with a month to sail in style in both directions tacked on. The thought of getting away from the heat, the flies and the foreignness always turned them giddy.

'You lucky man. Wayne's the name. Rupert Wayne. I'm in dyes.' Harry held out his hand and Simon Armitage, Deputy Land Officer for Cha Tao district, took it, not realising he was about to stand Harry two drinks before telling him the address of his house in Mid Levels that would be empty while he was away, apart from a Number One Chinese houseboy and a *wash-amah*. From the way Armitage described Number 8 May Road, it was the kind of house that would suit Harry Cole down to the ground.

Two

Harry Cole gave one last satisfying thrust into Mrs Parkhill and withdrew noisily. He gave her rump a slap, watched the flesh, with its silvery stretch marks, ripple for a moment then slumped over onto his back, gasping, letting the down-draught of the squeaky ceiling fan chill his naked skin.

She squatted there on all fours, dark hair plastered to her forehead, breathing heavily, rivulets of sweat streaming down her breasts. 'You, Mr Wayne,' she finally said, 'are a selfish bastard.' He smiled, because they both knew it wasn't true, at least as far as the sex was concerned.

Harry was pleased with the way things had turned out with the Colonel's wife, especially as his Rupert character had nearly blown up in his face, following the hugely successful Ladies' Night he had orchestrated. His masterstroke, apart from hiring a piano trio from the Peninsula, had been teaching Jimmy, the young Chinese barman, how to mix a proper pink lady.

'No yolk,' he had told him. 'Very important. Whites only. Like up on The Peak? Got it?' He poured the separated albumen into a cocktail shaker. 'And no bits of shell. OK?' He took the gin from the refrigerator, tossing it by the neck and catching it with a satisfied smile. 'Nice chilled gin. Not warm. Don't rely on ice cubes. Harry's gin is always in the refrigerator. Remember that. Now, not too much grenadine. Some say a tablespoon, I say that's too much. Give it a good shake. Pour, slowly and . . . there you are. How's that?' Jimmy sipped and beamed a comical grin and Harry said to him: 'Now you do it.'

Egg yolk, bits of shell, too much grenadine. This was what they'd been drinking at the club these past few months? Harry made him do it again and again before going on to tackle the over-limed Gimlets and medicinal Manhattans. Jimmy did get it, quickly. He was a bright boy. He'd come to the colony from Kong Moon in the Kwangtung province – where they knew him as Yiu Sun – and a clansman found him work as a tea-carrying coolie for Douglas boats. There, he was spotted by one of the senior recruiters for the British Army who, as was the custom, charged him two months' wages – repayable with interest – for recommending him to the service. However, he used to earn just two dollars a week shifting tea; now he got four times that with none of the great welts the wooden chests left on his shoulders.

'What are you thinking?'

Mrs Parkhill's voice brought him out of the slumber he had been drifting into. She ran a finger across his chest and played with his nipple, which made him wince. She was in her mid thirties, two kids in school back in Blighty, with a face that still had the outline of her youthful beauty, slightly blurred by an accumulation of soft fat under the skin. She was still a fine-looking woman, though.

'Sorry. Miles away. Business.'

'It's meant to be pleasure, Rupert.'

'It is, Lilith. It is.' He stroked her hair.

He liked to pay attention to women. Listen to what they say, give it equal weight to any man's opinion, involve them in the conversation, rather than treat them as mere adornment. It went a long way to explaining why Harry had what they euphemistically called 'a way with the ladies'.

It was Harry playing the trumpet that had brought them together. Without the trumpet, she might have dismissed him as just another busy bar steward. At close of play on that first Ladies' Night, however, he hadn't been able to resist joining the Peninsula band on a couple of choruses of 'Ain't She Sweet' with the battered Chinese horn he had picked up in the Night Market.

Three days later, Mr Rupert Wayne, flushed with victory after having persuaded the Armitage houseboy that his master was letting him rent 8 May Road during his absence, had strolled into the Peninsula. There, he bumped into a puzzled Mrs Lilith Parkhill. Despite the suit, the panama and the glasses, she recognised him immediately as Harry, the trumpet-playing bar steward. He had wheeled her off to a quiet corner, where he spun and spun his story, explaining that he was an undercover policeman, trying to root out widespread corruption in the Civil Service and army. It was imperative the Colonel didn't know and he finished by requesting her discretion.

He got more than her discretion. Soon Lilith was asking her husband if she could borrow his car, and Harry the driver, to do some househunting. She didn't want to live on the barracks, was tired of her rooms at the Repulse Bay Hotel. She wanted to look around, see what was on offer.

What was on offer were regular sessions making love with Harry/Rupert at Armitage's house in Mid Levels above the harbour.

'Do you realise how dull it is to be a married woman in Hong Kong?' she said, lighting a cigarette. 'Nothing but petty rules and conventions. You can't work because white women don't work, not white married ones. You can't even do housework, because there is always some dirt-cheap servant to do that for you. Bridge, *mah jong*, tennis, dinner, those bloody awful dinner parties, and more bloody bridge and *mah jong*. My God, it's no wonder we end up fucking the staff.' She paused and glanced at Harry, who feigned a pained expression. 'Well, you are staff. Sort of. How long before you've cracked this racket you're investigating?'

'How long till I leave, you mean?'

She nodded.

'I don't know. A week, a month . . .'

'A year?'

Christ I hope not, he thought. He'd be bored with her well before that. 'Possibly, darling, possibly.'

He slid off the bed, grabbed a towel and walked to the window. Simon Armitage's place was a well-appointed dwelling: teak floors, high ceilings, plenty of fans, and a grand view of the neat row of steamships moored along the Praya.

'When you go, can I have this house?' asked Mrs Parkhill, reading his thoughts. 'It's quite the nicest one I've seen of late.' She reached over and nibbled on one of the biscuits she had bought at the Lane, Crawford grocery department, letting crumbs drop onto the bed. 'No Chinks too near, either.'

The well-off Chinese tended to concentrate on Conduit and Caine Roads below them; here, on May Road, they were a bold minority. Above was The Peak, site of the colony's most desirable homes and overwhelmingly European, almost exclusively British.

'Can't do it. Crown Property. Would have to go through . . . the proper channels.'

'Oh, rot. You mean bribe the right person. Fill his washbowl or whatever the term is.'

He laughed. 'I'll find out who the land agent is and tip him the wink. Fill his ricebowl. How's that?'

'Oh, Rupert, that would be wonderful.'

'Does that mean you want me to hurry up and leave Hong Kong?'

'Not at all, you rascal. Come here. I'll show you how much I want to get rid of you.'

He stole a glance at his watch on the bedside table. He should be opening up the bar soon. 'I've got time for a quick one.'

She produced a ripe chuckle. 'We'll see about that.'

Harry, dressed once more as Rupert, approached Mister Eric's place twenty minutes after he had dropped off the Colonel at the Peninsula, giving the man plenty of time to get inside the house and out of his way. Parkhill wouldn't be out for at least an hour. Eric was leaning against the red lacquered door of the brothel, a cigarette clamped between his stained teeth.

'Hello, Harry.'

'Mister Eric. Is he in there?'

'Ten minutes now.' Eric spat noisily into the dust.

'Did you . . . ?' began Harry.

Eric nodded. He pushed himself off the door and walked across the road, weaving through the coolies and waving at Harry to follow him. 'Come. Talk over tea.'

'Suki won't sleep with you.'

Harry tapped his forefinger on the table as Mister Eric refilled his cup. They were at the little *chai* stand a few streets away from the house where the Colonel was being entertained by Suki. He felt his throat go dry. He had asked Eric if she would take him as a client. He said he doubted it, but Harry insisted he put the request in.

'Why not?' Harry asked as he sipped the scalding tea. 'Why won't she sleep with me, when she'll *dui* Parkhill?'

'What your wife called?'

Harry studied Mister Eric's face, but it was an unreadable mask. Eric must have known that he was, in the army's eyes at least, too young to have a wife.

'I don't have a wife,' he said at last. Mister Eric looked over his shoulder and Harry followed the glance down the street, past the row of *comprados*, the grocery and dry good shops, each barely three feet wide, to the pair of white police officers walking towards them. Harry looked away and carried on as if nothing was more natural than Anglo-Chinese fraternisation. He felt the coppers' stares bore into his back as they slowly paced by.

'The girl that interests you will only' – Mister Eric made an obscene gesture – 'officers and married men.'

'What?'

'Officers, because she is expensive,' and he said in pidgin, '*forty dollah*.'

Forty was right at the top end, almost off the scale. For forty Hong Kong dollars he could go down to Kennedy Town and get himself twenty girls, all clean, all willing to do whatever he wanted. For six dollars a week, he could have what soldiers called a *dahnomer* – a down-homer – a girl in one of the laydown cubicles for his exclusive use, with sewing and washing thrown in. But, even at her extortionate price, he still wanted Suki, had done for every waking moment since the day he had spied on her. Having to be hitched, though, as well as finding that kind of cash? It was an insult.

'Stone me, Eric, surely marrieds, they're the last people that need her services.'

'Maybe so. But she think married men safer.'

'Safer?'

'Take a lot more care. They not want to give the Japanese disease to their wives. They careful.'

The Japanese disease was obviously the same as the Cuban

thing. The clap was always some other country's fault. 'Well,' said Harry glumly, 'I'm fucking the Colonel's wife. Doesn't that count?'

Mister Eric flashed his gold teeth as he laughed loud and dirty enough to make the two policemen stop and swivel their heads, sure something fishy was going on. Eric raised a placatory hand. The pair glared and moved on.

Eric giggled and said, 'I'll ask her again.'

Three

'Where are your family from, Cole?'

Harry flicked his eyes to the rearview mirror and tried to interpret Colonel Parkhill's expression, wondering what had caused this sudden interest in his antecedents. 'Hoxton, sir.'

'Hoxton. Don't know it. East End of London, is it?'

'Sir.'

They drove on in silence for a few minutes, north towards the barracks, past a cluster of locals outside a shop, arms waving, teeth bared as they chanted incomprehensible slogans. Two policemen and a knot of soldiers pushed them back.

'Must be a Jap shop,' said the Colonel. 'Officers' *nappy-wallah*'s a Jap.' It took a moment for Harry to realise he was using the old Indian Army phrase for a barber. 'Says the Japs are all getting a lot of stick around town. A lot. Be worse if they take Canton.'

The Japanese had shelled the outskirts of Canton, killing close to a hundred people. Many people in the city had relatives up there, hence the unrest and attacks on their businesses.

'How'd you get your stripe, Cole?'

'I busted a racket, sir. Back in Blighty. Boots and blankets. Selling them to civilians they was. Right under everyone's noses.'

'Really.'

'Criminal, sir.'

They swept through the barrack gates, the sentries on duty snapping to attention as they went. 'You'd know all about that, I suppose, Cole.'

Ah. It dawned on him that the Colonel must have seen the ERAS on his file. Early Release for Army Service. He'd knocked three years off his sentence in the Scrubs for burglary by volunteering for King and Country.

'All behind me now, sir.'

'Excellent. Pleased to hear it.'

As Harry pulled to a halt outside the CO's office, two regimental policemen stepped smartly forward from the shadows, one either side of the car. They were big men, with no necks to speak of, and clearly very hard.

'There are certain irregularities in the bar accounts, Cole. And some complaints about, shall we say, the quality of the drinks.' Parkhill beamed a smile of pleasure that threw deep creases across his face. 'Now, you can try telling me you are an undercover agent for HM Government if you wish, but those things work rather better with my wife.'

'Never give a bloke a second chance, eh? Once a crook, always a crook?'

The Colonel stepped out and leaned back into the car. 'In my experience, that's about the size of it, Cole. I'm sure the do-gooders and social engineers and communists at Wormwood Scrubs saw it differently. My office, now.'

The policemen pulled Harry out of the Austin, barked for him to stand to attention and quick-marched him into the CO's office. Harry's brain whirred, trying to put everything together. Lilith had let something slip about Rupert, possibly trying to goad or belittle her husband, and now he was blown wide open.

Parkhill took the seat behind his desk, an air of victory settling around him. He left Harry at rigid attention while he examined a list of figures.

'Well, Cole. We seem to have a shortfall of several hundred Hong Kong dollars.' He looked again. 'No, my mistake. Eight hundred and twenty-five.'

'Sir.'

'Is that all you have to say? I need hardly remind you this is a court martial offence, Cole. I think you'll find military detention rather different from your time at Wormwood Scrubs.'

'Sir. Permission to speak, sir.'

'Of course.'

'Wasn't me, sir.'

The Colonel chuckled. 'I suggest you come up with a better defence than that.'

Harry took a deep breath. It was time to pull something out of the bag. 'Thing is, sir, I knew something odd was going on. I did a little digging. I can prove it wasn't me.'

Parkhill looked bemused. 'Really? And how can you do that?'

'Permission to show the evidence, sir.'

'Go on, then.' There was a hint of doubt in his voice.

From the top pocket of his tunic Harry took the creased brown envelope, stepped forward and handed it over. Parkhill flipped it open and eased out the contents. He sucked air through his teeth and hissed, 'I see.'

'Yes, sir.'

'Cole. So who does this implicate? Your assistant, I suppose? The Chinese boy?'

Harry nodded. No way out of that one. Sorry, Jimmy. It's the way the *chim* sticks fall. 'Looks like it, sir.'

Parkhill glanced at the regimental policemen. 'Sergeant. Jimmy the barman at the Officers' Club. Detain him. Now.'

'Sir,' snapped the sergeant and the pair wheeled around and left.

'Permission to stand at ease, sir.'

'You bastard,' said Parkhill slowly.

Harry slouched and, the charade over, sat on the edge of Parkhill's desk. 'Mister Eric takes every client's picture, Colonel. It's an insurance policy.'

Parkhill let the grainy photographs drop onto the desk, and Harry could make out the blurred shape of him and Suki intertwined in a variety of positions. 'I suppose these aren't the only copies?'

Harry picked one up and examined it, marvelling at the smooth curve of her back, a creation of exquisite proportions. 'Good God, no,' he said eventually. 'Got a whole library of them. I have to say, sir, you have impressive stamina for a man of your—'

Parkhill slammed the desk in fury. 'That's enough.'

Harry reached over and helped himself to a cigarette from the teak box on the desk and lit it with the ornate table lighter.

'Where do we go from here, Cole?'

Harry took a few puffs before answering, 'An honourable discharge.'

A bitter laugh. 'On what grounds?'

'Medical. Malaria. Repeated bouts, very debilitating, I hear. Passage to Blighty on the next transport. Very convenient, and gets me out of your way as well. Sir.'

'And the Japs' way too.'

'There is that.'

'Very well,' he spat, the irritation making his mouth twitch. 'I'll see the MO.'

'And a letter of recommendation —'

'You've got nothing to recommend, Cole.'

'I think Mrs Parkhill might disagree.'

A tic started in one of Parkhill's cheeks. 'Get out before I shoot you where you sit, you slippery bastard. One day, Cole, you'll come unstuck. And if there is a God, I'll be there to watch the whole thing.'

'Yeah, they'll probably be sellin' tickets by then.' Harry slid off the desk and stubbed out the cigarette. 'I'll make sure you and Mrs Parkhill get the best seats in the house.'

'OK, Suki says will see you.' Harry's heart leapt as a terse Mister Eric delivered the news. The brothel manager wasn't too thrilled that Parkhill had cancelled his visits indefinitely. Harry had told him the Colonel would be back – he knew how hard it was to resist the lure of Suki. In the meantime, Harry had offered to fill the man's shoes, and Eric's wallet. 'Wait over at the tea shack,' Mister Eric instructed.

Harry crossed over the road and walked through the narrow alley, holding his breath against the stench of urine, to the stall, where he ordered his *chai* and sat nervously on the bench.

It was fifteen minutes before she appeared, a clear head taller than the mass of people that she was pushing through. Despite the heat she was wearing a full length black cotton coat but her covered form was even more seductive than seeing her naked through the screen. He was suddenly very parched. He sipped at the cold tea in front of him and cleared his throat.

She sat lightly on the bench opposite him, as if scared to put her full weight down. Her face was astonishingly smooth and symmetrical – if she was mixed race as Mister Eric insisted, hardly any of the British blood had diluted the oriental features.

'I'm —' he began croakily.

'I know who you are.' She looked at him steadily. Her voice was neutral, almost accentless. 'Eric tells me. Here.' She slid a pad and pencil over to him. 'Write your name, your date of birth and your job, please.'

'What?'

'If you want to see me, you must do this.'

He did as he was told, writing musician as his occupation. He certainly wasn't going to be in the army much longer, so it was as good as anything.

'Wait here.'

And she was gone. He gazed at the back of her head until it was swallowed by a sea of pointed straw hats.

He took a refill of tea and moved into the shade, watching the coolies rush back and forth. One of the scrawny black-clad Hakka women came by at a more leisurely pace than the others, a trussed hen under her arm, the silent bird en route to its messy death at the temple in some ritual beyond Harry's understanding.

Then it came to him. His date of birth. His writing. These people never did anything without consulting a fortune teller. She had gone to confer with some phoney astrologer about whether to take him on. He pressed down on his anger. All she should worry about was whether he could manage her *forty dollahs*, not his damn' star sign.

It wasn't Suki who returned a half hour later, but Mister Eric, his face clamped into an expression that tried to convey regret.

Harry half rose. 'What does Suki say?'

'She says . . . no.'

Harry slapped the flimsy table hard, cracking it down the middle, sending the cups crashing to the ground, prompting a stream of abuse from the stall holder.

'Why? Tell me that. Why?'

Mister Eric squatted down and frowned, an unhappy bearer of

bad tidings. He put a hand out and touched Harry's leg before saying quietly: 'She asked the astrologer, Harry. Then the *chim* and even the *bui*. All said same thing. *Zao gao*. Have nothing to do with him. You going to come to a bad end, Harry.'

Four

London, 1938

'And which side does sir dress the male person?' asked the tailor crouching before him, tape ready to measure his inside leg.

Whichever bloody way it feels like going thought Harry, but he replied: 'Left.'

'To the left. Very good, sir.'

For his new suit, Harry had chosen one of the lesser Savile Row houses. It was a step up from a cat's face – the first premises opened by a cutter eager to make a name for himself – but not yet fit to mention in the same breath as Huntsman or Poole, so the tailor was keen to attract the titled and the military on its books.

Harry asked: 'Business good?'

'Can't complain, sir,' said the tailor. 'Although not for suits. Thirty-three and one-eighth.' An apprentice repeated the figure and then scribbled it down on Harry's order form. The tailor stood and looked at Harry's shoulders, checking they were level. 'Most orders are for dress uniforms at the moment.' He picked at a bit of fluff on Harry's lapel. 'All this talk of war, you see. But every cloud has its silver lining. There, all done. Now would sir like an extra pair of trousers?'

Harry nodded. Why not?

'Fine. First fitting in three weeks.'

'Can't rub in a PT?'

The tailor raised an eyebrow that a customer should know the Row's slang for working during lunch breaks to speed up an order. Harry, though, had friends who had worked as juniors for many of the tailors and outworkers in the East End.

'Well . . .' The tailor scratched his head, pondering.

'I don't mind a guinea or so on the final cost. Just that most of my clothes seem to have dated rather since I went overseas. Shapes have changed.'

'They have, sir. As I said, ours aren't quite as extreme as Mr Valentine's, but . . .'

Harry had asked for the boxed shoulders, wasp waist and pleated trousers that he had seen on the dandies at the Café Royal in Regent Street the previous night. His own suit, one of Kumar's, had seemed stiff in comparison. It turned out that a tailor called Bobby Valentine had created the radical new cut that was fashionable among the fast set. So much so, the waiting list for a genuine Mr V was upwards of six months.

'Shall we say two guineas, plus half a crown each for the cutters?' suggested Harry.

The tailor smiled. 'We shall see what we can do.'

'Tuesday?'

'This isn't Hong Kong, sir.'

'No, I'm forgetting. Friday?'

'Friday. We'll do our best.'

Harry slipped on his Kumar jacket. 'I'll see you then.'

'We'll look forward to it, Colonel Parkhill.'

The smartly clipped moustache helped to give a man in his late twenties, as Harry was, the gravitas to pass for a colonel. The rest was a matter of a little grey at the temples, an upright bearing, and a great deal of bluster. He also made sure he conspicuously flashed the papers that Mister Eric had reproduced from Parkhill's genuine set, lifted during one of the Colonel's early sessions with Suki. It was the best identity he had for the moment, even if his youth did occasionally spark the incredulity he could see flitting across the face of the Riley salesman, a young man with the big-boned face of good breeding.

Harry stroked the top of the Sprite Saloon and asked: 'Fast?'

'Very fast, sir. One and a half litre Riley engine, light body, gives a top speed of ninety-five . . .'

'And it's how much?'

'Three hundred and ninety-eight pounds.'

'I'll need a test drive.'

'No problem, Colonel. If you'll hop in, I'll take you for a spin.'

Harry looked aghast. 'No offence. But I'd rather drive by myself. Only way you can get the measure of something like this. One to one. Don't you find?'

The salesman adjusted his tie. 'Sir, if it was up to me . . . but company policy . . .'

Harry looked wistfully out of the window onto St James's and across to Jermyn Street. His tongue ran over the back of his incisor teeth, worrying the little ridge, still unused to the recent repair that masked his chipped tooth. Harry had decided it had looked rough rather than raffish after all. 'London's changed, hasn't it?'

'How do you mean, sir?'

'When I left, a gentleman's word was his bond. Now look at it. All treated like common criminals. I think I'll go across to Jack Barclay, see how he feels about a test drive.'

'Just a minute, sir . . . There must be some way we can compromise . . .'

'Look, I'll leave you my service papers and watch as security. Will that satisfy you?' He unfastened the clasp. 'Damn' thing's worth more than the car.'

The salesman left and consulted with the manager who glanced up as he examined the pay book and the Omega watch and gave the nod. The manager knew that no soldier would give up his pay book lightly.

The doors were pushed back and Harry climbed into the saloon, turned the flimsy key and pressed the starter. The little Sprite fired into throaty life. The salesman leant in and gave the Colonel instructions on the instruments and the best route for him to take, along Piccadilly to Knightsbridge, through the park and back round in a big loop. He stood back as Harry gunned the engine and roared off, leaving a faint haze of blue smoke in the showroom. The manager winced. The demonstrator was only two days old. 'You told him it needed running in?' he shouted across.

The salesman nodded glumly.

The manager looked down at the watch, wondering when he could afford one of these nice Swiss jobs. It was only when he saw the spelling Omego that the first misgivings began to flutter in his stomach.

Five

Two weeks after his final fitting as Colonel Parkhill at the tailor's, on a glorious autumn afternoon, Harry drove the Riley Sprite, now a fetching deep red colour, through the Blackwall Tunnel en route to Tunbridge Wells. By the time he reached Bromley most of the city's horse-drawn traffic and the costermongers' donkeys had fallen away. With a clear road ahead, he let the little car stretch her legs and wound down the window to blow out the last of the heavy cellulose and thinner fumes from the re-spray.

Harry was as well turned out as the car, in his bespoke Valentine-ish suit, polished brogues and new cravat. He had been moving along quite nicely himself since his return from Hong Kong. He had quickly slotted into his old world of boozers and spielers, the ad hoc gambling dens that were all over the East End of London like a bag of fleas.

At the Moon Under Water pub in Shoreditch he had bought the key to a council flat in the Dunstan Houses near Stepney Green, using some of the forged fivers that were for sale at thirty bob a throw at Daddy Ho's in Limehouse. The flat was a nice place by local standards – it had its own lavatory, no sign of bed bugs or mice, and a fine view over to St Paul's, or it would have been if the Civil Defence hadn't placed two vast barrage balloons in the way.

And, as a bonus, he had acquired Dottie, who stayed over a couple of nights a week to keep him company. She was the girlfriend of Micky Codling, one of his Hoxton pals from way back. He and Micky had undertaken their first crimes together, graduating from stealing off the barges down at the Shadwell Basin to breaking into Auntie Queenie's cat-infested rooms when they were nine, in search of the great wads of money rumoured to be in there somewhere – Queenie was the local moneylender – only to come away with thruppence each from the gas meter. Hardly a promising debut.

Now Micky was in the Scrubs, having progressed from gas meters to post offices. He'd been nabbed with a Webley pistol in his hand in the PO down on the Commercial Road and his fiancée, the cherub-faced little Dottie, didn't expect to see him in natural light for another nine years. Her arrangement with Harry developed on the night he had taken her out to cheer her up after the trial.

Lying in his bed in the flat the following morning, Dottie had explained at length how she had been a nippy in Lyons Corner House. She was sacked after pouring scalding tea into the lap of a customer who thought the nickname for a waitress meant they wouldn't mind a quick pinch on the bottom. Now, she worked as a chambermaid at the Charing Cross Hotel.

Harry had almost drifted off when something she said shook him awake. 'You wouldn't believe what people leave in their rooms after they check out. Amazing stuff.'

'Such as?' Harry had asked.

A Wing Commander Gilbert, it transpired, had abandoned his cheque book, log book and driver's licence in room 410. Dottie had meant to hand them in to lost property, but they were still in her uniform when she came to wash it. She had put them on the mantelpiece at her mum's place, she explained, unsure of what to do with them.

Harry changed down for the long climb up the hill towards Sevenoaks. In his inside pocket were the twenty-three cheques and the Wing Commander's log book. Unlike Dottie, he knew exactly what to do with the windfall: exchange them for cash. He would avoid the banks, of course, since they had lists of stolen and lost cheque books, but would target hotels.

As the car touched sixty across the rolling hills of the Weald, Harry ran through his forthcoming performance as the Wing Commander, talking out loud, trying to get the conspiratorial tone just right. He would go to the large hotel on the hill in the centre of Tunbridge Wells an hour or so after the banks had closed, and ask for the manager. 'My name is Wing Commander Gilbert,' he practised, 'I am engaged in some extremely sensitive work for the RAF in the area and, rather embarrassingly, I have something of a shortfall in funding. Now, normally in a situation like this, I would put in a request for the Ministry to wire a cash authorisation down to a bank . . .'

He carried on, outlining to himself how the Air Ministry would reimburse the hotel within a day or two, forcing himself to wriggle into the skin of the Wing Commander, until Harry from Hoxton was nowhere to be seen or heard.

Don't be too greedy at the hotels, he reminded himself, fifty pounds a time should do it. Success at two establishments a day and he'd be rolling in it. Wing Commander Gilbert was potentially a worthy successor to Colonel Parkhill. Harry had a feeling the pair of them were about to move up in the world.

Six

Le Touquet, France, early 1939

'I am afraid the manager is not here today, M'sieur. I am his assistant. Perhaps I can help?'

Harry looked around the lobby of the Hôtel Atlantic to make sure nobody else was in earshot and leaned over the desk. 'If we could talk somewhere in private. This is a sensitive matter.'

The Frenchman nodded. 'Of course. If you would like to step into the office, M'sieur . . . ?'

'Gilbert. Wing Commander Gilbert.'

As Harry had anticipated, Tunbridge Wells had gone very smoothly. In fact, most of the hotels had been only too glad to co-operate with a member of the services in such uncertain times and had been happy to advance fifty pounds. The run of successes stretched right across the winter up until The Grand in Brighton. Harry was punting cheque number twelve by then, but on that occasion he had seen doubt and suspicion in the manager's eyes. It couldn't have been his performance, that was word perfect. However, it was just possible that warnings about a cheque book fraudster had been circulated by the police or banks.

He had made a hasty exit from the hotel, and Brighton, just to be on the safe side and had decided to try his luck – armed with a newly minted WC Gilbert passport made in Stamford Hill – among the Anglophile enclaves of northern France. That meant trying the hotels of Calais, Boulogne, Dunkirk, Dieppe and now the Atlantic Le Touquet, an imitation of The Ritz in Paris, only with even more brocade and imitation Louis XIV fittings. A lily well and truly gilded, thought Harry.

The Assistant Manager indicated a chair for the Wing Commander, who said he preferred to stand. Harry moved smoothly into his story as the Frenchman examined Gilbert's log book. He had inked in some extra flights to account for his presence in the country, carefully copying Gilbert's tiny, dense writing. His fiction had never really been questioned on the continent because, if anything, the French were even more terrified by the ever-present rumours of fifth columnists and war than the English, and were relieved and reassured that undercover allied agents were abroad in the land.

'I am afraid I am not authorised to help, Wing Commander,' the Assistant Manager said glumly as he handed back the papers. 'Much as I would like to.'

'Oh.' Harry was taken aback. This had never happened before.

'The house rule is that only M'sieur Bourg, the manager, can authorise such payments. He will be here in the morning.'

'That's jolly unfortunate.'

'I'm sorry. He'll be in first thing.'

'I have to be on my way to Calais by eight.' Before the banks open, that is.

'He is here at seven thirty, Wing Commander. Are you booked into the hotel?'

'Uh, no.'

'Well, if you spend the night with us, I am sure M'sieur Bourg will gladly help in the morning. He was in the air force himself, in the Great War.'

Harry hesitated. This was a dangerous development. Get in, get the money, get out, that was his normal rule. But the thought of what was doubtless a supremely comfortable bed, and perhaps a bottle or two of wine, was tempting.

'Sir?'

'Yes, sorry. A room would be excellent. I'll get my bags.'

'Very good, sir. And will sir be joining us for dinner?'

'I'm travelling rather light, to be honest, old chap. Bit short in the dinner jacket department.'

'I'm sure the concierge will be able to assist, Wing Commander.'

'In which case . . . yes. Why not?'

The meal was taken at a vast communal table scattered with rose petals and adorned with heavy, gleaming silverware. He was seated with a mixed bag of Europeans, with just one fellow countryman at the far end of the table, a Henry King who was something in the moving picture business. Despite the pair being comprehensively outnumbered, however, the conversation was conducted in mostly impeccable English, which was just as well because Harry's French was rudimentary at best.

As he scanned the table he found his eyes flicking back to the woman who had introduced herself to the company as the Contessa Hellie von Lutz, who hailed from Alsace. He tried not to stare, but she had a rather delicious laugh and for a moment when she caught and brazenly held his gaze he felt himself start to redden, like a schoolboy caught peeking. He ran a finger round his dress collar, which felt half a size too small. He may have mastered the accent, but the penguin suits were still tricky for him.

As they moved on to dessert Hellie von Lutz insisted that the men all rotate, choreographing the changes with waves of her fan, and he found himself parted from the dull wife of the Michelin executive and directed next to the Contessa. She waited until the conversation sparked into life around them before she put her mouth close to his ear.

'So, a spy?'

Harry almost spluttered. He turned to face her and he could smell sweet wine on her breath. This close he could see she was well into her thirties, with pale skin, deep brown eyes and a mouth framed by two faint crescent-shaped lines that deepened when she smiled.

'What on earth gave you that idea?'

She shrugged. 'You think you can keep secrets from Hellie?'

'Clearly, the Assistant Manager can't keep anything from you.'

'Few men can, chéri.'

He wondered whether she was drunk, but those eyes were clear and sparkling.

'So,' she continued. 'Who do you spy for? No, no, don't tell me. Let me guess. The English is too obvious. You're clearly not a Wing Commander of anything, are you? The Germans? Maybe. The French? No, the DTS would never trust a foreigner. The Americans? No, they aren't even sure where France is. Or do you mostly spy for yourself ?'

Harry was uneasy. She was clearly teasing him, and for the first time in many weeks, he felt as if Harry Cole was showing through. He stiffened in his chair and pulled himself upright, putting a little Air Ministry frost into his words. 'What makes you say that?'

She lowered her voice even further. 'Because all spies spy for themselves, really. They don't do it out of patriotism. They do it out of love.'

'For their country,' he said curtly.

'No, for the love of the game. For the love of spying itself. The sheer excitement. Which is why you get double agents . . . spies who don't care who their masters are, just as long as they can continue to play.' She took a sip of wine. 'That is my experience, anyway, Wing Commander.'

'Have you known many spies, Contessa?'

'Not so many that one more would do any harm.' She threw her head back and laughed, causing some of the other guests to look over at them disapprovingly.

He excused himself and went to the lavatory, wondering if he had misread the signals. Signals? They were more like bloody distress flares. But he wasn't comfortable with the conversation. She had sniffed something all right, but she wasn't quite certain what the scent was yet. The sensible thing would be to break off. She was, though, he thought, as he buttoned himself up and adjusted his dress, a rather handsome woman.

When he returned to the dinner table the matter had been decided for him. Hellie was deep in conversation with a Dutch diamond merchant who had slid into his seat and was intermittently stroking her hand. She flashed Harry a what-could-I-do look of regret, but he suddenly felt relieved and tired. Certainly, he was too weary to start any sort of antler-locking with a wealthy and amorous Dutchman. He said his loud goodnights to the table and left before brandy.

It was six thirty the following morning when he realised the rapping wasn't in his dream after all, but someone at the door. The manager, perhaps. He opened it to find the Contessa, resplendent in a silk dressing gown, leaning in the doorway, a cigarette drooping lazily from her lips. She swept past him, letting the gown fold onto the floor, and stubbed out the cigarette, exhaling a cloud of smoke into the room.

'Thank God. You never gave me your room number. I've tried

three floors and been fucked five times on the way.' She struck a Louise Brooks pose, totally naked and unabashed. 'Well, I'm here now.'

Harry burst out laughing, unsure whether she was telling the truth, but unable to resist bringing her score up to the full half dozen.

There was swell on the Channel on his return crossing, making the ferry feel as if it was wallowing from one trough to another rather than making headway. He had the deck almost to himself as he watched the Dover cliffs grow larger with each peak, a tired smile on his face at the memory of the Contessa Hellie von Lutz and the thought of the thick wad of high denomination notes in his pocket.

Wing Commander Gilbert had done well again, adding three more hotels to the tally after the Atlantic. And he still had five cheques left. On the train from Dover he read a *Daily Mirror*, despite the fact that a Wing Commander would almost certainly have taken *The Times* or the *Telegraph*. It was time to give the man a rest anyway, he realised. His weariness was partly from the strain of having to keep in character for hours or days at a time. Still, there was a lot of cash in his pocket, enough for him to consider moving up West, breaking free from the low horizons of the East End, finally making something of himself, something that might even be legal. A share in a bar or a café, maybe a swank restaurant. He'd make an excellent host, he was sure.

The newspaper alarmed him with a recommendation that, in the wake of Mussolini's invasion of Albania and the trouble brewing in Europe, conscription be re-introduced. Harry didn't like the sound of that. He didn't want to see the inside of another barracks ever again, and certainly not when he was about to get a leg up in life.

He alighted at Charing Cross, wondering if he should wait for Dottie to come off shift from the hotel, but had decided to head back east when he became aware of the two men, one either side. He could smell a cologne on one of them, far too delicate for his big, square frame. They sandwiched Harry, pushing him towards the exit far quicker than he would have liked.

'I say —' he began, indignantly.

'Be quiet,' Mr Cologne barked as he snatched the overnight case from him.

Harry snapped his mouth shut and allowed himself to be frog-marched outside. A black saloon was waiting on the forecourt, blocking the taxis. Mr Cologne pointed a finger like a pistol barrel at the nearest cabbie, who was leaning on his horn, and the noise stopped abruptly. Harry clearly wasn't the only one to recognise that you didn't argue with Mr Cologne. Harry was forced in the back of the Morris between his two escorts and the driver pulled away.

Mr Cologne unfastened Harry's bag and began to rifle through the contents, spilling his soiled shirts and underwear on the floor.

'Look here,' Harry tried again. The fist hit him hard, clicking his jaw sideways, almost out of its socket, snapping his head back and loosening his hat. He didn't struggle when the trilby was removed and the canvas sack was dragged down over his face.

Sir Claude Dansey of the Z organisation heard the Morris saloon pull into the yard outside the warehouse. He buttoned up his jacket and strode across the dusty concrete and took his place at the rickety desk, lowering himself stiffly into position, careful not to stress his back. He was getting too old for all this, too old to be running a private intelligence service, too old for enforcement duties.

The gloomy brick building had once been an abattoir, back

when this part of south London was all fields and farms, but now, after service as a garage and a warehouse, it was an empty shell, the interior illuminated only by a pair of sooty skylights. These days it was used only as an anonymous venue for Dansey to have a few quiet words with those who crossed him.

Dansey blinked as the main door slid back to admit daylight along with the three silhouettes, then slammed shut again. His two operatives dragged the Gilbert fraudster into the centre of the room. Dansey was sitting mostly in shadow, aware that he presented a vaguely threatening presence in the half-light.

'Take off the hood,' he said.

The man grunted as the sacking was yanked off him. Dansey nodded and a hard punch to the kidneys was delivered. The man staggered forward and a kick behind the knee sent him to the floor. Dansey watched impassively as his two men alternated kicks, their victim rolling into a ball, grunting and yelping under the blows.

Dansey had no compunction about the beating. Potential threats had to be dealt with swiftly. The Z organisation was his own creation, a force doing the government's job of gathering intelligence, a task the real MI6 was far too enfeebled to perform. Using well-off businessmen, bankers, engineers and even film-makers – the producer Alexander Korda, the man the public knew only as the force behind *The Private Life of Henry VIII* and *Things To Come*, was one of his best sources of information – Dansey gathered material across Europe and reported directly to Winston Churchill, who used it to needle the spineless government of the day. This was on the understanding that, should circumstances change, then Z, and Dansey, would be welcomed into the official fold.

'Stop,' said Dansey after a few minutes. A wisp of vapour hung in the air from his breath.

The room was silent but for the laboured breathing of his men, sweating after their exertions, and a thin whine coming from the tangle of limbs at their feet.

'Search him.'

The man was rolled over and money and papers were placed on the desk before Dansey.

'Wing Commander Gilbert,' he said with a sneer. Dansey flipped open the envelope containing the cash. 'RAF pay seems to be getting better. And in francs. How very European.'

'Look, I don't know who you are . . .' The voice sounded frightened, the words blurred as they came out through swollen lips.

'No, you don't know who we are. It is best you keep it that way. I don't suppose it occurred to you, Wing Commander,' Dansey said slowly, 'that there might be genuine agents operating in northern France.' He nodded and another kick was delivered, powerful enough to send the impostor sliding across the floor. 'That a foreign spy could overhear your stupid fabrications and report back to, say, Berlin.' Another blow. 'Which would mean our men – the genuine article – are threatened with detection and exposure, compromising the security of this country.' He paused to let this sink in. 'OK, pull him up.'

As he was lifted to his feet, the conman shook his head to try to clear it, droplets of blood flicking off onto the floor.

'You stupid, pathetic idiot,' said Dansey. 'No more. You understand? No more.'

'Yes,' the man managed to croak, spitting out part of his front tooth as he did so. 'No more. You have my word.'

'No, no, no,' laughed Dansey. 'You have *my* word. Next time, if there is even a hint of a next time, it'll be a bullet behind the ear.' He waved the post office book under Harry's nose to indicate the business was over. 'We'll see the money gets back to the rightful owners. Get him out of here.'

Dansey waited until he heard the Morris drive off before he rose and left himself, pausing only to rub the sole of his shoe in the largest of the glistening pools of blood on the floor, scraping it back and forth until it merged with the dust and dirt.

Within minutes of getting home Harry's body had started stiffening up and turning a particularly sickly shade of yellow. His back ached, his piss was like rose water and his vision was distorted and flickering at the periphery. He felt like Max Schmeling after Joe Louis had finished with him in the rematch. He managed to pour himself a scotch and down it before he made it to the bed.

Dottie found him a couple of hours later, lying rigidly at attention on the candlewick bedspread, whimpering like a dog with toothache, his forehead covered with a slick of sweat. She quickly boiled kettles and helped him into the tin bath she positioned in front of the gas fire, feeding the gas meter to keep a stream of hot water coming, tutting and hissing at his wounds, calling him poor love this, poor darling that.

As she sponged him down as gently as possible, dabbing at the crusts of blood, she finally asked: 'You going to tell me who it was?'

'I don't know, do I?' he snapped irritably. 'Three of them jumped me after I got off the train. Took all the money, Dots. All of it.'

'Not the savings, though.'

'They took the post office book, Dottie. It'll all be gone.'

She pursed her lips in irritation at the news they were poor once more. 'You could've reported it. I mean, a robbery like that in broad daylight.'

He raised an eyebrow, and even that hurt. 'You know better, Dottie.'

'You should've gone to a hospital at least. Look at you. I don't know how you got home in that state.'

'Neither do I, love. Do I look terrible?'

She scanned the puffy face with its closed left eye, split lips, chipped tooth and deep gash on the cheekbone, leant over and kissed him. 'Pretty as a picture, Harry.'

'Yeah, I can imagine what kind of picture.'

'I'll go and get us some crackling and chips, eh? Make us both feel better. All right?'

'There's a fiver over by the window.' He pointed at the stack of phony notes secured under a West Ham footballer paperweight.

'I turn up at Charlie's with a brand-new fiver and they'll know there's something fishy apart from the rock. My treat, Harry. Just this once.'

Harry managed a smile, but inside acid was eating through the lining of his gut. The beating had hurt, but that would pass. It wasn't his first – when he was sixteen he'd had his nose broken in Limehouse by a copper who had caught him climbing over the dock fence on his way to a little pilfering – and he couldn't guarantee it wouldn't be his last.

The pain of having to start all over again, though, the horror of being sucked back into the mindless routines of Hoxton and the East End, of pubs and crackling and chips, and forged fivers, all that panning for fool's gold, just when he was so close to breaking free, that was real agony.

The spieler where Harry started his money-washing campaign was in a spartan side room of The Lord Taverner, a pub just on the edge of the City, near Spitalfields market and the Hawksmoor church. Closed off from the public bar by a mangy green velvet curtain, this was where, by invitation only, those known to Reg, the publican, could spend the night playing three card brag, rummy, Watch The Ten or Napoleon. Harry was a familiar face to Reg from the days when they'd both ditched school and become bookie's runners.

Harry's strategy was to exchange his supply of forged fivers for the real thing by winning some hands, losing others, getting the money nicely mixed up, but one thing hadn't gone according to plan. At The Lord Taverner that night he'd won every hand. He simply couldn't stop. The money flowed towards him in great waves, piling up at his side, watched by a wide-eyed Dottie, who sat at the bar sipping gins, occasionally coming over to ruffle his hair.

Round the table with him were Jimmy, a sometimes doorman at Daddy Ho's gambling and opium operation in Limehouse; Tony Smethurst, who was Harry's cousin, and whose dad owned the café along the street, Fred Lombard, a pimp, and, sitting in on some hands, Reg Smalls himself.

For most of the night, Harry was pleased with his progress, although he dared not calculate his winnings before the session was over – the one-sided success put him under a little more scrutiny than he would have liked.

Then, around four in the morning, the Maltese and his minder came in, sat down at the table, and soon the flow had reversed. Harry couldn't get up and leave, not after pounding the boys all night, not if he wanted to be welcome at any gambling table in the East End again. He just had to suffer the fact that the newcomer had brought a freshly minted piece of luck with him.

The Maltese's minder, who stood behind his employer, kept glancing over at Dottie in a way that irritated Harry, even more when she smiled back. It had been a mistake to bring her, he concluded, ruining his concentration like that; next time she could stay at home.

At almost seven in the morning, the last of his money crossed the table and Harry threw down his cards, his mouth dry and stale. He was suddenly aware of how bad the room smelt, of damp and roaches and rancid failure. Harry glanced around the table. Smoke-reddened eyes stared at him. He could expect no favours or sympathy. After all, someone had to be the first to crash out, and his fellow players were simply glad it wasn't them. The scar on his left cheekbone, still vivid from where a ridge on the warehouse's concrete floor had cut deep, began to throb.

Harry got to his feet, summoning as much dignity as he could, took out the last two notes from his wallet and threw them down. 'Thank you,' he managed to say. 'Be seeing you soon, gents.'

It was then that the Maltese burst out laughing, a long rattle that settled into his throat until it became a deep rumble. Harry froze. The Maltese was examining the last two fivers Harry had put on the table. He tossed one of the big white, crisp notes across at him. 'Is mine.'

Harry kept calm. 'They all are now.'

'No. Is one of mine. I made the fuckin' thing.' The man examined his pile of winnings closely, screwed another and another into a ball and tossed them at Harry's head. 'You come in here and play with gash money? *My* gash money?'

'Harry . . .' Reg began to tut.

'Shame on you, Harry,' added the self-righteous Tony.

Harry puffed out his cheeks. 'I must have mixed up my stash. Picked up the wrong one. I mean . . . you seen how good they are. Easy mistake to make.'

'In which case, you won't mind going to get the real thing, will you?' said the Maltese very quietly.

'What? No. No, of course not.'

'We'll swap it back.' The Maltese lit a cigar and puffed for a couple of seconds. 'One of yours for one of mine. That's reasonable, isn't it?'

'Right. Yes. OK by me. Take me, what? An hour.'

'We'll be here.'

He held out his hand. 'Come on, Dottie.'

'No.' The Maltese shook his head firmly. 'She stays.'

Harry looked over at Dottie, took in her pinched, terrified expression as the minder reached over and gripped her upper arm. She knew there was no second stash of real fivers.

It was Tony, the cousin, who laid it out for him: 'We'll only keep her till you get back with our money, Harry. You don't show, she works off the debt. I mean, Fred here could always do with an extra girl. Yes?'

Fred the Pimp sniffed loudly as he appraised her, before nodding his assent. Harry backed away, trying not to look at Dottie, mumbling his reassurances to the gamblers.

As he left through the darkened public bar, he heard Dottie call his name, the forlorn sound cut off as the greasy curtain swished back into place behind him and he stepped from the pub into the smudged light of another grey day.

Harry headed south, walking aimlessly, trying to get his mind around the dilemma. Nothing came, nothing that would save Dottie. Too many of them to take her out by force, no way of getting the money back to the gamblers within an hour. No, he'd got his wish, he was out of the East End for good, even if it wasn't quite the way he wanted. She'd be fine, he told himself over and over again. It was all bluff. They wouldn't turn her out just for a few fivers. Would they? He blinked back a tear and rubbed his temple in agitation, scratching at the skin until it was almost raw, as if he could erase the thought.

He realised what day of the week it was when he saw the little lads hanging around Fournier Street, hands in pockets, stamping against the chill morning air. Sabbath goys, the kids who earned a few bob by doing household chores for the Jews on Saturday – putting coal on the fire, lighting candles and heaters, boiling water and the like.

Which meant The Lane would be closed, of course. He'd been unconsciously heading for one of the market's breakfast stalls. A warm drink, a bit of company, someone who didn't know him, or what he had just done. He had enough change in his pocket for that. Not today, though. Keep walking, he told himself.

Eventually, he found himself on the Strand, footsore and weary, his bitterness replaced by fatigue, and he still hadn't convinced himself Dottie would come out of this all right. There was nothing he could do about that, he decided. Forget Dottie, he had to think of himself now. Another couple of hours and his name would be blackened all over the East End and he would be shunned in every pub and café where he did business.

As he looked up to check his direction, it appeared as if the world was softening, losing focus: a London Particular was rolling in off the river. Soon the city would be blanketed in its lung-burning filth.

He slowed and turned up the collar of his jacket at the thought of the smog and it was then that he saw the recruiting office. The army had got him out of trouble before, perhaps it might again. He went up to the darkened door with its picture of a comically fierce British Tommy and checked the opening times. Nine o'clock. Around an hour to kill.

Harry sat down on the step, waiting to find out exactly what his country could do for him, as the first tendrils of gritty mist began to curl around his feet.

Seven

France, April 1940

Harry buttoned up his greatcoat and pulled on his gloves, ready for his excursion into town. As he adjusted his cuffs he smiled at the three bright stripes on his arm. Sergeant Harry Cole. It still amazed him – how the bloody hell had he become Sergeant Harold Cole? He had never managed higher than lance-jack before.

Harry stepped out into air that was pin-sharp cold on his cheeks. His billet was a converted garage on the outskirts of Croux, a small town north-west of Lille, almost on the Belgian border. The Royal Engineers had commandeered the industrial complex at the northern edge of the village, converted two warehouses and stables into accommodation blocks, put the brass in the hotels and the non-commissioned officers into the old Citroën concession.

As his boots crunched on the road he was aware of the weighty swirl of his coat. Every British Expeditionary Force solder had a 'housewife', a sewing kit, and Harry had put his to good use, creating a warren of pockets in the lining of his thick greatcoat, each one capable of holding a packet or two of five Weights. As he strode towards the perimeter fence, Harry felt like a mobile tobacconist.

On that grim morning in the Strand six months ago, the recruiting sergeant had questioned him closely on his former career. When he heard Harry had been instrumental in building up the defences of Hong Kong against the Japanese, and that he was a talented electrician (well, it was true he could re-wire a car's ignition), the sergeant had recommended him for the Royal Engineers – plenty of defences going to be needed over the next few months, m'lad, he had said, and always work for good sparks.

And so, welcome back the prodigal lance-corporal, complete with, it appeared, a commendation from Parkhill in Hong Kong attached to his records. In an army being hastily cobbled together from raw, green recruits, perhaps it wasn't so surprising that the authorities at Aldershot had concluded that Harry was a soldier with just the right degree of experience and polish, yet retaining the common touch, someone who could move effortlessly between the disparate worlds of the men and the officers. In short, a perfect NCO.

Harry got his third stripe on 2 September, 1939, the day before war was declared. He still remembered when his new colleagues in the Sergeants' Mess had burst into loud cheering at the thought of 'giving old Adolf a taste of his medicine'. Bloody idiots, Harry had thought.

As he strode along towards the main road that led into town he could hear the thump of feet as the two men who had drawn stag – guard duty – stamped up and down against the cold and damp. It was spring, but the waterlogged flatlands on the Belgian border were in no mood to give up winter so easily. As he ducked under the flimsy two-inch striped pole that marked the barracks' entrance, he heard Evans, one of the sentries, say: 'Evening, Sarge.'

Harry didn't reply, just stared out across the darkened marshy flats, sniffing the fumes from the sulphide-heavy sluggish water that lay a few hundred yards hence. Somewhere out there under the crystalline stars, the British sappers were extending the Maginot Line. Whereas the latter was by all accounts a model of modern comfort and efficiency, the so-called Gort Line that the BEF engineers were creating was little more than a series of slit trenches. As they excavated they kept discovering the gruesome reminders that someone had passed this way before – rotted trenchcoats, rusted bayonets, the fragments of skulls. Chipping away day and night, the engineers were building exactly the same charnel pits as their predecessors had constructed twenty-five years previously.

He sniffed the air once more and rounded on Gascoyne, the second sentry. 'You been smokin', son?' Harry liked to keep his charges guessing, so they were never quite sure which version of him they were going to get. He moved between affable Harry Cole, just one of the lads, who liked a pint, a joke and a sing-song as much as the next man and Sergeant Harold Cole, strict enforcer of rules and regulations. He tut-tutted loudly. Gascoyne had got the latter. 'On stag?'

'Had one just before I came on, Sarge.'

Harry looked at his watch. 'You been on two hours, son. I can still smell it. Either you're lying, or you need to do something about your breath. Let's see them.' He clicked his fingers impatiently. The soldier handed over a pack of ten cigarettes that was already half empty and Harry took one. 'Du Mauriers? They're too posh for the likes of you. Where the bloody hell did you get Du Mauriers in tens?'

The last thing Harry wanted was upmarket competition from

the likes of Du Maurier, not when he had a shed full of Players to shift. 'Well?'

Gascoyne hesitated for a moment. 'Doyle, Sarge. Doyle's got 'em. Better for me chest than Weights.'

Harry threw the pack back and said with disdain: 'Tipped ciggies. You think the Wehrmacht'll worry about the kind of army where the soldiers smoke tipped ciggies. Now you watch yourself, my lad.'

Evans cut in before Gascoyne could answer. 'I need a piss, Sarge,' he said.

Harry considered telling him to do it in his pants, but he decided he'd done enough of the hard man. 'Go on, then, at the double.'

Harry left them to it and strolled round the perimeter fence towards the first of the neat redbrick houses that made up the bulk of the town. This was a friendly posting – there was no anti-British feeling, in this part of the country at least. In the Great War, Croux had been smashed, invaded, liberated, invaded and liberated again – by which time there was precious little left. The current BEF garrison was seen by locals as the next generation of brave Tommies, returned to defend them once more. Brave, maybe, but ignorant. It astonished Harry that very few of his comrades actually knew where they were and what they were meant to be defending.

He supposed this was normal, that soldiers lack any kind of overview of war, leaving it up to the top brass. However, the apathy of even the NCOs in trying to get a sense of place took him aback. 'Be out of here next week,' one of them had said by way of explanation. 'Another town, another country, another set of orders we know nothing about. No point in frettin' it.'

Well, Harry knew exactly where he was, which direction to Paris, how many miles to the coast, knew they had the majority of the French forces a few miles to the east, a few more divisions to the west. He had also noted how the BEF were busy scrounging guns off the French, notably the one-pounder anti-tank guns that didn't look as if they could dent a dustbin. It was worrying, that, both the Brits wanting to filch them, and the French willing to give them up.

He came to Julie's *estaminet* and entered, the warm fug of beer and hot breath washing over him. There was the usual split between locals and soldiers and at the squaddies' end of the bar someone at the piano was promising to hang out his washing on the Siegfried Line.

Julie was behind the bar with her mother, both dressed in floor-length white aprons. Julie was twenty, a sparky brunette with a sexy, toothsome smile, and he had got to know the daughter while setting up a little business transaction with the mother, who owned the bar. Her name was Madame Dubarry and she liked Harry, and liked his cheap NAAFI cigarettes and whisky even more, although she didn't trust him, not, at least, with her daughter.

'Madame Dubarry, you look lovely tonight.' His French was only good enough to give the most bald-faced of compliments, but it did the trick, as always. You fix the mother's electrics, mend their stairs, generally make yourself useful around the house, and they soon get used to the idea of you courting their precious one. He shrugged off his cigarette-laden coat and Madame Dubarry leant across the bar, took it from him and hung it in the backroom. When he picked the coat up, it would be considerably lighter.

As soon as she was out of sight Julie whispered, 'Eleven-thirty. Canal bridge,' and slid him a frothy beer. He smiled, gulped half of it in one, winked at Madame Dubarry and sidled off to the piano for a few choruses of 'Smile For Me, Yolande'.

★ ★ ★

It was midnight before he heard the clatter of her heels on the steel bridge and looked up. He'd been leaning over watching the grey water swirl lazily in the moonlight, smoking a cigarette cupped in his hands, as had become a habit, and had noticed the wires trailing in loops under the frame of the bridge. He wondered if it had been mined by the engineers. Another part of the big picture mere cannon fodder like him weren't allowed to know.

She came alongside, slipped an arm through his and let his lips brush her cheek. He pulled her closer. She wriggled to loosen his grip and produced a roll of francs. 'A present from Maman.'

He took the payment for the NAAFI cigarettes and slid it into his tunic pocket. 'Good, thanks.'

'I've got ten minutes, Harry.'

'That's no time at all, Julie.' He moved to kiss her again, but she placed two hands on his chest.

'I have to help finish cleaning up, Harry. No time for any of that.' She smirked. 'I know what you soldiers are like.'

'I bet you do.'

She slapped him playfully on the arm. 'That's a horrible thing to say. You know it is not true.'

Unfortunately, she was right: he knew exactly how chaste she was. So far they had had a couple of meals together – with Mother always close by – a few snatched meetings like this one, nothing even close to a moment of passion. He wasn't sure whether Julie even liked him or if Mother had asked her to keep him sweet – at least, up to a point. So why did he bother? Because, he guessed, he liked a challenge and she was the prettiest, and most coveted, barmaid in town.

'They've invaded Norway. The Germans.' She said it with a chilling matter-of-factness.

Harry stepped back in shock. So it had begun. 'Christ. Nobody told us. When?'

'I don't know. Yesterday, perhaps. It was on the radio just now. That might mean the Germans will move against us here. And you'll all have to fight.' Her lip quivered as if she were about to cry. He knew how she felt.

'Not likely. Norway'll keep them busy, Julie. The Germans can't invade every bloody country in Europe, can they?' The question sounded hollow even as he asked it.

'You'll be shipped out, won't you?'

'It's possible. It is also possible we'll just sit here and wait for them to come to us. Nobody tells us anything. Shit. I was hoping you could come to Paris with me.'

She shook her head. 'Maman would never have allowed it anyway.'

'No, I suppose not.'

She kissed him on the cheek. 'She likes you, Harry.'

'She likes my fags.'

'No, no. She thinks you want to go places. Not an ordinary soldier, she says.'

He laughed. 'No, I'm not an ordinary soldier.'

She was closer to him now, and his lungs filled with her scent, and he was remembering the easy, lazy way it was with poor Dottie, no guilt and no Maman to worry about. It clearly was never going to be like that with Julie. He shut Dottie out of his mind. It didn't do to dwell.

'If we do go away, I'll come back for you.'

She gave a sigh of disbelief.

'No, really,' he insisted.

'Why would you?'

He stroked her hair, running the dark strands between his fingers. 'Because I'd want to. How can I convince you?'

It was her turn to touch his face and he enjoyed the sensation of her fingertips across his cheek. 'There is a ring . . .'

'A ring?' he said, as non-committally as he could.

'In Van Roy's. It'd give me something to hold on to when you go into battle. To pray with. To remember you by.'

Go into battle? he nearly shouted. Are you out of your fucking mind? 'We're the Royal Engineers. We don't really do battles,' he lied, 'not as such.'

'It wouldn't have to mean we were engaged or anything, if you didn't want. It's a . . . token.'

'I'll take a look at it.'

She smiled and said quickly, 'In the window right at the far left, white gold with three diamonds.' Just for a second he wondered whether the hustler was being hustled, but when he looked at her, there was no sign of it in her innocent face, just a pair of eyebrows raised in a silent question.

'I'll see what I can do. Sergeants don't find the money for white gold and diamonds easy to come by.'

She stuck out her lower lip and pouted. 'Harry, I know you get more than a sergeant's pay. My Maman gives you . . .'

'OK, OK. I said I'll see what I can do.'

She kissed him. 'I have to go. Let me know how you get on.' Harry watched her hurry away into the dark, listening to the echo of her footsteps reflect off the houses, fading until all he could hear was his rapid breathing.

He looked back north and saw a flare rise in the far distance and hang in the air like a low-slung star. Was something afoot out there? Or was it just another nervous sentry, spooking at every movement? He couldn't worry about the implications of Norway right now – it was a long way away and he had business of his own. Obviously progress with Julie was determined by whether he thought she was worth a ring in Van Roy's jewellers. Plus he had Doyle and his fags to worry about. He'd have to construct a way to scupper the rival cigarette trade in its tracks; there was, after all, room for only one Harry Cole in any fighting regiment.

After asking around some of the seedier *estaminets* in town, Harry found his man in Lille, down a backstreet, cobbling shoes and cutting keys in a lock-up shop that smelt of rubber heels and foot odour. He showed him the drawing of the Van Roy ring he had sketched through the window glass and they haggled and then the cobbler said he could make a copy in one week and Harry said five days and they shook hands and that was Julie's 'token' sorted out. Doyle was going to be trickier.

Private Evans was miserable. Not only was he fed up with the cold, with the sloppy food, with the digging of trenches and the guard duty, he was really annoyed by the size of his bladder. It didn't seem to be able to hold more than a cupful and he'd stupidly had a couple of pints of dark Belgian beer and now he felt fit to burst. He looked across at Dobson, his oppo that night, who was scanning the horizon with an intensity that suggested he expected Germans to appear at any moment.

'Dobbo, I need a piss.'

'Again? Well, go on then, boy. Be quick.'

Evans re-slung his rifle, rushed over to the large stack of packing cases, unbuttoned himself and sighed with relief as the high-powered stream splashed against the plywood. He was just doing his flies up when he saw the shadow move a few hundred yards to his left. He slowly slid his rifle off his shoulder. The dark shape stopped and the weak wall light briefly illuminated a face. Sergeant Cole.

Evans waited, torn between getting back to his post and wondering what the Sarge was dreaming up. He watched the black form hesitate once more, then unlock the big double door and slide inside. Strange, what would Cole want in the Officers' Mess at this time of night?

A low-flying plane, probably one of the Potez bombers stationed nearby, reminded him there was a war on, and approaches to be watched, so he ran back to his post as quietly as he could, quickly forgetting Cole for the moment.

Dawn was little more than a dirty smudge in the sky when the corrugated metal doors to the old storehouse that doubled as a barracks squeaked open. Captain Malone stood in the doorway, waiting a few seconds before he yelled at the top of his voice, the barking reverberating around the triangular metal roof supports, amplified by the corrugated roof. Evans opened one eye, cursing. He'd only been in bed two hours. You were meant to get a lie in after late stag.

'Everybody up. Come on, look lively.' Evans peeked out from under the blankets on the cot bed and noted the officer had come with a couple of Redcaps in tow and Sergeant Cole.

Malone pointed his swagger stick at Evans, who had made no movement, and the Captain repeated the order, with more force. Reluctantly Evans slid out onto the chill concrete floor and started to dress.

Across the room, Dobson dared to ask: 'Is this an exercise, sir?'

'Of sorts,' Malone spat out. 'Twenty-five pounds missing from the Officers' Mess. A break-in, looks like.'

The words should have sunk in right there and then, but Evans's brain was too befuddled to make connections.

'Stand by your bunks. OK, Sergeant,' said Malone, summoning Cole forward.

Harry moved through the dorm and began to point out men to the Redcaps, and beds were stripped, bedding piled onto the floor, lockers turned out of meagre belongings. Harry wandered casually over to Doyle, the Du Maurier merchant, who was looking at him from heavy, sleep-filled eyes. Harry opened the man's locker. No cigarettes. No, not stupid enough to keep them there. He picked up Doyle's .303 rifle and worked the action. The tightly rolled tube of notes, bound with a rubber band, came flying out, bouncing onto the floor.

'Sir!'

The Captain picked up the roll of money from under the cot bed, brandishing it in Doyle's face. 'I suppose you don't know how this got there?'

'Don't know how it did, sir. Won some money at cards, sir. Dobson'll back me up.'

Dobson said quietly, 'Fair and square, sir.'

'But I didn't put it in me rifle, no, sir.'

'What was it you said, Cole?'

'One of the missing notes had some ink spilt over it, apparently, sir. Blobbed across the note. Bar steward'll swear to it.'

Malone unrolled the tube and flipped through the pound notes until he came to one splattered with Parker & Co's best blue-black. He snapped at the Redcaps, 'All yours.' Doyle, a genuinely puzzled expression on his face, was hustled away.

The Captain turned to Harry. 'Well done, Sergeant. Always one, eh?'

In his best NCO tones, Harry agreed: 'Yes, sir. There's always one.'

The rumours started a few days later. The Royal Engineers were being moved into Belgium. No, they were falling back to the ports, they were staying where they were. The Germans were suing for peace. Harry, his attentions elsewhere, wangled a day pass, rarer than Hitler's balls now that something was finally starting, and went off to meet Julie.

The summer weather had finally arrived and she was sitting outside a café on the main square of Croux, sipping coffee, looking neat and pressed in a white sleeveless blouse and pleated skirt. Her hair had been braided and put up, and she was wearing brighter lipstick than Maman usually liked.

Harry pecked her on both cheeks before sitting. 'Missed you.'

'I missed you, too, Harry. So has Maman. She's running low.'

He ordered a beer and said, 'Tell her I'm trying my best.' Problem was, since he had staged the robbery to get rid of Doyle, security everywhere had been stepped up and already there were rumblings about the NAAFI cigarette inventory. He couldn't risk it just yet. He'd been trying to find out where Doyle's Du Mauriers were hidden, but to no avail; the men had closed ranks against him.

Julie closed her eyes to let the sun warm her face, and he realised again just how attractive he found her. Harry offered her a cigarette, which she refused, and lit up himself. From his pocket he took the small velveteen Van Roy's box and placed it carefully on the table. Julie gave a small cry of surprise and reached for it, but Harry snatched it away playfully.

He edged open the lid of the box, allowing her to see the edge of the band of white gold, the first glint of what, to any layman, looked like diamond.

She hesitated, then frowned. 'What's that noise?'

Harry glanced across the square. A Jeep had squealed to a halt and inside were a pair of regimental police with Evans, who scanned the café's customers and quickly pointed out Harry to the Redcaps.

Harry rose from his chair, and realised Julie hadn't meant the noise of the Jeep, that she was looking skywards. The two policemen striding over the cobbles towards him broke step as they, too, raised their eyes to the heavens.

Harry followed their gaze. He had now caught the alien sound, not the dull thrum of the Potezs, or the gnat-like whine of Dewoitine fighters, but a low growl. Harry scanned the sky until he found the formation, now almost directly above the village, twelve black cruciforms silhouetted against steely blue. As he watched, the leading three shapes dipped their port wings and began to slide from the sky. The rumbling engine noise was suddenly drowned out by the rising shriek of the dive bomber's siren, and Harry felt a new kind of terror rise from the pit of his stomach.

The first explosion was outside the square, a single, ear-punching eruption and a plume of smoke spiralling upwards as the Stuka swooped over them, its propeller wash blasting through the café, snatching at napkins and tablecloths.

Julie was shouting at him, but he couldn't hear her words. They reeled back as the second bomb took the patisserie and hairdresser's opposite, reducing the frontage to matchwood and dust, the force of the shockwave flipping the Jeep onto its side and sending the Redcaps and Evans sprawling across the cobbles.

Harry could feel something stinging on his face. He reached across to Julie, to grab her hand, his instinct to drag her away from this place.

The third detonation lifted the cobbles and rained them across the plaza. One of them smacked into Evans's head and his neck snapped to one side.

Another glanced off Julie's outstretched arm, snapping it. Then the glass-laden blast peppered her exposed skin and pushed everyone and everything deep inside the café, creating a bloody pyramid of bodies and furniture and crockery.

When the smoke cleared, Julie stirred stiffly. With her good arm she reached up and stroked her face with her fingertips, feeling the bristles of glass and metal across her cheek, each one a locus of burning pain. Where was Harry? She managed to stand and, supporting her broken limb as best she could, picked her way among the tangle of groaning bodies and smashed furniture, but there was no sign of him. It was as if Harry had been vaporised.

Part Two

Eight

Calais, France, May 1940

The retreat to the sands just outside Calais from the ruined little village of Coulogne took the best part of a day. Before he could leave the town, Lieutenant Anthony Neave was ordered to destroy the secret sound location parabolas that his Searchlight Battalion had brought over. Designed to detect the sound of enemy engines, they had proved next to useless, and it was with little regret that he overturned a French oil tanker and immolated the lot, only regretting the waste of fuel as the thick black clouds rolled through the village streets.

The wind changed and the choking fumes followed his group as they fell back to the coast, a retreat covered by the resilient Colonel Goldney, who used Brens and a solitary anti-tank gun to slow down the Panzer advance. When Neave finally made the shore, he and his corporal, Dacre, and a group of volunteers from the Searchlights were ordered into town to help back up the rearguard action being fought along the Boulevard Leon Gambetta by the remnants of the Rifle Brigade, trying to thwart the German probings coming from the west.

Neave led the men from the beach, trying his best to give them direction and confidence, even though he felt neither himself. His corporal, a proper soldier, should have been in charge, not a barrister like Neave – one who hadn't even had time to practise before war was declared – who had never fired a gun in anger until today. Dacre had served in Borneo, Malaysia, Hong Kong and Singapore. He had actually been shot at with real bullets long before Calais. However, Neave was a product of Eton and Oxford and the Bar, the corporal came from a two-up-two-down in Stoke, so it naturally fell to the Old Etonian to get these men through the day in one piece.

He placed the bulk of his unit in a house overlooking the railway tracks, and he and Corporal Dacre went to establish a fallback position. Within seconds they were dodging through the rubble-strewn streets, the air zinging with bullets, the pavements exploding into vortices of dust where heavy machine guns had opened up. His corporal started zig-zagging wildly, and Neave followed, his heart beating frantically, wondering if his first day of real war would also be his last.

As they made the Place Albert, its central monument reduced to a heap of stones, a pair of Panzers appeared at one end. A British A9 cruiser wheeled noisily forward from a side street and fired, a well-placed shot that tore the tracks from one of the German machines. The second Panzer returned fire, rocking on its haunches with the recoil, its shell neatly slicing the turret off the A9, sending it whipping down the boulevard like a discarded saucepan. There were six crew in there. A chunk of wall exploded above Neave's head, the shower of grit stinging his eyes, and the corporal tugged at his sleeve. They had to keep moving.

He and Dacre pressed north, past small groups of Tommies behind makeshift barricades, heading for Calais Nord, the citadel and the harbour. The massive walls of the old fortress were disappearing under columns of smoke and dust as more German shells found their range.

Fresh bullets smacked around them as they ran, and they found themselves among a group of elderly citizens staggering along the pavement, carrying an old woman, her dress stained dark round the middle.

Whether they drew the fire onto the group or the gunner fancied some sport, Neave would never know, but the machine gun opened up from a rooftop and suddenly the street was dancing with shrapnel and ricochets and bodies were tumbling.

Dacre pushed Neave into the doorway of a *pharmacie*, the shattered glass of the windows crunching as they slumped down. A pocket of the British Expeditionary Force fired from behind their barricades and the German gun fell silent. Out in the street most of the old people lay still.

It was then Neave felt the blood trickling inside his tunic.

'You all right, sir?'

Neave looked down and gasped when he saw the raw mess of intertwined fabric and flesh on his left side. A little tremor of fright went through him.

'Here, take this.' The corporal passed over a flask and Neave took in the heady whiff of good cognac. Very good cognac, for a corporal, but this wasn't a time for questions. He took a heavy slug. Dacre examined the wound and said, 'I think it's just taken a chunk out of your muscle. Be all right.'

The corporal consulted his map. 'No idea where the regimental aid post is. There's a hospital up there, sir.' He indicated towards the walls of Calais Nord. 'Think you can make it? It's about half a mile, maybe a little less.'

A machine gun rattled again, finding the flimsy shelter across the street, the soldiers dancing until the firing stopped and they, too, lay motionless. 'Can't stay here,' Dacre said calmly, but

Neave was staring at the dead. The corporal touched his arm. 'We can't stay here, sir,' he repeated.

They ran, heads down, guns held low, weaving as best they could, the whine of stray rounds urging them forward. At the top of the boulevard there was a kink in the road, which took them out of the immediate line of fire. Beyond it was an infirmary, a gaunt, gothic building, with makeshift Red Cross flags fashioned from sheets dangling from each window. On the steps was an agitated group of civilians, mostly women, and in the centre of the mêlée a young olive-skinned nurse, clipboard in hand, tried to establish some kind of order. Her face was smudged with dirt, she had lost her cap, and sections of her dark hair had become unclipped, falling to her shoulders, but she still exuded a sense of calmness, the still centre in a whirl of panic and despair.

Dacre propped his lieutenant up against the wall, lit a cigarette, and put it between Neave's lips. Neave was sweating now, and not just from the run. He looked over at the confrontation on the steps and was surprised when the nurse detached herself from the group and walked over to them, reclipping her hair as she came.

'You are hurt?'

She was only a few inches shorter than Neave, slim, possibly too slim, it was difficult to judge underneath her uniform's bib and short cape, her features and colouring more Mediterranean than those of northern France. She asked again: 'You are hurt?'

Neave nodded.

She examined the side of his tunic and probed as gently as she could. 'I can't tell how bad. Not without cutting it away. It needs cleaning.' She glanced over her shoulder at the desperate crowd at the entrance to the hospital. 'We are full in there. Not one centimetre of space, Lieutenant.'

Neave was staring into her eyes. There was the slightest of casts to one of them, but the imperfection had a strange effect, making it feel as if the gaze was drilling into him, almost pinning him to the spot. Perhaps he was giddy through loss of blood.

'We should get you to the Gare Maritime. There is a medical station in the tunnels off platform one. Orderlies are tending British and French wounded there. You know where it is?'

'I can take him,' said Dacre. These were his last words as the shell blast pitched him into the street, little columns of smoke rising from his ruined body.

Neave came to with a roaring in his ears and found himself on top of the girl. He stuttered an apology. 'Mam'selle, I . . . I . . .'

'I'm all right,' she said brusquely. With an expert movement, the nurse rolled him off her, pulled him to his feet and started forward. Neave looked back at his corporal. The round had detonated inside an apartment block and the blast had channelled out through the windows, killing Dacre outright, but leaving them alive. Neave made the nurse stop for a second, so he could retrieve his rifle and say a small prayer for his corporal.

As they crossed the street, an old van, its bodywork pocked from small arms fire and the windscreen webbed with cracks, slithered to a halt inches from them. A helmetless French soldier was at the wheel, his eyes wild. The nurse spoke to him, rapidly and with a tone that brooked no argument, and the next thing Neave knew he was being helped into the back, to lie, gratefully, among rotting shreds of cabbage.

The aid post was a vaulted niche in the huge station wall, perhaps eight feet deep, full of medical supplies, water canisters and half a dozen wounded. Others were laid out on the low continental-style platforms, some clearly dead or dying, the occasional sharp whiff of decay suggesting some had been deceased for a while now.

Wagons-lits were sitting at each platform, the carriages heavily punctured with holes from strafing Stukas. A derailed hospital train had jack-knifed across the approaches to the station, its doors left hanging open where the wounded had been lifted out and walked, dragged or carried the last few hundred yards. Nothing would be moving in or out of the Gare Maritime by rail, that was clear.

Neave was laid at the entrance to the tunnel, with a view of the ruined quays down at the port, their cranes sprawled at drunken angles. He could glimpse stacks of apparently abandoned equipment. Only much later would he discover that they consisted of piles of three-inch mortars, supplied with two-inch rounds, of machine guns so tightly packed in mineral jelly it would take 48 hours to have them operational, and of radios without crystals. Worse, an entire motorcycle unit had been landed, while their machines were still at Dover.

Within the harbour breakwater, a number of ships lay half submerged, waves lapping over their warped decks. Out at sea, nothing was visible, just the thin line of the Dover cliffs, shimmering like a mirage. No rescue craft, no destroyers, no Royal Navy to pull them from this fire. The last ship, the *Kohistan*, its deck covered with wounded, had left hours before. No more would be coming. Something else Neave would find out later – Churchill had ordered the garrison to fight to the last, to buy precious time for the events happening further east at Dunkirk. They were to be sacrificed. From the streets of Calais-Pierre to the south he could hear the unknowing soldiers of the BEF, the 60th and the Rifle Brigade, refusing to give an inch. Answering them, the deep whump of German Panzers and mortars.

Neave was drifting in and out of consciousness as the young nurse cut open his battle dress.

'What's your name?' he managed to ask her.

She hesitated for a moment, as if this were privileged information. 'Odile.'

He nodded. 'Thank you.'

'Oh God, no. Not again.' Odile stood up and covered her ears.

The Stukas were swooping once more, tossing bomb after bomb after bomb onto the soldiers of the QVRs and the 60th along Gambetta and around the canal.

Columns of fresh smoke pinpointed the spots where the explosives had detonated, curling up from the general haze that had obscured all the landmarks apart from the citadel and the tip of Notre Dame to the immediate south of them. Odile knew that, somewhere beneath this veil of smoke, the infirmary must have taken direct hits. She began to cry.

An orderly, dressed in the classic blue French overalls, but adorned with prominent Red Cross arm bands, came across and placed his hands on her shoulders.

'Come on, Odile,' the newcomer said in strangled French. Switching to English, he looked down at Neave: 'Well, at least this one's breathing.'

The rifle report was so close it made them start and all three looked around to see a young soldier slump down onto the platform, a neat, self-inflicted wound in his forehead. Odile put a hand to her mouth as the body twitched one last time and Neave groaned at the casual waste of a life. The situation was slipping away into despair, he realised. Inexperienced soldiers were taking what they thought was the honourable way out.

The orderly knelt down and examined Neave's tunic where it had been partly cut away from the wound. 'Odile.' He looked at her and repeated: 'Odile. We can save this man.' Neave could tell he was trying to snap her out of it, and slowly she turned and looked down at her patient.

'Odile. Please.' The orderly reached up and touched her arm.

'You can't do anything about that one.'

She finally nodded and crouched beside him and Neave passed out as Odile began to work on the wound again.

Neave came awake with a jerk, to find his side bandaged and no sign of seepage. He touched it and winced a little, but at least his insides felt more in than out now. His head was swimming, though, and he had a raging thirst. He looked around for Odile. Nice name, he remembered. The orderly, though, had spoken in English. Strange.

It was morning. The shelling had stopped, although the atmosphere was still heavy with dust and smoke. He could hear the sporadic crack of rifles, the BEF clearly conserving ammunition. At least someone was still holding out, though, and the thought made him feel proud.

He did a double-take when he saw the uniform of the man striding across the tracks towards him. A German officer, a Walther pistol in his hand, with a strange metal crescent bobbing around his neck. Behind him, cautiously crouched over their weapons, were a dozen or more Wehrmacht soldiers. Neave automatically reached for his rifle. A pile of Enfields lay stacked at the end of platform two. He'd been disarmed. They had surrendered. Or, in his case, someone had surrendered him.

The German officer with the metal necklace seemed surprised to see him sitting there, leaning against the dank wall, a blanket across his legs. He came and stood before him.

'All over, is it?' Neave asked.

The officer nodded. 'Sichelschnitt.' The voice sounded muffled and Neave realised the constant explosions must have affected his hearing.

Sichelschnitt?

The German made a scything motion with his left hand. Ah.

Sickle-cut, although Neave had become more concerned about the Walther pistol in the man's right hand, which, he realised, was pointed at his heart.

'You kill him and you'll have to kill me.' The voice rang out across the platform and the German spun round. It was the blue-overalled orderly, now emerged from the front of a wagon-lit, wiping his hands on a grimy cloth, speaking in French. Then he repeated the sentence in bad German. The German hesitated, looking down at his gun as if surprised to see it. Neave was fairly sure the man had no intention of killing him, but he might just be wrong.

'And me.' It was Odile, stepping down from the rear of the carriage. 'Captain . . . ?' That's it, thought Neave, get the bastard's name.

The officer slowly holstered his gun. 'Sonderführer Diels. Feldgendarmerie.' So, thought Neave, the strange necklace indicated he was military intelligence of some sort. Diels looked down at Neave. 'And this man is a prisoner of war. I have responsibility for interrogation and removal of all enemy forces from this area. All men who are fit to be moved will be transported out to a transit camp.'

Neave was suddenly weary to his soul at the prospect.

'He's not fit to be moved,' said Odile firmly.

Diels hesitated, then, as he turned to go, he said, 'We shall be back as soon as he is, then.'

'Come on, old chap. Wake up. Must have worn off by now.' It was the Red Cross orderly, speaking perfect English. 'Come on, Neave, snap to it, we didn't give you that much.'

Neave opened his eyes, blinked hard, and focused enough to take in his surroundings. It was afternoon, another hard, bright day. He could see German troops, and a small column of British walking wounded lined up on a far platform, a column of grey, drained men, leaning on each other for support.

The orderly unwrapped something and handed it to Neave. A sausage roll. A British sausage roll, albeit a rather squashed one. He realised he was ravenous and gratefully took it.

'How long have I been out?' asked Neave as he chomped.

'Off and on . . . a day.'

'Christ. What's happening?'

'Rumour has it Jerry is knocking seven bells out of Dunkirk now. As for here, well you can see, old boy, those that can walk are being taken off for what they call processing. The rest of you have a little time while they organise transport. I have to get you into one of the carriages.' He indicated the nearest wagon-lit.

The orderly gave Neave a sip of water and helped him to his feet. His legs felt feeble, and he was grateful for the support. 'You're English?'

'I'd rather you didn't shout about it, old chap, there's a good fellow.'

Neave nodded. 'But . . .' He couldn't keep the distaste from his voice. 'Are you a deserter?'

'Hardly.' The man chuckled at the very thought. 'Just keeping a low profile. Picking up what I can.'

They reached the carriage and Neave was half carried, half pushed through the corridor and into a couchette that smelt of carbolic with, underneath, the faint, ferric tang of blood.

Neave slumped back. 'What did you give me that put me out for so long?'

'Drop of morphia.'

He felt his side spasm. 'Well, it's wearing off now.'

'Don't worry, you're pretty well patched up. Couple of grazed ribs, although you lost a fair bit of juice. Head'll clear in no time.'

'Who are you exactly?'

'Name's Mason. And I'm no deserter. Been here since thirty-nine off and on.'

'Ah. So, you're . . .' Neave couldn't think how to put it delicately. 'One of the intelligence chaps?'

Harry Cole hesitated, before tapping the side of his nose. 'No names, no pack drill. You should know that, Neave.'

'Yes, yes of course. You're an officer of some description, I assume?'

Harry smiled. 'Captain Harry Mason. But no need to stand on ceremony. What we've got to do is get you out of here.'

'I knew a Daniel Mason. At Eton?'

Harry racked his brains quickly, dredging up Wing Commander Gilbert's background. 'We Masons were always Winchester chaps.'

The door slid back with a screech and Odile stepped in. 'How are you feeling?'

'Bit fuggy,' said Neave. 'Could do with another drink.'

Odile nodded. 'Listen, the Germans are bringing trucks tomorrow morning for those who aren't mobile. If you can't walk you will be driven to a camp. I told them you were still too weak to move, to buy some time.'

'Is there any way you can get me out before then?'

'I don't think so,' she said. 'There are Germans everywhere.'

'We could put him with the burial detail,' blurted Harry.

Odile shrugged. 'I suppose. I thought you were taking that slot?'

Harry found himself saying, 'I think I can do more good here in France. I think the Lieutenant can do more good if he isn't in some POW camp.'

Neave blinked hard and nodded. 'Well, yes. Could be you're right, Mason.'

'The next burial detail is first thing tomorrow,' Harry

explained. 'At the citadel grounds. There'll be one German guard if it follows the same drill as this morning. There are two French soldiers on burial duty who have agreed to help. It won't be hard to slip away. But we can only misplace one cadaver per trip. If we lose too many bodies, someone'll notice.'

'Worth a shot,' said Neave. 'But I don't fancy being buried alive if it all goes wrong.'

'If we get the German guard distracted, there is a culvert deep enough to hide in. It runs for a thousand metres downhill, then you are on the coast. Beyond that . . . you're on your own.'

'It's worth a try. Uniform's a problem, though.'

'We'll get some civilian clothes to put under it. You can strip off the uniform in the culvert.'

Neave coughed and grimaced. Odile checked his bindings and asked Harry if he could fetch some water. As Harry opened the door to leave, Neave said, 'Captain Mason . . .'

Neave didn't see the strange look that flitted across Odile's face at the mention of the name and rank. 'In case I forget, thank you. I'll remember this.'

Harry smiled thinly as he reluctantly left the two of them alone.

Neave was aware of someone in his compartment at three in the morning, over near his few belongings. He raised himself on one elbow. 'Who's that?'

'Me.'

Harry stepped forward so that, in the glare of the dockside krieg lights shining through the carriage windows, Neave could see his face. 'Oh.'

'Hoping for someone else?'

Neave laughed and felt a spasm in his ribs. He lay back, his breathing shallow. 'She is prettier than you, Mason.'

Harry couldn't argue with that, but wasn't sure he liked Neave noticing. 'Well, there's not much meat on her.'

He saw a flash of teeth in the half-light. 'Hard to tell under that uniform.'

Harry shrugged. 'I think that's the idea. Cigarette?'

'Yes, thanks.'

'So what will you do here, Mason, after I've gone? How will you wage your war?'

'You sound as if you don't approve.'

'I'm not sure I do. Skulking around, pretending to be someone you aren't. It's . . .'

'Ungentlemanly?'

'Well, it's unconventional.'

Harry sat on the compartment's metal fold-down chair. 'I think this is going to be a rather unconventional war, Neave. There are times when conventional soldiering just won't do.'

'And that's when they wheel out people like you?'

Harry nodded. 'What about you, Neave? What will you do? Report back to your unit?'

Neave snorted. 'My unit is either dead or behind barbed wire, I suspect. I don't know, in truth. I don't know what happens next.'

'The Germans cross the Channel.'

'Then our job is to stop them, Mason.'

Harry laughed. 'What, between us, you mean?' He felt his accent slip and corrected it. 'Me over here, you over there? A pincer movement?'

Neave laughed as well, but in short bursts to protect his damaged side. 'They could . . . they could do worse. I'm not sure about how you chaps fight your wars, Mason. But I wish you luck.'

Harry got up and put a hand on Neave's shoulder. 'You too.

Now rest up, you've got two more hours before you get to play dead.'

'I'm looking forward to it.'

Harry left the compartment without bothering to rearrange the items he had been rifling through when Neave awoke. Nothing worth having anyway.

Nine

As the first curvature of the sun rose above the horizon, Harry watched the dozen bodies being loaded into the back of the old baker's truck, the limbs occasionally flopping out from the soiled windings as they were carried by the two weary French soldiers and slung onto the heap. Nearby, the sleepy German on guard duty kept an eye on proceedings, glancing more often at Odile, who stood next to Harry.

They tried not to stare when the next-to-last body was lifted, that of Neave, but the phoney corpse sagged and the head lolled free in a very convincing manner. Pretty good acting, thought Harry, better than he would have managed.

Harry scratched at his cheek stubble and looked at his fingernails. They were thick with grime and blood and pus, the hands of a dedicated worker. It might be a strange role for Harry, but this was pretty much the only option in town at the moment. Death and glory or POW being the others. No thanks. Best stick with his nice nurse with the wall eye, he reckoned, see where that might lead.

After his narrow escape from the Stukas – and the Redcaps – at Croux, he had headed west to the Channel ports to try to get back to England. On the road, in the chaos of a whole country on the move, he had heard that non-fighting personnel – 'useless mouths' in the army's charming phrase – were being shipped out from Calais.

He had purloined a motorcycle and ridden to the port, but without decent papers he had been unable to get past the bureaucratic bulldogs who were in charge of embarkation. Then one of them had noticed his leg. The wounds to his face had more or less scabbed over, but his thigh had taken something heavier.

In the aftermath of Croux he'd bandaged it as best he could, but the quayside guard had noticed the seepage and packed him off to the hospital, where a nurse called Odile had removed the offending items – two pieces of metal of unknown origin – and cleaned and dressed the wounds, telling him how lucky he had been not to have bled to death.

As she tended him, Harry gave Odile his standard cock-and-bull story about being a downed pilot on a secret mission – not dissimilar to the old Gilbert tactic – but he had also offered to help her in her work. There was something about her – and it wasn't just those dark looks – that made him want to assist, to make sure she got through this nightmare intact. Accepting his offer, she had packed him off to the Gare Maritime, where an aid station was treating less serious wounds to the battered and demoralised troops falling back into the city.

Harry couldn't fully explain why he hadn't run when the bombardment began, but had adopted the guise of a French orderly as the Germans got closer, telling Odile on her daily visit that he would be shot as a spy if they discovered who he really was. To top it all, he'd now given up his best chance of escape to Neave. Harry was beginning to think he was losing his touch.

Odile gripped his arm and he looked up to see Sonderführer

Diels, with a Schmeisser-wielding soldier, the machine pistol held threateningly at waist height, heading their way. Odile flashed a signal for the two French soldiers to get a move on and they pushed up the tailgate and headed for the cab. As the engine stuttered and caught, issuing an alarming cloud of black smoke, the Schmeisser man detached himself from Diels and stepped onto the running board next to the driver. The sleepy German shrugged, tore his eyes from Odile, slung his Mauser over his shoulder, and took his place at the opposite door. The truck pulled away with double the number of Wehrmacht escorts they had expected. Odile uttered an oath under her breath.

'Mam'selle. Good morning.' Diels didn't acknowledge Harry's presence.

'You are up bright and early, Sonderführer,' Odile said.

'I thought you might need a decent breakfast. We have a field kitchen—'

'Thank you, Sonderführer. No.'

'It's not much—'

'I'm not hungry. Thank you all the same.'

Diels changed tack. 'You speak English, don't you?'

Odile nodded.

'We have over twenty thousand prisoners. We are short of English interpreters. We brought along plenty of French speakers, but we didn't quite anticipate such a haul of British soldiers.'

Odile smiled. 'I am a nurse. Not an interrogator.'

Diels shrugged. 'Not interrogation. Just the collection of a few simple facts.'

'All the same, no. Thank you.'

'As you wish,' he said, his tone hardening. 'It does mean you must leave. This entire area is to be cleared of civilians by tomorrow. We can offer you transport to Lille.' He turned to go. 'The English Lieutenant. What happened to him?'

'Dead,' she said quietly. 'Septicaemia.'
'Ah. One fewer to worry about.'

Neave could feel the mass of bodies pressing against him as the van bounced over the ruined streets, bucking in and out of potholes. He understood now what was meant by a deadweight. As the gruesome cargo tossed around him, he worked himself free of the bindings, ready for the signal that he should make a run for it. One of the Frenchmen would distract the guard with a cigarette around the far side of the truck, and then feign a coughing fit as he lit his own. They had promised Neave he would be laid out next to the culvert, which he could roll into and sprint down before the German noticed. Remember to take the sheet with you, they had stressed.

The last of the drugs seemed to have left his system and the vagueness they had inflicted had gone, leaving a bone-aching tiredness. God alone knew how Odile and that Mason felt, they could hardly have slept at all. Mason was a bit of a strange fish. He'd always hated being called 'old' anything, boy, chap or man, and Mason had a sackful of the damned things. Very odd, him being there. Decent of him to give him his place in the burial party, though, to donate selflessly his own chance of escape. He owed him that.

The whine of ineffectual brake linings announced their arrival well before they ground to a halt. Neave took a last lungful of stale air and let his muscles relax, willing them to rubber.

He felt a weight removed from him as the first body was lifted and then hands grabbed him, neck and feet, and he let himself sag like a hammock. He allowed the breath to leak gradually from his body and was glad he did because he hit the ground with such force, it would surely have exploded in a tell-tale burst. He closed his eyes and squeezed, trying to focus away from the pain of the sharp rock in his back, and waited for the sound of false camaraderie and the cough.

Voices. German to his left now. And German to his right. Two Germans: that wasn't correct at all.

He heard the dragging of more corpses to the tailgate, the grunts of the Frenchmen, the thunk of the lifeless on earth. He counted. All out now, all lined up. Time for the distraction.

The burst from a machine pistol set every nerve in his body firing, and with dismay he felt his left leg twitch with the shock. He tensed himself, wondering what the hell was happening. Had they shot the French soldiers? No, he could hear them protesting, the note of panic unmistakable.

A second burst, closer, and he could imagine the 9mm slugs ripping into sheets, the shrouded bodies convulsing under the impact.

A third thudded closer, and he felt a stray cartridge bounce off him. Neave twisted and flailed and was finally free, pulling the sheet away and screaming: don't shoot, don't shoot. He looked at the line of shrouded bodies laid out on the earth, but there were no bullet holes. One of the Germans smiled, pulled back the bolt on his Schmeisser and let a small burst thud harmlessly into the earth. Bluff. It had been a bluff to flush out anyone who was playing at being dead.

The other German with the rifle indicated that Neave should get back in the truck. As if to reassure him, the man used a phrase he had clearly been uttering over and over for the last few days: 'Pee-ohh-double-u.' POW. Neave shuffled forward, his spirits sinking with each step.

'Harry.'

'Yes.'

'Not Paul.'

'Sometimes Paul.'

'Not RAF.'

'No.'

'Huh.'

Odile was a little drunk. They were sitting at the rear of one of the carriages, on seats perforated by cannon fire, looking out through glassless windows at the never-ending activities of the new masters of Calais, now busy rigging up yet more lights so that dock repair could go on round the clock. You use all your efforts to blow it to pieces, then use all your skill to put it together again. The British would come along and blow it to kingdom come again soon. Or would they? Twenty thousand prisoners the man said, and no RAF in sight. Did the British have anything left?

'So why did you tell me that story? About being a pilot?'

Harry shrugged. It had been a long day. For an hour of it she had been shouted and screamed at by Diels for the Neave deception. The Abwehr man was all for shipping the medical staff off to camps as well, but Odile held her ground, arguing that Diels himself said they had more prisoners than they knew what to do with, and that it was an officer's duty to escape.

Eventually Diels let her go, although, as he had threatened, they were to be shipped out of the Calais zone the next day.

Harry took the wine from her, refilled his tin cup, and handed it back.

'You weren't in the RAF?' she repeated.

'No. Trouble is, Odile, you get into this habit of lying. You lie so often, you forget to tell the truth. You run up the story that's most convenient.' He sighed. 'That's a spy's life. I'm sorry.'

He heard a distant crackle of rifle fire. There were still small bands of British and French soldiers out there, trying to slip away, desperate to avoid incarceration. Heavier machine-gun fire answered it, and all was quiet once more, but for the distant spluttering and hum of welding torches.

'So I'll never know the truth about you?'

Harry moved closer. 'Well, there is one you can take to the bank.'

'What's that?'

'That I like you.'

Odile laughed. 'Of course you do. Every man you take a bullet or a splinter from looks up at you and sees some nice tits in a uniform and falls in love. It's only natural.'

'I didn't say love, did I? But look, there is something I'd like you to have.'

From his pocket he brought out the ring he was going to give to Julie. Odile slid it onto the third finger of her left hand. 'Lovely. You must have paid all of thirty francs for it.'

Harry burst out laughing. 'They're diamonds.'

'It's a bad fake, Harry. Like you.'

'Odile—' he said softly.

'Tell me about this,' she said, reaching out and touching the scar on his cheek.

'Hopping.'

'What kind of hopping?'

'The vegetable kind. I was brought up in east London. And east Londoners go hopping, to Kent. You get a free holiday, sleep in big huts, and you pick the hops for the farmer. Great time. Special trains used to take us down from London Bridge. Trouble was, if you had a big family, it'd work out expensive. We little ones used to hide under Mother's skirts. The train people got wise to this and they gave the conductor a big hat pin, and if they were suspicious, they'd go stab' – he made a thrusting motion – 'into the skirts, see if anyone squealed. One year they got me, but I didn't cry out. Just stayed there, quietly bleeding.

Well, it went bad and left me with this, but my mum was right proud of me.'

Odile giggled tipsily.

'What's so funny?' He thought it was a much more likely story than being dragged across a concrete floor by members of the security services.

'I think you're full of shit, you know that? That is not an old scar from boyhood. I don't know if you are a captain, a corporal, a secret agent, a shipping agent, a shipping clerk, and part of me really doesn't care. You did well these last few days.'

'Thanks.' They sat in silence, sipping the wine, both pondering the same question, until Harry finally asked: 'What happens now?'

'To you? Or me?'

'Both.'

'I can only answer for me, Harry.' Odile stood up and went to the carriage window, sucking up air to try and clear her head. She would regret the wine in the morning. She watched the tiny figures beavering away under the dockside lights and reminded herself that they were Germans out there, the men who had over-run her country with humiliating ease. She felt a fury start to rise within her and gripped the window frame, flinching as a shard of glass sliced her palm. She licked the blob of blood away. 'Perhaps it isn't over,' she said out loud.

'What isn't?'

'The war. The fight.'

Harry stood and joined her at the window, listening to the shouted orders drifting across to them, the sound of hammers on steel and hobnails on concrete. It looked pretty over to him. He put a hand on her shoulder, but she shrugged it off.

'I feel ashamed, you know.' She turned. 'Ashamed of my country, ashamed of its men, its soldiers.' The last word was loaded with derision. She pointed at a group of Wehrmacht gunners tugging a howitzer into place behind sandbags. 'It shouldn't end like this.'

'There is nothing we can do here—'

'I think there is something we can do.'

Harry felt his heart sink slightly, realising it was he who had started using the plural. 'Against that lot?'

'There are British soldiers all over. Ones who haven't surrendered. In the dunes. In farmhouses. Dozens. Maybe hundreds . . .'

'How do you know?'

'Everyone is talking about it. For the moment, the Germans are too busy to sweep the whole countryside. What if we got these British undercover, find clothes, papers, houses that will take them, before the Nazis do.'

'Why?'

'Why? So they can get back home. So they can carry on the fight. I hate to say this, Harry, but you British might be our last hope. You and that few miles of water out there.' She returned to the seat and emptied the dregs of the wine into her cup. Tomorrow be damned. She sat and seethed, irritated with Harry, that he couldn't see what had to be done. 'If we do nothing . . . then we deserve what we get.'

'Let's suppose you do start rounding up stragglers—'

'Oh, I'm going to do it, Harry, don't you worry.' Her voice was hard with determination, and he didn't doubt that now she had a plan, no matter how vague, she was going to act on it.

'How do you think that the Krauts will react if you are discovered doing this?'

'I thought you were a secret agent? That you were used to such things.'

'Yes, but you have no idea what you're getting into.'

'Which is why I need you to help me.'

'Help you?' He sat down next to her. 'Me?'

'Help me, help me, help me. Yes. Help me.' She leaned forward and he could smell the sourness of the wine on her breath. 'Let me tell you a secret, secret agent. I like you a little, too. But right now—'

He kissed her, short, sharp, quickly, but she pulled away. 'Help me. I have to do this thing. OK, so maybe gathering up a few soldiers is pathetic, a pinprick to those bastards out there. But, Harry, we have to do something.' Outside an engine coughed into life and a half-track with a makeshift bulldozer blade on the front lurched into view, ready to carve a path through the worst of the debris. 'Before it is too late.'

He could feel her eyes drilling into him, willing him to join her. There was an energy crackling from her, as if her rage was generating a massive voltage. It was a seductive mix, a beautiful woman, a good woman, stoked with passion. Why not? thought Harry. Why not be on the side of the angels for a change? Why not be on Odile's team?

'Take this as a yes,' he said and kissed her again. This time she didn't pull away.

Once the decision had been made, Harry threw himself into the work, following her lead in creating a few safe enclaves for some of the hundreds of soldiers still lost in France, using his well-tuned sense of character to sniff out those locals willing to help.

After just two weeks, they had something approaching a network in place, centred on Lille, and he had sent willing helpers off down the line to create a point-to-point system stretching down the length of the country. 'Like the bloody Pony Express,' as Harry put it.

Odile had found him a base on the outskirts of the small town of Madeleine, a few miles north of Lille. Three weeks after leaving Calais, they celebrated their success in a modest restaurant-with-rooms in the city centre, although dinner was somewhat soured by the crush of Feldgrau uniforms in the room, and the leering glances that flashed Odile's way every now and then. He didn't blame the Germans. She looked radiant, alive, her skin glowing with good health. She loved all this, he realised, loved the subterfuge and the rebellion, the feeling of achievement, of fooling the oafs crowding the bar. Deceit and deception were, as he knew only too well, powerful drugs, and Odile was becoming addicted.

Harry was clean-shaven, with no hint of the rough stubble he had cultivated back when he was impersonating an orderly. His once-savage army haircut was growing out, albeit slowly, and Odile had oiled it to approximate a French style. He was still uncertain of his accent, so he kept his voice low while the room filled with smoke and the hearty laughter of the invincible.

'I have found a job,' she said. 'At the hospital.'

Harry nodded.

'Nursing again.'

He picked up a tinge of disappointment. 'It's what you are. A nurse.'

'My father is a doctor. My brother, a doctor. My other brother, a lawyer. I'm a nurse.'

He wanted to say that she shouldn't be ashamed, that nurses were very valuable, but a little voice warned him to be quiet.

'If I had been given proper schooling . . .'

'Then what?'

'What do you think? I would not have been a nurse.'

'Oh. Is it too late?'

'It was always too late. For the daughter, the sister.'

The penny dropped. 'They have woman doctors here, don't they?'

'Not in my father's world they didn't.'

'If you'd become a doctor I might not have met you.'

Odile laughed at this, causing more stares from the Germans. 'Oh, that's all right then. Better to meet Harry than become a famous surgeon.'

'Is that what you want? To become famous?'

'My father is famous. Was famous. He's dead now. In the twenties he developed a procedure for removing tonsils quicker and cleaner, with less bleeding.'

His grasp of the language still wasn't up to anatomy, and it was a few moments before he was clear what she meant, until she opened her mouth and pointed, making a loud gurgling noise.

'Tonsils? Famous for being able to take out tonsils? Christ, that's not real fame, is it?'

'It was in my house.'

'You talked a lot of tonsils in your house?'

A chuckle. 'I suppose we did.'

'There's a soldier who keeps staring at your back. Can you feel it? Christ, I think he's dribbling.'

She shrugged, as if the gaze could be swatted off like a fly. 'I have a present for you,' Odile said softly.

Harry simply raised a quizzical eyebrow.

Odile stood up, held out her hand. He took it and they rose, Odile leading him through the knots of soldiers, silencing them with a wink and a smile as she took Harry up the squeaking wooden staircase. Someone let out a ribald cheer, but was silenced. Dozens of eyes were on Odile as she sashayed ahead of a red-faced Harry, still holding his hand, signalling the bar that she had made her choice, and a Frenchman had won.

The bedroom was small, made even more cramped by a vast

wardrobe that could have held most of Printemps' stock. The beds were narrow singles and Harry stood looking at them, balefully.

'Was that all just for show? For the benefit of the Wehrmacht?'

'Help me push these together, and we'll see.'

After they had rearranged the furniture, she turned off the yellowy overhead light and lit a candle. There was a knock at the door, and Odile opened it a couple of inches, taking an opened bottle of wine and two tumblers from an unseen figure outside.

Harry felt lost. Normally the room and the wine and the candles would have been his idea, but here she was peeling his jacket off, taking control. She stopped as she saw his expression. 'You don't want to?'

'Yes. Of course. I'm just . . .'

She pushed him back onto the chimeric bed, which creaked alarmingly under their weight. She giggled. 'This should make for quite a show in the restaurant. What's the matter? Don't worry, I don't make a habit of this. In fact, I have only had two lovers . . . both doctors. Of course. Nurses and doctors. Such a cliché,' she said sardonically. 'Does it worry you? That you aren't the first?'

He laughed. 'The only thing worrying me is me.'

'You're nervous? Harry? Surely not?'

'Not nervous . . . just . . .' He tried to think of a word that would explain the feeling of being caught in midstream, caught in an unexpected eddy. For all his life so far, he had more or less known what he was doing and why. The why being to benefit Harry. Now he was helping a woman in a scheme which, on the face of it, had no percentage at all for him. Furthermore, he was letting her seduce him. 'Confused,' he said finally.

She kissed him on the cheek, close to his lips and he moved his head so their mouths met and now his fingers were at the buttons of her blouse. Her hands ripped at his shirt and he heard a button or two go, and then she was at the fly. He was having trouble with a clasp on her blouse.

'Leave my clothes,' she said, pushing his hand inside her skirt and up her smooth, stockingless thigh. 'I seem to have forgotten my underwear anyway.'

Suddenly, Harry was no longer confused.

Ten

London, October 1940

The grass of the park was crisp underfoot with a stubborn frost as Sir Claude Dansey crossed from Broadway Buildings towards St James's, musing on his narrow escape that morning. If things had gone differently, the political wilderness, rather than a good lunch, might have been beckoning. There had been moves afoot to censure him and his boss, Sir Stewart Menzies, universally known as 'C', for their intelligence failures, but it had been squashed in cabinet by Winston Churchill, the Prime Minister.

Dansey may be deputy to 'C', but whereas Menzies (whose main judge of a character was the ability to pronounce his name correctly – Mingiss and you were in) concerned himself with making sure the security services got credit where it was due within Whitehall – and credit even when it wasn't – it was Dansey who nurtured and lubricated the various Circulating Stations, the everyday machinery of intelligence gathering.

Most politicians realised how pivotal Dansey was, and when the blame for the French fiasco came to be apportioned, fingers were quickly pointed at him. Why hadn't the Secret Intelligence

Service known that France had no spirit for a fight? Because SIS had relied on his Z men in northern France for far too long. A group of privateers could never compete with a properly funded government organisation, which MI6 had not been since the 1920s. His counterblast was that they were lucky to know as much as they did, thanks to the patriotism of men like Alexander Korda and Henry King, the filmmaker's chief location scout, who worked for scant reward. Luckily, Churchill had bought it.

Dansey's spying career spanned back through the decades to the Boer wars in South Africa, where he had met Churchill, followed by Borneo, Congo, Somalia, even the United States, where he had helped set up their own fledgling intelligence efforts. Throughout the 1930s he had run his Z organisation and, as promised, once Winston was Prime Minister, he had been brought back to operational headquarters, where he was hastily trying to repair the damage done by years of institutionalised neglect.

Dansey skirted past a pair of ack-ack guns, snouts elevated to the steel-blue sky, but the only things up there were the bloated barrage balloons over the House. Less and less daylight traffic now, more and more night raids.

However, no matter how grateful Churchill had been for past efforts, after the fall of France he had given Dansey a hefty slap by making sure that the new Special Operations Executive was effectively beyond his control. True, Dansey had slipped a couple of his people in there, notably the journalist Kim Philby, but day-to-day, it was free of SIS influence apart from the fact the new boys had to use the MI6 communications system, which was useful happenstance.

Dansey couldn't let another organisation slip out of his control, though. He had to make sure that MI9, the hastily cobbled-together outfit in charge of bringing escapers and evaders home, stayed within his sphere of influence. He hated the thought of soldiers and pilots running through France willy-nilly. It could be Edith Cavell all over again. During the First World War the matron had used the nursing home she ran in Belgium to hide Allied servicemen from the Germans. When this was discovered, she was shot and became one of the war's great martyrs. To Dansey, though, she had been a dangerous amateur, totally lacking in the skills needed for such work. To make matters worse, her activities had exposed a number of British and French secret agents who used her hospital as a cover, blowing a whole network. He couldn't have that kind of thing happening to him.

It reminded him of the report on his desk from his old Z operative Henry King, explaining that there was a chap in Lille who had successfully been feeding airmen to Marseilles and over the Pyrenees since the summer. The Lille area was a transit point for all German traffic to the Channel defences, which is why it was designated as part of the northern Forbidden Zone, closed to casual travellers, even those from the occupied areas. This was where Dansey desperately needed intelligence. So whoever this Scarlet Pimpernel was, he'd have to be watched, brought under the cosh.

King was the man for that. Henry King had proved his worth over and over again, to the point that Dansey felt he was an extension of his own arm. When he clenched his fist in London, King delivered the blow across the Channel, with few questions asked. That was Dansey's kind of agent.

He suddenly decided to lunch at the Travellers Club on Pall Mall. He usually went to Brooks's in St James's, but there were times when the more discreet Travellers was better suited to his needs, such as now, when he needed the space to think. Of course he could have eaten well enough in the SIS executive dining room, but Dansey liked any excuse to get out of the suffocating confines of Broadway Buildings with its gentlemen spies and Old Colonials, not a real professional among them. He'd make an exception for someone like Philby, who had the making of a first-rate agent, but mostly there was a lot of dead wood to cut out.

Dansey detoured around the two murky brown bomb craters in the park's lawn, crossed the Mall and started up Marlborough Road, now re-opened after the unexploded incendiary scare of the last few days. There was still a war reserve constable posted at the end of the street, a WW1 veteran with a large drooping moustache who saluted smartly.

The odd thing about the Lille man, who seemed to be called Mason, was that, according to pilot debriefings at London Cage, a requisitioned mansion in Kensington Palace Gardens, he claimed to be SIS. Yet they had no Mason on their books.

He was nearly at the Travellers and Dansey began to pull his gloves off in anticipation. He knew that the kitchen had secured some decent game, and he was about ready for a bit of rich, red meat.

As the ancient doorman hurried to let him in, Dansey made a mental note to get King to give Mason a once-over as soon as possible, see if there was any mileage in him.

Eleven

Lille, France, Early Summer 1941

Bernd Diels studied the list on his desk and chewed his lower lip. Mines de Dourges, the metalworkers at Compagnie de Fives-Lilles, the textile workers at Stalar mills, the Anzin mines. Every single one on strike. He'd thought that they'd diminish after the winter, but no, women were still turning up at pitheads demanding increased bread and fomenting protest strikes. It wasn't good enough.

In fact, it was generally unsatisfactory that he should be bogged down by petty disputes like these at all. His transfer to the Feldpolizei, the plain clothes section of the Abwehr, came with a brief to seek out spies and saboteurs, not deal with strikes over the ration system and distribution of food. But his superiors decided that anything that threatened the flow of goods to the Reich was an Abwehr matter, so he had to pay some attention to the strikers.

Diels poured himself a glass of water and sipped. He had spent a good weekend in Paris, relaxing at the shows, forgetting, for a while, that his fiefdom was the most boring section of the country

– flat, industrial, populated by the miserable and the curmudgeonly. Coal miners, for instance. Was there any nation in the world where they weren't a pain in the arse? In any other industry, you could threaten to send in replacements. Replacing a miner – finding anyone stupid enough to do the work – was not easy.

There was a knock at the door and Pieter Wolkers entered. The fair-haired Dutchman was wearing a large grin. Wolkers was a Brandenburger – a volunteer from a conquered nation who instinctively knew where to place his allegiances. Diels had no illusions about the sort of man he was. Before the war in Amsterdam he was probably a petty crook or a horse trader. Maybe even a diamond smuggler, Diels never asked, and he didn't care. All that concerned him was ensuring that Wolkers used his dubious skills to prise information from a tight-lipped population.

He threw a folder down on Diels's desk. 'You owe me a drink, Bernd.'

'Do I?' He flicked the corner of the document. 'What is it?'

'The names of the Comité Populaire. The ones behind the Stalar Mills and Fives-Lille strikes and I'd wager the others as well. Ten of them.'

Diels smiled. This would make Generalleutnant Niehoff a very happy man. Already the area commander had closed theatres and cafés, banned alcohol and reduced the bread ration in an attempt to flush out the Comité. Now his little ferret had done the job. 'Certain?'

'Certain? I spoke at their last meeting.'

Diels burst out laughing. 'Very good. Very good.' He stood up and sat on the edge of his desk.

'But I cannot show my face at the mines again.'

'Don't worry, we have plenty for you to do. You read English. Look at this . . .'

He threw a dog-eared newspaper across to Wolkers. The *Daily Mirror*.

'Page five. A pilot shot down over Dunkirk, made it back to his squadron two months after he was believed dead. A real morale boost. Now, he must have come through here, down one of these ratlines I keep hearing about. Stories like this make us look bad. And they make the locals think they can thumb their noses at us.'

'What do you want me to do?'

'Find me some pilots who need rescuing.' He paused and then winked. 'Some friendly pilots.'

Odile called first at the hairdresser where Harry had a room out back. Annette, despite being in the middle of a permanent wave, greeted her warmly, but Harry wasn't in, she said. Odile remounted her bike and began pedalling towards Povan, the next village, trying to stop the panic from rising in her chest. Everything was in danger of crashing down around their ears.

As she rattled over the cobbles, her breath coming hard in the afternoon heat, she wondered where the hell Harry had got to. After twelve long months of operations, he had six or seven safe houses he scuttled between and she had been to four of them now. At the back of her mind, there was always the fear that one day Harry would move on, the way she was sure he'd moved on all his life whenever things got sticky.

It was sometimes difficult to steer him away from the black market, livestock deals, tobacco smuggling, all the other temptations that would engage the Harry of old. Odile, though, made it clear that wasn't the Harry she wanted or needed. Sure, there was time for a little dabbling, just to 'keep his hand in' as he put it – and to top up their larders – but for the most part she insisted that the Harry she shared her bed with had to be the one who had worked out dozens of dodges to fool the Germans.

It was Harry who had noticed that ration coupons were issued according to the population size of the towns as they'd been before the Germans arrived. But many people had fled in May 1940, and 300,000 of them had not been allowed back by the Germans. So the surplus ration books provided a means to feed the escapers and evaders – mostly downed Allied airmen – who were slowly filling up the available barns and outhouses across the region.

He'd come up with ways to forge the identity coupons, blanks of which were available at any *tabac*, and co-opted a printer to make the stamps. He knew which make of typewriters were used by the Gendarmerie, the Marie and the Offices of the Occupation, purloined one of each make, and taught himself to rattle off letters of authorisation, apparently written by important-sounding bureaucrats with enormous, florid signatures and sealed with brutal, eagle-headed stamps.

In Paris, he had created two safe houses, one a brothel near les Halles, the other at the rear of a restaurant where the escapers could get a decent meal. Whether they were offered the services of the other establishment, Odile declined to enquire. She had made it clear what would happen if Harry took advantage of such an offer, even if it was on the house.

From the Marie in Lille, Harry extracted a card which stated he was deaf and dumb to cover his French which, although improving, still lapsed when he was excited. Harry thrived, she suspected, because fooling the Germans was something he'd been preparing for all his life, albeit unwittingly, with his lies and half-truths.

She knew there were those in the escaping business who didn't like Harry: Faucomb and Trotobas, Madame Preyier and old Berclau, the ex-mayor. They'd all expressed their doubts about the cocky little Captain, but they had to face up to one fact –

nobody came close to matching Odile and Harry's track record when it came to hiding and moving pilots and soldiers.

Odile was beginning to rely on the Englishman far more than was healthy, and she knew that was a bad thing even before she saw his bicycle chained outside the Court Restaurant.

Harry reached over and poured another glass of Fleurie for the woman opposite. It was late afternoon, they were two bottles down, and even in the gloom of the restaurant – Hugo the owner kept the shades drawn day and night – Harry could see the flush on her cheeks.

He'd forgotten just how much he enjoyed this particular chase, the hare and the dog, and the hare was slowing, he could sense it. Lucienne Dievart had something he wanted and today, she was going to give it up. Which was just as well, because the black-market lunch had cost him a small fortune.

He sipped his own wine. 'In return, Lucienne, I can get you a travel permit to Paris. Hell, I will even come with you.'

'But they are gold dust.'

Harry laughed. *Ausweise* could be forged, copied, stolen, or even used several times over – they bore no photograph, and he had used a single pass to get as many as a dozen pilots across the Abbeville bridge in the course of two days.

'And I am a gold mine.'

'So I have heard . . .'

Harry bristled slightly. 'What have you heard?'

'Oh, things. That you have a mother and her daughter as lovers . . .'

No, that was Keiller the Scotsman, who had been living in Madeleine for six months and was lucky not to have been caught.

'That you had a treacherous woman shot in her hospital bed.'

No, that was Trotobas, who arranged for two bogus doctors to finish off a woman who had been turning in downed airmen.

'That you have a young French fiancée. A very young fiancée. Some might say, too young.'

No, Odile may be French but she was neither too young nor a fiancée. He shook his head.

'That there is a reward of ten thousand francs on your head.'

This was news to him. He was about to ask Lucienne where she had gleaned this last gem of gossip when he saw her eyes widen.

He knew the look. It was the terror that showed whenever Germans walked into a room. Always stay calm, he reminded himself. He had papers, he had his deaf-and-dumb certificate to fall back on, and he had more front than Barker's of Kensington.

The blow stung his left ear and he couldn't help but cry out. He half-turned and feathers filled his mouth and face, the quills leaving red weals on his cheeks. He rose from the chair but the pheasant hit him again, sending him staggering back.

Odile was being restrained by Hugo, who was appalled to see one of his expensive birds plucked off the rack and used for common assault. Now she was hitting the restaurateur, and he started to retreat under the rain of feathery blows.

'Odile—' Harry took a step back to avoid another faceful of feathers. 'For God's sake.' Odile held up her hands, signalling for quiet. The only other remaining diners were two bloated executives from the coalmines at Bethune, pigging out on the proceeds of their own black-market operations, now staring at this impromptu floorshow in disbelief.

'You . . .' She pointed at Lucienne and flung the bird at her, smashing the wine glass and drenching the woman with Fleurie. Lucienne leapt up, staring down open mouthed at her ruined clothes, and began to scream. Hugo panicked and pushed Odile towards the door. She shrugged him off, turned on her heel and swept out. One of the coalmen began to laugh but a glance from Harry silenced him.

'Lucienne, I'm sorry, I'll be back. I must . . .'

'You can forget your damned house! And keep your precious travel passes . . .'

'Ssshhh. No. Please, Hugo.' He held his hands, pleadingly, out to the owner. 'Help me out here.'

As Hugo took over, trying to calm the hysterical Lucienne, Harry raced outside just in time to find Odile cycling off. With no time to unlock his own bicycle, he ran in pursuit, arms and legs pumping.

Odile was furious with herself. She had let a petty jealousy, a moment of anger, swamp her judgement. She knew better than to draw attention to herself, to them. It was even possible, it dawned on her, that she had misjudged the situation. She slowed when she saw the German staff car, a swastika fluttering on its bonnet, approaching and pulled the bike to a halt at the kerbside. A breathless Harry appeared beside her, took in the Opel and leaned over and kissed her as hard as he could. As soon as the slow-moving Opel had purred past she pulled away and spat into the road, her anger flooding back.

'For God's sake, woman.'

'For God's sake? What about *my* sake?'

'What the bloody hell was all that about?'

'What? How can you ask me that? You are in there with that whore, eating and drinking black market—'

'Keep your voice down.'

'How much will all that cost?'

'A damn sight more now I'll have to pay for the pheasant,' he said with feeling. 'And probably a new dress for Lucienne.'

Odile cracked a sardonic smile. 'Well, at least something good came of it. That was a hideous outfit.' Then the burning feeling in her stomach again. 'You are a shit, Harry.'

'I was working—'

'Oh, yes, nice work if you can get it, Harry. Look, I could get all kinds of information by fucking a few Germans. You want me to do that?'

'I wasn't fucking her.'

'Not yet . . .' She began to act out him stroking her hand. 'Oh, chérie, just let me slip this in, you won't feel a thing . . .'

'Yes, she damn well would,' he said with mock indignation.

'Darling, why don't you just put your lips round this big fat sausage . . . Oh, yes, darling . . .'

Harry suddenly felt his own temper flaring. He grabbed her upper arm. 'Lucienne's father has a house near the Somme bridge. It's not used. It would be perfect. We could hide ten, twenty men there at a time. It would mean not exposing ourselves so often between here and there . . .'

'Harry. Harry. Look at me. It's Odile. Not some tart with her brains in her buttocks. *Odile*. Don't give me any more of your shit. You start fucking around, I start fucking around. What's the expression? Good for the goose . . . ?'

Harry raised his hands in surrender. 'Agreed. But I wasn't going to fuck her.' Odile moved with the speed of a snake and grabbed his balls, giving one of them a painful squeeze between thumb and forefinger.

'Ow, shit.'

'If you did, you wouldn't have anything left to do it a second time. Chéri.'

'Bloody hell, you bitch. Let's get off the street before someone takes too much notice.'

Odile nodded, feeling her eyes fill up, the fury replaced by remorse at her impulsiveness. 'I'm sorry, Harry. I don't know . . .'

He pulled her head onto his shoulder. 'It's OK. This bloody

war makes us all do stupid things.'

She looked at him. 'It's this bloody war I came to see you about. There's a problem at Goutard.'

'I'll get my bike.'

As Harry walked back to the restaurant, Odile watched him go, annoyed with herself that, despite her best efforts, she'd gone and fallen in love with him.

As the pair pedalled away they passed the Café Central, where Dansey's Henry King was sitting on the terrace, sipping bad coffee, pretending to read the newspaper. From his vantage point he could see right into the Court Restaurant, and he had witnessed the whole performance with a mixture of curiosity and horror.

'He can't stay here. He can't stay here. He can't stay here.' The old woman was beginning to fray Harry's nerves. They were in the gloomy living room of a farmhouse near Goutard where the pilot before him had turned up unannounced, asking for sanctuary. Madame's husband was a prisoner of war in Germany, and clearly she thought it would go badly for him if she were discovered to be harbouring an Allied prisoner. She'd been threatening to turf him out all day; only Leverin, the young boy they used as a runner, had prevented her, while Odile went off to fetch Harry.

'Be quiet, Madame,' Harry snapped. 'Get us a drink, please. Anything.' The woman went off to the kitchen, still grumbling. He turned to the glum-looking pilot. 'Your name is . . . ?'

'Rola. Jan Rola.' It was a thick, indeterminate accent. He was dressed in a mixture of civilian and RAF clothes. His flight jacket had been replaced by a coarse wool coat a couple of sizes too small, but the blue trousers with their sharp creases would have him singled out as a downed pilot within ten minutes on the street. No matter what happened, Harry knew they had to get him a fresh outfit.

'And you are based at . . . ?'

The pilot raised an eyebrow. 'I cannot tell you that.'

'You are going to have to.'

'I can't.'

'Look, I hand you over to the Germans, you are a prisoner of war, no harm done. I feed you into the system and you are a stooge . . .'

'I am no stooge!' Rola said angrily. 'I flew Potez bombers for the French. I was shot down, got across the Channel. I am with . . .' he tailed off. 'The Free Polish Air Force.'

'Where did you do your English course?'

'Sorry?'

'All Poles take an English course before being allowed to fly.'

'I didn't need one. Good English.'

Something wasn't right here. The man was too chippy, too confrontational. Or was that just the Polish way? The woman returned with two small glasses of orange liquid. Harry watched as Rola tossed it back in one and shuddered with pleasure. Harry sipped his. It was sweet and sickly. He smiled insincere thanks at the woman.

'What did you say you flew? Spitfires?'

'Ha! I wish. Hurricanes.'

Harry looked over at Leverin. He was seventeen, a boy, who looked even younger, but he was quickly learning more about the RAF than most of the downed pilots. The lad nodded slightly. Hurricanes were more common among the volunteer squadrons.

'OK, Odile, get François to bring his van.' He looked at the boy. 'Go with him to Povan, put him in with Mahoney.' No, that could be a disaster, if the Pole was a plant. 'On second thoughts put him at the farm. The barn. OK? And get him some decent clothes.'

'Thank you,' said Rola as he stood.

'Don't thank me. Nothing happens till we find your parachute and confirm that a Hurricane went down.'

'But—'

'But nothing. Listen, there is a man in the rue de l'Arc in Lille who likes to sew the fingers of Frenchmen and women together, just to start them talking. When he is finished with fingers, he starts on other parts. That's what happens to people who get betrayed. So you stay put till we are sure you are who you say you are. Understood?'

Rola went pale at the thought of enforced suturing and nodded. 'I'll tell you exactly where I went down.'

Odile snuggled closer to Harry as the explosions became more frequent and then turned into one long, low rumble, the flashes of the bombs seeking out the gaps in the blackout curtains of her bedroom and playing across the ceiling. The chemical works was getting it tonight, ten, twelve miles away, but it felt like the next village as the bed creaked and shuddered under the impacts.

The ack-ack was pounding away steadily, audible in the pauses between the bomb clusters. Harry knew from bitter experience that the fields for miles around would be showered with hot, twisted metal from the exploding shells.

'More customers,' he said and she buried her head in his chest. 'For you or me?'

Odile was still working at the hospital in Lille, and would often see the results of what the Germans called 'the callous targeting of civilians' by the RAF terror bombers. Like most, she would find her loyalties strained by the sight of maimed innocents, especially the children. There were times, in her darkest moments, that she really did believe the bombers unloaded their cargoes without bothering too much about whether a factory or houses were below.

'Both.'

She snaked up his body and kissed him. 'How much longer can we go on?'

He pressed himself against her. 'I reckon I can manage it one more time.'

She slapped his chest. 'That's not what I meant. It's not going to get any easier, is it?'

He shook his head. 'No. It'll get worse before it gets better.'

'How long have I got you for, Harry?'

He rolled over to look at her. It was a strange question, but he knew what she meant. It was no good giving Odile happy-ever-after. She wouldn't fall for that. She'd take happy-for-however-long. 'A thousand and one nights.'

'A thousand and one nights is almost three years. Three years of this. Jesus, my nerves won't stand it. Sooner or later someone will . . .' She couldn't finish the sentence. Betray us. 'You know that for every night there was a shadow night?'

'A what?'

'You know the stories? A Thousand and One Nights?'

'Not really. I mean, I know about, what's her name . . . ?'

'Scheherazade. My father told me about her and the stories. I think he fancied himself as Richard Burton. The great explorer.'

'I thought he was into tonsils?'

'That's what paid the rent. He saw himself as a more glamorous figure. Eventually, a few years back, he went to the Congo ostensibly on a medical mission, but really, I suspect, just to see how it felt to do some exploring.'

'And?'

'He died of malaria.' She paused and he looked at her as the white of an explosion flicked over her features. She was dry-eyed. 'Anyway, he told me that every story had several versions, different endings, that these were called the shadow stories and Burton said there were a thousand and one other nights, darker nights. I wonder if these are our thousand dark nights?'

He paused, as if considering his answer, trying to hide his befuddlement, before saying: 'I think you are talking rubbish.'

She laughed and pinched him and he kissed her forehead and she suddenly asked: 'What about the Pole? What do you think?'

They had discovered that a fighter had gone down into the marshland, as the Pole insisted, but it wouldn't be the first time the Abwehr had switched pilots to try to infiltrate a line. 'I can't tell. I know a man who can though. Gérard in Paris. He has a Polish waiter. Old boy. Sharp as a knife, though. He'll tell me what's what.'

'It means you'll have to risk him as far as Paris. That's six, seven people exposed in the chain.'

'I know. We can't sit on him for ever.'

'What if he's a spy?'

Harry clutched her as the windows rattled and the mattress bucked. A stray bomb, a big one, had fallen nearby. When the noise subsided they could hear the desperate bleating of wounded livestock and the shouts of a farmer. A few moments later, the flat crack of a shotgun.

'God, that's Jean-Pierre,' she said.

Yes, thought Harry, and there might be fresh mutton available tomorrow.

'Harry?'

'Hhmm.'

'What if he's a spy?'

'What do you think?'

Another shotgun blast from the fields answered for him.

★ ★ ★

Harry kept his contraband in the rear of an abandoned baker's shop on the edge of Povan. The owner was too old to cope with rationing, he claimed, and had shut up shop and moved to be with his daughter in Paris. Harry rented it for a few hundred francs a week. Now he had filled the racks at the rear of the shop with tobacco, wine, ration books, blank passes, torches, currency pouches, parachute silk, cigarettes, canned goods, ladies' underwear and precious shoes. As a collection of bargaining tools it was quite a resource.

He found the pistol at the back of one of the racks, a heavy Webley .38 that one of the Wellington navigators had given him as a token of thanks. He was just checking the cylinder when he heard the footfall on the dank flagstones and instinctively spun round, pointing the gun at the stomach of the elegant, square-jawed man before him.

Unfazed, the stranger took out a pack of cigarettes and offered Harry one. Harry shook his head.

'Who the bloody hell are you?'

'Henri Rex, Service Général de Contrôle Economique. Anti-black market.'

Shit, Harry thought, these guys were making sure people got twenty months for trading a bit of coal or meat. He had enough on the racks for eternal damnation with no parole. Still, he was the one with the gun. 'I hope you've got some friends with you.'

The man lit his cigarette and took his time inhaling, before he said in English: 'That's a bloody awful French accent. You sound like a dustman. Real name's Henry King.'

He held his hand out, but Harry eyed it suspiciously.

'You don't remember me?'

'Should I?' Harry asked warily, trying to place the unfamiliar face.

'No, you only had eyes for the Contessa as I recall.'

Harry's mind slid back to the dinner two years previously in Le Touquet. 'The Englishman? In films?'

'Correct. Location scout for London Films. A very handy cover.'

'That wasn't a coincidence, was it?'

'That I was at dinner? Absolutely not. I'd followed you around for a couple of days. You were causing frightful trouble. They had to shut you down.'

Harry touched the scar on his cheek. 'Oh, they did that, all right.'

'You didn't know what you were getting into, Harry. Out of your depth. That had to be made clear to you. Trust me when I say you were lucky. Uncle Claude isn't always so considerate.'

'Uncle Claude?'

It was Dansey's nickname throughout the security service, an ironic reference to the fact that he was as far removed from a kindly relative as imaginable. 'No matter,' said King. He'd been with Dansey a long time, and he knew that few emerged from a tussle with Uncle Claude with just a souvenir scar. King admired Dansey. He also owed him because he was pursuing the one wartime career he ever coveted. He came from a long line of conventional soldiers but King felt he was modernising the heritage, as profound a change as the cavalry switching from horses to tanks. He agreed with Dansey that the future of warfare was intelligence and all its dark corners, the places where people like Harry Cole dwelt.

'And you've come to shut me down again?'

'You can put the gun away, Harry. I'm here to help.'

'I don't need any help.'

King delivered the next sentence as off-handedly as he could manage, dangling the bait casually. 'Everybody needs twenty thousand francs.'

Harry put the gun down.

'Good.'

'Twenty thousand francs?'

Got you, King thought, with a tinge of disappointment. This was too easy by half – it was meant to be a game, and it needed two to play. Harry was too easy to read, the greed thick in his voice. 'Not here, in Marseilles.'

'Marseilles?' Harry felt a niggle of doubt. 'Why Marseilles? It's a long way to go. Even for that much money.'

'Relax, Harry. It's not a trap. That's where the banker is, and believe me this banker wants to look everybody over before he parts with his cash. Go to the Seamen's Mission. Give your men to Caskie there.'

Harry nodded. He knew the routine, and he knew of Donald Caskie, the minister who ran his mission as a staging post before the last hazardous leg over the mountains to Spain.

'Afterwards go to this address.' He handed a piece of paper over. 'Simple to remember?' Harry nodded. King took the note back and set fire to one corner, waiting until it had caught before he let it drift to the floor. As he did so, Harry noticed his nails, bitten down so savagely that the fingertips were little more than misshapen lumps of skin. 'Tell them Rex sent you. There is a Belgian chap who'll give you the once-over. Bloody fussy. But without his say-so, no twenty grand. And no back up from London Central.'

London Central? Harry couldn't help but let his jaw drop. He knew war made for strange bedfellows, but it appeared that the very people who had once beaten the shit out of him were now trying to recruit him.

'And what, exactly, do you want for your money?'

King reiterated what London had told him. 'You get all sorts of chaps down your line, don't you? Soldiers, sailors, aircrew. People who have seen a lot of things. Things they might not know they have seen. We need them debriefed. Everything about any military activity that they may have come across.'

'Why not wait until they get back home?'

King sighed, as if vexed by a stupid child. 'Because that could be an age. They sit around here for weeks, in Marseilles for months on end. They get into Spain, they may end up interned. You can be the best spy in the world, Harry, but unless your information gets through quickly, it's just so much useless paper. We need the information now. I will give you a list of questions. We'll pay for it, of course.'

'Over and above the twenty thousand?'

'Yes. I'll give you a dead letter drop for reports in Paris. In return, you'll find a consideration in an envelope. But you tell nobody, understood? Nobody at all. Alpha-Need-To-Know basis. You understand what that means?'

'I can guess.'

King laughed. 'You'll need to learn the lingo if you are ever going to be a proper spy.'

They both jumped as Odile entered the room.

'Ah, Mam'selle. I was just leaving. Henri Rex . . .'

'Of?' she asked suspiciously.

'The SGCE.' He waved a hand around the room. 'But you have nothing that interests me here. Goodnight, Mam'selle.'

Odile waited until he had left and snorted. 'Ugh, what a reptile. What did he want?'

Harry shrugged and rubbed thumb and forefinger together.

'Like all of them, a bribe to look the other way. Where the hell have you been?'

'You were right about us getting new customers. Dozens. The Lannoys had one, but someone shopped them. By a miracle they missed the pilot. He is in the safe house down near the Somme.

There is another above the hairdresser, with Madame Druse. Leverin says he has heard of another two living rough in the sugar-beet fields. It's going to get crowded.'

Harry thought for a moment. 'I'll get the Pole and Mahoney out tomorrow. I'm going all the way to Marseilles. It's about time we had some proper recognition.'

'Marseilles? Are you mad? It means crossing the demarcation line. Twice.'

'You think I can't do that?'

'No, but—'

'I'll be gone a week at most. I want to follow the ratline all the way through. Make sure it is absolutely secure. Then we can start feeding the pilots through faster. The longer they stay around here, the more danger we are all in. Come on, I need a drink.'

Harry walked through the shop, stepped out into the street, holding the door open for her to follow, but she hesitated for a moment, rummaging in her bag for the stub of her precious lipstick, re-running their conversation, unable to shake off the feeling that she had missed something important.

Twelve

'How much longer?'

Harry turned to look at Rola, who was dropping behind as the trio trudged across the field. A group of redstarts were whirling overhead, as if keeping them company on their shortcut, and they could hear the persistent yapping of a far-off dog. The sun was dropping rapidly now, but the effort of crossing fields had made all three hot and sweaty and they were being attacked by voracious horseflies. Mahoney, the young English pilot who had been hidden in Povan, and who was also making the run south, had a cluster of bad bites on his face, which he kept scratching.

Harry slapped Mahoney's hand down. 'Leave it. You'll infect them.'

Harry was fuming that they had missed the local train from the next town to Paris, the safest route he knew, which meant an overnight at a hotel. Not a good start to the trip to Marseilles.

The car breaking down on the way to Lille station hadn't helped, even though Harry had used the Wehrmacht motor pool mechanics to get it going again, while the pilots sat in a café and watched Harry berate the German mechanics for their unfamiliarity with Renaults. His forged papers as an inspector of mines meant he could throw his weight around with impunity, suggesting that delays were an insult to the Reich.

The first train journey had been uneventful, but slow. Sections of rail were being repaired after the bombing raids, meaning parts of the network were single-track, adding an hour to the travelling time, hence their missed connection.

'How much longer?' repeated Rola.

'About thirty minutes to the bridge,' Harry said. 'I know this is a round-about way, but it misses out two security checks. Over the bridge, we are out of the Forbidden Zone.' Harry checked his watch. 'Look, we'll have to get the first train tomorrow now. I know somewhere we can stay without registering.'

They tramped on for a while through sugar beet and corn, Harry waving at a farmer who, after a moment, waved back. Sometimes you just had to take a chance that not everybody reported strange men traversing their fields to the Germans.

'What got you?' asked Mahoney. Harry turned, but realised the Englishman was addressing the Pole.

'Ground fire,' Rola said slightly shamefaced. 'Of all the damn' things. It all went wrong from the beginning. We were scrambled. Bandits over Kent. I got in the Hurrie to fire her up and the self-starter jams on. Terrible fooking racket. You know what it's like?'

Mahoney: 'Don't I just.'

Rola carried on: 'Mechanic whacks it with a hammer and it frees up and off we go. Got myself a one-oh-nine and followed it down through the cloud. Too low. Next thing I know, I have wings like a . . . What's it called . . . lacy thing?'

'Doily?' offered Harry.

'Yes, doily.'

'Bad luck,' said Mahoney.

'Stupid.'

'At least you got one of them.' Mahoney couldn't be more than nineteen, had already marked up two kills, and he was desperate to get back into the fight, with a fervour that, to Harry, bordered on the suicidal. 'I got hit by a one-ten.'

A rook took to the air with a lazy cawing, and Harry stopped still. He thought he caught a faint metallic sound, just before the bird had opened its big beak.

'Shut up. Get down.'

He waved an arm and they crouched down into the beet. Ahead was a narrow asphalt road, and after a while the pilots, too, heard the lorry, its badly worn gears grinding as it negotiated the bends. It passed, a six-wheel Mercedes truck, the canvas back snapping as it went, seemingly empty of passengers.

'OK, chaps, no talking unless it's in French now. Save the war stories till we are at the hotel. We have to follow this road north for a while. Any traffic, you duck into those trees. Two miles, perhaps a shade more, there is a bridge, cross that, we're into the hotel. First big hurdle over.'

'Well, at least we can have a nice meal,' said Rola.

'No we can't. We stay in the rooms. Bread and cheese. There's some chocolate in your cases. Don't eat it all. You might need it.'

'Chocolate? What for?' asked Mahoney.

Harry dropped his cardboard case over the wire fence and onto the grass verge, then stepped over into the road, glad to feel something solid underfoot. 'You never know when chocolate will come in handy,' he said enigmatically.

Claude Dansey studied the daily reports from his usual stool at the Rivoli Bar of the London Ritz. It was against the rules to remove the documents from Broadway Buildings, of course, but as he was the one who made and enforced the regulations, he felt pretty sanguine.

The glass and maple art deco Rivoli Bar, its famous etched and frosted windows defaced by crosses of blast tape, was drearily quiet. It was late afternoon and the normal Ritz crowd were still either hard at their war work or sleeping off the previous night's excess. He was alone with the young barman, who ostentatiously displayed his limp, just in case his customers should wonder why he wasn't in uniform. Dansey ordered a double port and leafed through the mundanities. It was all low-grade stuff. Even he wouldn't risk removing anything that originated with Station X.

He stopped at the one-page report from King, concerning Mason, then chuckled to himself. It was, astonishingly, that chap from the shed, the bogus wing commander. A nasty, amoral opportunist as he remembered. Ah well, maybe opportunity was finally knocking for this opportunist. King had recommended letting him run, to try to make use of his talents. So be it. Just as long as it didn't blow up in his face.

He scribbled an instruction to be sent to King the following day and turned to the next problem. Which desk should he give the resourceful Kim Philby after he had done such sterling work reporting to him on the SOE shambles from Beaulieu?

Contrary to what he had impressed on the pilots, Harry had to get out of the little hotel, which was oppressive in its unclean mustiness. He'd put the two of them in separate rooms with a warning not to fraternise with the locals or each other and dumped his stuff in the musty shoebox he had been allocated. After he had paid the owner the bribe for non-registration, had given them their bread and cheese, he took himself off to a small bar down the road where he sipped pastis and thought about Odile.

More precisely, he reflected on the hold she had over him. He'd been able to walk away from every other woman in his life, to disregard what they thought. Poor Dottie. Little Julie. He had never wished them harm, but with both of them, he had played the only hand he had. It hadn't been his fault. With Odile and her funny eyes, well, to his surprise, he'd even been thinking about marriage. Yet he was certain she'd turn him down. 'You should judge each man by his finest day,' she had once said ominously. 'This is yours. Make the most of it.' God, she was full of shit sometimes.

He was aware of the man bouncing onto the stool next to him, but made a point of not looking up until he heard the thick accent order one of the watery beers. His head snapped around and he found himself looking into the smiling face of the Pole.

'Jesus – what the bloody hell are you doing here?'

'I needed fresh air. That hotel stinks.'

'That's why we use it – it can't afford to be fussy.'

'The cheese was mouldy. The bread was sawdust.'

'Oh, excuse me.' He looked around to make sure they weren't overheard. 'And what do you think the food is like in a POW camp? Caviar and chips? Or do you already know?'

Many a captured pilot had been offered a deal if they would work for the Abwehr, the SD or the Gestapo. This man could easily be a renegade Pole, Norwegian or even Dutch flier.

'You still don't trust me?'

'It's my business not to trust anyone.'

'Mine too.'

'Meaning?'

'Your friend Mahoney. I don't know what he has flown before, but not Hurricanes.'

'How do you mean?'

'Hurricanes don't have self-starters. They have starter trolleys.'

'All of them?'

'All of them.'

'Shit.'

'I'm with the 302 from Duxford. You can check. It's a Polish squadron. Under Squadron Leader Jack Satchell. The squadron he told me he belonged to? Blenheims, not Hurricanes. Switched two months ago.'

Harry nervously shredded the bar coaster in his hands. Mahoney was a stooge, a rat, a ringer. One who must know the risks, what would happen were he discovered. He thought of the floppy-haired young boy in the corn field and tried to equate him to this treacherous subterfuge, but the two wouldn't gell. 'What the bloody hell are they doing sending him along?' he finally snapped. 'He's just a kid.'

'That makes him more dangerous, not less. He has something to prove. Look.'

Rola brought out a fistful of paper scraps, each with dense, scribbled writing on them. Names, addresses, safe houses, false identities. The boy had been very thorough, keeping his eyes and ears open. Harry felt panic for the first time in an age, the thought that those bastards could come after everyone who knew him, from Odile down.

'What's to be done?' asked Harry, trying to stop his voice shaking with anger.

'Don't worry,' said Rola evenly and for the first time Harry noticed the size of his hands as the Pole curled them into a gripping, strangling action. 'I've taken care of it.'

Odile realised she was getting tipsy, but took another sip of the brandy anyway. She was enjoying herself. It was almost like old times. Round the table in the scruffy bar were Thérèse and Iva, her two oldest friends, Madame Chalon, the owner, and Guy Chalon, her leathery husband. It was after hours, and the only thing marking this out from the pre-war days the heavy blackout blinds drawn over the windows, sealing them in.

Odile had spent the day bringing two Scots RAF men across the border from Belgium to her house at the edge of Madeleine. That made a total of seven living in the outhouses of what had been her parents' house and was now jointly owned with one of her brothers, the lawyer she hoped was somewhere safe down south. Only one cryptic card in all that time, one of the ones with preprinted phrases. *Am OK. Don't worry*. It only made her fret more.

'Do you think it is wise to keep all these men at your house?' asked Guy.

'Are you offering to take some?' Odile asked, emboldened by the drink.

Guy cleared his throat. 'The Germans come in here all the time . . .' He shrugged in an I'd-love-to-help fashion.

'Often best to hide under their noses. That's what Harry says – hide in plain sight.'

Iva snorted. She was no fan of the Englishman, but Odile suspected there was a tinge of green-eye at work. 'He certainly does that. I saw him go into the Marie in these strange trousers . . . he looked like, like . . .'

'An idiot?' offered Odile.

'Well, that'll do to be going on with.'

Odile smiled. The bizarre plus fours did make him stand out in a crowd as somewhat eccentric. Yet Harry knew that. In the same way he knew if you sat in a train and tried to hide behind a newspaper, you'd be the first one the Gestapo or the Gendarmerie or the Field Police would pick on. So Harry was always there, out in the corridor, whistling, singing, joking in his clunky French.

'And have you seen his deaf-and-dumb act?' asked Thérèse. 'My God. It is like Popou.'

Popou was a popular musical hall entertainer in Lille, a local man who had taken Paris by storm with his pratfalls. Odile couldn't stand him, but she took the point. 'Again, who'd think a secret agent would act so stupidly?'

'Is that what he is? A secret agent?' Thérèse again, with a sneer.

Odile flushed and shifted. She was no longer certain what he was. 'Well, not exactly. I mean, we're all secret agents now, aren't we? Look, I know most of you don't like Harry—'

A chorus of half-hearted protests.

'But at least he is doing something. How many Frenchmen are taking the same risks?'

'Young Lepers. Leverin. The priest in Abbeville. Doctor Tannery—' began Madame Chalon, obviously intending to go on for some time.

'OK, OK. But nobody is as good at getting men through as my Harry. Are they?'

Murmurs of reluctant agreement, even as they all noticed the possessive pronoun.

Madame Chalon reached over and touched her hand. 'Don't worry, my dear. We appreciate what he is doing. And you. Just that these are strange times. And when it is all over, we're sure you'll find a nice French boy to settle down with.'

French boy? She could hear the faint echo of her father uttering the very same words, warning her that a career was not an option, that she would only find a nice man, settle down and have children, and all her training would be wasted. Odile felt a hot anger well up in her, but swallowed the harsh words forming on her tongue. She rose as steadily as she could, grabbed her coat and slipped out the back door into the oppressively warm night. French boy, indeed.

The body was already beginning to smell when Diels walked into the hotel room, the air thick and heavy with the stink of excrement. The Abwehr man looked down at the figure on the bed, the stains on the cheap bedspread, the grimace etched into his face as the life was choked out of him. He glanced at Wolkers. 'How long?'

'Twenty-four hours, maybe more.'

'Twenty-four hours?' Diels asked incredulously. 'Don't they ever clean the rooms? Are there no chambermaids in France?' He looked around. The thick layer of grime on the window ledge gave him the answer. 'I want the entire staff transported for war work in the Reich.'

'For bad housekeeping?' asked Wolkers. 'Isn't that a bit harsh?'

'For not registering guests.' Diels could see by the smile on the Dutchman's face that he had been joking. He wasn't sure he approved of his Brandenburger displaying a sense of humour at a time like this.

'Shall we stop the trains?'

Diels shook his head. 'No, but check on traffic over the bridge in the last few days – question each guard shift, see if they remember this man and who he crossed with. Get a photographer up here, try and get the tongue back in.'

'What are you going to do, Bernd?'

Diels lit a cigarette to mask the smell of the corpse and walked to the window, looked across to the café opposite, at the morose faces of the customers as they studied their bastardised coffee and wished today was a cognac day. Alcohol or not, it was a beautiful afternoon, and he was hot in his unseasonably thick tweed suit. He must have some lighter clothes run up next time he was in Paris. In fact, he would like to move to the capital permanently, away from the depressingly sullen people of the north.

'Sir?'

Diels spun round and back to reality. His cigarette was almost gone. 'I'm going to catch the bastards. We can't have this. It's anarchy. Rewards. That will be the answer. Rewards. A hundred thousand francs for each airman. How does that sound?'

'Expensive,' said Wolkers.

Diels raised an eyebrow. 'But worth it.'

'Is it? We could hire ten of me for that.'

'Perhaps, but I think we should let the locals work for us. From the inside. I know these French.' He looked back across at the glum patrons in the café. 'Right now they would give up their grandmother for a bag of decent coffee or a shot of brandy. We'll get these pilots, Pieter. And soon.'

Thirteen

Gérard held up the glassy-eyed perch and pressed a finger to its scales, which yielded easily under the pressure. He looked dolefully at Harry, before throwing the fish back into the basket with the others and wiping his hands. 'That fish last saw water before you did, Harry.' Gérard wrinkled his nose at the smell of body odour. 'What have you two been doing?'

Rola, who had been given the all-clear by Gérard's elderly Polish waiter, was busy slurping a bowl of vegetable soup. He stopped and looked up from the ancient wooden table which dominated the kitchen of Gérard's Paris restaurant, its surface a mass of scar tissue from a thousand chopping sessions. 'Walking mostly. Your friend Harry decided it was easier to walk here than catch trains. My feet—'

'A precaution,' said Harry when Gérard looked at him quizzically. 'We caught a couple of locals. The expresses are getting too dangerous.'

Gérard put a large arm round him and directed him away from Rola's earshot. 'Talking of which . . .' He leaned in close, as if he wanted Harry to smell the garlic and aniseed on his breath. 'I will have to put my prices up.'

'Up? We're going to put four, five, six at a time through. Couple of hundred a head, we agreed. That's a fair whack for one meal and a bed. I could always put them in René's knocking shop. He'd throw in a couple of girls.'

'Oh, yes, that's very secure. And they're some of the most pox-ridden creatures in Paris. The English'll get their pilots back, but they'll be too worried about their cocks dropping off to fight Messerschmitts. And how much does he charge you?'

'Nothing.'

'Nothing?' The expression showed his disbelief.

'We pay you because you provide food and your beds aren't as crusty as the ones the tarts use. But don't push it, Gérard. Everybody else does it out of love for France.'

Gérard made a harrumphing sound and tugged at his beard. 'And why do you do it, Englishman?'

Harry paused, reached up and took a salami down from the rack and cut himself a thick slice. 'Me?' he said between mouthfuls. 'Because I'm good at it.'

Nobody knew why she was called Tante Clara. Harry had never met anyone who claimed her as a blood relative, but Gérard had told him that if he ever needed a bed for a night, or a loan, or a large bosom to sink into, Tante Clara was his woman. Her apartment was on the edge of Les Halles, in those streets that never seemed to shake off the clinging odour of decaying vegetables.

Harry usually parked the pilots either at the brothel or Gérard's and headed to Clara's for a decent night's sleep. It meant if there was a raid by the Gestapo on either of those premises, Harry was well out of it, which suited him just fine. Her spare room belonged to her son, a gunner, missing since the invasion, who she forlornly hoped was lost in some camp in Germany.

It was midnight when Harry arrived, and Clara made coffee and a huge sandwich from grey bread, filled with thick goose pâté, her favourite.

Clara was a portly woman, probably close to seventy, with hair dyed a strange shade of brick-red. She dressed like any other working class Tante, but Harry had seen the outfits in her wardrobe, elaborate concoctions of silk and feathers and gold lamé. She had been rich once, back before the last war, but her husband had lost everything in the 1914–18 conflict and disappeared. Now, she let out the rooms below her floor to generate an income, the scruffy building the rump of a once great fortune.

When he had finished the sandwich she gave him a splash of whisky. 'How is that girl you told me about . . . Odette?'

'Odile. Well, you know . . .'

'You are blushing, Harry. I bet you don't do that very often.'

'It's been known.' Only where Odile was concerned, though.

'Oh, I doubt that. I think you are used to being a heartbreaker, Harry. Not the other way round.'

'You think Odile will . . .' he yawned. 'Will break my heart?'

'I think, from now on, broken hearts are the order of the day.'

He stood up, walked over and kissed her hair, which smelt of lavender. 'I'll try to keep mine intact.'

She slapped him lightly on the arm. 'And hers.'

'Yes, and hers. Goodnight, Tante Clara. Next time I'll come earlier. We'll play cards. And I'll fix that water heater.'

'That'll be nice, Harry.'

She watched him leave the room, such a helpful young man, a credit to his country.

The next day Harry and Rola took the train south, from the Gare d'Austerlitz. Harry secured them a compartment and did all the talking. His French may not have been perfect, but it was better than Rola's. The Pole fell asleep, but Harry forced himself to stay awake, despite the soporific rocking of the slow-moving carriages. They had cases, and in the cases were things he wouldn't want SNCF inspectors or the Field Police or anyone else to see.

They disembarked at Saint-Martin-le-Beau, had a late lunch of slivers of meat, and Harry walked them through the town down to the Cher riverbank, the glistening water criss-crossed by dog-fighting dragonflies. Normally he turned back here, entrusting the last part through the ZNO, the non-occupied zone, to Lepers or one of his other helpers.

Once across the river, they would have a coffee at the little café, then walk on until they could find somewhere to spend the night, before catching a train to Marseilles. He explained all this to Rola who grimaced at the thought of more walking. 'I would have taken more care about choosing my shoes,' he complained. 'The Frenchman who had these was a midget.'

'They'll sort you out in Marseilles. The Seamen's Mission always has a supply of clothes. I reckon two more trains and . . .' He hesitated and lopped twenty-four hours off. 'A day on foot and we'll be home and dry. Then we get you a guide, across to Barcelona, Gibraltar, back in Blighty within the month. One more Pilot Officer returns to fight another day.'

'Sergeant.'

Harry stopped and grabbed Rola's arm. 'What?'

'Sergeant. I'm a Flight Sergeant.'

Harry squeezed it to make sure he had Rola's full attention. Behind the Pole, the river glistened in the late afternoon sun and a cruising swan gave them a quizzical glance. Part of him wanted to lie down and chew a reed and close his eyes. Instead he said with slow deliberation: 'Don't ever say that again. Pilot Officer. Understood? Pilot Officer?'

'Why? What's the problem?'

'The guides who take you over the Pyrenees get forty pounds for every officer. NCOs and enlisted men – it's twenty.'

'You can't be serious.'

'Absolutely.'

'That's unbelievable. But one pilot is much like . . .'

'I know, I know. Orders from London. Officers are worth twice as much as everybody else. Therefore if a guide has a group of enlisted men and it looks like trouble ahead . . . well, they'll leave you to the mountain. Or Miranda.'

Miranda was the hellish concentration camp where would-be escapers unfortunate enough to be caught by border guards or army patrols were sent to languish. The consulate at Barcelona had the devil's own job getting them out, so he'd heard. 'So what are you?'

'Pilot Officer Rola. Free Polish Air Force.'

'Good.'

As they carried on walking along the bank he heard Rola mutter: 'Fastest damn promotion I ever got.' He could tell that the Pole had a lot to learn about why the RAF might deem one pilot worth twice another, depending on which Mess they ate in.

By now, they were both tired and hot. The sun may have been falling but it seemed to be getting fiercer as it did so, and Harry opened his case and they both took a drink of water before crossing the river. The heat hadn't done their supply of chocolate any good, he noticed, glad he had rewrapped his in greaseproof paper at Gérard's.

The rowing boat the ratline used was tied to a small jetty. They clambered aboard, Harry took the oars and started to pull. 'You'll like this café,' he said to Rola. 'It was always a rendezvous for cyclists and walkers using the riverbank. Not being on a road, you don't get any Germans, except maybe at weekends when they bring their French floozies . . .'

'What day is it?' asked Rola.

'Thursday.'

'They've come early, then.'

'Who have?'

'The Germans.'

Harry risked a glance over his shoulder. On the dilapidated wooden jetty on the south side, a mirror image of its companion on the opposite bank, stood a German officer and his sergeant.

'Bollocks,' said Cole. 'Are they armed?'

'Pistols,' replied Rola.

Every half-hearted pull brought them closer, and he skimmed rather than dug the blades to slow their progress, but he knew there was nothing for it. Trying to escape in a row boat didn't bear thinking about. 'Do not say a word. Not a word, OK?'

Harry felt his neck burn under the gaze of the soldiers as he pulled slow and steady, edging towards the inevitable confrontation. The boat swung in the eddies near the bank and the German sergeant reached down and grabbed the bow, yanking them to a halt. Harry muttered his thanks and stepped out.

Rola handed up the cases and followed, perspiring heavily. The officer held out his hand in a mime of the classic demand to see some identification. They both handed over their documents and the two Germans peered at the identity cards, permits and ration books.

'Where are you going?' the sergeant asked.

'We have an appointment to see a doctor. My friend here—'

'I asked him,' the sergeant snapped.

Rola grinned inanely and shrugged.

'He's simple,' said Harry, pointing at his own forehead and making a twirling motion with his forefinger. 'That's why we need to see a doctor. He's getting worse.'

'You can go,' said the officer, handing back the papers. Harry grabbed the pile and stuffed them into his jacket pocket, not waiting to be told twice.

'No,' said the sergeant, pointing at the pilot. 'I want to hear him speak.'

Rola had managed to work up enough saliva to execute a convincing dribble down his chin, but still the sergeant persisted. 'What's in his case?'

'You don't want to look in there,' said Harry.

'Open it.'

The officer had lost interest and was admiring a flotilla of ducks making their way downstream.

Rola slowly opened the case and Harry quickly pointed at the sticky brown mess and exclaimed, 'Look. He has shat in his own case. I told you he was simple.'

Rola gurgled an embarrassed who-me? laugh and the officer grabbed his horrified sergeant. 'Enough of this. We have a ten-minute walk to the road.' The sergeant offered no resistance as he was pulled away, his face contorted in distaste at the sight of excrement in the case.

Harry waited until the Germans had passed the café and were walking across a field before he said quietly, 'I told you the chocolate would come in handy.'

As the train finally entered Marseilles and approached the centre, Harry could smell the Old Port, feel its pull. What he had heard of it suggested prime Cole territory, full of cobbled streets, seedy bars, flophouses, whorehouses – a Free State of sordidness, fuelled by drink, drugs, greed and sex. Harry Cole could be happy here, he thought, there'd be an angle or two to play. People wanting a boat to Africa, a guide across the mountains, new passports, cards testifying to non-Jewish origin, travel permits to the Occupied Zone, passage to Lisbon or Gibraltar and then England. It was a bazaar, and Harry Cole liked bazaars, particularly when it was human vices, foibles and bodies for sale or rent.

But he wasn't Harry Cole, he reminded himself as they walked through the streets. He was Harry Mason, soon to be His Majesty's secret agent, and he had a package to deliver.

The Seamen's Mission stood on a corner, looking as grim and unwelcoming as its name suggested, a place of last resort. Harry made Rola stand in a doorway opposite for ten minutes, smoking a last cigarette together. The mission was well known enough to be an open secret, and Harry wanted to make sure there was no obvious police stake out. As he sucked the last lungful of tobacco he said, 'Off you go.'

'You're not coming in?'

'No, I'm like Moses. I don't get to see the promised land. Hot baths, billiards, company. All yours.'

'What are you going to do?'

'I have an appointment,' Harry said cryptically.

Rola held out his hand. 'Thank you, Harry.'

Harry thought of the dead stooge in a hot, stinking hotel room and said: 'No, thank you. Give my regards to London.'

'Will do.'

'Oh,' said Harry, as if it was an afterthought. 'I might as well take your fund.'

'My what?'

'The escape fund. The francs you were issued with as part of your escape kit. You won't need them now, Caskie will give you money for the next stage, and we can certainly use your cash up north. In a good cause.'

Rola hesitated and waited for Harry to crack a smile, to let him know he was joking. When he didn't he shook his head and laughed himself. 'Harry—'

'You can't spend them in London.'

Rola reached inside his coat and extracted a small fold of notes and tossed them over. 'Have a drink on me, Harry.'

Rola turned away and had taken just two steps when Harry hissed after him, 'Good luck, Pilot Officer.'

Rola raised a hand to show he'd remembered his new rank, crossed the street, knocked on the door and was let in. Harry had an impression of a strong, no-nonsense face framed in the door crack, the eyes quickly taking him in before the opening disappeared. So that was Caskie, that was what a really brave man looked like.

Harry felt the usual deflation after a delivery. Once you handed them over to the next stage, like a runner's baton, it was a terrible anti-climax, a feeling of bereavement almost, coupled with fresh fears for your former charge. They had a lot of other obstacles to get through, and there was nothing you could do to help them. All that was left was to retrace your steps and start again.

He shook his head to throw off his melancholy, made sure he remembered the address of the apartment that King had given him and started off through the alleys. He hesitated before a grimy-windowed bar, the interior thick with smoke and laughter, generating a freewheeling gaiety he hadn't experienced for many a month. He lit another cigarette and ducked inside. One drink before the rendezvous. He fondled the money he'd taken from Rola. One drink on London. Surely he'd earned that. Where was the harm?

Pieter Wolkers took a cigar, sniffed it, inhaling the deep aroma of fine tobacco, and placed it back in the humidor. He wished he smoked them, he really did, especially after Diels sent over a box after his successful penetration of an escape line operating in the Dunkirk area.

He was sitting at his desk in the drawing room of his house in the northern suburbs of Lille, on the edge of the band of coalfields that were causing such problems. He already thought of it as his house, this twelve-bedroom confection with its massive grounds. Of the original owner there was no sign. So, to all intents and purposes, it was his.

He looked at the woman in front of him and felt a flash of contempt. She was scribbling as if her life depended on it. Names, addresses, rumours, unsubstantiated gossip, page after page, pouring out first her heart and then her bile: *Madame Lascelle hides Allied pilots. Worse, she fucks them. And her poor husband away doing good work for the Reich. Marcel Loubet. Black marketeer. Always has petrol, food, chocolate, cigarettes. A disgrace.* And so on, and so on.

The trouble was, Wolkers was compelled to act on the information. If these busybodies just kept quiet, he could leave the lesser offenders alone. Now, though, once the report was written and signed and witnessed and filed, he must go after the horny Madame Lascelle, pass on the names of black marketeers to one of the economic enforcement bureaux springing up across the Forbidden Zone. It did not endear him to this nation at all.

The woman paused. 'Is that all, Madame?'

She chewed her pencil for a second and bent forward once more, the pencil squeaking as it flew over the paper. 'Not quite.'

Wolkers stood and paced, noting the carpet had become dirty over the past few weeks from the constant tramp of boots and shoes. The staff had left with the owner. He must hire some more. Servants and cleaners were cheap these days. Even those who found working with a Brandenburger distasteful had to eat.

Wolkers's father had been German, so he felt a kinship with the Reich, even though he hated seeing the Netherlands, his mother's country, over-run. His choice to work for the Germans had been practical, though. He had no great ideological battle to wage, not like some of the civilians helping the Abwehr and SD. He, too, had to eat and get on in this world, and he had to face it, the world belonged to Germany now. Was there much difference between cleaning the house of a German and working for them in other ways? No. Not at all.

The woman stopped again. 'There is one thing . . . an Englishman . . . organising the escapees.'

Wolkers suddenly stopped pacing. Diels liked English escape organisers. One would be worth a lot more than a box of cigars. 'Where?'

'I don't know exactly. I have just heard there is one in this area.'

'Well, I think I could have told you that, Madame.'

'I have a name.'

Well, that might be something. Wolkers took out the pile of occupation Reichsmarks and stripped out a bundle without counting. 'I know you are doing this out of patriotic duty, but some expenses are in order—'

She pursed her lips, creating a thousand tiny furrows. 'I would prefer francs.'

'And I would prefer more information.'

'Mason, they say.'

'Is that a first or last name?'

'I don't know.'

'Well, it's unlikely to be his real one.' It was an overheard snippet, he was fairly sure, with no more depths to explore. 'Is that it?'

She nodded.

'OK, get out.' He pointed at her depositions. 'I will have these typed up. Anything leads to an arrest, we'll let you know.'

The woman got up and crossed to the large double doors, fiddled with the locks for a second, flustered in her haste to be gone from the scene of her connivance with the enemy.

Mason. Not much. But, as he knew only too well, a name could be a hammer to beat the enemy or a key to unlock further information. He just had to use it well.

Fourteen

Marseilles, Summer 1941

It was only when he walked into the swanky apartment that Harry realised just how filthy he was. Not so grubby as to stand out from the crowds who flocked to railway stations and walked the countryside these days – that would be almost impossible – but among the gilt mirrors and fleur-de-lys wallpapers and silk and brocaded chairs and polished tables, he could smell the days of travel rising off him.

His hosts, a Belgian and a Scot, were sitting in two of the more padded armchairs, while he paced the rug, going over the story of his trip into the Unoccupied Zone, careful to highlight the dangers and his resourcefulness, although he kept losing the thread. He was beginning to think the drink or two in that bar had been a bad idea.

'Just missed a sweep by a cunt hair,' he said. 'But luckily we saw them and hid under a freight truck. When they'd gone we crossed the lines and got on the train. Walked the last five miles.' He sniffed his armpit. 'Sorry, must be a bit high.'

The man on the left, the Belgian, raised an eyebrow at his turn of phrase. His companion nodded and said: 'We'll let you get cleaned up soon enough. Sure Lucy won't begrudge you some soap.'

'Lucy?'

'Owns this place,' said the Scot. 'Married to a local. He's got business in Spain, which can be very handy. You'll like her—'

The Belgian coughed to interrupt him. Too much information, he seemed to be saying. Harry was aware that these people were no fools. Being deeply sceptical was going to keep them out of the hands of the Vichy police, and he had no problem with them refusing to give their names or responsibilities.

For the next half hour, they fired more questions at him about his route and its security and he answered those he felt able to, without giving exact locales and addresses, showing that he, too, knew all about discretion. The Belgian grew frustrated, but the Scot was more understanding. Meanwhile Harry had his eye on the whisky bottle sitting on the mantelpiece, framed by two cut-glass tumblers, clearly lovingly polished each day and just waiting to be filled with the rich, peaty liquor—

'I said, would you mind waiting next door?' It was the Scot, breaking into his day dream. 'We have a few things we'd like to discuss in private.'

Harry nodded and headed off for the bathroom where he ran a long, hot soak, liberally sprinkling in the mysterious Lucy's bath salts and sliding into the water. He watched with satisfaction as a layer of scum floated off him and disappeared into the froth. He ducked under the water, holding his breath while the dirt dissolved from his hair, surfacing in time to hear a heated argument from next door. It was hard to know who was for or against him. Or, indeed, if it was him they were discussing.

Harry ran some more hot until the water was lapping over the edge onto a floor so highly polished the drips pooled like mercury. He hopped out, wrapped one of the big fluffy towels around himself and got busy at the sink with Lucy's husband's razor, scraping away at the bristles, but leaving himself the beginnings of a moustache, his first since his Wing Commander Gilbert days. A change of look never did any harm.

He stopped as he heard a third voice, another male, from the adjoining room and laughter this time. He rinsed off, pulled on a robe and went to the door, pressing his ear against it.

'—uniform was fine until we got under the bloody arc lights – began to glow bright green. So near . . . I had the . . . bicycle in my hands . . . surrounded me. Wasn't just the uni . . . unGerman bearing they said. Put my damn hands in my pockets. Very Brit . . . Two weeks in solitary for that one.'

There was a pause and then the voice became indistinct and then started up again. 'Ballet Nonsense the show was called.' He began to sing a particularly awful song, like something from a pantomime. 'Pat Reid was the lead ballerina . . . and very fetching he was too' – laughter from the Scot – 'I was the bloody headmaster.' More guffaws masking the next sentence. 'Curtain came down and we were off. Bloody Lutyens made me walk like a Jerry for weeks on end, but it paid off. Proper officer bearing this time. And his German, absolutely perfect – he even made an NCO salute him. Two days later, Switzerland.'

Harry, by now sure of the voice, replaced the towel with a robe and strode into the drawing room, startling Anthony Neave, who almost dropped his pipe to the floor. 'Bloody hell. I . . .' Neave looked at the Belgian. 'But I know this man. Helped me at Calais.'

Harry held out his hand. 'Neave. Sorry you didn't make it from the burial detail at Calais.'

Neave shook his head. 'Not your fault. Good effort.'

'He did make it out of a place called Colditz. Our first home run,' said the Scot proudly. 'All we have to do is get him to Gib, then Lisbon and home.'

'Top hole,' said Harry and before they could stop him he took three paces to the whisky, unscrewed the cap, and poured two big slugs. 'You deserve a drink, old man. Bit of a toast.'

'I don't think you ought—' began the Scot.

'What the fucking hell are you doing?'

Harry froze with one glass halfway to his lips and another halfway to Neave. Each man in the room stood still, the woman's American accent having sliced through the air like a blade. She pointed a long, red-tipped finger: 'Pat. I let you use the apartment and you turn it into some faggot's bordello.'

Harry looked down at himself, wrapped in her robe, drink in hand. The woman was about thirty, tall, blonde, with a husky smoker's voice and languid eyes that, under other circumstances, might have stirred an interest in Harry. As it was, the scowl on her face pretty much negated that. Under one arm was a small bundle of fur he guessed was a dog.

'Is that my whisky, fella? Is that my fucking whisky?'

She came across at a fair lick, despite the tight skirt of her suit, grabbed one of the glasses and tossed the drink into Harry's face. He gasped as the scotch stung his eyes.

'I say—' began Neave.

'I was saving that for Liberation Day. You knew that, Ian.' The Scot looked down at the carpet, as if studying the thread count. Lucy gave a huge sigh and poked Harry in the chest. 'Get out of my robe and out of my place.'

Harry raised both hands in surrender, hoping she wouldn't notice one of them still held a glass, but, after placing the dog on the floor, she took that, too, and sloppily poured it back into the bottle.

The Belgian got up and said, 'Lucy, I'm really sorry.' He glowered at Harry as he spoke.

'Later, Pat,' Lucy said curtly. 'Has the bastard left me any hot water?' She turned to Harry. 'And get out of the robe.'

Harry went into the bathroom and reluctantly changed back into the same clothes he'd arrived in. He'd find a room and get a new suit for this evening, then discover what delights the Old Port had to offer. He was pretty sure that Neave's approval would mean the Belgian would agree to fund him, despite the misunderstanding over the whisky.

As he shuffled out of the door, Harry hesitated in front of Lucy and tried to offer an apology, but there was a yelp as he managed to pin some indefinable part of the dog to the floor with his boot. Lucy scooped up the furball and cuddled it, nodding at the door.

Down on the street, the shadows were lengthening as the afternoon wore on. The other three men were about to go their separate ways, but the residual taste and smell of whisky made Harry want a drink even more. He suggested Neave tell him all about his Colditz adventures in a bar across the street and they took their leave of the Scot and the Belgian. As he shook his hand, the Scot said sadly: 'Bit of a poor show in there. You know, Mason, I wouldn't make an enemy of Lucy Hodge if I could help it.'

Harry raised his arm as if waving the thought away, but carefully filed it for further consideration.

Neave walked across to the table in the corner of the bar and placed the beer in front of Harry. He picked up where he had left off a few minutes previously. 'You know, Mason, he's a sad creature, the prisoner of war. Stuck in limbo, facing an indeterminate sentence, left to feel terribly guilty. Guilty that he got caught, guilty he didn't try to escape, guilty he is alive and his fellow men dead. It's a tragedy with no crime to expiate, except personal folly. It gnaws away at you, day after endless day. You see the bitterness getting to them, clouding the soul as month drags into month. Strong men, not the ones you expect to go under. Brooding, brooding, brooding. And the atmosphere . . . I wished I was an NCO, I really did. They seemed to cope better than the officers. Something about the camp brings out the worst in the public schoolboy. And you had to know your place . . . otherwise, God help you. Saw men ostracised for stepping out of line. I tried to write for the prison magazine, but they told me I was too flippant and simply not talented enough. Couple of them had worked on university rags, thought they were bloody Beaverbrook. After that, what else was there to do but dream of escape? It was the only way to take on Despair and Boredom, the twin terrors of the POW. And I tell you, Harry, your fellow inmates will eventually drive you to make an attempt, no matter how futile.' Neave paused to take a large gulp of his beer. 'You see, every one of their mannerisms, every little tic becomes a giant irritation, an itch you want to scratch by punching the poor fellow as hard as you can. The one who hums all day long, oblivious to it, the scrounger who only appears when you rustle your Red Cross parcel, the over-competitive table tennis player, the preener, combing his hair all day long, the miserable cuss or even worse, believe it or not, the relentlessly cheery chap who is always telling you to look on the bright side when you really want to throttle the bugger . . . Ready for another?'

Harry nodded, feeling as if he was serving a prison sentence himself, wondering at what point the free drinks would no longer compensate for another dull tale from Colditz.

'It sounds pretty miserable. But, look, how exactly did you escape?'

'How do you mean?' asked Neave, as if it were a foolish question.

'What were the mechanics? The technique?'

'Technique? There's no . . . Well, there was the uniform. That was pretty crucial.'

'Is that all it is? Having the right uniform?'

Neave puzzled for a moment or two. 'There are a few pointers, I suppose. I think, first, never give up. Always keep your eyes open for an opportunity. Second, once you've made your play, it's a question of attitude. Cockiness, I think it is. That I-belong-here swagger.'

Harry almost smiled. It sounded like his manifesto. Copying the posh swagger of the privileged always worked wonders for him. 'Third?'

'Third? Have a prop. It might be a person, a pile of wood, a document. If you have something about you, you look as if you have a purpose in life and are less likely to be challenged. And fourth . . . a lot of good luck.'

'You should write it down.'

'What?'

'A guide to escaping. Imagine if every pilot, every gunner had a blueprint for escape.'

'There you go again,' said Neave, clicking for a refill. 'Thinking like a spy.' But he suddenly went very quiet.

Harry raised his glass, feeling the first stirrings of drunken camaraderie, and said, 'You're a brave man, Lieutenant Neave.'

'Me? No, I think you are the brave one, Harry.'

'How do you mean?' asked Harry, taken aback.

'I have come through France once, and that was bad enough. You do it almost daily, moving people around, getting them on trains, feeding, clothing them. All these things that could get you shot. I'd say that was bravery.'

It was Harry's turn to fall quiet. He'd never before thought of himself as brave.

'Come on,' said Neave, tossing back his drink and slapping his new friend on the back. 'One more for the road.'

Lucy Hodge threw an arm across the bed and felt only a cold sheet where her husband should have been. For one second she thought perhaps Henri had risen to fetch a glass of water, but her sleep-fuddled brain remembered that the chill was long-term, the bed empty for too many weeks now.

She let herself think for a second of what it would be like back in New York at that moment, to be in a city where conversations concerned something other than war, routes across the mountains, boats to Algeria, where gossip was about illicit trysts, consummated flirtations, secret abortions, hidden mistresses, not betrayals, forged travel passes and the amount of Jewish blood flowing through your veins.

She opened one eye to try to focus on the clock in the dark and was astonished to see it clearly and, even more bizarrely, the wooden case casting a flickering shadow on the wall. She rolled over, instinctively pulling the sheets to her throat, feeling vulnerable, wishing she had worn a nightdress for once.

On the floor was a low, fat candle, its yellow flame waving in the breeze from the doors leading to the small ornate balcony, doors that she was certain she had bolted, but which were now open enough to billow the curtains.

The gun was in the drawer right next to her, a small Italian automatic, that felt feeble and ineffective in her hand. Strange, it had frightened her before. Now she wished she had something three times the size, something that might stop an intruder in his tracks. She slid out of bed and crossed to the closet, quickly wrapping a robe around her, pulling the cord tight so there was no chance of it falling open, swapping the pistol from hand to hand as she did so, noticing the crimson petals strewn across her carpet to the door.

Henri?

Possibly. It was conceivable that a few weeks' absence had turned him into some incurable romantic and he was out there at the table with flowers and champagne, but she doubted it.

Lucy stepped out into the corridor, and gasped at the thick river of petals, apparently carelessly tossed across the polished floor, but forming a pathway to the entrance of the apartment.

She stopped, feeling ludicrously melodramatic as she pointed the gun held, as she had seen in the movies, at waist height, describing an arc of a few degrees, left to right and back again. She listened carefully, hearing only the everyday creakings of an old building.

There was nobody in the apartment, she was sure of that. She would sense it, the displacement of the air, the breathing and the companion beat of a second human heart. All she could hear was the soft snoring of Liberty – confirming her status as the worst guard dog in the world – in her basket in the kitchen.

She stepped quickly alongside the flowers, the red triangles fluttering lazily in the draught of her passing, and pulled open the door to the common hallway. She pushed on the timer light. More petals, a softer pink this time, snaked across the marble floor, stopping at the foot of the stairs and hopping up, one small heap per step, and disappearing as the flight turned, the shifting yellow blush on the stairwell walls suggesting another candle. She pocketed the gun in the robe, but kept her hand round the butt, and, aware of the slap of her bare feet on the cool marble, followed the fluttering trail, up the stairs to the next landing where, finally, there stood a large wooden box, topped by two pewter candlesticks and an extravagant vase of flowers, petals intact. She stepped up to it and suppressed a grin. A case of whisky.

She reached down and took the note and saw the address, a bar in the Old Port, and the time, and screwed it up into a ball, tossing it over the banister. Bracing herself, she lifted the case and struggled back to her flat, kicking the flower trail as she went, still alternately smiling and smarting. As if he could get round her that easily.

Fifteen

The bar entrance was a scruffy doorway with a hastily hand-written sign, suggesting it had a new name and new owners – or at least new front people – on a regular basis. It was a couple of blocks, as she still called them, from the port itself. Inside, it opened up from a tiny entrance lobby to a vast space, still smelling sweetly from its days as a spice warehouse, overlaid with more than a hint of hashish in the air.

Lucy stepped in and felt eyes rake her. She had dressed down for the occasion, plain and well covered. Half the women in here would be whores she knew, and a large proportion of the rest on the verge of joining the business, as they realised that in this city, at this time, women's options were severely curtailed when it came to negotiable goods.

Why had she come? a voice asked her. Not because one side of her bed was cold and clammy in the night, that was for sure. She felt nothing like that for this man. Because of another voice, the one she had answered since she could remember: go on, I dare you.

She hadn't been in this particular dive before, but a dozen like it, and she felt confident enough to return the stares and flash a smile where appropriate. Straight ahead was a long zinc bar, to the left tables and chairs, beyond that a stage and a dancefloor. Musicians were milling around, blowing tentatively, plucking at strings, ready to start. She couldn't see Harry.

The clientele was mixed, the dress code running from grubby jellabas to tweed and wingtips. However, a strange inversion had occurred: the scum of the docks, the type who ran raggedy-arsed boats in all weathers, or knew those who did, moving tobacco or drugs or drink or people as the market demanded, they were the elite, the kings of this particular castle now, and the cultured, well-presented middle classes, they were at the mercy of the habitués of these dives.

Lucy shucked her coat at one of the tables and draped it over the back of a chair. She sat, lit a cigarette, ordered a whisky and soda, hoping they had the real thing and not the medicinal spirit they sometimes stuck you with, and watched the ebb and flow of customers, the small furtive groups constantly coalescing and breaking apart, as deals were done and undone.

The musicians began to tune up as a group, the dissonant sound causing most of the clients to flick a glance at the low stage. As the ripple spread, she spotted Harry, previously hidden from her by a cluster of over-painted women in tight dresses, talking animatedly in the ear of a tall, swarthy man who had to bend to catch the words. Cheb. Cheb ran boats across to Algeria, or had until he'd been shut down two weeks before. Rumour was there were other access points on the coast for his ramshackle fleet, such as Canet Plage, and she knew Guérisse, the Belgian who went by the name of Pat O'Leary, for one, was anxious to find out what he was up to. He might not approve of this crew, but any alternative route out of France was more than welcome.

She screwed another cigarette into her ebony mouthpiece and waited for Harry to look over. She had smoked half before his eyes casually flicked around the room and alighted on her and she could almost see the pupils dilate with pleasure. Harry spat a sentence in Cheb's ear and came across, lifting a bottle of Algerian wine from the bar as he went. He sat down opposite her, signalled for a couple of glasses and said, 'You got my message then?'

'It's not as good as the stuff you opened,' she said disdainfully.

Harry laughed, and said with exasperation, 'There's a dozen bottles.'

'Quality, not quantity. That's my motto.'

'Or both if you can get it.'

She gulped back the last of the whisky. 'Now that's a rare thing.'

He opened his mouth to speak, but at that moment the music began, a strange concoction of guitar, flute, accordion and a hand-played drum. It was a throbbing, simple beat, two chords, hammered over and over, the guitarist playing so hard his fingers ought to have been bleeding. There was a smattering of applause as the singer took her place, all diaphanous robes and kohl eyes, a caricature of Arab exoticism. There was nothing phoney about the voice though; it came out deep and throaty and heartfelt, its smoky tones stilling the conversation for a second, although Harry, like most people, had no idea what she was singing about.

'What the hell is this?' he asked Lucy.

Against her better judgement, she helped herself to some of the rough red wine.

'You know the story of the Blackbird?'

Harry shrugged. He had a feeling he was about to find out.

Lucy cleared her throat for the well-rehearsed tale. 'It begins in Baghdad when a freed slave, Zyriab, sang so beautifully he incurred the jealous wrath of the court musicians. He had to run for his life and he ended up in Cordoba, where he created the *nuba*, the basis of classical Andalucian music—'

The singer switched to French and, to Harry's surprise, there were a few boos, quickly silenced.

'Rebel songs,' explained Lucy. 'She sings for a free Algeria. Anyway, Zyriab was known as the Blackbird, and after the expulsion of the Arabs from Andalucia, the music he created ended up in North Africa. Now it's come back up to France, but to Marseilles, where it has got mixed with the music of the Camargue gypsies. Only here, in the Old Port, does it sound like this.'

He listened for a moment once more, but it was too atonal for his taste. 'I suppose that's something to be thankful for,' he sniffed. 'How do you know all that stuff?'

'I'm an amateur anthropologist.'

'Like Houdini?'

She gave him an indulgent smile. The wine was scouring her throat, but she could feel the effect starting to pulse in her temples.

There was a small scuffle at the bar that flared and died within a minute, the protagonists shaking hands, the very best of friends. Selling freedom as the prime commodity made for a very volatile market.

'How did you find Cheb?' she asked.

'Who?'

'The man you were talking to?'

'Cheb? I thought he was called Remitti.'

'That's probably just today. I mean, I guess you've been in town, what? A day? Two at most? Most people take a week to even hear of places like this, two to find Cheb.'

Harry took one of her cigarettes and lit it. 'Most people don't ask the right question.'

'Which is?'

'Where are the bad boys? Works every time. You carry on asking and people keep telling you until sooner or later someone says: "We are the bad boys. What do you want?" '

She laughed at this. In a town full of double dealing and subterfuge it was refreshing to hear such a straightforward approach. She stubbed out her cigarette and looked into his eyes, noting how the green was flecked with impurities of brown and even blue. 'And are you a bad boy, Harry?'

The band moved back to a pulsing Arabic drone, a song that made him imagine and smell places he had never seen, except perhaps at the Gaumont, Mile End. Was he a bad boy? Not for a long time. Not really. But now and then, he found himself trying to remember if all breasts felt like Odile's, if sex had been better in Hong Kong or London, but they wouldn't come back, those lovers, they were locked out. He would need to create fresh memories if he really wanted to know the feel and taste of other women. But did he?

'What the bloody hell are you doing here?'

There was such anger in the voice, a tremulousness suggesting a temper on the very edge of control, that Harry spilled a glob of wine down his shirt. He looked up and the Belgian had both fists on the table and was glowering at him.

'You were meant to be out of here this morning, man. For God's sake. You have thou—' he lowered his voice – 'thousands of francs on you. In this town they'd kill everyone in the bar for that kind of money. And Lucy . . .'

He turned to look at her, letting his disappointment hang in the air, but she drew on her cigarette and blew smoke at him. 'Oh, Pat, he was only trying to make amends.'

'He can make amends . . . by getting the fuck out of here and on a train north.'

Harry realised the Belgian wasn't going to move until he did and, reluctantly, he stood up, retrieved his jacket from the bar, and made to leave. As he passed the table where the Belgian had slipped into his seat, he leant close to Lucy's ear and took a lungful of her perfume.

'A bad boy? Only when I get the chance.' Without another glance at O'Leary, he turned and pushed through into the lobby and out into the warm embrace of Marseilles.

As he settled down on the train heading north to Paris, back in the grimness of the Occupied Zone, Harry thought about Lucy. Had the evening progressed to a second bottle and maybe a dance – if you could dance to that racket – would he have run his hands over that body, pushing her, and him, towards infidelity? A definitive answer wouldn't come.

The train stopped at Blois, the compartment suddenly crowded with bodies. The dodge for crossing back into the Occupied Zone had been easy. You picked up a discarded ticket that someone arriving from Paris had dumped, then queued up and pretended to want access to the ZNO, where a French gendarme and a German official examined papers and listened to your hard-luck stories. Harry's was transparently poor – the need to visit a sick mother routine – so they sent him brusquely away with a flea in his ear and a return ticket to Paris. Perfect.

The train jerked, women squealed, luggage shifted and they were off. He glanced up at his case, but it was still on the rack, still full of the lovely tightly bound wads of francs. Enough to run the line and then some. So, a night in Paris, maybe at a decent hotel rather than Tante Clara's spare room, a meal at Gérard's place – out the front instead of lurking in the kitchen – a new suit or a shirt perhaps and then back to Lille and Odile. She'd seemed, for a few moments in Marseilles, a long way away, faded and bleached like an old photograph in the bright Riviera sunlight; now coming home, he felt an overpowering need to hold her.

Then he sensed a new emotion, one he didn't even recognise for a moment. He wasn't sure if it was a reaction to the temptations of Lucy, the danger of the trek south or the giddy thought of all that money jiggling about above his head, the promise of a more comfortable life. Whatever it was, he knew he desperately wanted to marry Odile.

Sixteen

The Savoy Hotel, London, 1942

'Persecuted.'

Claude Dansey wiped his mouth with his napkin and smiled. He had asked the man opposite him how he had felt since his return to home shores. It wasn't the answer he had expected. 'Why?'

Anthony Neave took another bite of the Savoy's excellent steak pie and chewed for a second. 'Think about it. You turn up in Geneva, having scraped across the border, and they stick you in a hotel for a few weeks while they decide what to do with you and check you out. You come back through Vichy France to Marseilles, where everyone thinks you might be a spy – Pat O'Leary sends his regards by the way.' Dansey nodded. Quite why Guérisse should have taken an Irish nom de plume, rather than, say, Swiss, to obtain a neutral passport was beyond him, but the Belgian was unpredictable at the best of times.

'The guides deliver you to Barcelona,' continued Neave, 'where the consulate treats you like a bad smell. They get you to Gib where you are told you have had the temerity to turn up on a

Saturday afternoon when the consulate is closed and you are shipped back to Glasgow, then Liverpool and finally London, where nobody believes a bloody word you say.'

Dansey laughed. On the face of it the man before him, still showing signs of a prolonged bad diet, with sunken cheeks and poor complexion, was the kind of person he despised. Eton, Oxford, called to the Bar, a life of privilege, too much education by half. Yet his resourcefulness and bravery shone through, especially in the self-deprecating accounts he had given to all those Intelligence Officers who hadn't believed a word he said – Dansey had read every report – where he was careful to praise his helpers at every stage, rather than draw himself as something out of Sapper. 'I'm sorry there's not as much meat as there used to be,' Dansey said, pointing at the pie. 'But at least the Savoy don't use sawdust.'

Neave swallowed and smiled. 'When you've eaten . . .' He stopped himself, frightened of becoming a POW bore.

'So the feeling of persecution has gone?'

'More or less. I went along Jermyn Street and bought myself two shirts, a box of cigars, new cufflinks, tea at the Fountain . . . First time I felt able to let myself go without being consumed with guilt about the other chaps. The ones still in there.'

Dansey saw his opening. 'That's what I would like to talk to you about. How d'you fancy giving them a hand? Helping get them out. Stop some of them from being nabbed in the first place?'

Neave had been waiting for almost fifty minutes for Dansey to get to the point. He knew the man's reputation. A complete shit. But this at a time when complete shits might be the best men to have around. 'How?'

'You know Jimmy Langley?'

Neave nodded. 'I know of him. From Marseilles.'

'He's been working single-handed since last year . . . oh, damn, I didn't mean that.'

'What?'

'Langley only has one arm.' They both burst out with embarrassed laughter, causing a few other customers to sniff in their direction. 'He's a good chap. He's in Room 900, in charge of escape and evasion tactics. We need someone who has actually done it recently to go in there with him – to add the practice to the theory.' And someone who was his creature, he failed to add.

'Room 900? Is it part of . . . Ba—' He dropped his voice to the merest whisper, and used the accepted shorthand for the Special Operations Executive, an organisation he'd only been told about twenty-four hours previously, 'Baker Street?'

'No, it bloody well isn't. It's in the War Office. MI9. Don't get carried away – it was a tea room up until Langley commandeered it. We aren't talking big resources. But it is our show, not Baker Street's. Your job will be to organise briefings – lectures, that sort of thing – for all the services and to keep the lines running as best you can. You, of all people, know the ropes.'

'How many staff, sir?'

'I just told you. You and Langley.' Neave opened his mouth to speak. 'It'll grow. Actually, it's three. You've also got a madman you will have to keep reined in.'

'Madman?'

'Clayton Hutton.' Dansey lowered his voice. 'Supposed to be a fucking genius. He produces escape paraphernalia – pens with compasses, shaving brushes with currency, a cigarette holder that's a telescope—'

'Are you serious?'

'Everything all right, Mr Dansey?'

They both looked up at the maître d', Neave realising that the man wasn't using Dansey's rank. 'Excellent, as usual, Menetta.'

'Some more wine?'

'You have more of this vintage?'

'For you, Mr Dansey, there is always more.' He lowered his voice, exaggerating the Italian accent, 'To follow, some ripe Stilton.'

As he swept away with a flourish, the temptation of rich, blue veins left hanging in the air, Dansey said by way of explanation: 'Most of his relatives are interned on the Isle of Man. If he keeps me sweet he somehow reckons they'll be better treated.'

'And will they?' asked Neave, regretting the question as it left his lips.

'I doubt it. Some of the Italians are getting what they deserve.' Neave had been warned that Dansey had a long list of dislikes, starting with Albanians and ending up with Zionists, calling at all stations in between. 'What were we saying?'

'I asked if you were serious about this madman.'

'About Clutty? Yes, absolutely. Challenged Houdini when he was a boy. Said he could build an escape-proof box. Houdini got out, of course. Transpired he bribed the carpenter to make all the nails short, except two, which acted as hinges so he could push one side down. Clutty was furious when he found out. Been obsessed with escapes and illusions ever since. You can have him, you're very welcome. Just try to stop him writing letters, will you? Must send a dozen a day.'

'Who to?'

'Who to? Everyone from Churchill down. Winston' – this was Dansey's way of telling him he had access to the top – 'even wondered if he was worth the trouble.'

'Is he?'

'I'll let you decide.'

Neave leaned back and took a sip of the claret while the maître d' fussed with the fresh bottle. The warm glow coursing through him wasn't so much from the alcohol as the feeling of purpose creeping back into his life. The thought of doing something – anything – for those in the Stalags and Oflags, and of keeping the RAF boys away from them in the first place, it was a sure way to expunge the last of his guilt. Mason had suggested that something along these lines be set up, some kind of blueprint for the captured, and he was a resourceful fellow. 'When do I start?'

Dansey ran his substantial nose over the quarter inch of new wine in a fresh glass, nodded and waved Menetta away before he answered.

'Tomorrow. Langley's expecting you. Well, I knew you'd say yes. Had you vetted already.'

'Good. I mean, excellent. Thank you.'

'One thing – you met Donald Darling in Gib, I believe. Well, Darling says he's a bit worried about one fellow who keeps coming down to Marseilles demanding more funds. Chap called Mason or Paul. Did you run into him?'

Neave nodded. 'Harry Mason. Yes. Bit of an odd sort . . .'

'But?'

'But he helped me at Calais. He's got quite a few people down to the coast. No, I'd say he was a good thing, overall.'

Dansey wagged his finger in agreement. Was it worth mentioning O'Leary's doubts? Probably not. 'That's what I think. I said to Darling, let him run. Let him run.' Then, almost casually, he said: 'Let Darling and O'Leary know you've given this Mason a clean slate, will you?' Neave nodded. 'Now? Pudding?'

Seventeen

France, 1942

Harry was out of breath by the time he had cycled to the brow of the hill outside St Doual, one of the highest points overlooking the marshy land on the Belgian border. It was an excellent meeting place. A thin copse of trees afforded some cover, while allowing the countryside to be scoured for approaching trouble. Right now though, there was just factory smoke and the whirling lift mechanism of the mines moving below. Mid morning, and honest folk were at work.

King was already up there, his coke-powdered car pulled over into a thicket. The ground was crunchy with frost, and both men shivered as they shook hands, King not bothering to remove his heavy leather gloves. As Harry took the flask that was offered and tipped a mouthful of cognac down his throat, he wondered if that was an insult. Shouldn't one gentleman remove his gloves when shaking hands with another? He gave the flask back. 'Thanks.'

'Thank you for coming,' King said affably enough.

'Everything all right?'

'Yes,' he lied, thinking of the communication from Dansey.

'Congratulations, by the way, M'sieur Paul.'

Harry took another hit. 'On what?'

'Your marriage.'

Harry shrugged, wondering how he knew. He had carried out the promise to himself, although it had needed a false marriage licence, an out-of-the-way church, and a new name, since Mason had been thrown out like bait across northern France, to try to flush him out. Seeing his name – even an assumed one – on Information Wanted posters in the centre of Lille had not been a pleasant experience. The reward was so tempting, he almost considered turning himself in.

The marriage itself had been simple, once he had persuaded Odile that it was the right move for both of them. Because he was a protestant, it took place in the sacristy of a small church in the northern suburbs of Paris, with just the priest, bride and groom and witnesses, Tante Clara, Gérard, Thérèse, all in their Sunday best. The wedding breakfast was prepared by Gérard, and Tante Clara treated them to a sumptuous room at the George V.

He had moved to Odile's house between Madeleine and Monveaux and, give or take his occasional excursion south, was pretty much settled in a routine, half-working for the line, half for himself. It was almost a job, or the closest he had ever had to one, gathering the evaders, getting them to Paris, sometimes to Tours, now and then all the way down to Marseilles. But he never lingered down there. Pick up the funds – or petition for more – and back. He was a married man, now, after all. Had a wife to think of and responsibilities.

'Thank you,' he finally said to King.

'She's nice. Your wife.'

'Look, can we get on with it? It's freezing.' Harry had on a thin overcoat – it didn't do to look too affluent – whereas King was swathed in a sheepskin.

'Did you hear about Hong Kong?'

'Of course. It was months ago.'

'Not the capitulation. About how the Japs did it?'

Harry shook his head, wishing he was back indoors. His ears were beginning to throb with the cold.

'Maps. They had detailed maps of all the defences, all the troop deployments. Knew where to stop and fight, knew where to go around.' Harry said nothing. 'You know how they acquired that information? Barbers. Most of the barbers in town were Japanese. Barbers and tarts. Pillow talk . . . the oldest espionage in the book.'

Suki. She only went with officers. She was of mixed blood, all right, but, he realised with a jolt, the other half wasn't English, it was Japanese. That was why she didn't look European. Because she wasn't.

She hadn't wanted the likes of Harry, not out of snobbery, but out of professional expediency. A mere lance-corporal didn't have enough information to be worth the effort. Mind you, such was his obsession at the time, there was no telling what he might have done to win her over.

'You OK?' asked King.

'So, what are you saying? Never trust a Nip barber?'

'I'm saying we want to do the same. In fact, are doing the same. We have barbers, whores, waitresses, secretaries, miners . . . all going on with everyday life, all reporting back to us in London, one way or another. All giving us vital information.'

'Hold on, hold on a sec . . . what are you saying? You told me you could get all this gen by debriefing pilots. Are you telling me I'm redundant?'

'Not completely. But most of it's shit, Harry.' King's voice was flat and weary, full of regret, as if Harry were a star pupil gone bad. 'What you are giving us is shit. Most of your pilots spent their time in a haystack staring up a cow's arse, not counting troop movements.'

Harry forgot the cold for a moment, a fury flaring up. 'Look, I did just what you said – I spend bloody hours making notes about cow's arses—'

King raised a palm to silence him. 'You heard of Edith Cavell, Harry?'

'I don't . . . the nurse? In the last war?'

'Yes. She was hiding escaped soldiers when she was caught. What most people don't know is that she inadvertently blew open a couple of intelligence operations. We are a bit worried that the same thing might happen. That if the Germans come looking for your airmen, they might find some of our people, their radios, their documents. They'll get caught in the crossfire.'

'What do you expect me to do about that?'

'Keep the lid on them, Harry. Keep your precious pilots undercover. No little shopping or drinking or whoring trips to alleviate the boredom.' Harry nodded. Such things were not unheard of. After a few weeks the evaders usually felt as if they were already in prison and needed to let off steam. 'That's how rumours start, and, sooner or later, rumours bring the Abwehr.'

'It's difficult to watch them day and night.'

'I don't care how you do it, but I want them nailed down tight till you can ship them out,' continued King. 'Nothing must be allowed that might arouse the Germans' suspicions and start house-to-house searches. That's all I ask.' That's all Dansey asked. 'Look, if you have any doubt about a house or a village being compromised, turn the pilots in.'

Harry was shocked. 'To the Germans?'

'Yes, to the Germans. They'll be well treated. Well enough, anyway.'

Harry looked at King's chapped face and tried to read

something into it, but it was blank, fathomless. King's hand shot out and Harry flinched, but he was only squeezing his shoulder, the leather gloves creaking as he did so. 'I know what you are thinking. God knows we need those airmen back home. But we need our people, yours and mine, Harry, to get on with their job as well. And they don't get shunted to an Oflag, as you well know. The security service's people get shot. So, as I say, if any of the flyers give you trouble by making a nuisance of themselves—'

'Yes, yes.'

'It's all a matter of not drawing attention to yourselves. It's like these sabotage raids.' King knew that Harry wouldn't know who the Special Operations Executive were, so he didn't bother with the acronym. 'Those jokers who blew up the synthetic oil works?' King pointed at the smudge of a smoke plume in the far distance. 'Lost a day's production and got fifty hostages shot. Three of our people gone. Is that a fair exchange?'

'I—'

'No it isn't.' Like Uncle Claude, King thought SOE and SIS were pulling in opposite directions, and he was very much on Dansey's team. 'Softly, softly, that's our watchword here, Harry. No explosions, no sabotage, just nice, quiet intelligence gathering. Look.' He reached into his overcoat and brought out a fat envelope. 'A wedding present. A bonus. Call it what you will. Buy the wife something nice.'

King punched Harry on the arm with mock bonhomie and walked off to the car, leaving Harry wondering why that light tap on the bicep was still smarting ten minutes after the spy had disappeared into the lanes of the cold, dull countryside.

The barn was around three kilometres from the home Odile now shared with Harry. Too near, really, but these great louts needed plenty of space to move around in. Put them in one of the tiny houses hereabouts and they were liable to explode.

As usual, that evening she cycled over to check everything was all right. She steeled herself for the normal complaints about the paucity of food, the stringiness of the chicken – a chicken! If only they knew how precious they had become – and the smell of the barn. Then there were those who wanted to party. Couldn't she send a few female friends along? They'd treat them right. Maybe get a gramophone, some wine . . .

She smiled to herself. Her idealism about the brave flyers had long since been eroded. They were just a bunch of young men like any others, mostly decent, some not, a few positively dangerous.

She pulled off the road, locked up the bike and gave the rapid knocking signals before she stepped into an atmosphere of sweat and smoke. Most of the evaders still wore the uniform they were shot down in, and wouldn't change until the last minute, just before it was time to move them. If they were discovered here, a uniform might make the difference between a train east to a camp and a bullet in the head. However, it certainly didn't help with personal hygiene.

Styles, the oldest of the group, and also the most polite, leapt to his feet, pushing his fringe back into place where it stayed for all of a second before flopping into his eyes once more. 'Hello, Madame. Any news?'

She shrugged. 'Harry says maybe four days. He is waiting for the other guide to come back. You will have to be split up into twos and threes, so we need all our—'

'You said that last week.' A sulky voice from the rear.

'And our man still isn't back,' she said firmly. 'It can take four days, it can take four weeks to get back through. It isn't just a case of hopping an express, you know.'

'Quite,' said Styles, shooting a glance at the moaner. 'We

wondered if you could get some more cards and perhaps some games? Chess—'

'I'll see what I can do.' From her bag she took some bread and sausage, the night's supper. 'I have some food. Not much, between twe—'

Odile stopped and looked up, scanning the barn. She didn't have to do a headcount to know they were a few bodies short. She tried to keep her voice level. 'Where are the others? It's getting dark.'

Styles cleared his throat and shifted his weight from foot to foot. 'Thing is, Maddox and Jenkins were getting a little, uh, stir crazy—'

'Driving us crazy more like.' The moaner again.

'So I sent them out for a walk.'

A walk? she wanted to screech. A fucking walk? Instead she asked calmly, 'When?'

'Lunchtime.'

Now she couldn't keep the exasperation at bay. 'Luncht—? In broad daylight? Sent them where?'

'Well, into town. Maddox speaks quite good French really—'

'Which town?'

The house was between two settlements. West was Monveaux, to the east, much nearer, was Madeleine.

'I . . . uh . . . They turned left at the gate.'

Monveaux. She threw the food down on the floor and ran outside, fumbling with the bicycle lock, stabbing herself with the key in her haste and cursing. She was aware of Styles looming behind her.

'Look, I'm sorry—'

The lock snapped open and she stood. 'It didn't occur to you they might be taken? That even now they are telling the Germans about this barn, about Paul, about Roland, about me?'

Styles's throat went dry. 'What should we do?'

'Nothing,' she said with as much sarcasm as she could muster as she pedalled off to get Harry, 'you've done enough.'

After she had cycled into Monveaux and located Maddox and Jenkins, she went in search of Harry, appalled at what she had found. Harry would know what to do, if they could get there in time.

She found her husband in the Café Football in the back streets of Madeleine, elbows on the zinc bar, laughing at a dirty joke with the proprietor, ignoring the fact that there were a trio of Germans playing *babyfoot* in the corner.

Harry looked up and smiled when he saw her. He was slightly drunk, she could tell from the lopsided grin. He went to indicate a drink for her but the flash of anger in her eyes stopped him short. He mouthed: 'What?'

'Trouble.'

She didn't need to repeat it. The word chased the clouds from his brain, sobering him up at once. He glanced in the Germans' direction, but they were intent on their game.

'You have your bike?' she asked.

He nodded, threw some coins on the bar and together they rode through the darkening streets, aware that the curfew had been moved yet again after the RAF bombing raids, and they had a mere thirty minutes to get Maddox and Jenkins out of Monveaux and to safety. As they cycled, Odile explained the situation, and Harry squeezed the handles of his bicycle so hard, it wobbled under him.

'In English?'

Odile nodded.

'Oh, fuck a duck.'

They parked up in a sidestreet next to the Monveaux Marie

and walked across the cobbled square, with its statue of Pétain – left standing by the Germans, unlike Madeleine's effigy of Foch, torn down because of his authorship of the hated 1918 Armistice – towards the café where she had spotted Maddox and Jenkins.

They strolled past the open doors arm in arm, and Harry casually glanced in. Yes, there they were, at the bar, slumped down, singing sporadically here and there, old Perrot, the nervous-looking owner, trying in vain to quieten them down. Harry also took in the uniforms of the two dozen or more German soldiers who were indulging in a hearty sing-song at the café tables.

Fifty metres past he stopped and took a deep breath. 'I think they are called Kampfgruppe Ostendorf. They are here for rest and refitting after the Eastern Front. A little light occupation duty after being slaughtered in the Demyansk Pocket.'

'How do you know this?'

He shrugged. King still regularly went through each of the regiments in the region with him so he could quiz those pilots that might have seen troop movements. 'You pick things up.'

'Does it matter who they are?'

'The Kampfgruppe Ostendorf is part of the Totenkopf regiment,' he explained. 'Our friends are singing four-part harmony with the Death's Head division of the Waffen-SS. In English.'

All Marcus Perrot wanted was a quiet life, a chance to run his bar for the locals, as he always had. It was not popular with the Germans, normally. They preferred the Golden Gate or Jerome's, where there might be women to ogle or chat up. He only had Collette, his toothless waitress, and none of the soldiers were that desperate. Tonight, however, the Occupiers had blessed him with their company, mainly because all the empty seats meant twenty of them could gather round and start their singing.

As they trooped in, he had warned the two men at the bar to leave. True, one of them spoke decent enough French, but with an accent that meant any local could tell he was English straight away. It was just possible that some of the Germans might also pick it up, especially as he was sure a couple of the new recruits, the fresh-faced kids without the hardened stares of the veterans, were Alsatians, now liable for military service since their home region had been incorporated into the Fatherland. French was their first language, or had been, until the Germans had started fining those who still used it in public. They'd spot the wayward vowels immediately.

However, it soon became clear that the English pair thought this was some kind of jape, something to tell the chaps back home, regardless of the fact that they would probably be shot if they were discovered. And him: he was sure serving drinks to airmen was a crime against the Reich. Everything else was.

The two Englishmen carried on drinking, winking to him now and then, even joining in the songs when they knew the words. All Perrot could do was keep the wine flowing in the direction of the Germans in the hope of distracting them, but the alcohol was beginning to make them maudlin. At first it had been popular songs, 'Lili Marlene', 'Liebling', 'Wenn Ich Traurig Bin', 'Hannelore', that sort of thing, but now the deeper voices of the veterans had taken over, and the unblooded recruits could only imagine what the old timers – some of them as ancient as thirty – were seeing when they sang 'Ich hatt'' einen Kameraden' or 'Alte Kameraden'. At least the Englishmen found it hard to join in the choruses on these.

Now, though, the two were getting dangerous. One of them had started humming 'We're Going to Hang Out Our Washing on The Siegfried Line', and a couple of the nearest Germans had looked over, puzzled. The pair were whispering together and sniggering and the big bruiser of a sergeant was glaring their way. It suddenly dawned on Perrot that it wasn't the fact that they might be English that had piqued his interest, but that they might be Frenchmen showing disrespect to a glorious fighting regiment and their fallen comrades.

Perrot hissed: 'I think you should leave. Now. They are beginning to notice you.'

'Fuck 'em,' said one, and they both laughed.

The sergeant was on his feet now, and had stopped singing. Some of his comrades had begun to snuffle, thinking of particular friends they had left behind, last seen crushed into the frozen mud by T-34 tracks. The big man had taken half a dozen steps towards the two at the bar when he was suddenly pushed aside, almost spinning him through a full circle. He shook his head at the impudence, until he realised it was a woman who had barged by.

'Albert, you drunken old sot,' she shouted at Maddox. 'Look at you. I suppose you'll come rolling home having pissed your pants, then think you can climb on top of me? Well think again!'

Odile snatched the glass of red wine and threw it into Maddox's startled face. The soldiers stopped singing and began to guffaw. Not all of them could understand the words that Odile was shouting, but they could certainly pick up the gist.

'You want to keep a wife, you come home right now. Right now.' She reached up and pulled him off the stool by his ear, tugging him towards the door. Maddox began to yell, which caused the soldiers to bang the table in delight. A few clapped their support for a wife at the end of her tether. Still yelling abuse and describing his habits in the most vulgar terms, Odile was almost at the door, when the German sergeant realised he had one victim left and turned towards Jenkins.

'You!' yelled Odile. 'Philippe. Yes, you. Come and help me get this oaf into bed. Now, or I'll castrate you like one of your pigs.'

Jenkins slid off the stool, collected his cap, and followed, looking down at the floor as the big veteran glowered at him, daring him to make one false move, such as catching his eye. Perrot reached under the counter and brought out a bottle of schnapps which he offered to the sergeant, with his compliments. The German grabbed it, managed something between a smile and a snarl, and wandered back to his table, the two rude Frenchmen at the bar suddenly forgotten, and began to lead his new comrades in the Division's filthy version of 'Leibe Wohl, du kleine Monika'.

Eighteen

What was the point of having a Waffen-SS Abteilung, a battalion of Germany's most blooded fighting troops, on your doorstep if you weren't going to use it? Just a show of strength was all Pieter Wolkers had in mind, a big stick to wave over villages for future reference. Diels had resisted Wolkers's plan for a week or two, and when he did finally put it to the Abteilung commander, SS-Obersturmführer Knochen, he found he was keen to let some of his men 'stretch their legs' as he put it. Wolkers had made sure Knochen understood him, that this was not a punitive action, simply 'housekeeping'.

The village of Monveaux was still sleeping when the company of 150 men under Knochen pulled up their trucks two kilometres away from the main square. Surprise was everything. It was the same principle as the lightning searches of every passenger arriving at Lille station. That had yielded thousands of kilos of contraband goods and dozens of travellers with incorrect papers. Now Wolkers would see what the search of a whole village would generate. He had picked on Monveaux because of reports of suspicious characters in cafés and bars speaking English a few weeks previously.

Roadblocks were set up to prevent anyone entering or leaving, and the Obersturmführer spread his men into a loose circle, a man every few metres, until the village was surrounded.

The noise of the cockerels and dogs was joined by three sharp blasts on a whistle and the men began to close the ring, pausing to rip open every shed and barn they came to. The circle tightened as they approached the outskirts and the soldiers bunched into four-man teams, each one taking a house in turn, pushing the occupants out, to be herded to the central square, then gutting the house, looking for contraband, radios, fugitives, anything.

Wolkers and Knochen drove into the square and waited under the statue of Pétain as bewildered locals, mostly still in their nightclothes, drifted towards them. A machine-gun post at either end acted as magnetic poles, repelling the gathering crowd towards the centre.

The first crackle of gunfire made Wolkers start.

'Relax,' said Knochen. 'They know what they are doing.'

More shots. A distant scream. 'It's a search mission,' Wolkers reminded Knochen. 'No instant reprisals.'

An older man with a livid bruise the shape of a rifle butt on his face staggered towards them, supported by his wife. They began yelling but Knochen signalled his Überscharführer to get them out of his sight. Wolkers began to feel uneasy. 'Obersturmführer—'

Knochen silenced him with a wave. He was a young man and had been in the regiment since its formation, when its main duty was to guard the KZs, concentration camps, and keep order. So he was familiar with how to deal with civilians. His doubts about reprisals had been buried a long time ago. 'I was thinking. We could transport all the men, evacuate the women. Burn the village. That would be a stronger example.'

'No,' said Wolkers feebly. 'This will be quite enough.'

The square was crowded now, the people huddling together for warmth, the children sobbing with cold and fear. The bodies parted as a young man was pushed roughly through and onto the cobbles. The exchange was fast. He had a radio, a transmitter of some sort. Wolkers had barely formulated the thought of how to use the equipment to his advantage when one of the soldiers raised his rifle and shot the boy in the chest, flinging him back towards the villagers.

'For God's sake—' Wolkers protested. 'Obersturmführer, please. This is an intelligence operation.' He knew he was wasting his breath. He was a civilian, a mere onlooker, with no authority to impose his will.

'Don't worry,' said Knochen. 'We've had plenty of practice with subduing hostile populations.'

Some of the soldiers appeared carrying ladders, a man at each end. Eight, nine, twelve of them. Twelve ladders. Why? Wolkers watched half a dozen soldiers run at the double, each carrying a coiled length of rope. He could hear his heart thumping in his chest.

'Listen, listen to me. Do you know what the population will do after this,' he spat in alarm. 'How they will react?'

Knochen grabbed his arm. 'I will tell you what they will do, Wolkers. They will do nothing. Absolutely nothing. Because after today they will know what will happen if they do.'

Wolkers watched the tightly twisted length of hemp reach skywards, and hang there in the morning light, stationary for a second, like the Indian rope trick, before it collapsed, and draped itself over the waiting arm of a lamppost.

It was then the members of the 3rd SS Division Totenkopf found the three airmen.

The early morning phone call to Harry was short. Something is happening at Monveaux. There was a panic in the woman's voice, and the line went dead before Harry could ask who it was, as if the connection had been cut.

Within five minutes he and Odile were cycling to the village where, just two weeks before, she had managed to avert disaster for Maddox and Jenkins. For all of them, in fact.

They passed the empty trucks and half-tracks first, crowded together at the edge of the field, a couple of hard-faced soldiers milling around, machine pistols slung low. Harry did a quick estimate. A hundred, perhaps more, could be seated in those vehicles. He felt his gut twitch.

'I think we should go back,' said Odile softly.

As they rounded the final bend on the approach road, they could see two six-wheeled armoured cars nose to tail across the road into Monveaux, a wall of field grey uniforms in front of them.

'Turn around,' said Odile.

'Only if we want to practise catching bullets with our arse cheeks,' said Harry. 'Just stay calm.'

They freewheeled to a halt and as the fresh-faced private approached, Harry said, 'What's going on, Grenadier?'

The young man's eyes darted about nervously. He lowered his voice. 'I would turn back if I were you.'

'No,' boomed a thick voice. An SS-Rottenführer, a corporal, swaggered over and indicated he wished to see their papers. They were handed over, given a cursory glance and flung back at them. 'What is your business?'

This was no time to be an inspector of mines or a dumb mute. 'We have a café,' said Harry. 'In town.'

There was the rattle of gunfire from this distance. A flight of birds passed overhead, and Harry thought he could detect panic in the rhythm of their wing beats. He kept his face impassive. Odile was shaking slightly, but her face, too, showed nothing.

The SS-Rottenführer stroked his chin. 'Two choices. You are welcome to go in.' The deeper thud of a heavy machine gun came up the road. 'Or you can piss off now.'

Harry and Odile reversed the bikes and began to pedal, slowly at first, then faster.

'Jesus Mary Mother of Christ,' hissed Odile. 'What are they doing?'

Harry didn't answer. They both knew what the SS were doing.

'Where are you going now?'

'The watertower at Wallous. It's the only vantage point we've got round here. Have we any binoculars?'

'At home, yes.'

'I'll pick them up. You stay there till I get back.'

'I want to come with you.'

He looked over at her. 'No you don't, Odile.'

He was right, she didn't. She didn't want him to go either.

The image through the cheap binoculars was blurred and chromatically distorted around the edges. Harry lay on his stomach on the cold metal of the water tower, pressing himself as flat as he could. If he was caught with binoculars, then there was no doubt what the Waffen-SS would do to him.

It took a few minutes before Harry pieced together what he was seeing. A German officer and a civilian at the centre of things, standing opposite the bar Odile had pulled Maddox from. On the ground, at least two dead bodies. Along one edge of the square, the bulk of the population, covered, but unharmed. The heavy machine guns he had heard were pointed at the crowd, but there was no evidence that they had been fired into it. Perhaps over their heads. It was only then that he saw the pilots, right at the periphery of his field of view, hands bound behind their backs. One of them looked as if he had been mistreated, his head lolled to one side; the others were relatively upright and alert.

Harry looked long and hard at them, scanning the faces. Not his. He had never seen them before. Another ratline, someone else in the business, God help them.

There was activity on the far side now. A tall house, with a German soldier on the balcony, pushing off the flower pots so they fell onto the pavement. Harry desperately needed a drink, his throat was dry. Two ladders were being pushed up against the balustrade from below. The man up top was wrapping something round the metal, which he let go.

Rope.

One of the soldiers on the ground took the end and, with the speed and expertise of an old salt, made a complex knot. Now, where there had once been a simple rope, there was a noose dangling.

Two ladders. Harry could see what would happen now. The executioner climbs one side, the victim the other. The noose goes around the neck. One ladder is removed from beneath the suspended victim, the feet kicking free, the fruitless struggle for breath. It wasn't hanging, it was slow strangulation.

He spat to try to get the sour taste from his mouth.

He scanned again, alighting on two figures gesticulating, the officer arguing with the tall, blond civilian. The civilian wagged a finger at the SS man and was irritably pushed away. As Harry followed his faltering steps backwards something else caught his eyes. A lamppost. The same set-up as the balcony: two ladders, a circle of rope waiting for a neck.

Again, to the left, another balcony, another thick rope, the free end quickly looped into a perfect sliding knot, ready for its customer. The whole square was sprouting lengths of cord, tumbling down like vines, swinging in the sharp morning breeze while Marshal Pétain gazed on.

They were going to hang the airmen.

Nineteen

London, 1942

Jimmy Langley kept glancing across at the newly promoted Major Anthony Neave, his co-worker in Room 900, wondering what the cause of Neave's Cheshire Cat grin was.

He and Neave were in their usual evening positions in the SIS flat near St James's, sunk into the large wing-back armchairs that faced the elaborate Adams-style fireplace, each with a tumbler of whisky in hand, the telephone placed on the occasional table between them within easy reach of either party.

They were rarely off duty these days. A ring from that white piece of Bakelite could have them scurrying back to the War Office in seconds, a telegram from Darling – Sunday as he was known to Neave's codename Saturday – or Cresswell, the diplomat in Madrid who was Monday, could mean a sleepless night while they tried to sort out one mess or another.

'OK, who is she?' asked Jimmy Langley, at last. 'Nothing else could generate an irritating smirk like that. Only a woman. You've been in a foul mood for a week, and now you look like a dog with two dicks.'

Neave stretched the grin further. 'Wouldn't you like to know?'

'Yes, that's why I bloody well asked. It was bad enough you being so damned sulky. I am not sure I can take much more of you beaming across the room at me.'

Neave sipped his drink. He still suffered from a black fog of depression descending on him, especially when he was forced to send agents across the Channel. He despised the risks he was exposing them to. Especially the women, the Little Cyclones, as he called them. It was true, though, that he had met someone who could disperse those clouds within minutes of her entering the room. He said to Langley: 'All in good time. Early days yet.'

Langley looked at his watch. 'How long does it take to get here from Hendon?'

'He's probably gone via a few pubs. I would in his shoes.'

They were awaiting the arrival of Whitney Straight, the American racing driver and pilot, who had been shot down over France. After several months of evasion, capture and escape, he had managed to make it home by boat from the south of France. A returnee was always a cause for celebration, particularly when the man had as much propaganda value as the glamorous Straight. The rigid bureaucracy of the London Cage debriefings and psychological tests at Hendon meant he had only just been released into the eager clutches of Room 900. However, it seemed the man who had crossed half of Europe to make it back to England was having trouble finding his way from north to central London.

The phone rang and, as usual, Neave got to it first. He clamped the receiver to his ear, expecting to hear Straight's polished American drawl. Instead, a voice suffused with fury barked at him, 'The name Monveaux mean anything to you?' Neave admitted it didn't. He heard Claude Dansey growl, before the man said very quietly: 'It soon will, m'lad. It soon will.' The line went dead and Neave felt that black swirl descending again.

Three days. It had been three days since Pieter Wolkers had slept properly, in a bed rather than slumped in an armchair or on a sofa, his coat pulled round him. He hadn't shaved or washed in that time. Now he was at the back of his favourite Lille café, having pushed himself deeper into the darkened recesses as the day wore on and the alcohol comforted him.

Wolkers had his back to the curtain that led to the shabby under-used kitchen out back. This was the kind of establishment where people came to drink, not eat, and his place in the shadows allowed him to watch the customers drift in and out. Occasionally someone would spot him and he would see them stiffen. They were wrong though, he wasn't here to spy on the customers. He was here to keep drinking, to try to block out what he had seen. What he had started.

After the atrocity at Monveaux, Diels had acted unsurprised when Wolkers complained about the hangings. Knochen had machine gunned some British POWs back in 1940, the Abwehr man had explained. Why didn't you tell me? Wolkers had asked. Because you have to learn about what happens when you wind up the Waffen-SS and let them go.

Six they'd hanged. Not the pilots, as he'd expected. They'd been made to watch, their heads clamped in position by a soldier on either side, yelled at and slapped if they dared to close their eyes, so they had no choice but to bear witness to each lynching in turn.

Six civilians, as an example to any village that might consider harbouring airmen and spies, Knochen had declared as he watched the victims ascend the ladders, one at a time, mostly in silent acceptance of their fate, apart from one. When the Death's Head troopers had selected a young man from the crowd, his father begged not to be separated from him. Knochen had thoughtfully hanged them from adjoining balconies.

It was then the airmen cracked, realising that the deaths would go on and on until there were no more necks left to stretch. They had promised to reveal everything, and were led away. The villagers were told to disperse, but many stood unmoving, gazing at the slowly rotating bodies.

Diels had invited Wolkers to interrogate the flyers, but he had refused. 'The trouble with you,' said Diels, 'is you think there are rules. Those soldiers have been on the Eastern Front, where you soon find out there are no rules at all. Total war, that's what the Waffen-SS believe in.' He paused. 'And so will you, eventually.'

It was time to move on, to get away from here. Ask for a transfer where nobody knew him. Paris. Paris would be good. Surely they needed a few good Brandenburgers there.

Wolkers felt the barrel press against his neck, the draught as the curtain was parted prickling the hairs on his neck. Assassin, Wolkers thought. Anyone watching that scene in the square would think he was part of it, had instigated it. He squeezed his eyes tight shut, waiting for the bullet to sever his spinal cord and exit in a cloud of bone, sinew and blood.

'How much would the Germans pay for every flyer within a hundred kilometres of here?' The voice from behind was low and muffled, and he strained to catch the words.

Wolkers opened his eyes slightly.

'How much?'

'Yes. How much? In marks. Every pilot, gunner, navigator, every safe house, every escape line.'

'And that's yours to give?'

'It is.'

'Who are you?'

'You know me as Mason. The one on those posters? Perhaps

you've heard of me as Paul. Or Cole. It doesn't matter.'

Of course, now he could hear the faint English accent. 'Why would you do that? Why give me your precious flyers?'

'Because I don't want to see what I saw the other day. No more Monveauxs. I want you to promise the airmen go to POW camps, that the French helpers will be spared execution.'

Wolkers snorted, thinking of how his protests had bounced off Knochen. 'I can't grant them immunity.'

'You can stop them being strung up like animals. You can recommend labour rather than liquidation. You can keep them away from the Waffen-SS.'

Wolkers hesitated. Could he? With a coup this size, perhaps he could. And with this feather in his cap, well, a ticket to Paris Abwehr or SD for him, and probably Diels, was guaranteed. They weren't hanging people from lampposts in Paris. Not yet.

'Yes,' he said slowly. 'Perhaps. I can do that. And in answer to your question . . . you'd be a rich man. How do you propose to do this?'

'I'll send you a messenger with the information. I'll be in touch.'

'If you are serious, Mason, I need . . . Mason?'

The gun was no longer pressing against his neck, the greasy curtain was back in place, the kitchen empty. Wolkers looked down at the drink before him and pushed it away. Clouds and silver linings, he thought. Maybe some good would come of the grotesque circus of Monveaux after all.

Twenty

'Do you believe in God?'

Odile stirred, opened her eyes and blinked. It was pitch black, except for the red tip of Harry's cigarette, wagging in the dark as he repeated the question. 'Harry, what time is it?'

'Two thirty or so.'

'I have to be on shift at seven.'

She felt him snuggle up against her, his knees behind hers. Not now, Harry, she thought.

'Do you believe in God?'

The words drifted over her with the smoke and she sucked up the fragrant tobacco. Harry always had good cigarettes. 'I used to. Turn over.'

He stayed where he was and she closed her eyes. It took her a while to realise something was wrong. It was beautifully quiet outside, the way it used to be. 'No planes.'

'Low cloud. Strange isn't it? No guns. No bombers. Nice. Sorry, I shouldn't have woken you.'

He turned over, stubbed out the cigarette, and pulled the blankets up to his neck and she lay for a second before she spoke. 'Why do you ask?'

'About what?'

She kicked him and he laughed.

'I was lying there, trying to discard all that I hate about this world. You ever do that? Just try and concentrate on the good things.'

'Like me.'

He laughed again. 'Well, possibly. In with a chance I'd say. After my mum. Anyway, suddenly I just felt this . . . this void.' It was a hole so dark, the very thought of it made his head spin. 'And I just thought . . . maybe that's all there is. Strip away what we've got now, and there is nothing.'

'Harry, what are you talking about? Are you getting religion?'

'I don't know. Just fighting some demons, I guess.'

She stroked his head, felt the beads of cooling sweat, realised he had probably had a good old-fashioned nightmare. 'I do believe in God.'

'Do you?' he asked. 'Believe that he's real? That you will see him one day?'

He heard her swallow hard. 'I think so. Don't you?'

'I don't know. It always struck me that the main difference between religious people and me is simple.'

'What?'

'They think that believing is seeing . . . I know seeing is believing. G'night.'

She lay there for another half hour, listening to him snore, trying to figure out what the hell he was trying to communicate. Odile suspected that inside her husband a continuous conflict was raging most days, as he fought to grasp exactly what it meant to serve a higher purpose than the purely venal.

Never mind God, she said to herself as she finally drifted away, could she believe in Harry Cole?

Harry became aware of his shadows just after he had left Quint, the butcher, having negotiated to supply thirty rabbits for the Wednesday after-hours opening of the shop, when rare cuts of sundry animals were sold at up to ten times the official maximum price of 20 francs per kilo.

The two raincoated men were walking parallel to him on the opposite side of the street. The moment they entered his consciousness, he swerved and looked in the window of the pawn shop. His eyes alighted on a trumpet, way over at the back. He hadn't played for years, not since the Officers' Club in Hong Kong. He puckered his lips slightly, as if he were going to blow a tentative G. He missed the touch of the mouthpiece against his lips.

In the glass, he could see the pair crossing over towards him and he doubled back the way he had come. He knew what they were. They always affected the same look – the hats pulled down low, the coats tightly buttoned and belted. The most conspicuous undercover police force in the world.

He quickened his pace, turned the corner and the Citroën was already waiting for him, doors open, its driver pointing a pistol at his stomach. He was trapped. He raised his arms and walked towards the Gestapo car.

Harry was puzzled when the men didn't take the road into Lille but headed north towards the border. The evening was thickening, the first stars flickering in the clear sky. Bombers' night. They'd be over soon, the small twin-engined Wellingtons, looking for the synthetic rubber and fuel works, the ball-bearing manufacturers, the tank turret presses, but dispersing their high explosives across the landscape like a wilful child scattering building blocks.

The driver switched on the blackout lights, and Harry asked

for a cigarette from the man next to him. He shook his head. Harry thought back to the last beating he had taken, in that cold south London warehouse, with the voice from the gloom telling him to lay off pretending to be a member of HM Intelligence Services. How would he hold out this time? About the same, he reckoned. He was no hero.

Possibly he could give Odile and the others enough time to get away. But how would they know something was wrong? Because he was late? That's Harry, they'd say. They'd give him a day, two, three. By which time he'd be telling these blokes everything they wanted to know. Maybe he could trade Odile for something else, someone else, anyone else.

The car took a familiar road, one he usually cycled, and the Citroën stopped at the brow of the hill, with its copse of trees and its rapidly fading view over the darkening fields below. The door opened, he was pushed out, and there, silhouetted against the horizon, the tip of his cigarette glowing, was King. He ground out the butt beneath his foot. Harry did a double take and said: 'Changed sides have we?'

King laughed. 'Who is brave enough to question the credentials of the Geheime Staatspolizei? Perfect cover.'

He beckoned him over. Right on cue, the drone of a bomber, high above. Over to the east, a bloom of white. Searchlights.

'Remember what this looks like in daylight, Harry?' King began to point out into the blackness. 'Coal, obviously. Mostly for the Ruhr. Precious little finds its way into French homes. Cement and concrete works. Mostly shipped to the Atlantic coast for gun emplacements. Some for the new submarine pens being built at St Nazaire. Over there, tank factory. Panzers. Here, gun barrels for eighty-eights. End up as ack-ack in France or Germany. Or knocking our tanks out if they so much as set a track in this country.'

'You've got better eyes than I have.'

'I memorised them. Every day I come up here, just to remind myself what we are up against. What sort of war this is.'

'Very touching.'

'Yes, isn't it? And you chaps are threatening it all, Harry.'

'I've done everything you asked.'

'You haven't kept a lid on them, Harry.'

'They aren't all mine.'

'I appreciate that. Even so.'

'Even so, what?' He jumped as flame spurted from a gun battery directly ahead, the deep thudding reaching their ears almost immediately afterwards. It was the eighty-eights opening up, hurling their big shells blindly into the sky. Now the search-lights, flicking back and forth, trying to trap some poor hapless plane, catch it long enough for the shells to blow the flimsy wooden framework to splinters.

'War never stands still, Harry. A year ago, when you were bringing out soldiers, sailors, pilots, we'd take all you could give us. Now . . . now we have people in deep cover down there' – his arm swept across the landscape dotted with light and fire – 'who are being harmed by your activities. You . . . well, the airmen, are fucking us up, Harry. Fucking us up.' He turned to face him. 'They were two of mine, Harry.'

'Who were?'

'Father and son. Both railway workers based at St Omer. They knew every single battalion that went through that railhead, told us where the wall was being reinforced, the quality of troops, when front-line men were replaced with the old and the infirm, with Romanians or Hungarians. They were mine, Harry. And they were worth fifty pilots to me.'

He resisted the urge to wipe away the spittle that flecked his face. 'Why are you telling me this? I told you, they weren't my flyers.'

'No, no they weren't. But guess what? Monveaux was chosen because of the rumours of a couple of Englishmen who sat at a bar under the noses of the Germans. Heard that rumour? The bar owner dined out on it for a week. And, eventually, the rumour got repeated to some V-man or Brandenburger who scuttled off to the Abwehr . . . *They* were yours, weren't they, Harry? The two jokers in the bar.' King sniffed, as if what he was about to say was of no consequence. 'I want you to blow your line.'

Harry shook his head in disbelief. 'You want me to do what?'

'Blow the line, every house down to Toulouse. I want the Mason Line dismantled. I've done the preliminary work. Borrowed your name for a little chat with one of the Brandenburgers. They're expecting you or your emissary to turn the information in.'

Harry spun on his heel and walked a few paces away, rubbing his neck. 'I . . . I don't understand . . .'

'It's simple. The Germans will think they have scored a big victory, and the pressure is off. Our people get to carry on their work in peace, without fear of lynching reprisals. The pilots just get sent to some Stalagluft in Germany.'

'And the French? The men and women in those houses and along the railways? They'll be shot or deported to Germany to die in some stinking—'

King cut him off. 'Harry. We have to try and see the bigger picture here. The greater good.'

'The greater good? You think blowing my own line is the greater good?'

King was behind him now, and placed a hand on his shoulder. 'I know this is an onerous task. London appreciates that as well. It is willing to make you an offer.'

'I don't want their money,' he found himself saying.

'Well, there will be money, Harry. My Brandenburger will pay a fortune for your line. A fortune. We'll even let you keep it.

London are offering something else, though. They are offering to expunge your file from the records. All of it. Harry Cole, con man, scam artist, forger, car thief, embezzler.' There was a pause. 'Deserter. Have I missed anything?'

Harry laughed hollowly. 'If I take your offer, you could add traitor and murderer.'

'Traitor? Oh, no, Harry. Patriot, Harry, patriot. Look, the Firm will take you onto the books. Rank equivalent to a commissioned officer, salary paid into an account in London. You'd be going legit, Cole.'

'Legit? You call selling out fifty, sixty people going legit? Jesus, I thought I was a bastard.'

He turned to face King, the man's features fitfully bleached by the distant muzzle flashes and bomb detonations. Acrid fumes were drifting across to them on the wind, the smell of high explosives. Up above the continuous low rumble of aero engines.

'Thirty years ago,' said King, 'our generals had to send men over the top, knowing they were going to walk into machine guns. That millions might die. It wasn't an easy decision to make. But someone has to do those kinds of things. And that someone is us, Cole.'

'You. That someone is you, not me.'

'Is that a no, Harry?'

Harry grabbed King's lapel with his left hand and he felt the man start, expecting a blow to follow, but Harry kept his fist down, if not his temper. 'It's a no. It's a no, it's a fuck off and don't come near any of my people.'

'Your people? Good God, Harry, I do believe you've gone soft on me. Is this the same Harry who lied and cheated his way across Hong Kong and France and London?'

He thought for a minute. 'No, I don't think it is.'

King took Harry's hand away and said, regretfully, 'Ah well, that's plan B then.'

Harry was about to ask what that would be when he heard the footfall behind him, the cosh landed on the side of his head and he crumpled into King's waiting arms.

Odile came home to the empty house, exhausted and wishing for once that Harry would be there with a cup of coffee. Instead, the fire was long dead, the house unwelcoming. She went upstairs, stripped off the nurse's uniform, and washed away the clinging smell of the ward. The still-raw memory of a flyer flashed before her – the arm that ended in a jagged knob of bone, the face crisped by flame, the sound of lungs scorched beyond use. Dead by the end of her shift.

There had been two other deaths on her ward, both old men, which shouldn't have affected her as much as the young pilot, but they did. They all did now. She touched her abdomen. Maybe it was something to do with her new condition. How would Harry take that news?

She threw water on her face, dried, slipped into a robe and padded downstairs, her wet feet leaving marks on the wooden treads. One way or another, Harry would probably confound her expectations when he found out about the child. But why should she expect Harry to be like other men? She knew what he was when she let herself fall in love with him.

When she saw the flowers she burst out laughing. The bastard did care after all. A great spray of lilies in the centre of the kitchen table, a mix of pink and white, the rich odour filling the room. She picked up the note sitting on top of a tightly wrapped parcel, opened it and began to read, her smile fading.

Twenty-one

Harry tried to raise his head, but starbursts exploded behind his eyes and he gagged twice. Near him he could hear low voices, the words difficult to make out over the whump of ack-ack shells. The earth was shaking as sticks of bombs detonated to the north. He lifted his head again.

There was a shape swinging in front of him, an oval of some kind, moving in the breeze. He blinked away the moisture in his eyes and it came into sharper focus. A noose.

'Get him up and get it done,' said King.

Hands slid under his armpits and Harry was lifted to his feet. The fake Gestapo men cursed as he slumped his weight against them.

'Do his wrists. Behind his back.'

Harry tried to struggle, but his muscles would not respond. He was unable to resist as his hands were yanked back and bound. His knees buckled again, and not just from weakness.

'You're no different from them if you do this, King.' Harry licked his lips. His voice was cracked.

'I never said we were, Harry. We all fight the war as we see fit.'

'Jesus—'

Another wall of tumbling bombs tore open the horizon and the slash of flame turned King's face crimson.

'King—' he started.

'String him up.'

The bag was forced over his head. Not here, not like this, not without Odile. He choked as the gag went round the outside of the sack, forcing the material against his nose, so he could hardly breathe.

'They'll think you betrayed your own people, Harry. And they took their revenge. It's neat, you must admit.'

Harry lurched forward, but rough hands dragged him back. 'You had your chance, Harry. Negotiations over.'

The rope slid down over his head and the thick cord slammed into his Adam's apple, slipping and burning the skin until it settled beneath his chin and forced him upwards. He was on his toes now, almost begging for the moment when the creaking rope pulled him free of the earth and it was all over.

Odile travelled to the address Harry had given her on the last tram into Lille before curfew, the parcel pressed to her body as tightly as she dared. She was so tired her head was swimming. She alighted from the tram at the outskirts of Lille, checked that there was a return in half an hour – again, it would be the last service of the night – and headed east, past the grand houses shuttered tight.

The streets darkened as twilight slipped away and she wished she'd remembered to bring a torch. There was little traffic on the roads, just the occasional cruising saloon, one of which slowed to examine her, but she turned her collar up and quickened her pace. Up above, bombers passed harmlessly over the blackened city, their target the factories on either side of the Belgian border.

What was Harry up to this time? Trust me, the note had said. That phrase always worried her.

The house she sought was one of the smaller of the mansions, but still impressive, with Dutch-style gabled roofs, spacious grounds, and the kind of forbidding gates that didn't need a sign saying No Hawkers, Salesmen or Beggars to tell strangers not to bother. She pressed the bell. She tried again, straining her ears to hear over the bombers' drone from above. A crack of light from a door and a stooped figure walked down the drive, boots crunching on the gravel. She explained, as directed by Harry's note, who she was, and the old Belgian retainer opened the gates and led her up to the house.

Pieter Wolkers tipped the last of the wine into his glass as the woman entered the brightly lit room, blinking. He watched her take in the surroundings, the beautiful plasterwork, the freshly cleaned carpet, the oil paintings – none of them first rate, but impressive enough – his leather-topped desk with the prominent humidor. She looked tired and drawn, and not a little frightened.

'Come in, sit down.'

The woman approached quickly, but did not sit. She placed a parcel down next to the humidor.

'Can I offer you something to drink? Eat, perhaps?'

'You're not French.' Her voice was firm and she was less intimidated than he had originally thought.

'Half German.' He watched surprise flick across her face. 'And half Dutch.'

'How did you choose which half to be?'

Wolkers shrugged. He was used to the question. 'Which side to back you mean? I am a betting man. Not a lot. Some cards, the horses. Enough to know how to add up the odds. Should I go with the countries that roll over and let an enemy army stream across their land in forty-eight hours? Countries whose armies do not fire a shot? Or if they do, it is their own officers they kill. Or should I go with the fastest, best-armed military force the world has ever seen? Let me see.' He tapped his fingertips together as if in contemplation.

She frowned, but not letting on it wasn't the answer she expected. She was dealing with a Brandenburger, the enemy. Now she really didn't know what Harry's game was. 'It's not all about winners and losers.'

Wolkers furrowed his brow. 'If war is not all about winners and losers, what is it about?'

'Right and wrong.'

'What makes you think the Germans are wrong?'

'Monveaux?'

Wolkers went quiet for a moment. He had spent long hours justifying that to himself. 'You want to read what Britain and France got up to in Africa. Or India. Or Algeria. Or South Africa.'

'You believe it was the same thing?'

'I believe it was worse in some cases.'

'I believe it was a long time ago.'

He shook his head at her naivety. 'I really don't care what you believe, Mam'selle.'

She realised from the sibilance of the last word that he had been drinking. The sourness of the belligerent drunk was upon him. It was dangerous to goad him further. Now she didn't care what Harry was playing at, she wanted out, quickly. 'I was told there would be a return package.'

'Indeed. If you don't mind, I just need to check I am getting my half of the bargain.'

He took his time opening the heavily taped parcel, snipping at the stubborn sections of string with a pair of nail scissors, until a thick notebook and a pre-war Michelin motoring map of France lay in front of him. He lifted a corner of the map, and grunted his satisfaction when he saw the red rings around certain villages, and dotted lines connecting them. He looked up and caught the stunned expression on her face.

From the drawer of the desk, he took a large envelope of money and tossed it in front of her. 'Deutschmarks as requested. Real ones, not Occupation, so be careful where you use them. I suspect your old life is over. I would think about moving. Tell Mason. We can help, of course, with relocation permits.' He looked at his watch. 'Now, I should arrange transport back for you, as it is after . . .'

She was still staring at the map and folder.

Slowly he said: 'You didn't know?'

A sob caught in her throat.

'You didn't know what Mason was doing, did you?'

Wolkers reached over and took a cigar from the humidor and, as usual, ran it under his nose. This was strange. The woman's surprise was not faked. She was shaking from head to foot.

There was only one way to be sure he wasn't being played for a fool here, and that was to act on the information at once. He could have Abwehr teams mobilised in the north, and gendarmes in the ZNO, before midnight. And the woman? He pressed the buzzer on the desk intercom. 'Georges? Yes, make up a room will you? Our guest will be staying over tonight. Yes, the Rose Room.' The most secure room in the house. 'I'm sorry, I will have to detain you for a few hours. Just while I check the veracity of the information. Then . . . you will be free to go. As long as there are no problems. Do you understand?'

But the woman didn't move, her body rigid with the shock of betrayal.

Harry had lost all feeling in his toes, and his calves had cramped, but his shoes kept their precarious contact with the soil while the rope sawed back and forward on his neck, chafing his skin until it was raw. The air raid had stopped, the guns were silent, and he imagined the countryside dark once more, apart from the dull residual glow of scattered fires that he could see through the loose weave of the hood. How long had he been here like this? He had dropped out of normal time; he no longer knew whether hours or minutes had passed.

His toes buckled and he felt his entire weight press against the noose, the air suddenly clamped off as his windpipe compressed. Harry desperately scrabbled for a hold.

When he regained his composure and balance, he realised that the bindings on his hands were coming loose. If he worked at it, he could get his hands free. If only his legs held out. He found himself praying to Odile's God, praying for the blood to keep pumping to his burning calves, just for a while longer, please Lord.

Twenty-two

'Listen, we'd all have a damn sight fewer problems if the bloody RAF could stay in the air where it belongs. Eh?'

Anthony Neave joined in Dansey's laughter, although with a growing unease. They were in the Colonel's Alvis, heading up the A11 towards Newmarket, making good progress on roads empty but for the odd army convoy. For the first time, Neave noticed how many American vehicles there were, both USAAF and US army, and the numbers increased as they headed north.

Neave stared out at a countryside distorted by war – every inch of free earth under crop, road signs missing, farmhouses almost swamped by sandbags, camouflage netting draped over the copses where vehicles had been hidden. He hadn't yet gleaned why Dansey had invited him for a day at the races, but the Colonel had insisted he be at the SIS flat above Overton's restaurant in St James's by nine, and to bring binoculars. He hadn't specified dress, so Neave had played safe and put on his uniform. Dansey was in a camel coat with velvet collar and a trilby. He was also in an exceedingly good mood, which, Neave knew, usually meant that, somewhere in the world, calamity was afoot.

'Married recently, I hear?'

'Sir.'

'Take some advice?' For once this was a question asked rather gently.

'Of course.'

'Tell her what you do.'

Neave was shocked. 'I can't, really, I've signed—'

'Not specifically, you fool. Just make sure she knows that your work is of a highly sensitive nature. That you're not just some desk jockey. Otherwise, all those missed dinners, late nights, weekends away without explanation, before you know it, she'll smell a mistress. Be as open as good sense allows. There. Today's sermon.'

'Yes. Thank you. I will.' Neave recalled hearing that Dansey had been married once. He wondered if he'd just been made privy to why the union didn't last. If so, that made it a very strange day indeed, because you rarely got personal insights into the murky past of Uncle Claude.

At the racecourse they parked in the members' enclosure. The crowd formed a sea of blue and khaki, interspersed with USAAF olive and brown from the nearby airbases. Neave was relieved he had opted for his uniform. Those few men of call-up age wandering around in civvies were speared with withering glances by many of the servicemen.

Newmarket was a course in reduced circumstances. Its perimeters had been sequestered as arable land, fences taken down, metal removed from the stands for recycling, and the number of meetings slashed. But at least it had avoided the fate of Epsom and Gatwick and Aintree, which had been closed for the duration. Most of the crowd had been bussed in from nearby military bases, the race meetings providing a useful pressure valve for the services.

As they watched the horseflesh in the paddock, Dansey suggested that Big Game's offspring would be worth watching and wagering on – especially as the horse had been sired by Bahram, the Aga Khan's triple Classic winner. Neave asked him how he had acquired such detailed knowledge.

'I was in the game for a while. Ran the stables for a chap called Bryan. American.'

'When was this, sir?'

'Late twenties. He wanted to win the Derby. Spent a fortune. I reckon we could have done, as well.'

'But?'

'He died. I was out of a job.'

'What did you do?'

'Went back to the only other thing I was qualified to be. A spy. Heard about Baker Street?'

Neave shook his head.

'Prosper network gone.'

Neave thought he saw a shadow of a smile cross Dansey's face, but when he looked again there was no sign. Prosper was the Special Operation Executive's spy network in the French capital, run by Francis Suttill, an enormous web of amateur spies and their helpers.

'All of it?'

'Whole of their set-up in Paris, bar a couple of strays. Disaster.' Dansey couldn't keep the satisfaction out of his voice and Neave shuddered. 'I told them, you send in clerks and teachers and dressmakers instead of professionals, you are asking for trouble.'

Dansey rolled his form sheet and banged the paddock fence decisively. 'I've seen enough. Let's find ourselves a bookmaker.' As they walked, Dansey said casually, 'By the way, Neave. You've got some bad news of your own.' He cleared his throat. 'I have a reliable report that one of your chaps has gone over.'

'Over where?'

'To the other side.'

Neave slapped down a flash of fury. Why hadn't Dansey told him before now? 'Who?'

'Mason.'

Neave's heart sank. 'Are you sure?'

'Gone renegade on us, Tony. Blew the line, turned in his wife, everything.'

'Bloody hell. When?'

'I heard this morning.'

And Dansey had dragged him to the damn' races and prattled on about bloodlines; fillies and the Aga Khan. 'I'd better issue a warning about him, and find out what damage has been done.'

'Got some of my chaps on that last point, don't worry. I knew you'd want to call this outing off, Neave. But we all need a break. Thing is, wasn't too sure about your Mason myself, nor was Guérisse, but, well . . . you vouchsafed for him as I recall.'

Neave said angrily, 'In a manner of speaking, yes, I suppose I did, sir.'

'You know, turns out he wasn't who we thought he was. Name wasn't Mason. Wasn't a captain, even.' He paused for effect. 'Sergeant who embezzled Mess funds.'

'A sergeant?' Neave felt himself redden.

'An oik, Neave, an oik. Oh, don't blame yourself. Pulled the wool over many people's eyes.' Dansey turned and smiled.

'What should we do?'

'Well, he's your problem. MI9's, that is. But if I were in your shoes . . .'

'I'd be grateful for any advice,' said Neave, his voice thick.

'I'd issue a Red Ribbon on him.'

Neave nodded. A red ribbon wrapped around a file meant just one thing. Shoot on sight. 'I'll get onto it as soon as we get back,' he said. A sergeant. An oik. He could sense how low he had tumbled in Dansey's estimation. The small amount of appetite he had for racing had evaporated entirely now, all he really wanted to do was get back, but he could tell Dansey was just hitting his stride.

'Excellent.' Claude Dansey pointed to one of the gesticulating bookies in his brown suit and bowler. 'Shall we try Phil Magas? He looks like an honest chap.'

Harry shifted his position in the darkness, fighting off the craving for a cigarette. She'd smell it as soon as she came in, and he'd lose the element of surprise. He could hear the muffled noises of the street, the loud conversations in the café opposite, the clink of glasses from the bar, a snatch of music from a club above the café, a ship's horn drifting across the harbour. These were the comforting sounds of a normal night in Marseilles. Except they no longer comforted him.

It had taken him many painful hours to get free from King's noose. By the time he had undone his hands and managed to open the noose and slip it off, he could no longer walk: the muscles in his legs had spasmed, and he crumpled.

The whole night had passed, hidden away in that copse on the hillside – had the blanket and water been left deliberately? – before he could manage to move, slowly. It was close to two days before he could get around without drawing attention to himself with his hobbling gait.

Once he could walk, he headed for his and Odile's house. There was a bunch of wilted lilies on the table, the room full of their decay. He had found the note, ostensibly written by him, and he knew what they had done, what King had done. Everyone had been betrayed.

Over the next few days he retraced the ratline routing. The

barn where the airmen had been held was still smouldering, but no sign of the occupants, other than a charred RAF tunic in the ruins. The forgery set-up in Abbeville was gone, the people disappeared along with the printing press; the safe houses en route to Paris, also gone. Lepers and the other helpers, missing. Gérard's restaurant had closed for a 'holiday' and the brothel had German guards stationed on the outside.

Tante Clara had survived, and he warned her that she should neither see nor trust anyone from the group now. Soon those who cracked in the cellars of Foch and Fresnes would be turned out onto the street to rope in others. He impressed on her that people would say he had done terrible things, and that she must not believe them.

Clara had hugged him, told him she knew he was in trouble, but that she loved him all the same. She gave him a roll of money, a gesture of solidarity that almost made him want to cry.

Harry travelled south again. The café at the river, another burnt shell. In Tours, most of the line's addresses had a saloon car parked outside, the occupants slumped down in their seats. A trail of destruction and misery and death was snaking through the country, cursing his name as it went. Who would believe him, how could he get a hearing amid the chaos of grief and loss?

Where was Odile? Had the Germans arrested her? Had she realised Harry was as much a dupe as she? Unlikely. The thought that she, too, was learning to hate him, snuffing out their love, was unbearable.

Harry heard the rattle of keys in the apartment's outer door. He stood up and unlatched the French doors behind him to give him an exit.

A rattle of cups from the kitchen, but no voices. She was alone.

The bedroom door opened and he saw her silhouetted there,

drink in one hand, purse in the other, the hall light shining through the cotton fabric of her dress.

'Don't turn on the main light.'

He had expected a scream, a protest of some kind, but she asked calmly: 'Who's that?'

'Me.'

'Speak up.'

'This is up.' His voice was a hoarse rasp.

'Can I put the bedside lamp on?'

'Yes.'

Lucy flicked on the small, yellow bulb and he saw her start. 'My God, I didn't expect you. Here. You . . . Pat O'Leary wants you dead.'

'He'll have to stand in line. I'm thinking of selling tickets.' He remembered Parkhill in Hong Kong. He'd promised him the best seats in the house.

'Why did you do it, Harry?'

'I didn't.'

'That's what they all say.'

'I'm not a traitor.'

She sat on the bed and removed her shoes, massaging her toes. 'The order is shoot to kill, you know.'

'No trial?'

'No.'

'Did anyone ask why? Why they wouldn't want to court martial me?'

'Beyond the pale, Harry. The full story came across from London. Hong Kong, cheque forgery, desertion. The lot. Plus all that money you got from here.'

'I know it looks bad.'

'You don't know shit, Harry.'

'Lucy. You asked me once if I was a bad boy. The answer is –

yes. But not that bad. My own wife? You have to believe me.'

'You want a cigarette, Harry?'

'No.'

'Mind if I have one?'

'Go ahead.'

Lucy opened the bedside cabinet and stopped. Harry took the little gun from his waistband. 'It's here, Lucy.'

She smiled faintly.

'Phone's disconnected, too. I need some money, Lucy.'

'I bet you do.'

'I can tie you up and search the flat.'

'No need. Here.'

She took a fold of notes from her purse and flung them onto the bed. Cautiously, he reached over and pocketed it.

'One more thing. Where is King?'

'Who?'

'King.' Harry gave a quick description.

'Doesn't ring any bells. Who is he?'

'The man who got me into this. O'Leary—' He fumbled for the Belgian's real name. 'Guérisse. He knows him as Rex. It was his doing . . .'

'Oh, Harry . . .' she said patronisingly. 'It's always someone else's fault, isn't it?'

He realised he was wasting precious time. 'I'm going to go out of these French doors and disappear. If you stick your head out I'll shoot it off.'

'I won't do anything stupid, Harry. You're not worth it.'

'I'm sorry you don't believe me, Lucy.'

'I knew when you drank my whisky you were no good. So long, Harry. Make the most of what time you have.' As he slid through the drapes, she raised her voice. 'Because they'll find you, Harry. Wherever you go, they'll find you.'

★ ★ ★

Harry checked into a flophouse near the port, shaved off his moustache and clippered his hair even shorter. Lucy had given him close to ten thousand francs, but after two card games, and an arrangement with two young girls and a sailor, he had quadrupled his stake. Just like old times.

However, he was aware that sometimes people looked too closely, and he was sure one man pointed him out across the bar. It was time to leave Marseilles. He couldn't use the same routing back north, though. So instead of heading north-west to Toulouse as usual, he took the train for Lyon. From there, he had a good chance of crossing the border into Switzerland, finding the British consulate in Geneva, perhaps making them believe what had happened. Or was that suicide?

Perrache, the main station for Lyon, was one of the most heavily watched in the ZNO, by French and German security services alike, so he alighted at Vienne and took a creaking charcoal-propelled bus to La Mulatière, where he boarded a trolley for the centre of Lyon.

He walked from the terminus down the Cours Lafayette towards the Rhône, enjoying the sun on his back and the clean air after hours inhaling other people's breath and sweat. He was depressed by the city. He had been through it many times, whenever he had to vary the route south, but now it was a shadow of itself. The butchers' shops showed thin wares, the *bouchons* were open for business, but the food on the plates had a meagre, synthetic look, the famous sausages filled with some kind of coarse oats or grain.

At a roadside stall, Harry stopped and stared at the oily black bodies lined up in neat rows. With a shock he realised they were crows, selling for ten francs each. Winter was coming, and it was clear it was going to be hard. Like the rest of France, stoical, hardworking Lyon had finally succumbed to the crushing hegemony of the Reich's war machine.

He crossed the river, walking as casually as he could over the bridge. He knew it'd be under observation, the crossings always were. Once over the Rhône, he veered south, heading for the enormous Place Bellecour, the focal point of the tongue of land between the two rivers, and the café on the north-west corner. He put his suitcase down, slid onto a metal stool, and ordered an Izarra, one of the few bottles remaining on the liqueur shelf that had more than a sticky centimetre left in the bottom.

A man could get lost in Lyon, he thought. Up above him were the high villages of the old town, and to the north the *traboules* of La Croix-Rousée, the old silk weavers' district, a network of tunnels, covered passages and secret doorways. The sort of people who used such clandestine passageways were his kind of people, the old Harry's kind at least. They would know how to get a man from here to Geneva, and they would know how to charge for it. He would need more than forty thousand francs. That shouldn't be a problem, though.

He scanned his fellow customers, but nobody caught his eye. There was a palpable feeling of unease. The barman wiped the counter in front of him and nodded at his cardboard case.

'Just got in?'

Harry nodded.

'Two hundred and eighty extra police came in yesterday.'

'Really?'

'Under some SS major. Looking for illegal transmitters.'

Harry smiled and shook his head. The man thought he had a radio in the case.

'If they are looking for a couple of old towels and a sponge bag, I'm their man.'

'Everybody's their man,' he said glumly and walked away to

serve another customer, who had made sure he stood as far away from Harry as possible. Lyon had never been a particularly friendly city, its inhabitants reserved, slow to warm to anyone, but it was clear that strangers were less welcome than ever. He should get off the streets.

Harry drained the liqueur, left his payment on the bar, walked back over the Rhône and checked in at the Angleterre, a hotel he had used before on his journeys south.

He took a shallow lukewarm bath while he thought about the money question. He had information that was worth a fortune to the Germans. Not around Lille, that was all shot to hell, but down in Marseilles. Caskie, Guérisse, Lucy, he could give them a dozen names and addresses.

But could he do it? After all, they were out to get him. He would just be saving his own neck. They had no compunction about condemning him to death. Self defence, almost.

He got out of the bath, dried himself, checked his neck was healing well, and dressed. He tried to shake off the image of Monveaux that kept coming back to him, the bodies slowly twirling at the end of a rope. That was why he couldn't do it now. He'd had a noose round his own neck. He couldn't do it to anyone else.

He heard the pass key in the lock and the door swung slowly open to reveal three men, two of them with guns. The one in the centre stepped forward. 'Harold Mason? Cole? Paul? Which is it?'

Harry shrugged. His papers were in none of those names. 'I'm sorry, gentlemen. My name is Joseph Deram. You are?'

'Triffe. DST.' Bloody hell, he thought, the Direction de la Surveillance du Terroire was French counter-espionage. 'I am arresting you on suspicion of being a German agent.'

'Don't be ridiculous.' Harry was stunned. Since when was

being a German agent in Vichy France a crime? 'What are you talking about?' he asked firmly.

'It is a crime to carry out espionage on French soil. Any espionage.'

Harry laughed out loud. 'Monsieur Triffe—'

'Colonel Triffe. This isn't the Occupied Zone. You people think you can come in and do as you please. This is Free France, my friend. So far in Lyon, we have arrested one hundred and eighteen of your fellow agents.'

'That's ludicrous.' Harry couldn't believe his ears. He had spent close to two years trying to avoid the hundreds of informers and V-men that infested the south. Now, finally, he meets the good guys?

'We have shot six,' added Triffe with some satisfaction.

Harry blanched and sat on the soft, saggy bed, trying to look relaxed. 'You must be mistaken.'

Triffe beckoned to someone on the landing and a familiar figure emerged from the shadows. Odile stared at him with utter loathing. Harry was halfway to his feet, trying to get some words out, when she spoke, calmly, 'That's him. That's Harry Cole. That's the traitor.'

Twenty-three

They had beaten Harry after his arrest. One eye was swollen shut, his lips had puffed up and a couple of teeth were gone. The little finger on his left hand was broken and a vertebra chipped from his being repeatedly flung to the stone floor. One of his nipples had been sawn off with a penknife. The soles of his feet were crisped with hot irons. His foreskin was torn, and bore the deep tooth marks from the pliers. Whole sections of his body were a glistening aubergine-purple.

At first Harry had insisted on telling his tormentors the truth. Then, when they dismissed his story as fantasy, he had tried to guess what they wanted to know. Finally he had asked them to tell him what they needed him to say for them to stop.

Now he lay in the fortress-prison of Fort Montluc, with lice running through his clothes and hair, vermin sneaking up and sniffing at him and a fever making his bones ache.

The cell was barely three metres square. A tiny slit high in one wall gave a view of the railway bridge and the tobacco factory. Now and then he heard the sound of keys being scraped along bars, a discordant jangle, sawing at already frayed nerves. Franzel, the warden, was adding his own little irritant to the mix.

Once a week, perhaps twice, they heard the soldiers' low voices as the firing squad was assembled. Then a few barked orders, the shots and the sound of a body being dragged away.

The key turned in the lock, the door opened, and the grey light of the main courtyard bled into the room, causing his one good eye to weep. Colonel Triffe looked down at him with his usual contempt. 'You should know this. I have sent a report to London on all you have confessed, all the damage that you have wreaked.' He neglected to add that London had demanded summary execution for Cole, but Triffe wanted this done according to French law. He knew very well how Red Ribbon actions could come back to haunt you years down the line, when, of course, the English SIS would deny any such order existed. By the book was best, Triffe had decided long ago.

'You can do one last decent thing. Maybe erase a little of the stain on your soul, who knows? You can save the girl. Technically, she handed the network to the Germans.'

'I need some water.'

'Later.'

'Who are you?' Harry asked, aware that no normal DST man would report to London.

'A patriot.'

Harry smiled, as best he could. 'That's what every shit says.'

Triffe grinned back without humour. Over his shoulder Harry could see the silhouette of Odile framed in the doorway.

'Odile . . .' he managed to say.

Triffe stood, blocking his view of her, and barked at him: 'Do you confirm that you betrayed Frenchmen to the German field police and security services? And used this girl as your unwitting dupe?'

It was clear now. He was to take responsibility for everything, the evil puppet master who pulled Odile's strings.

'I'm sorry.'

'A yes or no,' Triffe barked, pressing his boot against Harry's thigh.

Harry took a deep breath. 'Yes. She knew nothing. Me. It was all my doing.'

'Thank you.'

They withdrew, locking him back into the darkness. Outside he heard Odile's voice, sharp and clear in contrast to his own. 'What will happen to him?' she asked.

Triffe's voice was much deeper, a rumble like summer thunder. 'We will follow the law. There will be a tribunal. You will be acquitted. Harry Cole will be sentenced to death.'

And so it came to be. November 16, 1942: Harold Cole, German spy, was to be shot at Montluc prison.

Part Three

Twenty-four

Paris, early 1943

Gérard the restaurateur walked through to the rear of the cellar that ran beneath his establishment and inspected the false wall that divided it. It was still perfect after three years, still capable of fooling all but the most careful scrutiny. Behind the barricade that had split his cellar in two was his stock of fine wines and champagne, kept from the Germans who had drunk the rest of his racks dry. Now he was down to serving very poor table wine, but at least he was able to charge Grand Vin prices for it.

He climbed the dusty wooden stairs back into the empty restaurant and made for the kitchen, where the meagre pickings he was meant to invent a menu from were laid out on the table. In his mind, he juggled combinations of the scrawny rabbits, grey potatoes, a few pigeons, some beans, a sack of gnarled carrots, a few strands of herbs and a slab of butter that he suspected had been adulterated – the white marbling that ran through it looked highly dubious to him. Like most establishments these days, Gérard served whatever he had been able to buy or scrounge, and the customer could take it or leave it.

He had re-opened the restaurant six months ago. When the arrests had started following the Cole treachery he had made himself scarce, staying with his cousin in Rheims until it was safe to return. But the Germans had his name, even if they could produce no airmen to prove his complicity. So he bargained for his continued freedom with scraps of information. They were as harmless as he could make them, and occasionally he could use his German contacts to nail a particularly repellent individual, but his collaboration made his skin crawl with shame.

He put on a pan of water and began skinning the rabbits. An officer of the security services was due any time now, and Gérard had precious little information to give him. He had heard that Jews were hiding out in one of the city's cemeteries, and he thought about offering that snippet. Too vague. The best he had were the names of the most prominent of the city's black marketeers, yet he relied on them to source his butter and eggs. He'd be cutting his own throat. Besides, many of them had protection at the highest level of the Occupiers.

He threw the kidneys and livers of the rabbits into the pot and gave it a stir, just as the bell over the door sounded. He wiped his hands on his apron and grabbed a bottle of Lillet. The discussions always went better with a liqueur.

The new man was in the full formal uniform of the Sicherheitsdienst, the German security service charged with countering the French Resistance, with high jackboots, jodhpur trousers and tightly tailored jacket. He swept the cap from his head to reveal cropped blond hair, so fair it was nearly white. His face bore duelling scars he was doubtless proud of.

'Ah, Oberleutnant,' Gérard said, taking a guess at the rank, feeling himself starting to sweat. 'Too early for a drink?'

He sloshed the liqueur into two glasses, handed one over, and it was accepted, the drink tossed back. 'I am afraid I have very little for you, Oberleutnant.'

'I am not an Oberleutnant. I am an SS-Untersturmführer.'

The voice was low, raspy, but something about it made Gérard look closely at the bullet-headed man. No, they weren't duelling scars. And the blond hair was dyed.

'Christ,' Gérard said slowly before he knocked back his own drink in one, 'Harry Cole.'

'Nine days after the Allied landings in North Africa, the Germans moved into the Non-Occupied Zone as a punitive measure. In Lyon, they found various prisoners who had been charged with being German agents. One of them had been sentenced to death. This, they thought, was outrageous.' Harry took a drag on his cigarette. 'I was taken to meet Barbie—'

'Barbie?' repeated Gérard. Word of the SD man's brutality had reached Paris. The young SS Untersturmführer was awarded his first Iron Cross in Amsterdam for battering to death an 'enemy of the Reich' – a Jewish ice cream peddler – in public because the man refused to salute him. Now an Obersturmführer, he had been given the job of Sonderbehandlung – special treatment – in Lyon, which meant cleansing the city of the Jews, which he was doing with characteristic zeal. A favourite ploy was the *souricière*, the mousetrap. Word was put out through the refugee organisations and contacts in the underground that extra food rations or medical care was available on humanitarian grounds to Jews at a certain address. Barbie's men would open up the phoney clinic on the appointed day and detain anyone who walked through the door. Next stop, Montluc.

The prison-fortress had been barbaric before, but Barbie had lifted it into another league. He had a new structure, the *Baraque aux Juifs*, built in the courtyard, and filled it with a ready supply of hostages, who were on tap should anyone dare to attack German soldiers. Or, in fact, for any trivial reason at all. The weekly firing squads became daily, then, it seemed, hourly. People arrived with the most obscene wounds from Barbie's torture with terrible burns, holes in their heads from repeated blows on the same spot, but there was no medical care. Especially not for those in the Jews' Hut.

'Such a small, unassuming man,' said Harry. 'Not physically large. Mild mannered. But when he gets a truncheon in his hand, watch out. So, Barbie decides that his enemy's enemy is his friend . . .' Harry had been lucky. Barbie and his SD men lived a life of arrest and torture and murder during the day, but at night they caroused through the city's bars and clubs, always welcomed, always offered treats on the house. Somewhere along the way, Barbie had caught a dose of clap and returned to Germany for treatment. One of his hasty recommendations was for the wrongly imprisoned Harry to be released, on condition that he 'helped' now and then. First in Lyon, and when his face became known, a transfer to Paris.

Gérard walked back to the kitchen to check his bubbling stock and returned, wringing his hands. 'But Harry, you are working for . . . the Gestapo.'

'SD.'

'Don't split hairs. There is no difference.'

'I'm not really working for either. I'm working for Harry.'

'Then why the uniform?'

'This?' He plucked at the tunic. Strictly speaking, he wasn't really entitled to wear it, as he hadn't been through the SS school at Bernau, near Berlin, where Barbie had gained his lightning bolts (presented, the man had proudly told him, on April 20, Hitler's birthday) and dagger. Such was the intimidating power of the outfit, however, he, along with a handful of other trusties, was given dispensation to don it when it was deemed a useful tool. 'It's a means to an end. All I do is advise them on certain things. Perhaps have a word in an Englishman's ear, let them know the score.'

'But Barbie is an animal.'

'I have nothing to do with that,' Harry said firmly. 'Not there nor here. And let me tell you, the Allies are not the angels you think they are.' He outlined what King had engineered, the duping of Odile into handing over the escape routes and his near-lynching on the hill.

'Harry, I agree, that's a terrible story, but you are playing with fire and damning your soul.'

'Don't be melodramatic, Gérard. What choice did I have? One side tried to hang me. Look.' He pulled down his collar to show the crinkled friction scar on his neck. 'Then the French warders tortured me.' He showed a scar on his arm from a knife cut. 'Then sentenced me to death.' Triffe, his captor, had managed to escape Lyon before Barbie discovered that the Frenchman was in touch with London.

'The Germans at least kept me alive. Gérard, all I do is tell the captured English agents to behave. To co-operate. To save them the bloody pain.' Gérard was about to interrupt. 'No, listen. I know terrible things go on. I hear them, for chrissake. Some of them even happened to me. Oh, yes, the Gestapo don't have a monopoly on torture, Gérard. And remember this. When an English agent not in uniform is captured, the Germans are completely within their rights, under the Geneva Convention, to shoot them.'

'Are they?' Gérard had not heard this before.

'Yes. Absolutely.'

'And to pull their toenails out? And drown them in bathtubs? I hear your friend Barbie is very fond of that,' said Gérard quietly.

Harry banged the table. 'You are not listening. I try to stop such things.'

'By getting them to betray their friends and colleagues.'

'A German spy caught in England is liable to be hanged, Gérard. Both sides play by the same rules.'

'You have a strange notion of playing, Harry.'

Harry went quiet. It was hard to make people understand. When he had returned to Paris from Lyon, only Tante Clara hadn't doubted him, had given him food and drink and her son's bed once more. When he had appeared, unannounced, at her apartment, she had hugged him for a long time and told him that everyone was making compromises, even if they wouldn't admit it now and would certainly deny it in the future. She had cupped his face in her hands and kissed him.

'I have been in Paris only a few weeks,' he said to the restaurateur, holding out his glass for a refill of Lillet. 'Who knows? Maybe I can do some good?'

'Nobody can do any good in that uniform,' Gérard said brusquely. 'So, why come to me, Harry? I have nothing for you. No interesting snippets or rumours. Unless you want to know where to get fresh eggs. Then I can help.'

'I want King.'

'Can't help you.'

'And I want to see Odile.'

'She's not here,' he said. 'I mean, in Paris.'

'How can you be so sure? She's not in Madeleine, not in Lille. I think she is here. Isn't she?'

Gérard shook his head. 'She won't see you.'

'I need to tell her what really happened.'

'You think she'll believe you?'

'Do you?'

Gérard hesitated for a beat too many. 'Of course.'

Harry laughed. 'I can do a better job of convincing Odile.'

'You are too convincing all round, Harry. Nobody knows when you are telling the truth.'

Harry sat down and lit himself another cigarette. 'Gérard. This is simple. You get a message to Odile for me and I'll call off the dogs.'

'What does that mean?'

'It means you can give up working for the Gestapo, Gérard. No more information, names, rumours. You can take back the moral high ground.'

There was a long pause before Gérard said: 'I'll see what I can do.'

Twenty-five

Paris, early 1943

Harry sat close to the door at Le Rosebud café off Boulevard Montparnasse, nursing a coffee that tasted only of roasted barley. He was back in civvies, as usual, the suit carefully chosen, well cut, but clearly of a decent age. Newer threads would mark him out as a familiar at Foch or the Lutetia or one of the other security outposts. Unlike most Brandenburgers, he didn't like to advertise the fact that circumstances had brought him to the Germans' door.

Harry took a sip of coffee and a man at the bar – another of those Parisians who made desperate efforts to stay elegant in increasingly threadbare clothes – noticed him curl his nose.

'You know, I can dream the taste of real coffee,' said his neighbour. 'I can't summon it during the day, but some mornings I wake up with the smell in my nose.'

'Is that good or bad?' asked Harry.

The man laughed. 'Bad. I spend the morning trying to recapture the sensation.' He pointed at his own empty cup. 'Only to be disappointed every time.' He looked over at the proprietor. 'And he burnt the barley. I think I'll go and see what's in the Lies today.'

He stood up, adjusted his green bowtie and walked across to the street where he thumbed the stack of newspapers – the Lies as they were now universally known – trying to find the one with the fewest untruths.

Harry saw her from the corner of his eye. She must have come out of the Metro, crossed Boulevard Montparnasse, and was now standing on the opposite side of Delambre, looking left to right, clutching a cheap handbag in front of her. The fresh-faced girl, the feisty nurse, had gone, replaced by this nervous creature, with its sharp cheek bones and sad eyes, but, after he had stared at her for a few moments, he could see his Odile shining through.

He stood and stepped, feeling his jitters affect his stride.

Mr Green Bowtie at the kiosk had bought his paper and was standing with it spread wide. Next to him, browsing the magazines, was a rougher sort, in blue overalls. To the left, a couple of German soldiers were walking imperiously through their city, chatting with an officer. There was an ease between the ranks that would shock the British, thought Harry; they sometimes even ate the same food in the same messes. Ahead, to the right, was his Odile, still unmoving at the kerbside.

The Bowtie man with the taste for good coffee let the newspaper flutter to the ground. Odile had seen Harry now, but her face did not change expression. He glimpsed the sorrow in her eyes, moments before she squeezed them tight shut.

Harry heard the snick of a handgun's slide being drawn back directly in front of him. Green Bowtie man was standing legs akimbo, a Browning automatic raised and aimed in his right hand, the left bracing the wrist.

The blue-overalled man had produced a Sten gun and was pointing it from waist height. Harry looked back at Le Rosebud, thinking the Resistance was about to hit someone within the café; half a dozen faces stared back at him, open-mouthed.

Harry was the target.

She'd told them.

Harry tried shouting to Odile, to tell her she had it wrong, to call them off, but the first shot snatched the words away as the bullet plunged into his flesh and spun him around.

There was a rapid chatter from the Sten and more punches into his body, this time across his shoulders, sending him crashing into Le Rosebud's window, which wobbled and shattered around him. Harry lay still, listening to the blood roar out of him.

There were shouts, and more shots as the German soldiers opened fire and the screech of locked brakes as a car swept up to take the assassins away. He was aware of someone kneeling next to him, talking.

As more figures crowded around him, he managed to raise his head and look up across the street, at the empty space where Odile had stood only a few moments previously, before he slumped back into blackness.

Twenty-six

London, June 1943

It is odd how the death of strangers can affect you, thought Anthony Neave. He had never been a fan of actors or movie stars, but he had heard Leslie Howard on the Brains Trust and enjoyed some of his rousing patriotic speeches, and when the news came that the BOAC DC-3 carrying him from Lisbon had been shot down over the Bay of Biscay, he was strangely moved.

The initial scare that Winston Churchill was on board had caused a terrible panic but Dansey had quickly doused that rumour. What was peculiar was that no airliner on the Lisbon–London route had ever been attacked before, and this one was blown out of the sky by a whole squadron of Junkers 88s.

Neave, still pondering the tragedy of Howard's death, managed to find Kim Philby's Chelsea house easily enough. There was a loud burble of conversation and laughter spilling out of the open doors and windows. He didn't have to knock, but pushed open the door and stepped into a Technicolored world, far removed from monotone London. The women wore bright floral dresses or blouses and most of the men were out of uniform, many wearing sweaters Neave thought more suited to the golf course. Expensive art adorned the brightly painted walls and glasses were so full that the contents were being slopped onto the wooden floor. He felt stiff and overdressed in his Major's outfit.

The air was heavy with cigarette smoke and garbled, almost hysterical talk, with a rich seam of American accents running through the babble, which probably explained the informality. The house itself was light, airy and grand. The flooring was oak, the doorknobs crystal, the chairs Hepplewhite. Philby must have married well to afford all this, Neave thought, as SIS salaries didn't usually run to Hepplewhites.

Neave pushed his way through to the rear, where French windows had been thrown open into the garden. He could smell food, proper sausages cooking, and there were bought biscuits, not misshapen homemade efforts, and a bowl of oranges that he stared at for a second, as if they were something alien, the dimpled skin almost obscenely lurid. And there were great decadent piles of chocolate on the sideboard, another contribution from Uncle Sam, no doubt.

He found Philby opening a bottle of champagne in the kitchen. None of that awful South African sherry which had become the party staple for everyone else. Philby had yet another promotion to celebrate, and he was doing it in war-be-damned style. 'Neave! Glad you could make it. H-here, hold this glass.' The stutter was much diminished from the odd occasions when he had bumped into the man around Broadway Buildings or the Foreign Office. In fact, so casual was their acquaintance, Neave had been surprised at the invitation.

'Diana here?' Philby remembered the name of Neave's wife.

'No, bit under the weather I'm afraid. Sends her apologies.' In fact they had had one of their first rows. Neave had foolishly let slip he wanted to go on one of the Motor Torpedo Boat runs across to Brittany and she had exploded at the thought of him being captured again. He'd tried to explain the feeling of cowardice that overtook him when he had to send others into the field, but she would have none of it.

Diana knew all about covert operations, as she worked for the Political Warfare Executive on the black propaganda broadcasts to Occupied Europe that came out of Bush House – a fact that Dansey must have known when he recommended at the racecourse that Neave tell her what he did. He never did get round to clarifying the nature of his work to his new wife, and neither did she, and they had only discovered that they were both in intelligence when they bumped into each other on a restricted floor of the War Office.

The argument had ended in a stalemate, mainly because she knew the PWE had lost agents on those MTB runs. The evening had been soured by the unfamiliar hostility, and she had decided to skip Philby's summer party.

'Bit of a shock about Leslie Howard,' said Neave by way of conversation.

'What? Yes. Imagine the Krauts' faces when they thought they had killed Churchill and it turns out it's the manager of that chap from *Gone With The Wind*. Dead ringer for Winnie, apparently. Shame, but it was all in a good cause.'

'What was?'

'Well, letting it get shot down,' said Philby. 'It meant they weren't looking for Winston elsewhere and he got back into the country safely.'

'You mean . . .' Neave lowered his voice as someone pushed by. 'It was a deliberate decoy?'

Philby also dropped down to a whisper. 'Yes. We knew the Germans had targeted the flight, but couldn't let on, or they might have rumbled the source.'

Neave swallowed hard. 'Are you sure?'

'Look, two people were taken off that plane at the last minute. Just so happens, strangest coincidence, they were Dansey's agents.' He winked.

Before the scale of this monstrosity could sink in, Philby reached over and tugged at someone's sleeve, dragging him across. 'Ah, Graham, yes, come here, come here . . . Anthony Neave, Graham Greene. You two know each other?'

Neave smiled, suppressing the urge to blurt how much he had enjoyed *The Confidential Agent.* Didn't do to gush. He simply offered his hand and it was taken.

'Just talking about Leslie Howard,' offered Neave.

'I know,' said Greene gruffly, 'half the street probably heard you.' Greene had been in propaganda, for the Ministry of Information, until recently. He was now one of Philby's new recruits to Six, creating cover stories and backgrounds for agents, when he wasn't selling the film rights of his books to Hollywood for astronomical sums. Three thousand pounds, Neave had heard.

'Champagne?' asked Philby rhetorically. He found and filled a glass for Greene who slurped it appreciatively.

'Look, Neave, there is someone I want you to meet. Excuse us a moment, Graham.'

They passed out of the kitchen and through the hallway, Philby introducing people as he went. 'Muggeridge,' he said of one bright-eyed chap with an oddly strained grin on his face. 'One of us.' Meaning MI6, Neave supposed. 'Just back from Mozambique. Hence the tan. Tony Neave, first man to escape from Colditz castle.'

'First Englishman,' Neave corrected as they shook hands.

'Well, that's what counts, isn't it? The home team?' said Muggeridge as they moved on. 'Well done.'

They took the stairs, threading through chatting couples, and Philby pushed him along the landing.

Philby swung open the door to a bedroom and let Neave pass inside. On the bed was a young woman, staring out of the window, and for a second Neave was puzzled. He knew Philby had a louche side, and his friend Guy Burgess a bacchanalian streak a mile wide, but this was bizarre behaviour.

'She's not in a p-p-party mood, I'm afraid.'

The woman turned to face them and it took a moment for Neave to place her. He had to picture her younger, without the fine lines that had appeared around her mouth and eyes. Then he caught the slightly misaligned stare. It was the nurse from Calais. Odile.

After a while he found himself touching her face, not in any sexual sense, he told himself, just to reassure her, to try to convey his sympathy and his sorrow, although a small part of him admitted he enjoyed the tactile sensation. She didn't flinch when he moved to stroking her hair. Another Little Cyclone, with an astonishing story to tell.

She had been brought across the Channel by one of his fast boats, had been debriefed at the London Cage in Kensington Palace Gardens while he had been touring US bases in East Anglia, and so he had missed her. She had volunteered for SOE and her file had crossed Dansey's desk, who sent Philby to look her over, see if she was any use to SIS. Philby, after deciding that SOE was her best option, had nevertheless invited her to the party.

She told Neave everything that had happened to her since Calais. The betrayal at Lille. How, when she heard Harry had been spotted in Marseilles, she worked out that he would route through Lyon on his way north, and her alerting of the

Resistance. How they had watched all the bus terminals – she knew Harry was too sly to use the main rail station – his arrest, and the confession to Triffe in the cells. Then, her voice small and trembling, she explained about the baby. Harry's baby.

'Did he know that you were pregnant?' Neave asked quietly.

Odile lowered her head. 'No. After my baby was born I got Harry's note asking me to meet him in Paris. He could explain everything, it said.' She looked up at Neave, her eyes glistening. 'My baby was part of the reason I went to the Resistance, to tell them that Harry Cole had to be . . . dealt with. Once and for all.'

'You didn't let him try to tell his side of things?'

'Too risky. Harry could convince me the moon is made of cheese. When I was with him, I loved him. I knew what he said wasn't always the truth, but that part of my brain was deaf, dumb and stupid. Now, I think he might have killed every bit of love in me. It's a strange feeling.'

'Don't be too hard on yourself. He fooled me, too.'

'But how? Even I could tell he was not what he seemed. Not an officer or a gentleman.'

Neave couldn't explain that. It is true, in retrospect, all that Old Boy and Old Chap stuff was just too forced, but at the time, as Odile said, it was easier to accept him at face value. She described unemotionally the shooting at Montparnasse, the getaway car, the leaving of Paris and the journey to London.

'You really want to go back?'

Odile nodded. 'Yes. Of course. I have to . . .' She struggled for a word. 'Expunge what Harry did, somehow. Wouldn't you want to go back if you thought you could do some good?'

He flashed back to the argument with Diana and smiled. 'Yes. Yes, I would. At least you don't have to worry about Harry. He's dead now.'

'I wish,' she said with a sardonic laugh. 'Harry's not dead. He's not exactly alive. But he's not dead. The Sten gun jammed before the magazine was empty. He was hit, but obviously not enough. Before we could finish him off, two German soldiers started firing. It was a mess. We heard they took him to a German military hospital out near Vincennes, but it is almost impossible to get a team in and out of there. Maybe only a silver bullet can kill him.'

Neave leant over and kissed her, lightly, on the forehead and pulled her head onto his shoulder and said quietly: 'Don't worry.' He thought about the Red Ribbon Dansey had signed a few months previously. 'An ordinary bullet in the right place will do it just as well.'

Twenty-seven

Paris, September 1943

Missing Presumed Eaten. The notice with its wistful description of a much-loved cat, tacked to a tree at the edge of the Bois de Vincennes, made Pieter Wolkers smile as he walked down the drive towards the military hospital. It was about time something did. Paris had lost its sparkle for him, ever since Sicily had fallen, and now the Italians had gone and surrendered, his mood was increasingly bleak.

Yet his superiors were acting as if these were minor setbacks, as if they weren't up against the huge force looming behind starved, battered Britain, the USA. Of course, everyone in the various branches of the security services followed Hitler's official view of America – a country of children, run by gangsters. Wolkers knew better but he kept his opinions to himself. Since the pictures and descriptions of the camps in the underground *Combat* and *Liberation* newspapers, he knew where he would end up should he open his fat mouth.

He nodded to the nurse on duty at the desk, flashed his ID to the armed sentries, and mounted the stairs to the rehabilitation ward two at a time. There had been victories for his side, of course. Agents captured, broken, turned, their radios played back to London, but these were pinpricks. Barbie had picked up the elusive Jean Moulin in Lyon. A great coup, having de Gaulle's personal emissary to the Resistance, but then the fool Barbie had tortured him so badly, he died days after his arrival in Paris. So they gave him another Iron Cross. Unbelievable.

Harry was sitting up in bed in what had once been a very grand bedroom of the château, but, stripped of all furniture, carpets and art, it was cold and echoey. The window was open, and the first of the year's east winds was blowing. Harry looked at Wolkers with dull eyes.

He'd been warned that some of Harry's memory had been affected by the shooting, but that he would be out in a week or two. Wolkers had insisted he be assigned to his V-man unit. There was no argument from Diels, who had at last got his wish to move from Lille and was installed in Avenue Foch. The Reich's intelligence services were loyal enough to those who fell in the line of duty, but they didn't especially crave damaged goods.

Wolkers sat on the side of the bed, took a slab of chocolate from his pocket and handed it across to Harry, who broke off a piece and let it melt on his tongue.

'Nice,' he said in a low croak.

'Swiss.'

'Where—?'

'Don't ask. How are you?'

'Not bad for a dead man. I'm sorry . . . do I know you?'

'Wolkers. We had some . . . dealings together in the Lille area. You sent me . . .' He struggled for her name for a second. 'Odile.'

Harry flashed back to Monveaux, and the slowly revolving bodies in the square. This was the civilian who had been arguing with the SS. He knew who he was now, but what did he mean by sending him Odile? The mosaic slowly came together. This was the man King had contacted, using his name, to trigger the blowing of the ratlines. 'Of course.'

Wolkers said quietly, 'Harry, on your release you have been assigned to Section Fifteen. My section.'

Harry could smell alcohol on his breath. 'And what does Fifteen do?'

'The usual shit. Hang around bars, keeping their ears open. Watching for suspicious individuals, reading the denouncements that just keep coming.'

Harry shrugged. It didn't sound particularly elevating work, but he'd need some kind of employment. The Dutchman ran a hand through his hair and decided to make his pitch. 'Been keeping up with the news, Harry?'

'Off and on. Which bit of the news are you interested in?'

'All of it. The Russian Front. North Africa. Italy.'

Harry said, cautiously: 'I know what you mean. Doesn't look good from this end.'

Wolkers nodded, pleased he had correctly judged the measure of the man. 'The High Command prefer the word elastic. Meaning they expect themselves to bounce back.'

Harry dropped his voice. Like Wolkers, he knew they could be executed for this conversation. 'But you don't think so?'

'I told your friend Odile I was a gambling man. That I had totted up the odds, and backed the right horse. I still think I made a sensible bet.'

'But?'

'Didn't factor in the Americans. Didn't factor in fighting on two fronts.'

'You weren't alone.'

'No, but I seem to be one of the few prepared to admit it.'

'So when did the scales fall from your eyes?'

Monveaux, Wolkers wanted to say. That was when the cracks in his faith first appeared. It was an act by a people who considered themselves above common humanity. The award for Barbie, when he had clumsily murdered a potential trump card, added criminal stupidity to the charge sheet. 'A long time ago.'

'But you're still here?'

'Where can I go? We're tainted, you and me, Harry. Now we have to bet on the one thing we know is a certainty.'

'And that is?'

'Ourselves. You and me. We always looked after Number One, I suspect, and we should do so again. Once we start doing that, we'll be . . . what's your expression? Quids in. I have a proposition for you.'

'Whatever it is, I have a price.'

Wolkers walked over to the window, pulled aside the billowing gauze and lit a cigarette. 'It's dangerous, and if we are caught, we'll probably be shot.'

'I'm getting used to that.'

'Firing squads tend not to miss.'

'The last lot didn't miss, just in case you didn't notice. They just didn't hit anything too vital. Harry's luck is holding, that's all. Give me one of those.'

Wolkers lit a second cigarette and gave it to Harry.

'Swiss chocolate and British snouts. You are a man after my own heart.'

'That's what I thought.'

'Whatever your scheme is, and I bet I can hazard a good guess, all I want in return is for you to find me someone.'

'Is it a woman?' asked Wolkers cautiously, thinking of Odile.

Harry shook his head. 'A man. Called King. Or Rex. I can give you a very good description.'

'Why do you want him?'

'I want him to tell me a few things. Write them down. Sign it. Then I want to kill him.'

'You don't strike me as the killing kind, Harry.'

'Watch me.'

'OK. I'll tell you my side.' Wolkers quickly outlined his scheme to take them out of the war and into the good life. 'Well? What do you think?'

A nurse knocked on the door. 'I am sorry to interrupt, but we have some visitors from the Soldiers of the Fatherland charity. With some parcels . . . would you mind?'

Wolkers shook his head. 'Not at all. I was just going. We have a deal?'

Harry nodded. 'On that one condition.'

The four people from the charity came in before Wolkers could make his exit and he hesitated for a second, taking in the tall, striking woman with the elaborately wrapped package in her hands. She was dressed in a tailored white suit, with a large hat, decked with lace and feathers. She wasn't young, but something in the dark eyes made him quiver.

Harry pulled himself up in bed and stared at her, but for different reasons. It was the Contessa Hellie von Lutz. And the last time he had seen her, back in Le Touquet, he had claimed to be an English spy.

The Wolkers plan was straightforward enough. After each day's arrests, a sheet was posted in the SD operations office on the ground floor of 82 Avenue Foch. It gave the name and the address of the detainees, plus a code for the crime, indicating if it was being a Jew, a spy, a black marketeer; having an illegal radio; ration book or identity card fraud; being a communist or freemason; anti-social (ie anti-German) behaviour – or if it was preventative custody; no crime committed yet, but the potential culprits taken in as a precautionary measure.

After 24 hours a second code was added, which told Wolkers whether the individuals were likely to be released or were to be processed through Fresnes or Drancy and transported or executed. The names on the latter list were also dispatched to one of the approved French accountancy firms, whose job it would be to take a full inventory of the detainees' apartments and liquidate the goods on behalf of the Reich, keeping twenty per cent for themselves.

Such were the numbers involved during the round-ups of late 1943, that a backlog had built up. Consequently it was often three or four days after the arrests before stock was taken and the contents either sold or sent for cataloguing in the vast warehouses to the east of the city, to await shipment to Germany. This meant that should anything of value disappear from the empty houses or apartments between the time of arrest and the visit from the money men, it would not be noticed. As long as they were careful.

The first outing for the Wolkers plan was a second floor apartment in a grand block on the Avenue de Villars. The Jewish owners had been denounced by a neighbour, snatched by a team of gendarmes two nights previously and were being held in the unfinished housing complex at Drancy. The concierge of the block was bribed by Wolkers, using extra food coupons that some poor sap in Fresnes prison wouldn't be needing where he was going.

So when he arrived at Avenue de Villars, Harry had a full set of keys. He removed the Gestapo tape that sealed the entrance, ripping off small flakes of paint, which he would be careful to mask when he put the new barrier back. Once inside, he made sure all the curtains and shutters were closed before switching on the light. He paused for a moment at the sight of the dinner plates still laid on the table awaiting food, the cigarette with a two-inch-long ash on the sidetable, the sewing abandoned on the floor, all the signs of a normal life unexpectedly terminated. A white cat padded up to him and meowed plaintively. His resolve wavered, and he reminded himself of what Wolkers had said: the arrested with an NN after their name – Nacht und Nabel, night and fog, the code for the camps – or A, for Arbeiten, forced labour, they were as good as dead already. A slot in the Reich's vast machinery of misery had already been prepared. Short of a miracle – and miracles were in very short supply – they would never see the apartment again. So they were really only stealing from the bloodsucking accountants and Germany. It was almost an act of resistance.

Harry went through to the kitchen and found some pâté in a cooler box, which he put down for the cat, and returned to the living room. A quick glance told him there were good pickings here – white gold picture frames, solid silver tableware, a pair of antique snuff boxes. All went into his carry-all. Somewhere there would be the family's emergency stash which they may not have had time to access – diamonds, perhaps, even good old-fashioned money. Harry kept his mind focused on the work, and slowly filled up the bag.

Wolkers had arranged that the money they raised would go into an account at the Swiss Bank on Avenue Montaigne. Once there was enough cash to keep them going for a while, then they would head to Zürich or Berne or Geneva while Europe finished tearing itself apart. It was a good scheme, if only Harry could suppress the feeling of nausea that rose in his throat as he rummaged through the possessions of the disappeared.

He forced himself to recall the flipside of this pact. That, at Harry's request, a new question had been added by his partner to the interrogator's list in the cells of Fresnes and Foch: have you heard of a British agent called Henry King?

'And then she said to me . . . I've been looking on three floors and I've been fucked five times on the way!'

Harry laughed at the memory and Wolkers smiled indulgently. Harry had told him it before, more than once. It was early evening and they were in a scruffy bar in the Pigalle – chosen not for the peeling décor, but because it had a supply of coal for its stoves – celebrating the haul from the Avenue de Villars apartment. Wolkers's fences had given him eleven thousand francs. A fraction of the loot's true value, probably, but a healthy enough start to their retirement fund.

Wolkers clicked his fingers for a fresh round of drinks. 'You know who she is? I recognised her at the hospital straight away.'

'I know who she says she is,' said Harry warily.

Hellie had remembered Harry all right, despite the damage and bandages, and greeted him like an old friend. She had sent away the other members of her charity team and had sat and talked to him. It was only after a while he realised that she had created her own explanation for his presence in the Hôtel Atlantic. That on their first meeting, he had been a German spy posing as an English spy.

She had stayed for half an hour, locking the door and pulling the drapes and reinterpreting the whole concept of charity towards the wounded in a way no red-blooded soldier could object to.

'So who is she?' Harry finally asked Wolkers, still feeling the heat of her mouth on him. 'A fake?'

'Not at all. The von Lutzes were pretty powerful people. Her husband was an industrialist. German Alsatian. Bankrolled Bugatti for a while, until he realised that was going nowhere. Rumour has it, though, he did put cash into some of the Ruhr industries . . . Krupp and the like.'

'She didn't mention him when I met her in Le Touquet.'

'He was probably dead by then. Nineteen thirty . . . seven. Possibly early thirty-eight. He was sixty-odd . . . older than her anyway. But listen, Harry . . . he left her . . . hold on, in pounds, uh, five million. Give or take.'

Harry raised his refreshed glass. 'Take. Always take.'

'I think perhaps you should stay in touch with Hellie.'

Harry tapped his breast pocket, feeling his wallet underneath. 'I still keep her address close to my heart, from the first time we met. It's in Alsace somewhere . . .'

'I know it,' said Wolkers. 'Leave Strasbourg, heading south. Take the road to Mulhouse. Can't miss it. Second big fucking castle to the left.'

They both laughed, Harry flinching as one of the old bullet wounds objected. They had healed cleanly, but he still had trouble raising his left arm higher than head height, not the best qualification for a burglar.

'Where is the next job?' asked Harry.

'It's a house, in the sixteenth. Off rue de Passy.'

'When?'

'Tonight.'

Harry looked up to check Wolkers wasn't joking. His partner tossed a bunch of keys with an address fob onto the table. Harry pocketed them, drained his glass and raised his good arm to signal the waitress. 'In which case, I'd best have another.'

By the time Harry burgled the twenty-third apartment the hauls were averaging under five thousand francs per job. It seemed that, as another hard winter bit the capital, people were pawning the last of their valuables, trying to get through another Christmas without starving or freezing to death.

On number twenty-three the block concierge wouldn't listen to reason, so Wolkers had him pulled in for questioning on the grounds that radio transmissions had been traced to his block. Nonsense, of course. He'd be released after a lonely, nervous night in the cells with a brusque apology. Meanwhile, his pass key would be put to good use.

As usual Harry removed the Gestapo tape that stretched across the doorframe, opened the apartment, and slipped inside. He flicked the light switch but nothing happened. The power had been cut. He took a torch from his bag and moved through the rooms. In the bedroom he inspected the standard hiding places, discovering a pearl necklace in the underwear drawer, a couple of heavy gold cigarette cases behind the wardrobe. He moved one of the rugs, found a short, unnailed floorboard, lifted it and liberated the money and bonds nestling between the joists. He didn't bother to count it, but it felt like a substantial amount. This was better than he had expected.

He dropped the board back, replaced the rug, using the unfaded rectangle of floor varnish as a guideline, slung the hold-all over his shoulder and returned to the hallway, giving the place a quick once-over to make sure there were no tell-tale signs of his presence. As he opened the apartment door to leave, the harsh beam of white light played straight into his eyes and he raised a hand to shield them. He felt the barrel of the gun press against his forehead, forcing him back into the apartment. For a second he thought the scheme had been rumbled by the Gestapo, but then he heard the familiar voice behind the flashlight, speaking in English. 'Hello, Harry.'

Henry King.

Twenty-eight

London, April 1944

Colonel Sir Claude Dansey couldn't remember when he had last seen so many people at one venue in London. They had flocked north to the Tottenham Hotspur football ground at White Hart Lane by every form of transport – thousands on bicycles, others by train, tube and bus. They streamed onto the terraces and stands and onto the pitch, where folding metal chairs had been laid out around the raised boxing ring in the centre. Most of them were carrying their own refreshments – Spam or paste sandwiches, flasks of tea, a pork pie or a pastie for the lucky few, and bottles of beer – because the stadium's famous bagels were no longer on sale, replaced by soya-bean sausages, which had not attained their predecesssors' popularity.

Dansey took his seat three rows from the front, next to a Captain in the Signals, who shuffled sideways to give the larger man a little more room. The excitement in the air was palpable, with, thought Dansey, a strong whiff of Bread and Circuses: this gladiatorial contest was designed to keep the public, and the armed forces, sweet, distract them from all the speculation over the Second Front.

The dinner-jacketed MC, incongruous in the spring sunshine, stepped into the ring and began to fire up the crowd, encouraging them to chant their favourite's name.

That this fight was taking place at all was remarkable. Len Harvey was a Pilot Officer, his opponent, the challenger Freddie Mills, a mere flight sergeant. Gentlemen and other ranks never, of course, met in the ring, but Mills's manager had mounted a cunning campaign to swing public opinion behind changing such arcane, class-bound rules.

A comedian did a turn while the stragglers continued to arrive and find their places. He offered a Lord Haw-Haw impersonation ('Germany calling, Germany calling. Nine hundred Allied bombers shot down last night for the loss of one of our own fighters. London has collapsed into the Thames') and routines cribbed from Tommy Trinder and the ITMA radio show.

A pair of planes flew over, the new, fast American Mustangs in RAF colours, the sound of their thrumming Packard engines filling the stadium. One of them waggled its wings and a cheer went up that might even have reached the pilots. The great phalanx of blue serge in the RAF's corner was beside itself with joy.

All stood for the National Anthem and Dansey's neighbour, the Signals Captain, said from the corner of his mouth: 'Not my cup of tea, this sort of thing.'

Dansey turned and looked at Henry King, surprised that he objected to the sport. 'Tonic for the troops,' he said.

'Not this trooper.' King offered a cigarette, which was refused. 'I remember my father deciding a taste of the noble art would make a man of me. He was worried about my lack of sporting prowess. He'd been a Blue and all that.'

'And?'

'He let three local lads knock seven bells out of me before he conceded the only thing I would get out of it was a broken nose and two cauliflower ears.'

They sat as the anthem finished. King had been brought out of France by Lysander two days previously, and Dansey had arranged to meet him at the bout because he was concerned about security at Broadway Buildings. Nothing tangible, more a sense of unease he couldn't pin down. He'd had all the surrounding buildings swept for covert photographers, doubled the entrance security, instigated random desk checks, to ensure nobody had anything they shouldn't, but nothing had come to light. Still, the sense that everything wasn't as watertight as it might be would not go away. Dansey didn't want his efforts degenerating into the kind of fiascos Special Operations Executive were experiencing, so, for the time being, he was meeting key agents on neutral ground.

'How are things across the Channel?'

King risked a glance at Dansey and smiled. 'Much as you'd expect.'

His agent looked pale, the uniform loose on his diminished frame, but Dansey guessed that was true of most of the people over there. King was clever enough to know it didn't do to look too healthy or prosperous in an occupied land. 'You've done well,' said Dansey. There was genuine admiration in his voice.

'To last so long?' There was a slight hint of weariness, a desire to see it all over, to get back to some kind of normality.

'I suppose I do mean that,' said Dansey, 'given the numbers our friends in Baker Street keep losing.'

King nodded. Unlike his superior, he felt no pleasure in the SOE's mishaps. There but for the grace of God was his attitude. He'd been snuffling around in the murky business of espionage for a good six years before the war broke out. Which meant that he at least knew what he was doing. The people SOE sent over were like the replacement pilots in the First World War – if they lasted past the first forty-eight hours, they might be in with a chance. Many never made it beyond the drop zone or landing grounds. 'Still, at least we'll know who's been nabbed and who hasn't now,' said King. 'In Paris, at least.' He took out a buff envelope and passed it across. 'Everyone who is in the Foch cells. At least, up to a week ago.'

Dansey let a beaming grin play over his face before he remembered himself and wiped it away. From the old Z days on, he had always thought King was the agent closest to himself. Not quite as hard nosed, or practical, perhaps, but a master manipulator. He could overlook his streak of sentimentality when he delivered goods like this. 'How did you persuade him?'

King laughed. Twisting and turning a man like Harry Cole to your own ends was far from difficult. 'I told him I'd gone against my orders in Lille. That I had left an opportunity for him to escape the noose. That I was his friend.'

'And he went for it?'

King nodded. 'It's the truth. Well, the first part, anyway.'

'Don't remind me,' said Dansey, with displeasure chilling his voice. 'It is just as well your laxness paid off this time.'

That was what he meant by sentimentality. Cole should be dead by now, but then there would be no ferret in Foch even as they spoke, telling King, and ultimately him, which British agents had been caught, which radios were unreliable, who had cracked under interrogation, all the snippets a keen pair of ears like Cole's could pick up. King was lucky, but then, that was another attribute Dansey had always cultivated in his agents.

There was a time when he had considered bringing King in from the field and grooming him in the labyrinthine ways of Broadway Buildings, a political battlefield that was every bit as tricky to negotiate as operating in Occupied France. Two or three incidents had stayed his hand, such as King's hesitation in finishing off Cole in Lille.

Dansey had decided, after much consideration, to let King be, and to transfer his attentions to polishing Philby. He wondered if King realised he was overdue a recall, that he had been in the field for far longer than was usual. Dansey rather thought he did, in which case, he was curious to see how long it would be before he raised the matter.

A great cheer burst from the crowd as the two boxers emerged from the tunnel, arms pumping the air.

King said, 'They are mostly Baker Street's men and women. In Foch.'

'I'm sure.'

'So you will tell them.'

'Oh,' said Dansey, with a wave of his hand. 'When the time is right.'

'Are you going to watch the bloody fight?' complained someone from behind. Dansey ignored him. The two men were in the ring and the MC was making the introductions. Harvey was 34, but looked in good shape. Although he hadn't fought for three years, the famous legs that always kept him dancing until the final bell were knotted and muscular. Mills was twelve years younger, leaner with a wicked scowl, but, the word was, lacking in finesse. It was gentleman-versus-player.

King said quietly, but firmly, 'You must tell them.'

Dansey put a hand on King's shoulder. 'That's for me to decide, Henry.' Dansey knew that SOE was a diminishing threat to his empire. He had even extracted a promise from Churchill that the rival would be wound up at the cessation of hostilities anyway. So perhaps he would share some of the nuggets. He just had to make sure he got something in return. 'Please stick to your part of the job,' he warned King.

The bell for the first round sounded, and Dansey leant forward, listening to the thwack as leather gloves landed blows to head and body, the sweat already flicking off the fighters' faces. The three minutes went in a flash, and Dansey said: 'Close. Very close.'

King nodded. 'Yes, we are rather, aren't we?'

'Harvey'll have him though. Mills is just a rough-houser. Breeding will always tell.'

Seconds out, round two, and the crowd bayed as Harvey moved aggressively forward, in a manner not normally associated with his style. The Flying Officer usually played an elegant long game, concentrating on the psychological and physical attrition of an opponent, avoiding a messy scrap, but here he was surging ahead, firing three rapid punches that unbalanced Mills.

The Flight Sergeant staggered back, but quickly regained his footing and fetched a powerful left hook that lifted Harvey from the floor. The officer crumpled, and a raucous chanting of 'F-reddie. F-reddie' began from the other ranks.

On eight, Harvey was up, but swaying, and Mills was in again, combination punches flying, the famous Harvey pins looking decidedly wobbly.

A right hook snapped Harvey's head round and he staggered back towards the ropes, all balance gone. The momentum rolled him clean over and, to shocked gasps, he was out of the ring, landing heavily on the tarpaulin covering the grass. Every photographer in the ground rushed to get the frame that would fill the next day's newspapers.

Mills's hand was raised by the referee to a roar of delight from the ranks. A solitary red rose came arcing into the arena and Mills bent, clumsily picked it up with his glove and put it in his mouth.

The noise was deafening now, everyone was on their feet, some crying fix, many of the officers furious that their man should have lost, most of the other ranks jubilant. King looked at his watch and said wearily: 'Well, at least it only lasted four minutes. Looks like breeding isn't everything after all, sir. Ah well, back to the coal face.'

'The Harry Cole face,' said Dansey and looked pleased with himself.

King smiled, shook his head, and pushed his way through the over-excited masses.

Twenty-nine

Southern France, June 1944

The early morning cold had penetrated her jacket, two jumpers, a slip and her thin, over-washed underwear. She was shivering now, even though the first rays of the sun had pierced the tree canopy and were warming the patch of ferns where she lay on a coarse blanket, her eyes gritty from lack of sleep.

She rolled over and raised a hand to Patrick, her flank man, who signalled back. He crawled over on his elbows, rattling the undergrowth as he went, until he reached her and offered the flask of armagnac. Odile took a small swig. 'You OK?'

He nodded. 'You sure they are coming?'

Odile nodded. She knew that Tony Brooks, the young SOE man in charge of sabotage in the Lot and Correze regions, had made rail travel north all but impossible since the troops landed at Normandy. Now, the road at the bottom of this pretty valley between Toulouse and Limoges, lined by trees and creepers and wildflowers, was the only route the Germans could come. Which meant they would have to get through the four barriers of logs and boulders blocking it all the way to the little village of Cauliac, two kilometres away.

Hidden in the woods were her thirty men, mostly from the Armée Secrete, all Gaullists, all armed by her parachute drops. Normally, of course, they wouldn't be 'her' men at all, but whoever controlled the drops also commanded respect and loyalty, at least as long as the weapons kept coming.

She hoped she could remember all of Bob Maloubier's advice. He was a veteran of SOE action in Brittany and had been evacuated out to England with the Bugatti driver Robert Benoist in late 1943 and, like her, had insisted on coming back. He was operating in the Limoges area, to the north of her, but with the same objective, to harass reinforcements heading to the beachheads.

They had met two weeks ago at a training camp in a forest near Brive, where Bob had given her a crash course in hit-and-run tactics. Triffe had been there, too, her saviour from Lyon, now fired up with the chance to fight the Germans in the open, rather than as a spy. They all felt the same, happy that, as Maloubier put it, the gloves were finally off. Triffe was busy organising behind-the-lines drop zones for three-man training teams to be parachuted in, each comprising an Englishman, an American and a Frenchman, a combination that sounded like a bad music hall joke.

Patrick broke into her thoughts by letting a hand rest on her shoulder for perhaps a moment too long. Little Puppy some of the others called him, and it was true, he did flash those big saucer eyes at her once too often. Some other place or time, she would have taken this boy – he was not yet sixteen – and probably had some fun. For the moment, however, there was still an unexorcised ghost haunting her, a spectre who had drained dry her reserves of love and, more importantly, trust.

'Are you sure they're coming?' he repeated anxiously.

The noise answered for her, sending the birds racing for the sky, a deep-throated rumble, followed by higher, nastier barks, as tanks, lorries, kübelwagens, motorcycles, self-propelled guns and tow trucks all started on some unheard signal. Yes, the 2nd SS Panzer Division was on the move.

Paris was jittery. Salvation was at hand, the Free French, Americans and British were on their way from Normandy, but the hope of that salvation brought concerns at how, in the death throes of their occupation, the Germans were going to lash out. There was one name on everyone's lips: Stalingrad. Would the City of Light also become a pile of pounded rubble?

Harry sipped at his coffee on the terrace at the Dome and watched the early morning faces passing by, looking for a spring in a step, a sly smile, an act of defiance, but there was none. The population was wisely holding in any jubilation it felt. The Germans were not in the mood for any hint of rebellion. The waiter told him that some kids wearing a combination of red, white and blue clothing – a not uncommon act of subversion – had been whisked away by gendarmes this morning. Harry knew it was almost time to move on.

Wolkers slid in front of him and signalled for a drink. He looked tired, and hadn't shaved, but then he did have an increasing fondness for a certain brothel on the Left Bank. He might well have come straight from there.

Harry was aware of other customers looking at them. By now the regulars knew what they were, and some of them would be looking forward to the day of Liberation because of what they would do to men like Harry and Wolkers.

Harry had something, however, that Wolkers didn't. A chance of redemption. That night in the twenty-third apartment, King had sketched out a way back from his exile. One, he insisted, with zero risk to Harry, but the potential for great rewards: just tell us who is in Foch. The names of prisoners, of SOE and SIS agents, and we can take it from there. If we know who is in Foch and Fresnes and Saussaies, then we can warn others, we can even use it against the Germans. In return, there would be a clean slate for Harry, and more cash for the retirement fund.

Harry was no fool. This time, he got it in writing, and had placed the letter in a safety deposit box at the Swiss Bank. The work produced one other bonus. It helped his conscience counter-balance some of the stunts he was pulling with Wolkers as the thefts became more and more tawdry, even by Harry's standards. He consoled himself that it would all be over soon, when the first Willys Jeeps raced down the boulevards.

'It's a long way to Paris,' said the Dutchman.

'From where?'

'From Normandy.'

'What makes you think that was on my mind?'

Wolkers laughed, showing stained teeth. 'It's on everybody's mind. They've started emptying Fresnes and shipping prisoners east already. All the SOE people.'

'Why? What use are they?'

'Good question. Why don't they just shoot them? Perfectly entitled to. Bargaining chips, perhaps.'

'Possibly,' said Harry, not convinced. It was more likely that the well-lubricated machinery of imprisonment and deportation and enslavement simply demanded more and more raw material.

Wolkers accepted his coffee from the waiter and drank. 'Anyway, we are all assuming the Allies are going to make it this far.' He lowered his voice. 'I mean, like I give a shit as long as we are well clear, eh?' He winked. 'But I don't think they'll be coming up the Champs Elysées anytime tomorrow, somehow.'

Wolkers placed a newspaper on the table and Harry scanned

the stories. Allies bottled up on the beachheads. Crack reinforcements heading north to Normandy. Americans swept into the sea. Huge Canadian losses. Storms in Channel forecast. 'You believe that?'

'I believe a third of it. It's my policy. Official newspaper or underground rag, it's normally thirty per cent true.'

'Which thirty per cent?'

Wolkers shrugged. 'Storms in Channel?' He pointed at the blue sky. 'I doubt it. Americans swept into the sea. Hhmm. Even if they were they'd be back. Canadian losses. Well, maybe. Crack reinforcements head north? Yes, I believe that. There are some SS Panzer divisions down south which were regrouping, waiting for the new Panthers.'

Harry was shocked by Wolkers's loose tongue, but even so he decided to add that information to his report to King later that day. Must be worth a bonus.

'And when the SS arrive in Normandy,' said Wolkers with grim satisfaction, 'God help the people on the receiving end.'

As the noise grew louder, Odile's stomach contracted, making her feel sick. She could hear the massive tank transporters and the half-tracks churning the asphalt to black dust. This was a one-time passage. They wouldn't be coming back, so what did they care about the road surface?

Forty minutes had passed since she had heard the engines start and the roaring, grinding and clanking had grown steadily louder over that time. She had moved forward to the edge of the slope, just where the bracken-heavy valley walls began their descent. To her left was the first roadblock – three large trees interwoven with a dozen smaller ones.

The motorcycle was a shock. The BMW suddenly appeared and the rider skidded his machine to a halt in front of the barrier of trunks. The man dismounted, looking around frantically, and raised a hand at the truck that was behind, which reluctantly slowed and also stopped. Third in the convoy was one of the Schwerer Panzerspähwagen armoured cars, then a half-track. The rest of the vehicles were hidden by the foliage, but she now had a sense of how far the column stretched. A long, long way.

It's too soon, Bob Maloubier's voice said in her head. Wait until you have targets.

On the opposite ridge of the valley she saw the figures moving, coming out of their cover. No Germans, apart from the rider, had exposed themselves yet.

There was the flat crack of a Sten, and the motorcyclist sprinted for cover behind the truck. A grenade exploded, well away from any vehicle, harmlessly sending up chunks of dark earth.

She looked over at Patrick, unsure what to do for a second, then leapt to her feet, firing her own Sten at the canvas sides of the truck, fighting to keep the gun on target. A heavy Bren opened up from her right, but she watched a whole magazine wasted on thin air before the gunner found his range.

Across the valley, the Resistants had broken cover completely. They were standing in the open, totally exposed, pistols and Stens blazing, with no clear idea of what they were aiming at. Another wasted grenade, and she felt shrapnel snick at her skin. She shouted to Patrick, who was fifty metres away.

'Stay back!'

Ignoring her, he stepped forward with his gammon bomb. The tree to his left disintegrated in a shower of bark, and then the heavy machine-gun rounds flailed through his body, grotesquely convulsing him as his insides splattered red on the green leaves around him. She dropped and buried her face in the soil as his own grenade finished the job, leaving him a mess of smoking stumps.

Odile changed the magazine on the Sten, struggled to her feet, stepped from cover and fired three short bursts.

A German shell exploded among the trees across the road, splintering branches and sending a rain of steel and wooden slivers down into the men. There was less fire from her side now.

She found herself walking backwards as the 20mm cannon of the armoured car started to fire, biting chunks out of the forest, all but obliterating men caught in its path. Now the German ground troops were disembarking from the trucks, setting up sheets of covering fire. The way it should be done, she thought. Organised, concentrated, effective.

She turned and ran, aware that others were with her, leaping clumsily through the undergrowth as the fusillades increased, a lethal curtain of rifle, machine pistol, cannon and the rapid chatter of MG-42s.

As she went she took a quick head count. Just four men left. Christ, they could have lost a dozen or more, and not one confirmed German casualty.

The punch of a mortar round sent her splaying forward, her forehead grazed open by the bark of a stump as she slid along the earth. She struggled up and moved on. They had no range, this was just random probing and sure enough another detonation, but far to the right.

The guns stopped, engines started again: they'd cleared the first roadblock already. Her group's mission was to stop the 2nd SS Panzer Division reaching Normandy, giving the Allies time to break out of the beachhead. She had delayed it for nine and a half minutes.

She made it to the slope at the far end of the plateau and slithered down to where a motley collection of vehicles waited to take the survivors away. Patrick's father was there in front of his *gazogène* van, cap in hand, kneading it into a piece of shapeless fabric as she stumbled towards him, arms outstretched for balance. All she could think was: nine and a half minutes.

She only hoped Bob Maloubier could do better up the road.

Thirty

Paris, July 1944

Harry's weekly debriefing rendezvous with King took place in an apartment to the south of the city. Its entrance was off a dank courtyard, always flooded with grey, soapy liquid of dubious provenance, like an overflow from a laundry or sewer, but King liked it because it had two entrances. Both were watched during their meetings. To add an extra layer of security, King insisted that Harry turn up in his SD uniform. Nosy neighbours were still, even now Liberation was promised, very unlikely to risk complaining about the comings and goings of a Sicherheitsdienst man.

In the shabby living room with its basic furniture, Harry sat at a wobbly card table and laboriously encoded his findings for onward transmission from a place King assured him he 'need not know about'. King sat smoking at the dining table, drinking whisky, a battered canvas holdall at his feet. Inside was coffee, cheese, hams, and other staples that Harry would use to bribe his way through Foch and the other SS buildings. Any surplus, he would sell or give to Tante Clara in lieu of rent. Food was so much more valuable than money these days.

'You heard about Oradour?' asked King, flicking ash on the floor. 'Or are they keeping that from you?'

Harry didn't answer for a while, concentrating on ensuring there were no mistakes in the encryption. 'Oradour?' he finally asked.

'Or Tulle?'

Harry shook his head.

'When the Resistance tried to slow down the Das Reich Panzer division . . .'

'*Tried* to slow? I thought they had.'

'Well, they succeeded by a week. At Oradour and Tulle, the Germans took their revenge. They hanged ninety-nine at Tulle. At Oradour they burned the women and children in the church and shot the men. Hundreds. You must be careful, Harry. They are cornered rats now.'

Harry finished the last line of his report, asking for some sort of acknowledgement of his work from London. 'Why would you worry about me? You tried to kill me once.' He pointed at the mark on his neck. 'Remember?'

'Orders, Harry. And if I'd wanted you dead, you'd have been dead.'

'And if I hadn't been able to dance on my toes like a bleedin' ballerina for six hours?'

'You're a survivor, Harry. I knew you'd make it.'

'It was touch and go, King.' He shuddered as he thought of those hours breathing through the material, the cords slicing into his neck as he rotated to keep his balance.

King was irritated now, annoyed at being reminded how close he came to killing the goose that would one day lay the golden Gestapo eggs. He still wasn't sure what had stayed his hand that night at the lynching, why he had given the man a slim chance of survival. Perhaps it was some prescience that, one day, he and Harry's paths would cross to their mutual benefit.

King stood up, raised himself to his full height and brushed back his hair. 'Thing is, Harry, and it is very unprofessional of me to say so . . . I rather like you.'

'Christ, what do you do to people you dislike? It's a good job you had the gun that night in the apartment, King.'

'No it isn't. I could have persuaded you to work for us anyway, Harry. I know you are always open to offers, no matter who makes them. I've been doing this a long time. I went on an exchange to Germany in '33, and I tell you it was obvious even then what was going on, where it would all lead. When I got back, I was debriefed, informally, by someone from the office, as it were. They were impressed with my observational skills. The idealism lasted eighteen months, perhaps two years after I began. Then, you realise that intelligence is a war of attrition and exploitation. Particularly the latter. Find the weakness, exploit it. Sometimes, you are a weak man, Harry. For the record, once more, I'm glad you got out of the noose. Case closed.'

He took the coded report from Harry, and scooped up the one-time pad. 'I'll send and destroy as always, Harry.'

'If it is all about exploitation, why, then, should I trust the men in London?'

'Those were early days, Harry. Look, London is very grateful. Do you realise how valuable it is to know who has been in those cells? Whose radio is suspect? Whose word we can rely on? Do you know what that is worth?'

Harry nodded and pointed at the bag on the floor: 'I would guess a kilo of butter, two hams, some real coffee and maybe even some tea.'

King laughed. 'That's about the size of it.' He held up the paper. 'I'll make sure this is sent.'

Harry rose, grabbed the bag of contraband and asked, 'The other thing?'

King shook his head. 'Can't help you there. She seems to have disappeared.'

Harry nodded. King knew he didn't believe him. Despite what Harry suspected, it was true. Odile was somewhere in the centre of France. More than that, King didn't know.

After Harry had left King screwed up his message and set fire to it in the ashtray, then set about re-drafting the message, in a terse, professional manner that would give credit where credit was due. To him. After all, he had a career, a future in the service, his eyes on the French or Austrian desks. Once Paris was liberated, as it surely would be, the chances were Harry would have no future at all.

The Germans were in the forest. Odile had heard the snap of a tailgate, barked orders, the casual joshing and complaining of soldiers as they stretched their legs. Probably a patrol from the barracks at Laval.

She moved back into the woods as silently as she could and headed for the camp, sweating in the collection of woollen rags that covered her. At least she had good boots now, taken off the dead parachutist with uncommonly small feet she had found, still tangled in his lines. He'd been dead a week or more, and animals had been at him, but she had ignored that. After she had levered the boots free she cut the man down and had buried him as best she could.

After the Das Reich debacle, Odile had regrouped with the survivors and moved north, following the route of the Panzer convoy in many cases, witnessing their savage passage, to the area between Rennes and Le Mans. There, they been given new orders: Operation Sherwood. Round up all allied stragglers and group them into camps, hide in the forests and live off the land. We will come and find you, promised London. Yes, she thought, if the Germans didn't first.

She made good going over the hard ground as the foliage overhead thickened and the undergrowth thinned in the gloom. Far behind her she heard a single shot. There was no return fire. Perhaps it was just a trigger-happy trooper.

Twenty minutes later she found the makeshift camp again, in the clearing on top of the hill, fifty men, mostly crouched or slumped down on the spongy earth, their equipment scattered messily around them. Sitting against a tree was Marshall, the American, part of a Jedburgh drop team that had become separated from each other. He was looking for his English and French co-jumpers to make up his triumvirate, but the chances of finding them were slim. Langan, the sandy-haired SOE man who was her superior, was one of the few on his feet, seemingly incapable of immobility. Most of the others were flight crew, shot down in the past two or three weeks and now hiding out in the forests, as instructed, until the Second Front overtook them.

There were Americans, Canadians, South Africans, New Zealanders, Polish and British, with a smattering of *maquis* guards, a veritable League of Nations of evaders, and about as harmonious. Most of them had grown tired of this boy scouting and were becoming restive. Let them try it in winter, Odile thought, see how much they'd like it then.

'Well?' asked Langan.

It wasn't until she tried to speak that Odile realised how out of breath she was. Langan fetched her some water and she drank a mouthful, wetting a cloth and wiping her face with the rest. She had no illusions about how she looked. Her skin was criss-crossed with black, grimy lines, where soil and dirt had worked their way into her epidermis, her eyes were permanently red and sore from never daring to let go into a deep sleep, and her cheeks sunken from picking at food she wouldn't serve to a dog.

'There are Germans over to the west. We have to move east, to the camp at Fréteval.'

This was one of the mustering areas suggested by MI9 and passed on to SOE.

Langan nodded and indicated the men. 'Some of them want to strike out on their own, take their chances.'

Odile shrugged. She was too tired to argue. 'Let them. Just don't tell them where we are going.'

She shuffled over to Marshall, while Langan spread the word that they were striking camp, closed her ears to the mumbles of discontent and slid down the tree trunk to sit beside him. 'Thanks for the gun.' She offered the M3 machine pistol back.

'Keep it.' He tapped his sidearm. 'I've got a spare.'

She smiled her thanks, grateful not to have to go back to the unreliable Sten, which she had grown to hate. An argument was brewing on the far side of the clearing as dissident groups demanded conflicting courses of action.

'You think they're an ungrateful bunch, don't you?' he said, indicating the squabblers. 'Cigarette?'

She shook her head. 'Not ungrateful. They're just young and selfish.'

'Young? How old are you?'

'A hundred and five,' she laughed.

'You're not thirty yet.'

'Maybe not,' she snapped. There was a time when people mistook her for a teenager. 'But I think these war years are like cat or dog years. Each one is worth four or five normal twelve months. I'll be an old woman when it's over.'

Langan came up, his mouth grim, the freckles standing out on his pale skin. 'There's a little group of Aussies buggering off, the rest are with us. How far is it?'

'A day and a bit,' Odile said, trying to keep the weariness out of her voice. 'Mostly on woodland tracks. There is only one section of open fields and we cross that at night.' As Langan left to supervise the mustering and send the Aussies on their way, she stood and held out a hand for Marshall and pulled him to his feet. 'How is it?'

He took a couple of steps and winced. 'Better. But not perfect.'

He had wrenched his ankle on landing, which was why he hadn't been able to rendezvous with his Jedburgh group. She could tell he was putting a brave face on what he considered the failure of the mission – to co-ordinate behind-the-lines actions by the French *maquis*. He had trained for six months to achieve nothing.

She slid her arm through her rucksack straps and flinched as the metal frame found its permanent groove on her spine. She despised the sack almost as much as the Sten. One of the young *maquisards* had that gun now, and seemed positively thrilled. Don't hold the magazine, she warned the boy, it'll jam. It's what saved Harry, she almost added.

Marshall grabbed his pack, swung it on his shoulder, picked up the gnarled branch he was using as a walking stick and they, and their strange caravan of allies, started to walk east, along the forest ridge. 'Where is this place we're goin'?'

She kept her voice low. 'Fréteval? About eighty kilometres from Le Mans.'

'Really? Jeez, I always wanted to see Le Mans.'

'They won't be racing today, I think.'

He laughed. 'You ever seen it?'

'Oh, yes. My father took me . . . must have been . . . thirty-seven. Year before he died. He was very excited because two Frenchmen won. I thought it was so very boring.' Something else that didn't endear her to Papa – she didn't quite grasp the point of rich men driving stupidly fast cars round in a circle for a whole day and night.

They crunched through the leaf litter in silence, the only noises the huffing of men and the odd smart remark causing a little explosion of laughter, but most of them quickly dropped into the rhythm that would carry them through the next couple of days.

After twenty minutes of tramping, he asked: 'What did you do? Before the Occupation?'

'Nurse,' she replied flatly.

'Ah.' He tapped the strapping on his leg. 'Thought it was rather professional looking.'

'You?'

'Worked with my father. He makes fishing rods.'

'Fishing rods?'

'Yes. Someone has to. They don't grow on trees. Well, they do, but you have to do a few things to them before you can sell them. Marshall Rods? No, you wouldn't know them, but they're famous all over the north west. Best rods a man can buy. Great reels, too.'

'Is that where you are from? The north west of America?'

'Yup. Seattle.'

She shook her head. She had never heard of it.

The noise of an aero engine pulsed through the treetops and most of the column stopped, heads cocked, trying to pick up the signature. A Typhoon, seemed to be the consensus. Odile looked at Marshall, but he just shrugged. 'Can't tell one from the other. Strictly Army, ma'am.' He looked down at his foot. 'Look what playin' with airplanes got me.'

The trees on either side of the ridge thinned and they could see farmland below, dappled in summer sunlight, the only sign that there was trouble in Arcadia a farmhouse with a huge chunk torn out of its side, the table and dresser in the kitchen clearly visible, although both leaned at unnatural angles.

'Married?'

'What?' Odile turned back to the American.

'Are you married?'

'No.' It came very quickly now, no hesitation as there used to be when she debated each time if she and Harry were still together in the eyes of God. Once she stopped believing God had any eyes, it was easy to disown the bastard. Besides, she kept telling herself, it was all done on a forged marriage licence. Null and void: even His Holiness in Rome would agree.

'Then why the ring?'

Odile looked down as if noticing it for the first time. 'It keeps the flies away.' She touched her matted hair and laughed. 'Not that they need much shooing these days.'

'Now, look—'

'I wasn't fishing for compliments.'

'I wasn't going to give you any. None that weren't deserved.'

Langan was waiting for them as they entered the dark arch of the next section of thick forest, where the ground began to fall away again and early acorns carpeted the floor. 'I think you should take the lead, Odile. You know where you're going.'

She nodded and hurried ahead, past the slogging men, up to the front, wondering if Langan had separated her from Marshall on purpose, then discarding the thought. Few of them saw her as a woman any longer, especially not Langan.

They came to the open fields at around midnight and had made the outskirts of the huge oval of the Fréteval forest before first light. They camped in a clearing, bedding down as best they could, most of them slipping straight into a shallow sleep that would seem cruelly short when the sun came up and the first of the flies came to suck at their sweat.

Hoping they wouldn't be observed, she took Marshall into the darker sections of the wood and they made love, although she had to admit it was more fucking than anything vaguely romantic, and she had wanted it more, she suspected, than him. Afterwards she pushed him away and told him to go back to his place with the others and, cradling her new machine gun – with the magazine out, the safety couldn't be trusted – she fell into her usual restless, undernourishing sleep hoping that, just this once, Harry would stay out of her dreams.

Thirty-one

August 1944

On the day of what was to be his final meeting with King, Harry had heard that the Allies were out of the Cherbourg peninsula, and heading for Falaise. Wolkers had always said that if they got off the beaches, then nothing would hold them back. Hitler could launch all the revenge bombs he wanted at London, but the end was a foregone conclusion.

Meanwhile, he heard on the Foch grapevine that the sixteenth German spy had been hanged at Pentonville. Harry knew King was his long-term protection against suffering the same fate, that he had to square everything with him before they left the city, make sure that London knew he was back with the angels. So he'd told Wolkers to wait, one more day, he had a little business to finish, and then they could leave. They would be out of there well before the Allies arrived and the reckonings began.

Harry turned up at the apartment as arranged, only this time in a light woollen suit. The SS uniform was losing its menace; the bolder Parisians were risking stares of contempt.

It was dusk when he got there, the sultry heat of a blue-skyed summer day finally fading, only to find the ground floor apartment was empty. Harry sat down and waited in the gathering darkness, smoking three cigarettes before he realised King wasn't coming. He made sure the shutters were closed and turned on the light. On instinct, he looked through all the furniture, but the drawers had been cleared. Nothing. It was a good twenty minutes before he thought to look at the thin, blackened leaves of paper in the fireplace. The first few crumbled in his hands, but he found he could locate an intact corner here or there. They were the remains of his own messages, his laboriously coded signals to London.

You would expect an agent to destroy the evidence after transmission, he reasoned. Except King had always been adamant there was no radio in this building, none within the centre of Paris, because the German direction-finding vans were too fast to risk transmission.

The dots wouldn't join. He didn't want them to. Harry knew what they would spell out.

The next morning he presented himself at the Swiss Bank on Avenue Montaigne and gave his account number. The clerk left the desk and consulted the manager, who came over personally to tell him the news. Yes, he and Wolkers were co-signatories, but Wolkers also had sole withdrawal rights. It had been on the contract. Had he not read it? So, said Harry, I need Mr Wolkers to get access to my money?

Technically, yes, replied the manager. However, there are no funds left in the account. Mr Wolkers withdrew them all two days ago. And the letter from King he had deposited? Mr Wolkers had taken everything, it was stressed, very patiently, to him, including the contents of the safety deposit box.

That evening he went to Tante Clara's. He had spent an increasingly frenzied day scouring every known hangout of Wolkers, making a fool of himself at bars, brothels, even at Avenue Foch, demanding they tell him where the treacherous bastard was.

At Foch, a sympathetic Sturmbannführer Diels had quietly offered him safe passage out of the city as part of the SD convoy heading for Poitiers. It was only then he detected, rumbling beneath his own agitation, the sense of panic swamping the building, most visible in the reddened eyes of the French secretaries who would be left behind to face whatever punishment Paris felt inclined to mete out.

Elsewhere, he found files and documents being stuffed into boxes and there was a smell of burning in the air, wafting through from the square at the rear of the building. Scorched paper. The last of the cells had been cleared, the baths of freezing water emptied at last, old stains mopped from floors. The Sicherheitsdienst, at least, had made up their mind which way the battle for Paris would go.

Sturmbannführer Diels gave him a final word of warning. 'If you leave, stay away from Domont.' Harry looked puzzled. 'It's a village, just north of Paris. The Gestapo are using it to settle their old scores. You wouldn't want to get in the way.'

Harry thanked him and on his way out passed one of the ground-floor dining rooms, where a group of SD officers were cracking open cases of champagne, drinking straight from the bottle and discarding them half full.

He took a small red Opel from the SD car pool, making sure it had plenty of petrol, and drove through the streets of a Paris already giddy with excitement. The patriotic red, white and blue clothing motif was everywhere, and women walked with a skip in their step, or at least the best they could manage in clogs.

King and Wolkers. Harry, King of the Cons, had been fleeced

by his own. Once again. He banged the steering wheel in fury, and headed for Les Halles.

He climbed the stairs to Tante Clara's, expecting to catch the smell of the dishes she conjured up out of the meagrest of ingredients, but there was nothing. The door to the apartment was open and he stepped in, calling her name, softly at first.

The groan came from the bedroom, and he found her lying next to the ornate wardrobe that had sliced a chunk from her temple as she had fallen. Her false teeth lay on the carpet a few feet away, and her arm was buckled under her.

He tried to roll her over, but the groan turned into a gasp of pain. How long had she been there? She was in her day clothes, but the absence of cooking meant she could have been there for eight hours or longer. He examined the bruised face and touched the blood on her temple. It was hard and congealed. As he pressed, Clara shuddered, and one eye flicked open, the pupil barely visible. Harry stood and left the apartment as quickly as he could.

'I do not approve of bandit outfits running across this countryside willy-nilly, Major.'

Bandit? Neave glanced down at his corduroy trousers and his mud-caked brogues and suppressed a smile. In contrast, the American Colonel in front of him looked as if he was about to be inspected by General Patton himself.

Had Neave seen a British officer four years ago dressed as he was now, he would have put him on a charge. The years running Room 900 had altered his view of war, had put him at odds with the West Point correctness he had just collided with. These days, waiting for the US Third Army to give him permission to move forward was not to his liking at all.

'I have fifty, maybe eighty soldiers and airmen out in Fréteval

Forest, expecting me, Colonel. All I need is transport.'

'All you need is your head testing, Major. Look at your men.' The Colonel indicated the lobby of Le Mans' Hôtel Moderne, filled with Neave's ad-hoc force of rescuers, playing cards, smoking, dressed in bits and pieces of uniform, nobody's idea of a regular force. He had heard them referred to as Privateers. Well, Francis Drake was a Privateer, so there was no shame in that.

'You know the sort of German troops that are dug in out there?' continued the American. 'The sort that will make mincemeat of your boys. Spying and soldiering, Major Neave, are two different skills.'

'Are you refusing me?'

'Yes. And you can have it in writing,' the Colonel sneered, 'if you wish. I will not risk my men or resources on some crack-brained scheme to pull out a bunch of pilots who may or may not be there.'

'They've been there two weeks now.'

'Well, a few more days won't harm them.'

The Colonel turned and left the hotel. One of Neave's clerks brought Neave a terse message from Room 900, back in London. What was happening? Everyone, from Donald Darling, now running the office in London, to his wife Diana, was against him coming over, but Operation Sherwood, the gathering of evaders and escapees into forests, had been his idea, and he wasn't about to let the final stage be botched by someone else. The way things were going, it seemed, he was perfectly capable of botching it himself.

'Any reply, sir?'

'Tell them: "Fuck all".'

Neave turned and went into the bar, aware that someone was following him. He reached over the counter, looking at his fractured reflection in the damaged mirror tiles that backed this once-elegant corner of the hotel, and found the bottle of whisky he had secreted there. He poured himself a shot and turned to face the swarthy British Captain who had trailed him.

'Got another?' the man asked with a familiarity that momentarily took Neave aback, until he checked the shoulder insignia. Another irregular.

He fetched a second tumbler and poured the man an inch of the liquid. 'There you are, Captain.'

'Thank you, sir.'

'Tony Neave. I'm with . . .'

'IS9. Cheers.' Intelligence School Nine was the name they used in the field to cover all the roles of MI9. In reality, it was a building in Highgate where intelligence officers were trained, but it was a useful catch-all. 'Anthony Greville-Bell.'

They shook hands. 'How can I help you, Captain?'

'I couldn't help overhearing you and the Colonel out there. I think it's more a case of how I can help you, Major Neave,' said Greville-Bell with a cock-eyed grin.

Neave's heart leapt. Greville-Bell had drained his glass and Neave topped him up. 'How so, Captain?'

'Thanks.' He took a more moderate sip this time. 'In the square over yonder, I have thirty of my Special Air Service men sitting cooling their heels like you. We have two Jeeps with Lewis guns, and I know where we can lay our hands on fifteen or sixteen charcoal buses. You want to get your men out of the forest, Major, you talk to me.'

Harry was sure he had the right house. He knocked on the door and a face appeared at the crack. A woman, in her thirties. Yes, this was the one. 'I need a doctor.'

'There is no doctor here.'

'I know there is.'

The door opened a little wider and the woman said in a tone she would never have dared use three weeks previously, 'I've seen you. I know who you are.'

'No you bloody well don't,' he spat.

The door started to close and he threw his shoulder against it and the words tumbled out: 'Yes, you're right. You have seen me. You have seen what I can do. The Allies aren't here yet. I can still do it. Still tell them you are harbouring a Jew. Have been for, what? Two years. How long does it take to put you against a wall and shoot you? Or put you on a train? They're still running, you know. Every day. Now give me what I want.'

'What do you want?'

'Your Jew is a doctor. I need him. I'll take him, I'll bring him back. And then this didn't happen.' He puffed himself up as if he still had those twin flashes at his throat. 'If you don't . . .'

The man was pale, thin and frightened. Doctor he may be, thought Harry, but he'd never make a surgeon with those shaking hands. He wasn't much help in moving Tante Clara either, and Harry took most of the weight as they got her onto the bed, her screams now down to whimpers. Harry was sent off to get water, while the man went to work, occasionally pausing as if the skills of doctoring had long since deserted him.

Harry waited in the living room pacing the threadbare rug, his stomach knotted, his mind racing through his options. He could wait for the Allies to arrive, but how would he establish his story? No King to back him up. No letter. And enough people had seen him in SD uniform at Foch to make sure he would be arrested, or worse. He was in the shit.

It was gone ten at night by the time the doctor summoned him. 'She wants to see you. I've done all I can. Nothing broken . . . she is very lucky. Bed rest . . . and some food.'

'Thank you, Doctor,' he said. He reached into his pocket for money but the man raised his hand.

'No. Just don't come to the house again. Please.'

Harry nodded his agreement, and took the man back to where he found him. On his return, he went in to see Clara, who was sitting up in bed, one side of her face a purplish blue. 'Oh, Harry. I'm sorry . . .'

'No, no, don't be silly.'

She licked her dry lips in a way he tried to ignore. 'I didn't eat last night and this morning I had just put my shoes on and I stood up and I must have fainted . . . if you hadn't found me, I, well, I wouldn't be here.'

He picked up her hand and felt the bones under his thumb. 'I'll get you some food.'

'It's gone curfew. Nowhere will be open now,' she said. 'And there'll certainly be nothing left.'

'Everywhere is open all hours for Harry. And there is always something left.'

'There's some money under the floorboards. Beneath the rug.'

'No, I'm OK,' he said quickly.

He returned two hours later, his pockets filled with meat and vegetables, and a goose over his shoulder. It had cost him every favour he had left in the city. He made up a plate of charcuterie and gave it to Clara with a half glass of wine and a pitcher of water. She thanked him over and over again. He posted a note through the apartment downstairs, telling the couple what had happened and asking them to look in. Then he said goodbye to her, with a kiss on her ravaged cheek.

'Will I see you again, Harry?'

'I don't know, Clara. Things are falling apart out there.'

'Try and stay lucky, Harry.' She winced as she smiled, and

through the bandage and the bruises he saw a flash of the other, younger Clara.

'I will. Goodbye, Clara. Thanks.'

He wondered if she heard him, on his way out, pull back the rug, prise up the loose floorboard and help himself to all but a few thousand francs of the money. If she did, she never uttered a word.

As Neave walked into the square in the centre of Le Mans, its cobbles barely illuminated by the thin shafts of the new sun, he had to blink before he was certain what his sleep-filled eyes were seeing. There were indeed sixteen buses, but they were decked out as if they were going to some kind of exotic wedding, festooned with flowers and hung with French, American and British flags. Grinning civilian drivers, who clearly had no idea what they were letting themselves in for, sat behind the steering wheels. Greville-Bell was leaning against one of his Jeeps, smoking. He flicked the cigarette away as he saw Neave.

'Morning, Major. How's the head?'

'Functioning,' said Neave, annoyed with himself that he had finished the bottle with the Captain. His mouth was dry and there was a persistent knocking behind one eye, whereas the SAS man looked as if he was newly minted.

'Good. Shall we roll? Here. Just in case.' The Captain handed Neave a Thompson submachine gun and the two of them slipped into the Jeep, with Greville-Bell driving. Behind them a sergeant manned a Lewis gun mounted on a crudely welded framework. The convoy coughed into life, the engines rattling and belching, thick clouds of gritty dust filling the square until the sun began to fade to grey. After fifteen minutes, each one had managed to start, and they jerked forward, heading out to the forest.

Groups of US soldiers stared at them with puzzled expressions as they swept through the early morning streets, but nobody challenged them. It was just too bizarre a sight, the no-nonsense SAS men leading what looked like a parade of charabancs off on a magical mystery tour. Neave, the barrister, the Lieutenant at Calais, even the one at Colditz, would have been appalled at this affront to army convention. Now he was someone who believed in achieving his aims by any means at his disposal.

As they left the town and started through the fields towards the forest, Neave felt nervous. Farmhouses, haystacks, copses, any one of them could hold a cluster of German rearguard gunners. He slid off the safety and checked the action of the Thompson. At any other time he would have relished the warm summer air whipping through his hair, but now he wished the open-sided Jeep offered more protection.

'About thirty kilometres,' yelled Greville-Bell over the clattering of the engines. 'I reckon another ten before we are likely to see any Jerry.' He lit another cigarette. 'Is it true that you saved Chartres cathedral, Major?'

Neave laughed. 'I suppose it is.'

'And that the Yanks were going to shell it?'

'To be fair they thought there were snipers in the spire.'

Greville-Bell turned to him and said, 'I heard you walked in on your own to prove there weren't any. Up the spiral staircase to the bloody top and shouted out all clear to the Yanks.'

It was no big deal, as the Americans would say, although striding into the vast space, its stained glass removed to the safe haven of caves in the Dordogne, had been tense to say the least. 'There weren't any up there, that's true. But I couldn't shout, too high. So I waved my handkerchief for the all-clear. Felt like some bloody maiden in the tower.'

'You weren't sure, were you? That there were no Germans up there?'

'No, I couldn't be absolutely sure, no.' Indignation crept into his voice. 'But to blow up Chartres cathedral. It's just not on, is it?'

Greville-Bell chuckled and put his foot down.

It happened, as the Captain had suggested, after ten kilometres, the first warning a tapping from the side of the leading bus as the metal was perforated by a long line of black dots. Neave slumped down in the seat, scanning the fields, but the sergeant already had the snipers pinpointed and Neave was suddenly disorientated by the huge clattering as the antique Lewis gun fired and spent shells began to rain down on him.

Other SAS men returned fire – there was the lazy thud of the Brens from the buses – and Neave could see it was concentrated on the long, low barn that began to send out small puffs of smoke as rounds hit the rotten wood. The convoy hardly slowed, but the fire was dense and accurate, raking the barn from one end to the other.

'Anyone left, we'll get them on the way back,' said Greville-Bell. 'Quite right not to fire. You would never have hit it at that range.'

Neave looked down at the Thompson and realised it had never occurred to him to use it.

They found them on the edge of Fréteval, half starved and completely bedraggled. They ran from the treeline, shouting greetings as the SAS convoy approached, leaping up and down, arms waving. Neave felt tearful pride well up in him. Operation Sherwood had worked.

'Get them on board, quick,' said Greville-Bell. 'I don't want to be caught here. Too much cover for Jerry in the forest.'

Neave was pulled out of the Jeep by a weeping Pole, who

kissed him on both cheeks. A rather more diffident squadron leader held out his hand. Neave took it and nearly didn't get it back. Langan, the SOE co-ordinator, slapped his shoulder in an overfamiliar way, and Neave had to stop a spontaneous party breaking out among the Anzacs. 'Listen,' he yelled, 'there is hot food and cold drink at Le Mans.'

'And women?' an Aussie voice asked.

'Oh, yes, and women. And they'll all be very pleased to see you.' Not quite as pleased as they were to see the Americans, thought Neave, but let them work that one out for themselves. 'There are still German patrols in the area, so if you'll just get on the buses. Leave all non-essential gear.'

She was standing over to his right, back against a tree, machine gun dangling casually from one hand, smoking a cigarette with the other. He excused himself from Langan and walked over to her. It was only as he got nearer that he noticed the three bodies in the undergrowth, faces covered, one of them with a US flag.

'Odile.'

'Major Neave.' She touched her hair, aware of her appearance. 'How nice of you to come and get us.'

'Least I could do.' He nodded down at the bodies and asked: 'Who have we here?'

'One *maquis*, one New Zealander and an American called Marshall. A Jed-something.'

'Jedburgh,' he said. 'What happened?'

'A plane.'

'A German plane?'

She shook her head. 'American. Must have thought we were Germans. Strafed the woods. Killed the first two right off. Marshall,' she indicated the nearest form, 'ran out with a US flag, but . . .'

'I'm sorry.'

'Why? It's not your fault. It's one of those things.'

'You coming to have something to eat? I'll get some of the SAS to fetch the bodies.'

'A bath, Major Neave. I need a bath.'

'I'll find you one. A proper big one.'

'And then? Where are you off to next?'

'Paris,' said Neave.

'That sounds good.' She slid her arm through his and they walked back to the convoy, oblivious of the stares as she let her head rest against his shoulder.

Thirty-two

September 1944

After leaving Paris, Harry had headed east. The roads were congested in both directions, as if the Germans couldn't decide whether they were retreating or advancing, digging in or making a tactical withdrawal to the Rhine. He had bullied a tankful of petrol from an army sergeant at the Troyes fuel depot, flashing his Gestapo papers and muttering dark threats about defeatism when the man hesitated.

His path had been erratic, dictated by the needs of food, sleep and fuel, and also the desire to avoid those areas which the Wehrmacht had abandoned to the *maquis*. That was bandit country. The forged seals and letters he had prepared for himself before leaving Paris counted for something where the Wehrmacht or the SS roamed. Elsewhere, they could be his death warrant.

Even with the Germans you had to be careful. They were mean and spiteful and any hint of gloating by the locals could be lethal. He had seen the evidence slumped against walls, hanging from lampposts, or remembered with forlorn bunches of flowers at crossroads and on bomb sites.

The underpowered Opel coughed as it began to climb, heading for the switchback roads that would take him over the mountains and into the Rhine valley. The scenery should have lifted his heart, but it was just so much backdrop to him, the hills and peaks mere obstacles.

He tried to remember Odile, to stop the memory fading, trying to conjure up her face, her smell, her feel. It all went wrong for him when he lost Odile. If only he had played it straight with her, then he might not be a hunted man now.

The Opel wheezed up the final snake of road and crested the range at Bonhomme. Below him, he saw the hills and the vineyards and the river, a beautiful, forest-pocked vista, dotted with gingerbread villages, all seemingly untouched by the war. Yet he recalled that in Foch they talked about Natzweiler, a concentration camp near here, an extermination centre on former French soil. Of course, Alsace was German now. He had driven right into the lion's mouth.

Every deserter was heading west or north, trying to make it to the US or British forces. He was going in the opposite direction on Special Administrative Duties, as his papers had it. He would lay up for a while in Alsace and then head south to Switzerland. There, a new beginning. He was sure post-war Europe would offer him plenty of opportunities.

Harry stopped and consulted his map, turning north as he reached the foothills, threading through the forests, skirting the vineyards, waving at the odd bemused farmer bringing in the harvest under the looming grey skies.

The house was up an unmade road, and the car bucked its way up to the enormous gates, one of which was open. As he took the sweeping driveway, he smiled when the château came into view. Like Alsace itself, it was a curious mix, with a huge French mansard roof, but with schloss-style turrets at each corner, looking as if a princess could be imprisoned in each one. It wasn't pretty, but it shouted old money, a true aristocratic pile.

Harry pulled to a halt on the gravel and got out, craning his neck as he scanned the vast stone walls for signs of life. Nothing. He checked his tweed suit – the SD uniform was safely packed in the boot – loosened the Walther pistol in his inside pocket, and hoped he wasn't making the biggest mistake of his life as he stepped towards the fat oak doors with their ornate black hinges and pushed them open.

The hallway was grand baronial in style, with lots of dark, carved wood and a staircase which could take an army marching abreast. Its walls had once been lined with paintings of the ancestors, and illuminated by a chandelier of the kind that Errol Flynn or John Barrymore might swing off in a swashbuckler. Now, the dark wood had split into blooms of splinters where bullets had gouged it, the only evidence of the portraits the marks on the panelling where they once hung, and the chandelier was reduced to a frosting of shards on the parquet flooring.

The house felt cold and damp, as if it hadn't been heated in months, and there was a strange, sharp smell. He pulled out the Walther pistol and tiptoed over the remnants of the shattered chandelier, heading for the double doors with the huge family crest on each half that looked as if they led to the main chamber.

The room beyond was in semi-darkness, with most of the full-length window shutters folded across, but enough of the wintry daylight was leaking in for him to recognise her.

'Oh, Hellie,' he said softly to the Contessa von Lutz.

Her tongue was purple, squeezed between her lips, her hair had been clippered, leaving isolated tufts here and there, the front of her dress was ripped down to expose her breasts, and the makeshift noose had forced her head to one side. How long she had been there, he had no idea, but the odour suggested a while. He stepped forward to touch her.

'Hello, Harry, I was wondering if you'd turn up.'

He started, nearly pulling the trigger of the gun in shock. He flicked the safety off and advanced, trying to stop his hand shaking, keeping the gun level on the black form he could just make out. The figure was lying with his legs out straight, and Harry could see two empty bottles of Hock next to him. Harry reached across and slammed back a shutter, and looked down at the squinting, unshaven face before him. Pieter Wolkers.

Odile thought she had seen rowdy celebrations in Paris, but the racket coming from the foyer of the Hôtel Metropole in Brussels was deafening. At the entrance she took a step back as a great cheer went up. Neave was clambering onto the reception desk. He tried to signal for quiet, but the scores of men and women stamped their feet and whistled wildly.

Odile turned and ushered her four companions in. One was an RAF gunner, who had been in hiding for three years, the others Belgian members of the Comet line who had been betrayed and managed to go underground before the Abwehr got to them. All were pale, nervous and confused, but soon each held a container filled with champagne.

When it was offered to Odile she shook her head, but indicated it should be passed to the two armed men behind her in the doorway, the Frenchmen who made up her Rescue Team V. Neave had created a series of small mobile units whose job it was to scoop up evaders and their helpers. He had been disappointed that the big camp at Bastogne had not materialised. The airmen and soldiers in the area had suspected that Operation Sherwood was a German trap, and her job had been to find the stragglers and convince them this was a genuine operation.

'Ladies and gentlemen,' shouted Neave, 'thank you very much. I know you are all very happy to be here. I am very happy you are here. And to those who have been badgering me all day—' He glanced down at a small group of Belgians who quickly examined their feet. 'There will be an Awards Bureau set up in due course to reimburse expenses and to recommend decorations. But not now. I suggest that over the next few days you put your claims in writing, with dates and amounts and witness statements.'

Neave reached down and fetched himself a glass, a proper champagne flute. 'Now, I'd like to thank Colonel Murphy of the Supreme Headquarters Allied Expeditionary Force, who has agreed that SHAEF will sponsor our little celebration here. Thank you, Colonel.'

Odile looked over at the benefactor, who graciously acknowledged the roar of thanks. Odile was certain she had seen him in Paris, first heading up a documentary film unit, secondly as part of the group which had targeted the cellars of Paris's best hotels, with the express aim of drinking them dry, part of the orgy of hedonism known as the Ritzkrieg. She would put good money on him not being part of SHAEF, although who settled the bill was a problem for later.

Neave hadn't finished. 'I also want to propose a toast to all those brave Belgians who helped us, especially during the early years. All the members of the Comet line.' He raised a glass at a gaunt young woman near the front. 'And my Little Cyclones, the women who took appalling risks with no thought for their own safety. I give you . . . those who won't return.'

There was a rumble of murmured agreement and thin applause. Neave raised his flute and flung the contents down his throat. 'There will be reports and debriefing and paperwork and lots of it . . . tomorrow!'

Another cheer and the pop of more bottles. As Neave climbed down, a man in black jacket and pinstripe trousers approached. The manager. Neave bent forward, whispered something short and sharp in his ear and the man flinched and scurried off.

Neave pushed through the crowd, shaking proffered hands, occasionally stopping for a word, once or twice hugging a man or a woman. Eventually he made it to Odile who was still near the entrance, her machine gun slung over her shoulder.

'Odile. How did you get on?'

'We found four. What did you say to that poor manager? Look, he's shaking.'

'I told him we knew about his dealing with the Germans and if he didn't stop complaining about his precious champagne, I'd make an announcement about it and let the crowd have him.'

'My God. What had he done?'

Neave grabbed a passing bottle and refilled his glass. Odile noticed it was a '26 Taittinger. 'What had he done? Buggered if I know. It was just a wild guess.' He laughed. 'Hit a nerve, though, eh? You haven't got a glass. Here, have mine.'

She took it and sipped. It was warm and sticky, and she handed it back. 'It's OK, I don't feel like drinking.'

Now they were being pushed against the perimeter wall as more people arrived, drawn more by the drink and the noise of the party than any knowledge of IS9, she suspected. 'Are you all right? You look tired.'

Odile laughed. 'I've looked tired for five years. This is how I always look.'

No it isn't, he almost said, then realised he would be giving himself away, would be admitting he had looked in on her while she had slept, in Le Mans, fretting she was never going to wake.

'What now, Major Neave?'

A worried look crossed his face. 'Arnhem. Bloody fiasco. There are thousands of the First Airborne at large. We have to get them back.'

'You have to get them back, Major. I am returning to Paris.'

'Really? Must you?' A body thumped into him and he was thrust close against her, something he did little to rectify and, he was glad to note, neither did she. 'I'm not suggesting you come to the bloody bridge with me. There's enough for RTs to do.'

'No. I can't follow you round Europe, Major. I'm not a soldier.' She banged the side of her gun. 'I am just a nurse who got out of her depth.'

He touched her cheek. 'You never got out of your depth.'

'Harry Cole?'

'Sergeant Harry Cole was a bastard.'

She smiled. 'He wasn't all bad, you know.'

'There are men and women who aren't coming back because of him. Who suffered horribly. You suffered horribly.'

'I know, I know.' He knew she was referring to her child. 'But there was a time when he was a good man.'

Neave felt an anger whip up inside him. 'I don't believe you. There was a time when he chose not to behave in his usual despicable way, I might accept that.'

She shook her head. 'No. It was more than that. You liked him once.'

'Never. Please don't let time and distance soften your heart towards him.'

She laughed at the flowery phrase. Neave was tipsy from champagne on an empty stomach.

'He was a bad man,' continued the Major, grabbing her arm. 'Whose interests and ours coincided for a short while. As soon as they were no longer concurrent, he took the path best suited to Harry. That's the difference between a man like him and a woman like you.'

She gently took his hand away. 'Perhaps. Or perhaps we all do what suits us, and just dress it up as patriotism or altruism.'

Neave's eyes flashed. 'Try telling that to half the people in the room. They are heroes. So are you.'

'I don't feel much like a hero. Right now, I have to go back and pick up a life, Major.' Odile hesitated, then kissed Neave lightly on a well-shaved cheek.

'Major Neave.' The booming voice startled him and he spun round. Before him was a hatchet-faced man with a thin, tightly razored moustache under a beaked nose. 'Major Hugh Fraser,' he introduced himself. 'Special Air Service. I believe we have an appointment with a bridge at Arnhem.'

Christ, he thought, as Fraser squeezed his fingers together, who'd be a bridge? 'Indeed we do, Major. Hold on a second.'

Neave turned to say something to Odile, but she was no longer there, and the sensation of her lips on his skin, that had faded, too.

Thirty-three

Harry held the gun on Wolkers, wondering whether he should pull the trigger. Wolkers looked sweaty, greasy, with patches of dirt and possibly bruising across the nose and down one cheek. Then Harry noticed the pool of congealed blood under the calf of his left leg. The man was badly wounded.

'I should kill you,' Harry said finally.

'I think this'll beat you to it.' He nodded at the stiff limb stretched out in front of him.

'What the fuck are you doing here?'

'Dying, Harry, dying. Can you get me some more wine? There might be a couple of bottles left in the cellar that they didn't drink or take. Shitty anaesthetic, but it's all I've got. I made it down there once . . . can't do it again.'

Harry knelt down and pulled back the material of the trouser leg. It had already been slit with a knife and revealed a piece of metal shaped like a shark's fin protruding from the calf. The flesh around it was swollen and multi-hued, with flecks of pus squeezing out where steel and skin met.

'Jesus,' muttered Harry. 'How did this happen?'

'Pretty, eh? No, don't touch it. The wine? Please? Then you can kill me.'

Harry went back towards the hall, trying not to look at Hellie, noticing the darker patterns on the floor where rugs and furniture had once stood. Like the hallway, this room had been gutted.

The cellar, too, had been ransacked. Shelves had been pulled over, barrels split, bottles smashed, and the air was thick with sour fumes. He picked his way across to the largest pile of glass, then crouched, rolling the intact bottles aside, until he found one that was half full, and had, unusually, been re-corked.

On his return, the Dutchman drank it down gratefully. 'Thanks. Go ahead, shoot.'

'You took all the money.'

'You're just pissed off you didn't think of it.'

Harry almost laughed. 'I wouldn't have cheated you.'

'Crap. Had you thought of a way, you'd have done it. Harry, con men only get conned by con men and they don't see it coming because they are conning themselves.'

'How the hell did you get here?'

'Look, Harry. After I saw Hellie at the hospital and you told me about her, she wasn't hard to track down at the charity.'

'You fucked Hellie?'

'Yes, me and half of Paris probably.'

'So you took my money and fucked my woman—'

'She was hardly your woman.'

Harry fell silent for a moment, then pointed at Hellie. 'So who did this?'

'I don't know. She was like that when we got here. We got strafed—'

'We?'

'I had one of the Hungarians with me, from Foch. We got

strafed on the road from Strasbourg. I got this but we managed to make it here.'

'Why here?'

'I agreed it in Paris. With Hellie.'

Harry sniffed. 'Yeah, me too. Could've been an interesting party, that one. I wonder how many others she told.'

'Nobody else made it so far.'

'So who did it to her?'

'Locals, I guess. Maybe she had a German lover. Maybe they just fancied some new furniture and a drink and she got in the way. Funny things are happening at the moment, Harry.'

'And your Hungarian?'

'He left me here and went off to get a doctor.'

'Three days ago?'

'He isn't coming back. I didn't think to look for my bag till he'd gone.'

'The money?'

Wolkers nodded.

'All of it?'

Wolkers looked at him. 'I thought you were going to kill me.'

Harry shrugged. 'As you once said, I'm not the killing kind. It's my burden.'

'Well, I'm not going anywhere fast.'

'I can load you into the car. If you can stand it.'

Wolkers shook his head. 'No need. About half an hour before you came an American Jeep drove into the courtyard. I think they saw me peering out—' He flinched in pain and grabbed his thigh, waiting for the burning to subside. 'Out of the window. My guess is they'll be back with their pals before sunset. Thing is, Harry, I know you have a way with words. You best come up with the story of a fucking lifetime, my friend, otherwise Hellie's going to have company.'

★ ★ ★

'That's a hell of a tale, Captain Mason,' said Captain Dixon of the United States' 117th Cavalry Unit, one of the fast, mobile probing arms of the VI Corps that were racing to Germany. He had arrived with a dozen others in the half-track and three Jeeps parked next to the Opel outside. 'Don't you agree, Lieutenant Beiser?'

The Captain turned to his intelligence officer, who nodded. 'We can of course verify this with London?' asked Beiser.

'Absolutely, old chap, absolutely. But first, I think we should patch my friend up here. Don't you?'

Two GIs were lowering Hellie to the floor and wrapping her in a US army blanket.

'So what is your mission now, Captain?' asked Dixon. 'Why are you here?'

Harry's story had stuck closely to the truth, although it made out he had been parachuted in as an agent in 1941 to run the escape lines, had been captured, and then gone into deep cover as a double agent, working at Avenue Foch while reporting to London. Wolkers was a trusted SOE operative. Harry had played up his old clipped officer accent and, after initial scepticism, they seemed to accept his fabrications.

'Nazi hunting,' said Harry firmly. 'The worst of the bastards have gone undercover, posing as ordinary soldiers. We' – he pointed at Wolkers – 'saw many of them first hand. We won't forget those faces in a hurry.'

'Or what they did,' said Wolkers.

Dixon took out a pack of cigarettes and offered them round. 'I'll have to check you out.' He gave Beiser a look which told him that it would be the Lieutenant doing the checking. 'Make sure you didn't do a little impromptu justice of your own with this woman here. But we're picking up more prisoners than we can handle out there. Anyone who can help process them is very welcome.'

'We'll have to get you some uniforms. And have that leg seen to,' said Beiser excitedly, 'then we'll be heading east, gentlemen. Into Germany proper.'

Dixon held out his hand to Harry. 'Welcome to the Hundred and Seventeenth Cavalry, Captain Mason.'

Harry smiled as best he could. Just what he needed. Another bloody army.

Thirty-four

Paris, April 1945

Odile had found a place in St Germain, not far from the Rhumerie Martiniquaise bar. It was a simple room, off a courtyard, with a bed and basin and the usual restrictions on cooking. She wouldn't dare break this rule, because behind the desk in the office was a fearsome thing, a shrew-faced creature so intimidating she was almost afraid to ask for her mail. Strange really, to be able to face up to Nazis and traitors, and still find yourself at the mercy of the Parisian concierge.

So she would eat her sole meal of the day among the communists at the Bonaparte or at the Royal St Germain, with its jazz musicians, which she preferred, or the apprentice intellectuals at the Flore. Sometimes she would drink a solitary cocktail at the Rhumerie, and join in with the laughter at the tables.

The heady days of the Liberation were fading fast now, although the infatuation with all things American remained – several bars had renamed themselves after US cities or popular American songs, the zinc tops replaced by fat, padded leather or plastic, the stern white-aproned waiters now transformed into chatty cocktail mixers or even pretty girls in tight skirts.

The *épuration sauvage*, the settling of scores, had also moved on from the mindless violence of the first six months. Paris had never been as bad as Avignon, with its lynch mobs, or Marseilles with its murderous 'people's police', or Lyon, where acquitted Vichyists were kidnapped, bound hand and foot, then loaded into bombers and dropped onto a concrete runway. No, Paris had lashed out at its collaborators initially, but now it was as if a truce had been agreed, and the agenda was to try to heal, rather than pick at, the city's wounds.

Odile had found a job in a nursing home, looking after French men and women who had been maltreated in Germany, either in concentration camps or on labour gangs. She knew that there was an office near the Palais Royal where those who had worked the ratlines could go for financial compensation or for consideration for various medals. She wanted none of that. The shame of being duped by Harry into handing the information over to Wolkers still tainted everything else she had tried to do. She didn't deserve a medal or thanks. She may have just been a dumb messenger, but if she hadn't allowed herself to trust Harry, to love him, then the disaster might have been avoided.

There was a young man in the nursing home. He had worked in the Volkswagen factory in Wolfsburg and had been wounded in an air raid. He had only one eye, and was missing some toes, but by the standards of the home he was pretty much intact, even psychologically.

They had sat and talked about the future, she perched on the edge of his bed, long after she should have left for home. His family were shopkeepers. He thought perhaps he would sell radios and possibly televisuals if a service ever got started. He had been reading about the British and American broadcasting trials. He believed that after the silence and furtiveness of the war years, the French would embrace big radiograms and record players and possibly even televisual sets. She liked his enthusiasm and optimism and his lack of bitterness.

So it was with a feeling of some joy that she left for work on that April day, skipping down the four worn steps to the courtyard and hurrying past Madame's lair until called back to take the letter which had arrived for her with the US army postmark and aroused the suspicions of the concierge. Odile thanked her and slipped the missive under her cape, her happiness fading. She didn't have to open the letter to know exactly who had penned it.

Harry and his army swept into Delgau at noon, after a long drive through the gently curved hills and the patterned farmlands of Württemberg. He was a passenger in a sleek silver Mercedes, driven by Hervé, a young Frenchman whom he discovered trying to 'liberate' it. Hervé had been a forced labourer in German factories, and when Harry had explained his scheme, the young lad had agreed to join the ad-hoc deNazification force. The only problem with the Merc was the lack of a back seat, but the space proved ideal for the mountain of C-rations, cigars and silverware they had gathered on their trek from town to town.

Harry was dressed in the US army captain's uniform Dixon had given him when they had joined the 117th Cavalry. It was while they were helping process prisoners that Harry had hatched his current scheme.

Behind the Mercedes came Wolkers in a Jeep, also in US army uniform, his leg now almost completely healed. He was accompanied by one of the two French women they had picked up along the way, Natalie. Suzy, the second woman, was in the Citroën driven by Jean, another Frenchman with scores to settle, along with their real prize, Jeff Hardman, a Lieutenant with the 101st who had been inducted into the OSS.

Impressed with Cole's English manner, Hardman had managed to get himself assigned to what he had convinced himself was a top British deNazification unit. His brief was to look out for any Nazi scientists, something they hadn't yet come across. In fact, something Harry wasn't at all interested in. There was no money in science.

The town was bustling with US personnel and DPs – displaced persons – French, Czechs, Poles, Hungarians, overcrowding what had once been a quiet, prosperous spa town.

As always, Harry would do the talking. The occupying forces were based in the best hotel in town, the Thermale, and Harry found the G-2 counter-intelligence officer in a comfortable bedroom on the third floor, the carpet covered in a thousand pieces of paper arranged in neat stacks. He introduced himself as Captain Mason and gave his letters of recommendation from Dixon and, the clincher, Hardman's OSS orders.

'Well, Captain,' said Lieutenant Powell, the G-2, handing back the documents. 'What can we do for you?'

'We have reason to believe that this town was selected as a rendezvous point for members of the SS in the event of the unthinkable happening. Like losing the war.'

This much was true. Wolkers beat it out of one of their victims in Gamisch. 'I believe, among the ordinary Wehrmacht soldiers, you may be harbouring war criminals.'

Powell scratched his head and indicated the papers on the floor. 'These are depositions taken from the prisoners. I am supposed to read them, report to CIC—'

'I can save you a lot of time and effort, Lieutenant,' said Harry smoothly. 'Trust me. We've been doing this for almost six months now. We can give you full recommendation to action after three, perhaps four days.'

'What will you need?'

'A base somewhere, free access to the prisoners, the chance to speak to them away from their fellow internees. Peer group intimidation, fear of reprisal, they are powerful disincentives to talk.' Harry grinned.

Powell sat down on the bed and sighed. 'I tell ya, I'm inclined just to send the whole lot back to where they came from. They're a sorry bunch.'

'And when it gets out that SS butchers slipped through your fingers? How will CIC feel about that?'

Powell nodded wearily, grateful to be able to hand the responsibility over to someone else. 'OK, I'll get the papers typed up. But I want a full report at the end of each day.'

'Of course. Be on your desk by twenty-one hundred each night,' said Harry.

Harry watched Hervé and Jean rain truncheon blows onto the German strapped to the chair. Every so often, Suzy spat in the man's face, until a mixture of blood and spittle coated his skin. There was no doubt the French enjoyed this part, exacting revenge of some sort for the years spent under Occupation and in their stinking workhouses.

Harry's time with the Gestapo had coarsened and simplified his response to pain. As long as it wasn't him under the cosh, he pretty much didn't care what they did. He didn't, however, enjoy watching and he walked out onto the verandah, trying to close his ears to the grunts and groans as more flesh split and teeth loosened. He'd have to stop them soon.

The house was a mile outside Delgau, a thick-walled former farmhouse set high on a flower-decked hillside. It belonged to a local SS man, a name Wolkers had also been given in Gamisch. He was unceremoniously turfed out with the promise that he would get his house back when they had finished with it, along with the threat that any protest would mean his name went forward to the local G-2 officer as someone worth detaining pending an inquiry into his wartime behaviour.

Once the verandah would have enjoyed a charmingly pastoral overview, but now the valley was blighted by the sprawling German POW compound with its metal huts and, on the opposite side of the town, the canvas tents of the Displaced Persons camp.

Harry lit a Camel and wondered if it was a mistake to have written to Odile, but he desperately wanted to see her. Like the DPs in the tents, he had a life he needed to pick up again. Two, perhaps three months more, if the chaos in Europe that allowed him to operate lasted that long, and he'd have enough cash to start over, in a place where he could build that new life. Maybe, he hardly dared even whisper it, with Odile.

He was aware of a figure at his side. Hardman, the American. 'Captain Mason—'

'Harry, please. I've told you before,' he said.

Hardman stuttered it. 'H-Harry. I think we are losing sight of the original mission.'

'Are we?'

'Yes, sir. I have to report back to OSS in five days, sir. So far . . . well, all we've done is beat up people. That might be the way you do it in the British army, but . . .'

Harry glared at him. 'These people are scum, Jeff. You understand? They tortured and looted their way across Europe.'

'That's no reason for us to do the same.'

'You didn't feel like that in Mengen.'

Harry had encouraged Hardman to take part in an interrogation and watched the American begin to enjoy knocking an SS man down, standing him up and knocking him down again. It was an important part of initiation into the group.

'I regret that now. I have no compunction about these people on the field of battle. But I overstepped the mark in Mengen.'

Harry realised he had to lose the Yank. Perhaps the game was drawing to a close sooner than he had hoped. One of these days, a suspicious G-2 would get a query through to London or SHAEF, the Supreme Headquarters Allied Expeditionary Force, about a group of freelance deNazifiers, and his cover would be blown once and for all.

Harry nodded, as if a sudden realisation had hit him. 'You're right, Jeff.' He stepped back inside and said quickly: 'Enough.'

Hervé and Jean took a pace backwards, breathing hard from their exertions, and the German looked up, his nose trickling twin streams of red down into his mouth, his filthy uniform speckled with dark crimson.

Harry knelt down in front of him. 'Come, come, I saw worse than that in Lyon. And in Foch. Stings, doesn't it?'

The man was considering spitting in Harry's face, but the thought of more blows stayed his mouth. Natalie emerged from the kitchen and handed Harry a drink. He sipped. Gin.

'All we need are the names of your SS colleagues in the camp, and you can go back. We know they are in there. This was a Werewolf rendezvous point, after all. Just pick them out for us.' Harry was fishing now. He had heard rumours of Werewolf, the plan for die-hard SS units to continue the fight as saboteurs and terrorists, but part of him thought it was pure fantasy.

'They'll kill me if I do,' the German said through split lips.

Harry indicated the Frenchmen, their chests still heaving from their exertions. 'Look, I wouldn't bank on what these guys will do if you don't tell me. And if you do, you don't have to go back to the camp. We'll get you shipped up to Stuttgart. Names. That's all I need. Names.' He paused. 'Oh, and where you keep your ratfunds. You know, the little nest egg you put aside in case this day ever came.'

'Ratfunds? What are you talking about?'

Harry smiled and turned towards the door. Hervé moved in again and he heard the German say: 'Wait.'

'I have some names.'

'And some funds?'

A slight inclination of the head.

'Good, very good.' Harry fetched a pen and paper.

Every one of the SS officers had something hidden away somewhere: paintings, gold, cars, cash, jewellery. Harry's deal was hard to resist. You offered them a clean bill of health, approval from this British-led International deNazification Unit, if they handed over something worthwhile. Otherwise you labelled them an SS war criminal and threw them into the court system. It wasn't surprising that many of them merely came to see it as a tax on their war booty, a form of reparation.

Wolkers entered just as Harry wrote down the last of the fifteen names and grabbed the list from his hands. 'Bullshit.' He slapped the man across the face and he reared up in protest. 'This is shit. He hasn't got the main one on here.'

'What main one?'

'I've just been down the camp. I was given a tour of the officers' quarters. He's here.'

'Who is?'

'Diels. Our old friend SS Sturmbannführer Bernd Diels of Avenue Foch is here.'

The first blow took Bernd Diels by surprise. He fell off the chair and onto the floor and looked up at Wolkers. 'How dare you?' he shouted. 'After all I did for you. What right have you to do this?'

'Do you box, Bernd?' asked Wolkers.

It was late now. The room was lit with gloomy wall lights and almost everyone, with the exception of Diels, was drunk. The girls were sitting, watching the show, Suzy perched on Hervé's knee, Natalie on Jean's. Jeff Hardman was sleeping off a lunch-time binge on the settee, a Thompson submachine gun laid across his lap. Harry was perched on a chair by the kitchen entrance, detached, strangely depressed by the scene. Diels, he reasoned, had done plenty of unspeakable things to others. So why was it giving him this sour feeling in his gut?

'Well, do you, Bernd?' Wolkers repeated. 'Box?'

'Don't be ridiculous.' Diels struggled to maintain some dignity and held up his handcuffed hands.

Wolkers pretended he was in the ring, punching and feigning. 'All we want is a share. A percentage. We know you SS boys have got lots of loot. You especially, Bernd. I was there when you were ordering all that art to be crated up. All those fine wines. All that couture jewellery. I was there. Say, sixty per cent?'

'That was all for others. For Kieffer. Kaltenbrunner. Not me.'

Wolkers went in with the old one, two, a left and a right, sending the German reeling back.

'Total war, Bernd, remember? You told me I'd learn the meaning of total war. Well, this is total peace.' He hit him again, generating a mist of blood. 'And we want some of it.'

'I did nothing,' insisted Diels. 'I took nothing.'

Wolkers unleashed a flurry of blows, so hard and fast that Harry recoiled. He could hear bone cracking and still they came, landing one after another, body and chest and head, wherever Diels couldn't cover with his manacled hands. Harry knew the Dutchman was out of control, but was powerless to stop him.

Suddenly Diels sprang at Wolkers, scooped his arms over his head, and twisted him round, working the cuffs under Wolker's chin and pulling, digging the chain into his throat.

Wolkers began to gurgle. Harry searched the low table for his Walther pistol. One of the women screamed.

The noise of the Thompson machine gun engulfed everything and they watched as Diels twitched under the bullets. He fell to the floor, dragging Wolkers with him, hitting the ground with a force that sent an arc of blood high into the air. The pair lay still, wisps of smoke drifting over them. Hardman stood swaying, the empty submachine gun at his side, a stupefied look on his face.

Wolkers's bloody tongue was protruding from his mouth. It was hard to say whether Diels had succeeded in strangling him before the stray .45 bullet had passed through his head. Harry stared at Hardman and said, 'Look what you've done now, you dozy fuckin' Yankee cunt.'

Thirty-five

Paris, May 1945

Odile had just made herself that most decadent of luxuries, a hot chocolate, when she heard the sound beyond the door of the small apartment, a breathy, metallic noise. She pulled the gown around herself, opened the door and froze when she saw the familiar slouch, one hand steadying himself on the outside wall. She felt that if she looked down she would see her heart beating through her robe, coming right out like one of those silly American cartoons. She shivered and he put a finger to her lips and eased her back inside.

In his hand was a trumpet, dull and worn.

'Listen,' he said softly.

She nodded, walked over and replaced the blown bulb in the small lamp by the window and switched it on, turning off the main light. The light was green, giving Harry a sickly look.

'In 1936, when Mussolini went—' he began.

'Harry.'

'Stop it. Just listen. No, not Mussolini. Let's say that when Hitler said he was going to annexe the Sudetenland, Chamberlain and all the other statesmen of Europe turned round and said: No. Enough, Adolf. We know what you are up to. OK, maybe it is time to reconsider some of the elements of the Treaty of Versailles. Let's talk sea corridors and ethnic Germans. But step out of line and we'll slap you down. Imagine that? What happens next? Nothing. No war. No Blitz. All the cities that would be intact. Berlin included. No occupation of Paris. No round-up of Jews. Maybe no extermination camps. Well, not on the same scale. Nineteen thirty-nine comes and goes. Over in England a chap called Harry Cole decides he has had enough of the bent life. He can play trumpet a bit.' He held up the instrument. 'Play a lot, really, if he practises enough. But he really only had time for that in prison. So, he knuckles down, he learns his scales.' Harry put the trumpet to his lips and played a quick, slurred arpeggio.

'Ssshh . . . The concierge. She'll kill us both. And then sell the trumpet to pay for the cleaning bill.' Odile found herself soothed by his voice, deeper than she recalled, but with the same rhythms, a few of the coarser edges knocked off from years of affecting other men's accents.

'Harry starts a band. The Harry Cole Hot Five. He goes on tour, all the best places. Bournemouth, Blackpool, Brighton, Torquay, Café Royal, Café Anglais, and then – the Continent. Le Touquet, Dieppe and eventually, Paris. There, he plays a little club in Montmartre, Bricktop's, say, and who should be in the audience but Odile, a nurse out on a date with a jazz-loving colleague. But she soon forgets the lemon next to her, because she only has eyes for the trumpeter, with his high licks and fast finger work. In the interval, she slips him a phone number. They get together two nights later, go dancing, and fall madly in love. They marry, he gives up the jazz life and becomes a mechanic, the best car mechanic in Paris, and she has three kids. Two girls and a boy, who looks just like his dad. They both die old and in bed and blissfully happy in, oh, the 1980s. How's that sound?'

'It sounds pretty good, Harry.'

'You told me once about those tales with shadow stories, remember? Alternative endings, other paths, just like life. I wish this one had had a different ending.'

She moved towards him and put her arms around his neck and he leant forward and kissed her, as softly as he could, trying to convey a promise never to hurt her again. Odile let him take her across to the bed and he sat her down, not wanting to rush things.

'I need to tell you my story, Odile.'

'Do you? Now?'

They kissed again, and he wanted to pull back the robe and feel her breasts again, and lower her onto her back and slide, as lightly as he could, on top of her, but he had to explain things first.

He stood and began pacing, the metre of his steps quickening as the words spilled out of him. He started at Lille, with what he did for King, and took her through step by step, to the noose on the hillside, the forged letter, the dismantling of the ratline, and as he reached the part in Lyon where she denounced him, Odile felt tears forming. Harry sat down again and stroked her hair. He carried on, slower, his voice flatter, emotionless, and brought her almost up to date.

'I don't understand,' she said when he had finished. 'Diels jumped your man . . .'

'And we had to shoot him. Well, an official inquiry was inevitable. Death in custody. Plus Wolkers, there would be questions about him.' He held her hand tightly. 'You have to understand, Odile, the odds were against me. The Americans would have notified SHAEF who would have contacted London, London would have found out who I really was. With my track record, I'd be finished. Even you think . . . thought I was a traitor.'

'So what did you do?'

'We buried the two bodies in the forest and disbanded. Sent the American back to his unit. Hervé drove me to Paris. I had to see you. I'm not asking you to start again.' He looked down, and said, in disbelief: 'You still have the ring.'

She looked down at her hand, the band of gold loose on her bony finger. 'I never took it off.'

'All over Europe people are making a fresh start, walking out of old identities into new ones, swapping sides from the bad guys to the good guys. We could do it, Odile. You were the only one who made any sense in my life. You could do it again.'

'Harry, I'm sorry.'

'What have you got to be sorry about?'

The door whiplashed back with a crack and the cup of hot chocolate smashed to the floor. Harry tried to get up, but three pairs of hands grabbed him, fingers expertly finding pressure points in his neck and arms, and he felt his knees give way.

The three Redcaps supported his weight while Major Donald Darling of MI9 looked him up and down. Odile could see that the Major's hand was twitching, that it was taking a great effort of self-control not to strike Harry. In the end, he just spat out: 'Take him to the Paris Detention Centre. Get him out of my sight.'

Harry tried to look back at Odile, but he was bundled out of the door. Darling took off his cap and dropped it onto the bed, brushing his hair back. 'You all right?'

Odile nodded, then from beyond the door, she heard the slap of baton on bone. 'What are they doing?'

'Making sure he doesn't run off. Don't worry, hurts like hell for twenty-four hours, that's all. Sorry it took so long. She called,' he pointed a thumb to indicate the concierge, 'as soon as she saw the green light in the window, but she had no idea how long it had been there. Said she'd dozed off.'

'You were fast enough.'

'It was the right thing to do. To come to us when you got that letter from Cole. Absolutely the right thing.'

'What will happen to him?'

'Oh, a trial. Depositions. Witnesses. Then . . .' He drew a finger across his throat.

She got up and shakily poured herself a small Dubonnet. 'It all sounded, the way he told it, so . . .'

'True?'

'Yes, true.'

Darling said: 'Harry Cole is a con man, Miss. It's his job to be plausible. You and I know what's the truth. He doesn't. Which is why he can make lies sound so convincing. Look, I'm going to leave a man in the street outside, just to make you feel better. If you have any problems or would like a hotel for the night . . .'

'No, really, thank you. You've done more than enough. I can sleep tight, knowing you've got him.'

'We'll get the door fixed first thing.' Darling picked up his cap from the bed and touched her arm. 'I'll tell Neave in the morning. They'll be cracking open the champagne in London at the news.'

As the door closed behind Darling, Odile noticed the trumpet on the floor, partially hidden under the bed. She picked it up. The bell was bent and the mouthpiece had come out. She found herself face down on the bed hugging the broken instrument, crying with huge sobs that racked her chest.

Thirty-six

Paris, June 1945

Neave found Malcolm Muggeridge and Kim Philby taking an early dinner in Fouquet on the Champs Elysées. The refurbished restaurant was gleaming – the gilt ceiling had been re-covered, the tired red drapes renewed, the chandeliers given brighter bulbs, the mirrors polished and filled with the reflection of the uniforms of a dozen nations, majoring on the US and Great Britain. The maître d' was being especially unctuous, perhaps aware that some others in his position had been accused of collaboration for being equally servile to the Germans.

It had taken Neave a week to disentangle himself from his work at the Awards Bureau in Brussels, then he had flown back to London to see his wife, and now, ten days after the man's arrest, he was finally going to get to confront Harry Cole.

He had been instructed to call on Malcolm Muggeridge before proceeding with his interview. Quite why, Neave wasn't sure. This was an open-and-shut case. Lord Haw-Haw, John Amery, Harry Cole. They would all have the same end. Seeing

Muggeridge, whose thankless task in Paris was to co-ordinate the activities of the various British security services, was just protocol, he supposed, something he was having to re-learn after the freewheeling months in France, Holland and Belgium.

When he called at the Army Intelligence Corps Liaison Office, which was located in the George V hotel, he learned that Muggeridge was with Philby, who had come over to see if Muggeridge could be of any help with his new Section Nine. As a reward for his work on various desks throughout the war, and unswerving loyalty, Dansey had given his protégé the anti-Russian desk, ready for the next stage of the ongoing global conflict.

By the time Neave arrived the two former journalists were a bottle down, with another already opened, and looked oddly relaxed in each other's company. On one side of the table, the austere, emaciated Muggeridge was picking at an omelette, whereas Philby seemed to have selected every exotic dish on the menu. They found Neave a chair and a glass.

'I have to say,' said Muggeridge, 'I thought my friend Stepson was going to get Section Nine.'

Philby grunted. 'Did you really? Or are you just saying that?' Neave noticed the stutter had almost gone, although his face was showing considerable drink damage. 'You're teasing me, aren't you?'

Muggeridge nodded. 'I suppose I am. He was bloody useless in Mozambique.'

'Well, he was worse than that in London. Don't you think, Neave?'

'I never ran into him,' said Neave, truthfully. He raised his glass. 'But belated congratulations, Philby. On the Nine desk.'

'Cheers. So, what's your brief here? Drink the wine and fuck the women like the rest of us?' Philby grinned and Neave found himself actively disliking him. A look of distaste flickered across Muggeridge's face, too.

'Oh, I have a few awards to dish out, a bad sort to interrogate, that kind of thing.' He was unwilling to elaborate. 'Finish my Nine's business.'

'MI9,' said Philby with sudden sarcasm. He sniffed his wine. 'How many flyers did you get out, Neave?'

'Nobody has done the sums yet. A guess? Three thousand.'

'Will anyone do the sums on how many French lives that cost?'

'I beg your pardon?'

'By my reckoning every single man you got out cost the life of a French man or woman. Maybe more. But one to one sounds about right to me.'

'If that is so,' Neave replied as calmly as he could, 'it is thanks to traitors—'

'Doesn't matter what the reasons are. Traitors, informants. You didn't expect the Germans to sit back and let you operate under their noses, did you? It's like with SOE. They claim to have sent in brave saboteurs and resistants, whereas the Germans gave us filthy underhand spies. A touch of the double standards there, I think. A spy is a spy is a spy. Anyway, I just wonder when they trot out the noble history of your Nine, whether those poor sods who died in the camps or up against walls will get a mention, or if it will just be the story of the brave British flyers who got away.'

Neave leant over and gripped Philby's forearm tightly. 'Those poor sods are the reason I am in Paris. To make sure someone pays for them. I'd thank you to keep your opinions to yourself until you know the facts.'

'No offence meant, Neave. Just a hobby-horse of mine. Nobody remembers the men at the coal face.'

'I do. Every one,' said Neave. Somehow, he couldn't quite square the thought of Philby as a defender of the oppressed and neglected with the man before him, tucking into a meal that must be costing all of five pounds.

'Sorry. Have another drink,' slurred Philby. 'Speaking out of turn.'

Neave turned to Muggeridge. 'How did you get on with Plum?'

Muggeridge sent the remains of his omelette away and ordered cheese and fruit. The noise in the room was rising now, and Muggeridge had to shout to make himself heard. 'Wodehouse? The man is guilty of nothing more than being naïve. Anthony Powell agrees. And that chap Orwell. Miserable bugger. But he's going to write an article in Plum's defence.'

Early in the war, after his internment in France, P.G. Wodehouse had made five broadcasts to America on German radio, intended to be humorous accounts of his trials and tribulations. Neave agreed he was naïve if he hadn't thought the Nazis would use his celebrity to their own advantage, and there was a line in one of the talks that had been seized on back home. 'Whether England wins or not.' It sounded like defeatism.

That Wodehouse wouldn't swing like that other radio propagandist William Joyce – christened Lord Haw Haw by the British listeners to his increasingly ludicrous rants from Berlin – was probably thanks to the author being associated in the public's mind with his creation, the brainless Bertie Wooster, the best defence a man could have. That and old school friends in high places.

'It's Cole, isn't it?' asked Philby suddenly, knocking back the contents of his glass.

'What?' Neave asked.

'You were saying about making someone pay. Harry Cole? It's him you've come to see?'

'Yes,' Neave confirmed, surprised he knew, but then, these

days, it was Philby's job to know everything.

'Ah,' said Muggeridge. 'Him. Well, that's a foregone conclusion, isn't it? Man's a traitor.'

'And an impostor,' added Philby. 'Went through the war pretending to be one of ours, didn't he?'

'Traitor and impostor,' agreed Muggeridge. 'Hang the bastard.'

They both nodded sagely, drink making their heads heavy, and Neave smiled to himself. Traitor and impostor. He wondered which they considered the worse crime.

After a week at the Paris Detention Centre, Harry's knee returned to its normal size and he had finally managed to get his hands on a typewriter. He had even convinced the night shift that it was too cold to type in his cell, and they had cautiously allowed him to work on his deposition in the guard room, near the pot-bellied stove.

Eleven days after his arrest at Odile's, he wrote the last page of his account, taking him up to his return to Paris, but stopping short of his arrest. He snatched it out of the typewriter and laid it face down on top of the stack on his left. There were well over thirty single-spaced sheets.

'Finished?' said the English guard.

The American put down a cup of coffee next to Harry. 'Thank God for that. Maybe we'll get some peace and quiet now.'

'Completely,' announced Harry. 'So that's that. He's coming tomorrow, is he?'

The Englishman pointed at the wallchart showing the week's appointments. 'Major Airey Neave, ten o'clock.'

Neave. Airey Neave. Could he be a relation? Not that common a name, Neave. Anthony and Airey, they could be brothers or cousins. Would that work in his favour? Could he call the other Neave as a character witness? They'd got on well in Marseilles, after all. He'd find out soon enough.

'Now, gentlemen,' Harry said with a grin, 'how about a game of cards before I turn in?'

Neave had left Fouquet early, still aggravated by Philby's remarks about MI9, and returned to his hotel. He had tossed and turned for an hour before sleep finally took him. Had his own escape cost anyone their lives on his journey? Not that he knew of. How could he be sure? A denouncement might have happened days after he left a farmer or bank clerk who had been hiding him. Neave's freedom might well have had a human price he simply didn't know about and the thought troubled him mightily.

Later on, at Room 900, he knew all too well that his actions had cost lives – men, and women, who undertook missions for him who never returned. Even so, the arithmetic wasn't that simple. If one person was caught for every airman returned, surely the combatants were more vital to the war effort . . . but no, he had trouble with that. He left the considerations of whether one life was worth more than another to people like Dansey.

It seemed he had only just nodded off when the telephone rang. He looked at the clock as he reached over for the receiver. Six thirty. On the other end was an alarmingly bright-sounding Muggeridge.

'Neave? Have I woken you? Listen, just wanted to share something with you. Strangest thing. We had just left the restaurant when Philby said: "I know, let's go to the Rue de Grenelle." Do you know what's there?'

'Soviet Embassy,' said Neave, suppressing a yawn.

'Absolutely right. Well, I didn't know that at the time. Should have, I suppose. So we go to Grenelle, and have a drink at this bloody awful place called, uh, The Blue Noon, I think. Kim talks about his new responsibilities and what a threat Communism is now and how we must prepare for the next phase of the war and how hard it is to penetrate a Soviet Embassy, how they keep a tight rein on everyone, right down to the lowliest porter. To make his point, he drags me out of this damned bar and carries on, talking far too loudly for my liking, and that's when I realise we are standing outside the embassy itself. He is shouting at the top of his voice at a building chock full of Russians, yelling about this that and the other, not exactly shaking his fists, but, well, gesticulating at the building.'

'Was he drunk?' Neave asked, rather superfluously.

'We both were, as you well know. But even so. With his job . . . of . . . well, I awoke this morning and thought: that's irregular. Well, reprehensible really. I mean, they were bound to be watching, weren't they? And bound to have seen me. What do you make of it?'

'An aberration I dare say,' said Neave flatly, wondering what he was meant to make of a bit of drunken idiocy. It was either that or Philby was deliberately showing Muggeridge off to the Russkies, but what would be the point of that? Unless he wanted to identify Malcolm Muggeridge, SIS's new Paris intelligence co-ordinator, to someone inside the compound. That, though, was unthinkable. Philby's appointed task was to fight the men behind those walls, after all.

'An aberration, yes,' agreed Muggeridge. 'Sure you're right. Sorry to trouble you. Good luck, Neave.'

'What with?'

'Good luck with that little shit. Good luck with Harry Cole.'

Neave thanked him and put the phone down and thought about the conversation for a moment before he crossed to the bathroom to run his bath. One day, decades later, he would wonder if, had he dwelt on it further, he might have come to the conclusion that the affable, clubbable Kim Philby was not what he seemed, that perhaps the previous night he had cracked the way all people living a double life seem to snap at some point, inviting discovery, just as men with both wives and mistresses often push the barriers between the two until they bulge and break.

That morning, though, Neave pushed the incident from his mind. He had bigger fish to fry.

Thirty-seven

It took Neave forty minutes to read the pages so laboriously typed by Harry Cole, during which time the author sat opposite him in the interview room, smoking his way through a pack of American cigarettes which he claimed to have won at cards. Funny how the man had distorted in his mind's eye. The image he had carried of Cole was bigger, coarser, with a weaselly, untrustworthy gaze. This one was the chap he recalled from Calais and Marseilles, direct, polite, almost charming in an offhand way.

At certain points in the narrative, Neave would look up and feel like punching Harry, again and again. At other times, he had to laugh at the sheer audacity of the man. As he finished the last page, Neave stood up and walked to the window, gazing across to the metro station at Porte des Lilas. Dansey's Red Ribbon was still in force on Harry, but it was difficult to execute once he had been brought to the Paris Detention Centre and formally charged. No, they would have to do this the old-fashioned way.

'What happened to Tony?'

Neave turned. 'Pardon?'

'Tony Neave? Why the name change? To Airey.'

'I never liked the name Airey.' Why was he discussing this with Cole? The reversion was because of his imminent secondment to the War Crimes Commission, which insisted names matched official papers, and so he had got back into the habit of using his given Christian name. 'It's of no consequence.'

'What's in a name, eh? Something else we have in common.'

'We have nothing in common, Cole.'

'Are you sure? I thought Tony and I understood each other.'

Neave shuddered at the very thought that he could be identified with this treacherous creature. 'I doubt it, Cole.' He put Harry's manuscript down on the table. 'I'm trying to understand from this where you went terribly wrong. Where you crossed the Rubicon, from hero to villain, chancer to traitor.'

'Maybe you're asking the wrong question. Maybe you should ask where it all went terribly right. At what point did I start working for the good guys. You should know, you were there. At Calais. At Marseilles.'

'Marseilles?'

'We had a drink, remember? We talked about escaping. You quite enjoyed it.'

'I don't remember enjoying it, Cole. We were just ships in the night.'

'Heading in the same direction.'

'Hardly, Cole, hardly. And anyway, your account varies somewhat from the facts there. By the way,' Neave said with some relish, 'Guérisse has volunteered to kill you.'

So Pat O'Leary, the Belgian who had adopted an Irish name, had survived the war. 'He never did trust me.'

'He was right not to, wasn't he?'

'Did you read that properly, Major?' Harry nodded at his typing. 'It doesn't vary at all from the truth. Perhaps your memory is at fault.'

'I don't know where to begin, Cole. It is an astonishing document, I'll grant you. Quite remarkable.'

Cole smiled.

'I assume like all good liars you have stuck as closely to the truth as you dare.' Harry opened his mouth to speak, but Neave's look told him not to bother. Neave lit his own cigarette. 'Do you know what happened to the priest from Abbeville, whom you fail to mention here, Sergeant Cole?' He spat out the rank as if it was diseased. 'Carpentier? Beheaded. Didry? Also decapitated. Dubois? Decapitated. I could go on. Shot. Strangled, gassed. How many? Fifty? A hundred? But some survived, Cole, oh yes, some survived. And they want to see you dead as much as I do. Guérisse . . .'

'I had nothing to do with Guérisse or anyone else in Marseilles being caught.'

'No, but he knew you were a bad sort from the start, Sergeant. And your explanation of working for this King fellow? For God's sake, man. It's like something out of . . .' He struggled to find the appropriate book, then remembered *The Confidential Agent*. 'Graham Greene.'

'Look—'

'And Odile . . . not a word of remorse for what you did. She's worth ten of you, Cole. The baby died, by the way, Harry.'

'Baby?' The colour drained from his face.

'Are you telling me you didn't know Odile was pregnant when you sent her over to the Gestapo man with the list of safe houses? A man with your intuition, your way with the ladies, might have guessed. It was born prematurely, Harry, and it wasn't strong . . .' Neave took a breath and let it out slowly. 'The things you've done, Sergeant Cole. How do you sleep at night?'

Harry held his hands out, pleadingly. 'Major, I know it sounds bad. That's why I wrote it all down. All these things you say . . . it wasn't me.'

'No, no, of course not. Possibly an evil twin brother?' Sarcasm cracked Neave's voice as he reached down into his case and brought out a thick folder, tied with a crimson ribbon. He undid it and flicked over a few pages. 'Everything we have heard about you over the last few years is here, Cole. Every rumour, sighting, chance encounter. It would be interesting to compare the two accounts, don't you think, Sergeant? For instance, you neglect to mention that in the case of the apartments you burgled in Paris, you had denounced the victims yourself, then ransacked the place while they were being tortured in the cells.'

'Nonsense. That's nonsense. You make me out to be a . . . a monster.'

'What really puzzles me,' said Neave, in control once more, 'is why you told the evaders to give your regards to Scotland Yard or SIS when they got home, as if you were legit.'

'I was legit.'

'You must have known it would get back to the powers-that-be. That they'd know they had no Mason or Cole on the books.'

'I was working for the powers-that-be. On the QT.'

'So you keep saying. How many nipples do you have, Cole?'

'What?'

'How many nipples do you have?'

'The usual. Why?'

'Well, according to you,' he indicated Harry's writings, 'they sawed one off in Montluc. Isn't that right? And circumcised you with pliers? How is that wound? Should we take a look?'

'What is the problem here, Neave? I told you—'

'Of course. I was forgetting. Not your fault. It was this omnipotent Mr King, one of our agents. He set you up for everything.'

'He bloody well did.' The first trace of anger, perfectly judged, thought Neave. 'Check the records in London.'

'You think I won't?'

Harry stubbed out his cigarette and said quietly: 'I don't know what you'll do, Major Neave.'

Neave strode over and slammed a fist onto the pile of typed papers. 'I shall take this pack of lies to London, Sergeant, that's what I shall do. I assume this will form part of your defence?'

Harry nodded glumly.

'In which case I will have it copied and returned. You will be assigned a lawyer, of course. Then it is a matter of formalities.' Neave put the sheaf of papers under his arm.

'What formalities?'

'Whether we hang you here or in London, Sergeant.'

Claude Dansey grimaced as he reached over to the pile of documents on his desk. The pain flowed from his shoulder blade down his left arm. He slumped back in the chair, sweat on his brow, irritated. He didn't have time for infirmity, not now. There were loose ends to be tied and long-term plans to be put into action.

He signalled by intercom for more tea and picked up the top folder again. It was a copy of Muggeridge's report on Wodehouse, suggesting no proceedings be instigated against the foolish man. It was already ticked by 'C' and he scanned it quickly. The author was just too high profile, Dansey thought. Never liked his stuff himself, but any trial would generate too many column inches, here and in the United States. And Menzies was a fan. He found the rubber stamp, banged it down and initialled the blurred 'No Further Action'.

The second document was a memo from Neave, and a file of perhaps thirty typed pages. After he had skimmed through it, he stoked a pipe, a rare treat these days, and lit it, before standing and walking with the file over to the fireplace behind him.

There was a knock and Maddy, his secretary, entered with his tea, placing it on the desk and looking over at him as he knelt before the grate. 'It's a little warm for a fire, isn't it, Sir Claude?' she asked.

Dansey watched the edges of the typed pages curl as the flames caught and he stood stiffly, his knees cracking as he did so. 'Just getting rid of some rubbish, Maddy. Thanks for the tea. Oh, and when you get a minute ask Duty Ops to track down King, will you? I'd like a word.'

'Certainly, Sir Claude.'

She closed the door softly and he watched the flames change from a feeble yellow to a more robust red as the paper blackened and flaked, particles of it spiralling off up the chimney. Too many column inches, he thought. Best deal with all this softly, softly. The war was all over for him now, he thought regretfully, it was time to pass the baton on to Philby and his cohorts, let them fight the next war, the one against the new empire in the East. All that was left for him was to tidy up the outstanding matters, like this fellow Cole.

Dansey suddenly found himself smiling as he sucked on the worn stem, amused at the thought of the man's desperate version of events, now a small pile of flaking ashes. Cole. He felt something flicker inside as he considered the man. What was it? Pity? Guilt? But no, he couldn't recognise it. Perhaps it was just the feeling that, under different circumstances, Harry would have been a perfect agent after all. Some other war, maybe, but not the coming one. Cole's time was at an end. Couldn't Red Ribbon him in Paris Detention Centre, much too public, but King would find a way round that. Dansey reached for the tea and cursed as the blasted pain ran down his arm once more.

Thirty-eight

Paris, late 1945

Harry walked from his cell to the guard room, cleared his usual space at the table for the typewriter, fed the first blank sheet of paper in and typed his name in capitals at the top. The English guard looked up and said, 'You still at it?'

'I think I need to be a bit clearer on some points.'

The American brought him a cup of coffee. 'I heard they might be moving you on at last.' Months had passed since the Neave interview. Messages filtered through about possible transfers to London, about further interrogations, but part of him was convinced he was being left to rot. Other prisoners had come and gone, leaving him to refine his version of events and to ponder what Neave had said about the baby. He should have asked what sex it was. It would have been nice to be able to picture him or her. And a name.

He reflected on his child breathing its last breath in an icy bedroom, Odile clutching the tiny body, trying to press some warmth into it. Another wasted life. He pushed the images away. He could not allow himself to get maudlin. Recriminations could wait.

Harry shrugged and said, 'I heard that too. I'm in no hurry. I'm almost getting to like you blokes.' He pecked at the keys, getting down the opening details about his time in Hong Kong.

'Why are you still bothering to write the story over and over?' asked the Englishman. 'You must have done ten ribbons.'

'He's still inventing the truth,' said the Yank with a smirk. 'Aren't you, Harry?'

'I haven't invented anything. That's the thing I can't get these bloody officers to understand. They seem more bothered by the fact I gave myself a bit of unofficial promotion than anything else.'

The Englishman laughed. 'A most heinous crime, my son.' He leant over and read the first paragraph. 'Gettin' above your station. What's a *daih fung*?'

'A big wind, and you're right,' Harry sighed. 'You've got to know your place in this army. No different from civvy street.'

The Englishman nodded. 'Yup. The workers get shafted every time. Roll on the revolution, eh?'

'Christ, a couple of Commies,' muttered the American. 'I'm glad I'm out of here.'

'Oh, yeah?' asked Harry. 'And how am I meant to win my fags if you leave?'

'You can get your fags anywhere you like, pal,' he said mincingly. 'As for the smokes, I'll leave you a couple of packs. I'm off to Berlin.'

'I hear it looks like the backside of the bleedin' moon,' said the Englishman. 'You can keep it. Me, I'm back home. Warm beer, skittles, Ovaltine, Tommy Handley – all the things you Yanks don't understand.'

'Hold on, hold on,' protested Harry. 'You're both goin'? What if I get a couple of half-decent card players as night duty replacements? I'll be scuppered then.'

The Englishman sighed and produced a pack of cards. 'Come on then, Harry, put the memoirs down. Let's play serious. We've just been feelin' sorry for you up to now.'

An hour later and six packs of cigarettes better off, Harry returned to his cell with his typewriter under his arm. The Englishman dutifully followed and turned the lock in the key as Harry switched on the feeble light. It wasn't until he had slid the typewriter under the bed that he noticed the small book of matches from a bar on the floor. The Blue Noon. He flipped open the top and squinted at the tiny writing on the lid, frowning as he digested the contents.

Odile lay in bed, haunted by shadows, from dead Americans in forests to a tiny, unformed soul born prematurely in a Resistance safe house, too weak to survive a single night. What happened to babies who died? Did they go to heaven as infants or toddlers, or did souls not reflect earthly age? She had talked it over with priests, but each had a different answer.

She wondered if Harry had ever found out about their son. She hadn't had time to break the news before the whole escape line collapsed, although he may have had his suspicions. He certainly hadn't noticed the growing bump in Montluc, and the boy had been born and died by the time she had Harry ambushed in Paris. Perhaps she should have told him when he came to her that night, but she had decided she didn't want to share her baby with Harry, even in death.

It only took two taps at the door to wake her fully. She felt her stomach contract in fright. Even now, long after they had gone, no French person could hear an early morning knock on the door without thinking of men with little lightning flashes at their throats. She glanced at the green dial of the alarm clock. Five o'clock.

Another rapping, more urgent this time.

She slid out of bed, found her slippers and padded across. She put her ear to the door and jumped when a fist hit the other side. Her voice was thin and broken. 'Who is it?'

'It's me. Let me in.'

Odile slid back the bolt, and in a blur he was standing in the room with his arms around her. She looked up at him. 'I thought it was . . .'

'I know. He hasn't been here?'

She stepped back and put a hand to her mouth. 'He's free?'

Neave nodded and she retreated across the room and found her gown, slipping it on, unable to stop shivering.

'How?'

'The bloody idiots had been letting him type his lies in the guard room. New roster on last night, green as you like and Harry said he'd just go to the lavatory on his way back to his cell, put the typewriter under his arm, picked up a US sergeant's jacket on the way out and walked straight past the guard on the gate . . .'

Just like he'd described walking out of Colditz to Harry. Neave realised that back in Marseilles he'd given Harry a three-part primer – uniform, attitude and a prop – in how to escape from prisons, and the man had used it faultlessly at the Paris Detention Centre.

Neave opened his case and took out the two weapons. One was a Colt .45 OSS automatic with integral suppressor, the other a compact Browning. He handed her the smaller pistol and she instinctively dropped the magazine and checked the action. 'You think he'll come here?'

'I don't know. If he has any sense he'll get out of the city.'

'I thought he couldn't touch me any more. I was wrong, wasn't I?'

He held her for a long time. 'Don't be hard on yourself, Odile.

And don't worry,' he said softly. 'Remember what I said about one ordinary bullet?' Neave held up the Colt. 'I'll make sure it's mine.'

Harry was sitting in the darkened corner of Billy's Bar, sipping a beer. His typewriter was at his feet, the US Army jacket turned inside out across his lap, and he was watching the GIs pour the cheap booze down their mouths and pass the girls between them with giddy speed. Most of the floor area was brightly lit, the walls mirrored, the music fast jazz, the dancers moving with heady abandon.

The proprietress slipped into the alcove beside him and he stiffened, ready to bolt. 'You're Harry?'

Harry was primed for a trap, but there seemed little point in denial. 'Yes.'

'I am Madame Herveaux. Pauline. This is my place. You like it?'

'Very nice,' said Harry cautiously. 'Very . . . lively.'

'And this is only Monday. You should see it on the weekend.' She pointed at a smooth-headed black guy who was leaning on the bar, beaming at his exuberant customers as the small dance floor filled with hot bodies. 'That's Billy. I named it after him.'

Harry flashed his book of matches. 'The Blue Noon? Where did that come from?'

'That's the old name. I still have two thousand books of matches with it on. What am I going to do? Throw them away? My husband wanted it to be called The Blue Moon. The printer didn't speak English . . . we got Blue Noon. I became rather fond of it.'

'Why did you change it to Billy's Bar?'

She lit a cigarette and blew smoke from the corner of her mouth. 'My husband left me. This place was just a hobby for him.

So was I, it seems. Everything changes, Harry. Billy's Bar sounds more American, most of our customers are American, Billy's an American . . . it's just a name.'

Harry nodded. 'Yeah. What's in a name?'

She put a hand on his knee. 'I have a parcel for you.' She placed a small brown package on the table and asked, 'You need another drink?'

'Yes, please.'

Pauline walked over to the bar, hips swinging. She was well in her forties, but she oozed a lazy sexuality, and Harry began to wonder if she would take to comforting a lonely Englishman. It had been a while.

He unwrapped the parcel, weighed the roll of francs in his hand and examined the rail ticket. Marseilles, one way. From there, North Africa, he reckoned, well out of harm's way. Underneath the money, a passport. Irish, made out in the name of Hickey.

There was no note, but he could guess who had set this up, and the message was clear. Get out of town, don't darken our door again. He hated being told what to do.

He rewrapped the stack of papers as Pauline sat down and he took a mouthful of the new beer.

'Cheers.' Pauline raised her gin. 'So. What now?' she asked.

'I was wondering,' asked Harry slowly, slipping the parcel into his jacket's side pocket. 'Do you rent rooms?'

Harry was lying on the bed in the gathering gloom of a chilly twilight, working on another draft of the letter, cursing the flimsy onion skin paper, so translucent you could only write on one side, when he became aware of someone else breathing in the room. He peered into the dark corner where he could see a figure. He admired the stealth of the man, and wondered if he had entered from the door or window. A Belgian pistol, traded for the typewriter, was within his reach, but he had a feeling he wouldn't make it. He swung upright. 'Hello, King.'

A match flared, and he saw that it was indeed him.

'Hello, Harry. Why are you still here?'

Harry pointed at the crumpled balls of paper which littered the floor. 'I have some unfinished business.'

King reached down, unfolded one of the sheets and read the letter. It was rambling and unfocused, a long cry of pain. 'You'll never get near Odile. While you're at large, she's wrapped in cotton wool with barbed wire on the outside. It's over, Harry.'

King stepped forward and reached into his jacket. Harry froze, but King produced a copy of the *Daily Mail*. King showed him a headline on page five: POLICE HUNT TRAITOR. COWARD WHO SERVED IN FOUR ARMIES SOUGHT. The piece was illustrated with an old army photograph, in which he looked very shifty.

'Fame at last,' said Harry.

'You should have left the city when you had the chance.'

'Now I'm an embarrassment.'

'You're a bloody fool. I gave you one last opportunity. You were meant to stay here a day at most. It's been weeks.'

'I wondered why you did it. Why you got me out of Paris Detention Centre. Because of what I might say in court?'

'Bloody hell, man, I'm in deep shit now you're still here. I said you'd disappear, off like the wind. London wanted a Red Ribbon on you once you were lured outside PDC. Shot dead. Resisting arrest, whatever. You are right, there are those who would rather you didn't have your day in court. Even *in camera*, Harry. I stuck my neck out for you . . .'

'I didn't know you cared.'

King ignored him. 'You've got this chap Neave lifting every stone in the city to see if you're underneath. Oh, he won't find you, don't worry. He's being called to Nuremberg I hear – his new superiors have little sympathy for him chasing a small fry like you, when he's supposed to be helping hang twenty-odd top Nazis. Even so, they are on alert for you in Lyon and Marseilles and Toulouse, so you've closed those doors by leaving it so late. Cigarette?'

Harry nodded and accepted one. His last, perhaps. 'Why did you have a change of heart about me?'

King shrugged. 'Oh, I haven't. You're still trouble, Harry.' He thought for a moment about the meeting with Dansey in London, the offhand chat about his future in the service once he had taken care of Harry.

If King had known Philby, been within his cosy circle, he was sure things would be different, but it was made clear he didn't figure in Kim's plans for Section IX, the anti-communist desk, shaping up to be the biggest, most powerful and well-funded section of the SIS. He'd been told to request a new posting, but he knew what would happen. King would ask for Berlin or Vienna and get Cairo or Tangiers. Like all the old Z-people, he was B-listed now, being put out to grass with his master. He hadn't seen why he should oblige those busy stabbing him in the back by dirtying his hands with Harry any more than necessary. His instincts told him that, should a scapegoat be needed somewhere down the line for SIS's handling of the whole Cole affair, he himself might prove a little too convenient to resist.

Eventually, King said: 'I told you in Paris I liked you. It was one thing I wasn't lying about. I know you did some pretty rum things, Harry, but there are men who did worse than you on the payroll now. You might have even heard of one or two of them. Klaus Barbie?'

'That bastard.'

King laughed. Harry didn't know how right he was. Barbie was a genuine bastard, a stigma in German society that could not even be erased by the parents subsequently marrying. According to his SIS file, it was probably that humiliation which drove him into the monstrous family of the SS at such an early stage.

'Barbie is playing tickle his tummy with us,' said King. 'You want to find a Nazi who'll play ball? Ask Klaus. Get a man working in the Russian zone? Ask Klaus. Find the man who designed the V-2 engine?'

'Shouldn't the *Daily Mail* be writing about that? Butcher of Lyon now works for His Majesty's Government?'

'If the press ever found out there'd be a D-notice on them so fast their mastheads would spin. You're exposed as a villain, Harry. Barbie may be evil, but he's useful, so he's a state secret.'

'Can you get me out, King? North? To Belgium? I can pay.'

'No, Harry. Too late. Now the newspapers have you as a big story . . . they want an ending.'

'So you're here to kill me.'

'No, Harry. I'm here to ask you to do it for me.'

Thirty-nine

THE DAILY MAIL

'For King and Empire'

January 10, 1946

**BRITISH TRAITOR DIES
IN GUNFIGHT
In Paris Flat**

From Walter Parr
Daily Mail Special Correspondent

A burst of shots from a French police inspector's pistol in a flat in Paris today ended the life of a London electrician who had an unprecedented career of murder, treachery and espionage during the war. Harold Cole, aged 38, was known all over the Continent by a variety of aliases including 'Captain Robert Mason', 'Sergeant Carpenter' and 'Joseph Deram'.

His death brings to an end a comb-out of western Europe by the civilian and military police of most Allied nations, who circulated an urgent message: 'This man is a dangerous traitor.'

Cole began his orgy of crime by deserting from the British Expeditionary Force in France.

He then posed as a French resistor and delivered to the Germans 150 *maquis*.

ESCAPED THEM ALL

He squandered large amounts of money intended for the Resistance in France, murdered a high German Secret Service official and was arrested in turn by the German, French, American and British Army authorities. But he escaped from them all, his last break-out being from the SHAEF gaol in Paris.

Cole might still be at liberty but for a love affair with a French woman, Pauline Herveaux, in whose flat he was hiding. Police, who had been searching for him area by area, heard of a man 'who seemed to be German'.

A detective called at the block of flats on the Rue de Grenelle. The porter told Cole people had been asking about the flat.

A FINAL DRINK

Cole merely said to the porter: 'Someone is after me, but I shall be gone soon. I take the train in a few hours for Belgium.' Then, turning to Mdme. Herveaux, he said: 'Come along, *chérie*, and have some champagne.' *The delay to have a final drink and a farewell celebration led to his death.*

A few hours later Police Inspectors Cotty and Levy climbed the narrow stairway leading to the flat and entered. Cole, realising he was trapped, pulled a Belgian-type pistol from his breast pocket and opened fire. One bullet wounded Inspector Cotty in the shoulder, but both officers immediately fired, killing Cole instantly.

[This chapter has been reproduced by kind permission of the *Daily Mail*.]

Forty

Paris, early 1946

Airey Neave slid his arm through Odile's as they walked along the gravelled path of the Thiais cemetery and he felt her shudder. It was an icy winter day, the trees stripped bare by the wind, the flowers on the graves sad and wilted. She was underdressed, in a simple black two-piece suit that offered little barrier to the easterly sighing through the monuments. He offered his jacket, but she refused.

'It isn't the cold,' she said quietly.

Neave took her to the plot, which was simply marked by a rectangle of carelessly laid white rocks around freshly turned earth. No cross, no headstone, not a single floral tribute.

'Will there be something to mark it?' she asked.

Neave shook his head. 'It's a charity burial. Nobody wanted to pay. Eventually the grave will be reclaimed, the remains placed in the ossuary.'

'Why didn't they ask me to identify the body?'

'Pat O'Leary . . . or Albert Guérisse as he is once more, he did it.'

'Guérisse? Harry was my husband, Tony. Why get someone else to do it?'

Neave shrugged. There had been a great sense of relief at Cole's death in London, and matters had been rushed through without consulting him in Nuremberg. This had been the first chance he had had to get away from the endless legal contortions of the war crimes indictments. 'Nothing about Harry Cole was ever straightforward. You know, if he'd just left Paris immediately after he walked from the gaol, he might have got away with it. Luck gave him that one last chance . . . and then luck ran out on him.'

'I can't believe it's him under there.'

Neave squeezed her arm. 'You can read too much into things. Maybe Guérisse wanted to make sure his old enemy was really dead. Christ, he'd been promised it enough times. Even Harry Cole had to die sometime.' He cleared his throat. 'Can I buy you lunch?'

'That's very kind but . . . no. I have another grave to visit, back in the city. It would have been his birthday.' She quickly brushed a tear away.

'I wish . . .' He hesitated. 'I wish I could have killed Harry for you,' Neave said at last.

She touched his face. 'You English have the strangest ways of showing affection. I'm glad we met, too, Major Neave. I'll catch a train back, if you don't mind. I need time to think.'

She turned and walked away and Neave knew he'd never see her again.

Later that day, at the second cemetery, she cleared the weeds that were growing through the white marble chips covering the plot where her son lay at rest. Already she was saving for a more substantial headstone than the thin, cheap cross that stood guard now. She wiped away the moss and dirt on the painted wood with her handkerchief; it would be some time before she would be able to afford to replace it. She stared at the long shadow of someone standing behind her for several seconds before she stood.

It was one of the groundsmen, holding an extravagant bunch of lilies. 'These were delivered here a few moments ago,' he said solemnly. 'I was going to lay them, but perhaps . . .'

'Yes, thank you.'

She took them from him, and placed them on the gravel, stripping away the thick yellow paper to reveal an envelope, taped to the stems. The card inside was pre-printed, with a slightly mawkish verse, but there was something written underneath it. A single letter and an X, a kiss.

Odile studied the handwriting for a long time. As the wintry sun dipped low in the sky, she couldn't move and she began to shiver uncontrollably. She could not decide whether the letter was an A whose apex had failed to meet or a hastily scribbled H.

Author's Note

The background to *The Blue Noon* is based on real events. Harry Cole, Claude Dansey, Colonel Triffe, Kim Philby, Malcolm Muggeridge, Airey/Anthony Neave and Pat O'Leary are genuine historical characters, even if their actions here deviate from reality in places. Dansey's Z Organisation, Room 900, and Operation Sherwood all existed. Harry's improvisation with a melted chocolate bar, his burglary of apartments, his time with the US army, the two airmen singing with the Waffen-SS and Neave's rescue of Chartres cathedral are also factual incidents. The Muggeridge/Philby episode outside the Soviet Embassy is described in the former's autobiography. Other characters are fictitious or amalgamations of several people.

Claude Dansey, deputy head of wartime MI6, died in 1947, from heart failure.

Airey Neave, who really did use the name Anthony during the war years, later architect of Margaret Thatcher's election victory, was blown up at the House of Commons by an INLA bomb in 1979. The relationship between him and Odile in this book is total fiction.

Suzanne Warren (the anglicised version of her real name,

Warengham), the inspiration for the fictitious Odile and the woman who married Harry Cole and had his child, later married an American, living first in California, then in London.

Kim Philby defected to Russia in 1963; there is still much dispute over how many agents he betrayed in his career as a mole. He died in Moscow in 1988, shortly after a visit from Graham Greene, who remained a friend to the end.

Sergeant Harry Cole, trumpeter, swindler, con man, deserter, Resistance hero, resistance villain, really did sit down and write his side of events in the Paris Detention Centre before walking off into the night with the typewriter, and the document, under his arm, neither of which were ever found. The thought of what he might have written to justify the terrible deeds associated with him inspired this novel. As Harry would have, I have changed dates (including the boxing match at White Hart Lane, which took place earlier in the war), names and places, while keeping the arc of his journey from Hong Kong to Billy's Bar (aka The Blue Noon) more or less intact.

It is, however, certain that the British Intelligence Services knew about Harry Cole's dubious pre-war track record when he was working the escape lines: 'We decided to give him a second chance' was the rather glib reason given for not warning others. It is also true that doubts persist over whether he was, in fact, a double agent under British control for some of his time while he was helping the SS. There were even some who insisted that the man shot at Billy's Bar was not Harold Cole at all, but part of an SIS cover-up.

My thanks go to film director Jack Bond, who first mentioned Harry to me. I am also grateful to David Miller and Martin Fletcher for seeing some spark of humanity in Harry, and for the latter's brilliant work on the manuscript.

Thanks also to Guy Barker, Don Hawkins, Kim Hardie, Katie

Haines, Christine Walker, Jonathan Futrell, Laurie Evans and Susan d'Arcy. Odile Triplet of the Columbus Hotel in Monaco kindly donated her name to the character.

I also owe a large debt of gratitude to Mark Seaman of the Imperial War Museum, who has done much research on the man's career, uncovering his Hong Kong background, and who discussed Harry with me at length. This, however, is my (or rather, Harry's own) interpretation of the story: Mark should not be in any way associated with my methods or flights of fancy.

There is also a diligently researched book called *Turncoat* by Brendan M. Murphy, now sadly out of print, which is a thorough investigation into the man he calls 'the worst traitor of the war'. Murphy quotes Alfred Lanselle, one of those brave men who forwarded evaders to Cole in 1940, and who later ended up in Dachau, who said, 'Harold Cole was not killed. It was staged by the Intelligence Service to get him out of the way, to bury the case.' He was convinced Cole made it back to England.

Suzanne Warengham is the subject of *In Trust and Treason* by Gordon Young, which also tells the Cole story, or at least one version of it, in depth.

Other sources include *Hong Kong Then* by Brian Wilson; *At The Peak* by Paul Gillingham; *Growing Up Poor in London* by Louis Heren; *The East End* by Alan Palmer; *The Quest for Graham Greene* by W.J. West; *Colonel Z* by Anthony Read and David Fisher; *Das Reich* by Max Hastings; *The Infernal Grove* by Malcolm Muggeridge; *War Games, The Story of Sport in WW2* by Tony McCarthy; *MI9* by M.R.D. Foot and J.M. Langley; *The Man The Nazis Couldn't Catch* by John Laffin; Airey Neave's *They Have Their Exits*, *Saturday at MI9*, *Little Cyclones*, and *Flames of Calais*, plus Paul Routledge's very readable biography of the man, *Public Servant, Secret Agent*; *MI6* by Stephen Dorril; *The Private Life of Kim Philby* by Rufina Philby; *Philby: The Hidden Years* by

Morris Riley; *Anthony Blunt* by Miranda Carter; *Soldiers, Spies and the Rat Line* by Col. James V. Milano and Patrick Brogan; *An Uncertain Hour* by Ted Morgan (a good source of information on Klaus Barbie); *Paris After the Liberation* by Anthony Beevor and Artemis Cooper; and *Few Eggs and No Oranges*, the war diaries of Vere Hodgson, 1940–45.

The whisky scene was inspired by an incident involving Harry and Nancy Wake. However, the character of Lucy Hodge is a fiction.

Harry's files were originally sealed until 2010, but, as part of a policy of more open access, the Public Record Office at Kew released three files on Harry Cole, KV2/415, KV2/416 and KV2/417 in 2001. The SIS files, of course, remained sealed.

Robert Ryan
London